INCURSIONS:

Book One of the Simulations Saga

J. A. Giunta

Brick Cave Media
brickcavebooks.com

Incursions: Book One of the Simulations Saga

ISBN: 978-1-938190-96-4

Printed in the United States of America.

Cover Illustration Artist: Christian Bentulan

Brick Cave Media
brickcavebooks.com
2025

For Bluffer, Ishakaru, Babagahnoosh, and the many other incredible people I've played with over the years.

Some of the best memories I have are of gaming with all of you. From leveling up to dungeons runs, guild raids to guild drama, all of it was memorable because of the people behind the characters. I still hope one day we can do it all over again in another game. Until then, I'll just have to make my own adventures and drag you along for the ride.

Also by J.A. Giunta

Available from Brick Cave Books

THE ASCENSION
Book One: The Last Incarnation
Book Two: The Mists of Faeron
Book Three: Out of the Dark

THE GUARDIANS
Book One: Knights of Virtue

TRANSCENDENT POWERS
Book One: Supernal Dawn
co-authored with Sharon Skinner

War Golem

The Warden's Legacy

J. A. Giunta

Brick Cave Media
brickcavebooks.com

- 1 -

Palmer hitched up his leather backpack as he left school. It was lighter than usual, since he'd left all his books in his locker. It was a Friday, with no homework or tests on the horizon. The weekend was all his. He checked his phone for new messages. As per policy, it'd been on do-not-disturb all day. Nothing, not even an update about the session planned for Saturday. It was going to be twelve straight hours of tabletop goodness. He even had a new set of polyhedral dice that glowed in the dark. The only issue was whether they'd be playing at Daren's or Sara's, since the former had been sick the past few days. He stepped into the parking lot, head down, lost in thought, both aware of and doing his best to ignore his surroundings.

Guy slapped the phone from his hand, sent it crashing to the pavement. He heard laughter from three others, egging Guy on. One of them had even been a friend of Palmer's, before joining track and getting popular. Then, suddenly, role-playing games had become a waste of time. Palmer bent down to pick up his phone. There was a new crack across the center, webbed into the others. He could hear his mother lose her mind about it already. Palmer sighed. It wasn't the first time; it certainly wouldn't be the last.

"Sorry, man," Guy said in a feigned apologetic tone,

"but you really shouldn't be walking and texting. That's how people get hurt."

Palmer tucked the phone into his back pocket. He nodded and walked away.

He wanted to say something snarky, hurtful, but knew better. Any kind of response would just make everything worse. If he made a snide remark, he was a smartass and deserved a beat down. If he stood up for himself, he was looking for trouble. God forbid, he should physically push back. Then *he'd* be the bully. It was simply easier to avoid confrontation. Barring that, keep things from escalating. His left clavicle still clicked from when Guy had broken it in the sixth grade—back when he'd thought fighting back might stop the bullying. Palmer was painfully aware of his own size. He was smaller than average in both height and weight, which had only gotten worse over time, as other boys his age had grown bigger. Even if he could somehow defend himself physically, the school had a no tolerance policy, all parties included.

It just wasn't worth the expulsion.

A loud *crack* broke through his thoughts, like the shattering of glass. No falling shards followed after, just the sound of rushing air and fleeing birds. When that too faded, all that remained was the terrible feeling something was wrong. It had come from down an alley to his left. He immediately stopped to look but saw nothing out of the ordinary or what possibly could have caused it. The dirt road was empty but for trash and recycling bins along the walls. Rows of single-story houses on either side went on for another block. Backyard trees encroached into the alley, with branches trimmed in stark square-shaped cuts to allow garbage trucks room to drive through. He was about to turn away when he caught sight of something odd. Farther down the alley, suspended in air, was a distortion.

He slowly approached, tried to discern what he saw.

It was as if the air itself had been struck and broken like a pane of glass. Light bent around and through the large central crack, golden at its center and silver at the edges. It spread out into smaller lines in an all too familiar pattern. It reminded him of his phone.

Smoke began to seep from the main break, a thick gray the light behind could not penetrate. Still, he walked closer, through the ominous quiet. No one was around. If a neighbor had heard, they were being uncharacteristically uninvolved. Was it smoke? It appeared more like steam or dense fog, swirling gray and white, impossible to see through. Unlike smoke, with its acrid odor, this had no scent at all. The heavy mist spread quickly but unlike anything he'd ever seen. It didn't billow out along the ground like the rolling in of a morning mist. It crawled along the broken air, up and down the cracks, until it formed an arched doorway.

Nothing of the rift hanging in air could be seen. All that remained was the swirling gray, with silver light between the roils and along the edges of each eddy. The arched doorway was a foot thick and stood at least two feet taller than Palmer's five and a half. It was deathly quiet; no noise escaped the mist. Even the alley was silent, as if it too were afraid to move or make a sound. The earth beneath the archway had darkened a much deeper hue than mud.

Palmer hesitantly picked up a small rock and, against his better judgment, tossed it in. It disrupted the haze with a dulling of light, followed by what sounded like a reverse *whoosh*, but didn't land on the road. It just disappeared into the mist, as if the rift were an actual passage to somewhere else. Despite what he had witnessed with his own eyes and ears, he couldn't bring himself to believe it was true.

The hell? he wondered. *That's impossible.*

He wanted to plunge his hand in but took a moment to come up with a less risky plan. He saw a low hanging branch from a nearby backyard. It hung over the beige cinder block wall by several feet. With a snap and some twisting, he broke a length of it away the size of his forearm. A worried grimace on his face, he poked it into the rift. The half he'd stuck in disappeared, disturbed the swirling gray with a silver circle of light, but was not gone. He could pull it back out with ease. The prolonged sucking noise was a bit disturbing, though. The rift seemed to *want* the branch while any portion of it was inside.

Palmer pulled the branch back and let out a deep breath. If he wanted to know what was going on, he'd have to take a little risk. He pulled out his phone, set it to record in his left hand, and gripped the branch in his right like a weapon. Hoping for answers, rather than a lost limb, he thrust the phone into the mist, ready to strike with his right. It wouldn't do any actual damage, but it might startle someone enough if he struck them. While he'd intended to get a short video and quickly pull his hand away, the rift had other ideas.

Something grabbed him by the wrist and pulled him in. Eyes closed tight against the rush of bright light and cold air, he more felt than saw the shift in environment. He knew in that brief moment he'd left his home behind. Stranger than the sudden change in temperature and atmosphere, the faint ticking of an old clock could be heard in his mind, its gears turning more slowly with each pass, until finally the sound was gone and replaced with that reverse *whoosh* he'd heard before. The grip on his wrist was so strong, it nearly crushed the fragile bones. His fingers twisted into a claw from the pain and he lost hold of the phone—along with his footing. He was pulled forward like a rag doll, fell to his backside and was dragged forward without relent. His shoulder burned with the twisting, as if it might break from the strain. He tried to fight back to his feet, kicking and pushing, but the grass was slick with rain. The thick layer of mud refused to oblige. In the commotion, he'd lost his branch and could only helplessly flail. He was briefly aware that the urban world he'd began in had changed to a wide forest, with tall trees spaced far apart and thick brush a deep hue of green. His only way back, the stormy doorway in the distance, was growing further away with each step.

It was the creature with a death grip that demanded his attention, the diminutive monster that handled him as if he were a child. Though it stood half his height, it was stronger by far. Not even adults had that kind of strength. It made him feel more insignificant than usual. That it was dressed in oiled leather armor about its forearms, thighs, chest, and shoulders was only mildly strange compared to its deep green skin, long tapered ears, sharp teeth, and pointed nose. He'd seen many just like it hundreds of times, in books, games, cartoons, and movies. No matter how much his mind wanted to claim it was delusion, the manifestation of anxiety, or some other reasoned explanation, nothing else made any sense. It was a goblin, pure and simple, a creature of myth. He'd painted miniatures of them, killed them in tabletop and online games, saw them in countless fantasy stories. Yet here one was, dragging him through the mud like a sack of garbage.

What the hell am I even looking at?

Palmer must not have been accommodating enough in his role as helpless captive. The goblin gave him a rough tug forward with a grunt, as they continued through the forest. The ensuing snap and cry of pain were proof his arm had either dislocated or broken near the joint. Pain and terror shot down its length, churned his middle and upended from the depth of his stomach. The expulsion spattered the goblin's boots and short legs.

It stopped with an incredulous look to its otherworldly face. It scowled down at the soiled armor and backhanded Palmer across the face.

His vision exploded into white. He'd never been struck quite that hard, which was truly saying something considering all the beatings he'd endured in his life. He blinked away the tears, tried to see straight. The goblin reached down and yanked him up by the collar. Palmer's eyes went wide at being choked with his own shirt, unintentionally or not. He struggled to pull the material away long enough to catch his breath but couldn't fit his fingers in for a decent grip. When he saw the long dagger tucked into the goblin's belt, he didn't hesitate. This was life or death, with time quickly running out. No matter how unbelievable the situation, he'd suffocate long before the goblin realized he was dead.

He grabbed the pommel with his right hand and pulled it free with all his strength. The long blade sliced along the goblin's waist as he did, just beneath the leather chest piece. The goblin let him go in sudden shock, looked down at the gaping wound and growing stain of black spreading across the tunic beneath its armor. Disbelief turned to anger and a sneer that promised a more than equal retribution.

Palmer wanted to run, to get away at all costs, but he knew there was no way out except to fight. He swallowed his fear and did the unexpected, the unthinkable. He fought back. He lurched forward with the dagger out, clutched tight in his one good hand. It caught the goblin in the leg, brought the monster low with a hiss. He pulled it free and stabbed again, this time beneath the shoulder, just outside the leather armor. It was the goblin's turn to fall to its knees, breath heavy and filled with pain. It desperately reached for a sheathed short sword at its waist. Palmer stabbed again, this time in the neck. It scrabbled backward in utter fear, eyes wide in panic. He'd left the dagger deep within, continued to frantically kick at the wet ground to back away, still grappling with the imperative to run. He watched the goblin yank the blade free. The dagger fell from shaky fingers. Dark blood spurted three times, before the creature fell over.

Breathing heavy, chest on fire from the pounding, Palmer watched the goblin fall on its front and remain still. He waited for it to get back up, but the goblin moved no more. He barely had time to wonder if the fight was over, if he was free to flee and find a way back home, when words appeared at the bottom left of his vision. They persisted no matter where he turned his head or how many times he tried to blink them away.

Congratulations! Promoted to player character.

***

Palmer did his best to fully calm himself. The threat had passed, but there was no telling what other creatures were in the forest around him. He took long, deep breaths, until he felt certain he was safe—at least for the moment. With each exhalation, the overwhelming fear let loose its grip, settled his shaky vision from anxiety. He stared at the goblin with unbelieving eyes, both that it existed and was now dead. Dark blood stained his muddied hand. Monster or not, he'd killed a living creature. Did that make him a murderer? What he'd done didn't feel like self-defense. Was his injury enough to warrant what he'd done? How could this be happening? And what were those words? Though they had disappeared from his vision, memory of them still haunted. Had he imagined them? He was keenly aware of how unreal it all seemed.

It suddenly felt quiet.

Chill wind and his breath were all that could be heard. The backpack shifted off his shoulder, sending a shock down his arm. The pain in his shoulder rushed back all at once and pushed aside all contemplation, reminder of an all too real injury. It stabbed downward and out, like a relentless wave of aching that reverberated up to his head and rang in both ears. He did his best to hold the dislocated arm in place with his other hand, but it did little to ease the throbbing. He felt the bottom of his stomach begin to churn.

No, he told himself and turned about, onto both knees, *let's not do that again.* His mouth was still tainted with the last upheaval. He eyed the pool of black blood in a ring about the goblin. *Is this a dream? Am I dead?* He had no way to explain it, but the more reasonable conclusion was...*In a game?* He looked around at the tall trees, wind blowing through the grass, the darkening skies and growing storm clouds overhead. *How am I in a forest? Was I teleported? What was that archway, some kind of portal?* He recalled the distortion in air, like the breaking of glass. *A rift in space?* He studied the goblin's features, the long nose with warts, pointed ears wide and long, the sharp teeth like an animal, and green skin out of a fairy tale. It was so small. It looked like a child...a terrifying, murderous child with the strength of a grown man. *Am I even on Earth?*

He heard grunts in the distance, boots trudging through the mud. He dropped his head and hunkered down, instinctively hiding like he would when he heard Guy and his lackeys approach. Though the grass was little more than a foot high, it was enough to keep him from sight—unless the wind blew any stronger, or they looked his way with any interest. There were three of them. A patrol of sorts, they were all armed and armored. While two of the goblins had short swords drawn, the third carried a tall spear. They didn't seem to be searching for anyone, be it a captive or a lost comrade. Long minutes passed before they faded behind brush and trees in the distance.

A wave of relief washed over Palmer. The reality of his situation would become moot in the face of danger. Delusion or not, those goblins would have killed him. Or taken him captive, to be killed later? That was actually an interesting point. Why *did* the goblin take him captive? Why keep him alive, unless it had plans? He mulled it over while setting down his backpack and checking the goblin for anything useful. Perhaps it had intended him to be food. Or slave labor. Entertainment? He'd never thought of goblins as more than low difficulty creatures to level up on. He shook his head and tried to focus on the task at hand.

He picked up the short sword, still in its scabbard. It was too heavy for him to wield in one hand. If he had to defend himself again, the dagger was a better choice—though it wouldn't be much use against the reach of a spear. Even if he couldn't use the short sword at the moment, it made sense to take it. He used a knee to hold still his backpack, unzipped it and stashed the sword. The leather armor was worn, with numerous gashes and broken laces. It was too small for him to wear and had the smell of fresh asphalt. The belt definitely wouldn't fit, but it might still have a use. He stashed that as well. He picked up the dagger and wiped blood from its blade against the grass. He'd feel safer carrying it, but he needed a free hand to nurse his shoulder.

If this was a game, he thought wryly, *shouldn't it have an invent...*

The dagger disappeared from his hand, its entire length of steel deconstructed like a reverse rainfall of silver pixels. He pulled his hand away as if he'd been bitten.

What the hell? He opened and closed his hand, saw nothing in the palm. *Where did it go?*

An Inventory screen popped up in the center of his vision. If this wasn't a virtual reality game, the delusion was very convincing. The dagger was listed there.

Dagger (I)

Its item text was gray, which was different from the rest of the system's pure white. He wondered if that denoted rarity, like in other games, where gray meant common. The Roman numeral one beside it could be a quality tier. Curious, he silently called for the dagger back. It reappeared in his hand, a quick fall of glittering tiny blocks that formed the item.

The way items appear and disappear looks digital, he thought, *and the interface works by thought. Or is it intent? Either way, that could be handy. And creepy. I'm definitely in a virtual reality.* He frowned. *Or I'm having a mental breakdown. I guess it doesn't matter. If you can't tell delusion from reality, what's the difference?*

Palmer put the dagger back in inventory and gave his leather backpack a try. Unsurprisingly, the system wouldn't allow him to store it. For whatever reason, games never let players store one container inside another. It was either that, or inventory only worked on items native to the system. He was able to place the short sword in inventory, though, which was one less thing to weigh him down.

He continued to hold his injured shoulder with the other hand. As much as it hurt to move, he had to get going. He did his best to retrace the path back toward the rift, staying hidden in the trees or low to the grass when no cover could be found. One advantage to having been bullied most of his life was he'd developed an intuition for imminent danger. It was a skill, knowing when to hide or when to quickly move to avoid attention. It was like a second sense, honed throughout the years. He could always tell when there were eyes upon him.

The trail his unwilling body had dug while dragged was not as easy to follow as he'd hoped. Where damaged grass and upended earth should have made the path apparent, bramble and brush between the trees obscured any obvious way. The goblin must not have taken them on a straight course. More than once, Palmer had lost the main trail and was forced to double back to try again. If he hadn't been magically transported to some other world, he might be able to call for help—assuming there was a nearby cell tower in this middle-of-nowhere forest. It didn't matter, he soon discovered, as the phone had been lost in the scuffle.

He looked up at the darkening skies, the clouds slowly moving closer as they grew. There was an odd hue of pale violet behind them that deepened toward the horizon. It colored the world in a lavender tint. It was a possible sign that night would be falling soon. Though the sun wasn't visible, there was still light enough to see by. How long that would last, he was unsure. It had gotten a bit colder, as the wind picked up. If a storm was coming, he wanted to be gone long before it arrived.

Memory of the words in his vision, like a computer screen, crept back into his thoughts. Though they had disappeared from the lower left of his view, each time he recollected them, the window resurfaced. It was like playing a game, where his eyes were the monitor. Even virtual reality goggles couldn't do that.

Are delusions that persistent? he mused, in a futile attempt to distract himself from the fact he was lost. *What did it even mean? Promoted to player character... from what? Was I a non-player character before?*

The first drop of rain struck his neck, the precursor to heavy showers. He'd done his best to ignore the pain, but each step had been like a shock down the length of his arm. He looked down at his worn sneakers, now caked in mud—much like the rest of him. Trudging through the mire hadn't made it any easier. He began to eye the trees for any kind of shelter. He didn't care there was a greater chance that lightning might strike. A small part of him even hoped for it.

He stopped long enough to open his mouth toward the skies, caught enough rain to rinse away the film of vomit. It was an odd mix of churning in his stomach, to be both hungry and nauseated. There was an old granola bar in the outer pocket of his backpack, in case of emergency. Considering how they tasted, that was the only time they were worth eating. With nothing to drink but dirty rain, he thought it best to hold off. Thunder rumbled in the distance, a rolling threat from behind. One last rinse, and he pushed on.

Within minutes, a full-blown drizzle had begun to wash the mud from his hair and backside. It allowed him, at least, to clean his hands and face. A blackened tree off to the right caught his attention. It was fairly large compared to the others, its leaves all but gone and lower branches discolored. A storm must have made it a victim in the past, living proof not to take shelter beneath a tree. The entire base was charred, and the burn marks ran upward in jagged lines. As he drew closer to its ruin, he could see there was a deep hollow. Where lightning had struck it open, rot had eaten through and left space enough for him to fit.

He was barely settled inside, when the storm came in full force. All howling and sideways rain, it struggled to reach him. Thunder shook the ground in a rolling grumble, accompanied by a bright flash. He eased himself further in, far enough to keep the wind at bay. He couldn't get any wetter. It was the gusts of cold that made things worse. With only jeans and a tee shirt, mud caked up and down his backside, he'd been shivering for some time. On any other day, he would have worn a hoodie, even if it was warm out. At the last minute, his mother had insisted on washing it. His hands were so cold he could barely feel his fingers. It made him wish he'd had the foresight for an emergency hoodie or extra shirt to go along with the granola bar.

He took a deep breath in through the nose and let it slowly back out. At least now he had time to think, to consider what was really going on. He focused on the lower left corner of his vision. The words reappeared, just as if they'd never left. The screen reminded him of an event log in an online game. Concentrating his attention on the words themselves did nothing, so he fixed his attention to the upper left.

If this was like a game...

A Statistics window appeared.

PALMER
LVL: 1
STR: 0, **CON**: 0, **DEX**: 0, **INT**: 0, **WIS**: 0
HP: 3 [4], **MP**: 0, **F**: 0%
SP: 3

"What?" he nearly shouted, angry at the implication. "Why are they all zeros? The hell is that even out of, ten? A hundred?" *What a bunch of bullshit.* And why was he missing a health point? Because of his arm? If his health points went to zero, by dislocating his other arm and both legs, would he fall unconscious, or would he die? *Why did F have a percentage? Fatigue? What's SP, Stat Points? Why isn't there a class? Is this a classless system?* He gave it some thought, and an idea occurred. *If this is a skill-based system, there must be a skill tree or a list somewhere...*

An Abilities list appeared in the center of his vision. It was blank.

"Great," he said to no one. There was an underlying concern of being found by other goblins, but the storm had gotten so loud, there was little chance of that. "So, how do I gain abilities? Is there a trainer or a shop?"

The Abilities screen was replaced with an Item Shop. There were three tabs listed: Gear, Items, and Ability Stones. In the top right of that screen was a balance showing he had ten gold. He assumed it was from the goblin. If gold was the game currency, the ten must have been auto looted. He certainly hadn't seen or picked up any coins. Another idea struck, as he tried to familiarize himself with the system. He tried calling a coin to his hand, like he could with inventory items. Nothing happened. That meant currency was non-transferable.

He focused on the Ability Stones tab. The screen changed, and a long list of ability names appeared, each with a gold cost. The scroll bar on the right led him to believe there were many more. Most were grayed out, because he couldn't afford them. There were four listed for free, though, and another four for ten gold.

The pain in his shoulder pushed to fore once again. It caused a throbbing at both temples that stretched around and down his neck. He had to do something about it, or his stomach would upend again.

The free heal spell caught his eye. It took little focus at all. He simply wanted it. A small window popped up, layered on top of the center screen.

Confirm: Yes / No

"What? Just do it!" He focused on the Yes box, as if pressing it by thought. A round stone appeared in his hand, the same way items appeared from inventory. It was smooth but porous, cool to the touch. A rune glowed in blue across its surface, no symbol he'd ever seen. "How do I use..."

The entire stone flashed a brief moment. Another window appeared.

Warning! Using this Ability Stone will activate the Healer class. Do you wish to continue?

That gave him pause. He didn't care about the game or whatever was going on. He just wanted his shoulder to stop hurting. But what if he was stuck here? Healer was a support class. They weren't completely helpless, but more often than not, they were reliant on other classes to survive. Maybe he'd be better off with a healing potion. The Shop switched to the Items tab. While there were healing potions available, everything was grayed out. The least expensive one was a thousand gold.

"What the hell do you want from me," he shouted at the system, "my credit card?" He clenched his jaw, biting back any further outbursts. As expected, no one was listening. "Fine."

He used the stone once more and confirmed when he got the warning. The stone grew very bright for a brief moment and dissipated into ash. He could feel the ability take hold deep inside him, as if he'd been physically changed.

Congratulations! You are now a Healer.
You have unlocked new Quests.

By thought alone, he navigated back to the Abilities screen and saw the new ability listed there. He focused on it further, and a description appeared.

Minor Heal (I)
Class: *Healer*
Active, Combat, Reversible, Necromancy
Cost*: 5,* ***Range****: Touch,* ***Duration****: Instant*
Restore 1-4 health points to a living target.

He'd already been holding his injured shoulder with his good hand. He tried to calm down, took a breath, and concentrated on using the ability to heal his shoulder.

You cannot do that.

He wanted to scream in frustration but settled for a quiet growl.

"Why not?" He looked over the details. "Does it need components or something? It's not a spell, it's an ability! Ohh!"

He had no mana.

Palmer looked over his stats. Based on his experience with a myriad of other games, he assumed mana was tied to intelligence. *Is SP stat points?* If so, that meant he had three to spend, most likely gained from reaching level one. *I could test it, I suppose.* He focused on INT with the intent of raising it just one point.

Confirm? Yes / No

He confirmed, watched his stats change. INT was now one, and his mana increased to ten. He tried once more to use the ability. Warmth welled up from his middle, rushed down his right arm and out through his palm. It encompassed his entire shoulder with a glow of golden light. He could feel the pain subside, as the joint slipped back into place. With the injury gone, it no longer hurt to breathe. He was down to five mana, but his missing health point had been restored.

He wondered if raising his INT had done anything else for him. He gave the system a disappointing look. There was a distinct lack of instructions to this game. Focusing on the stat itself did nothing. He now knew it directly affected mana, though he couldn't be sure if it would continue to maintain a ten to one ratio. What else? In other games, intelligence affected things like perception and awareness, the ability to sense one's surroundings, to measure the power of an enemy, to see traps or hidden passages, things of that nature. Since it directly affected mana, it should also affect spell damage, which meant it should also affect spell critical chance and critical damage. He wished the system would clearly define things for him. He was left with no choice but to learn by trial and error.

"This is ridiculous!" he said more to himself than anything else. If this was a delusion, then interacting with it was probably not the best idea. "I need to get home. I don't want to play whatever this is."

The allure of growing stronger, though. He could feel that in his gut. It was a hard temptation to deny, especially for someone who loved gaming as much as he did. If he put the remaining two points into strength, could he defend himself against Guy? As he looked out at the storm, any thought of dealing with bullies seemed like such a faraway problem. Besides, fighting wasn't really his style. He did like the idea of playing healer in multiplayer games, with all the utility they offered groups. Too bad it always required other classes to level up. Healers could do damage, but they couldn't solo very efficiently. Their offense was nothing compared to a mage or a rogue. Even tanks outdamaged healers.

Another idea occurred to him. He called up the Ability Stones tab in the Shop. All but two were grayed out now, including the free weapon and spell damage ones. He focused on Fire Blast, despite the system noting it as unobtainable.

You cannot do that. Prerequisite not met.

"Oh, crap. Did I just lock myself into a healer role?" He frantically looked through the system, opening as many screens as he could find. "There's no multi-classing? Can I make a new character? Undo!" he yelled at the screen. "Help! Support!"

The system ignored his pleas.

He went back to the Abilities list and tried to delete or sell the heal ability.

You cannot do that.

"Nooo!"

***

Palmer wasn't sure how much time had passed as night fell. He couldn't remember not having a phone to keep him occupied. Even if there were no bars, he could have still played some games. Though he kept both arms tucked in close to either side, his entire body ached from the cold and constant shivering. He sat with legs crossed, leaned forward into a ball to conserve warmth. At least the storm seemed to calm, with the rain more of a steady rhythm than a seismic downpour. Small mercy as it was, it was too late in the day to matter. Without a light source, searching for the rift would be impossible.

He stared at the heal ability, still mentally kicking himself for being helpless in yet another aspect of his life. Unlike the frail physique he was born with, this one was his fault. He'd done his fair share of pushups and running in a struggle to gain muscle. It just never quite worked out for him. He'd gotten a little stronger but always looked the same—smaller than everyone else.

The stupidity of choosing healer, though? he thought to the screen. *Yeah, that's all me. No amount of sudokus is gonna fix that.*

It'd been a brash decision, but at the time, the pain in his shoulder took precedent over rational thought. If the situation he'd found himself in could be called that. He'd played a healer before, in online and tabletops. This was very different. His actual life was at stake. He'd never dislocated a shoulder rolling to hit on a d20. Now almost getting his arm torn off because he tried to sneak one of Sara's Twizzlers...

One word in the ability description caught his attention: Reversible. How did he miss that? In at least one tabletop game he'd played, Swords & Sorcery, heal spells could be reversed to cause harm to the undead.

Is that what this is? He chewed his lower lip. *It wouldn't do any good against goblins, but it's a start.*

Healers weren't always unable to defend themselves. In some MMOs, like Towers of Ruin and Spellfall, they could be considered top tier damage classes. It was especially true of games that allowed multi-classing or advanced jobs. Healers weren't always completely reliant on others to level, either. Even the weakest support class had a modicum of offensive capabilities, and clever use of mechanics could turn utility into advantage.

The description specified living targets, he noticed, *so no healing constructs or undead. Did that mean the reverse version affected the living too?* With something to keep his mind occupied, he wasn't quite so bothered by the cold. *If the reverse did something different, shouldn't it have its own listing and details? And what exactly constitutes a target? Trees are alive. Can I heal trees and plants?* Target was probably more clearly defined somewhere in the system he wasn't privy to. *That's what happens when you play a game with a terrible interface.*

His mind wandered back to the log, the words taunting with his mistake. Even worse was the line that followed it.

Quests, he thought with disdain. *Nope! Hell if I'm going to gather garbage, collect crap, or escort anyone anywhere. Quests are for chumps.* After a moment of realization, he let out a breath in defeat. *Like healers. Might as well look at them, I guess.*

Daily Quests

Defeat three enemies [1/3]

Class Quests

Use a heal ability three times [1/3]

There was nothing he could do about the first one. Honestly, he wasn't sure that he wanted to. The goblin had been terrifying. Could he really face another one? That's if he was lucky. The patrol he'd seen earlier had three. He had little to no chance of surviving that encounter. The second quest, however? That would be easy. He placed his right hand over his chest and activated the heal ability.

You cannot do that.

"Figures." While Palmer was all about efficiency, some games didn't care if the healer wasted mana. "Lucky me." A devious idea came to mind. "I mean, if I have to be injured, and the spell's reversible...Oh, wait." He was about to activate the ability, when he recalled its damage was a range and not a constant. "Am I gonna kill myself with this?"

He debated between going through with it, potentially risking his life, and playing it safe by putting a point into constitution for more health points. On the one hand, he would get an answer to the question of what happened if his HP reached zero. On the other, he might be too dead to appreciate the knowledge. He did have two stat points left to spend. If he put them into INT, his max mana would increase. Theoretically, it should also make his spells stronger and more effective. Focusing INT in a caster class to become a glass cannon was a solid strategy. Overpowered and easy to kill was always fun. Wisdom was usually the better choice for healer, though, with the increase to mana regeneration and magic resistance. Then again, this system had some quirks that made it different from anything else he'd ever played.

The delusion is pretty strong in this one, he thought of himself. *If I keep thinking this is a game, I'm gonna die for sure. But what else could it be? If it looks like an orc and snorts like an orc and kills you like an orc...*

With every other stat at zero, and this being only his first level, it didn't really make sense to think long-term. He wouldn't have considered playing a character in another game without careful planning and a clear leveling path. He just didn't know enough about this one to do that. All he could do was make educated guesses based on the information at hand. He'd have to save experimenting for later. For now, he needed to focus on surviving long enough to get back home. He put a point into CON and confirmed. His current and maximum health points went to ten.

See, now that's good information. He'd been keeping a tally of mental notes about the system's intricacies. *If current HP didn't go up, I'd be pretty mad, not gonna lie.* While he couldn't use stats points to heal himself, he could use them later on to avoid death by raising max health points mid-battle. Assuming the system allowed allocating points during combat. *Okay, here goes.*

He activated the reverse ability against his chest. The blinding flash of golden light was almost as much a shock as the fiery pain. The blast hadn't just seared him from the outside, it felt as if it'd reached deep within and scorched his soul. It was so overwhelming to the senses, he didn't even scream. He just sat there, taking in quick sharp breaths, as smoke rose from the burned tee shirt and smoldering wound over his heart. Tears blurred his vision no matter how much he blinked. The rush of air from holy fire still rung in both ears. He swallowed hard, tried not to look down, tried even harder not to puke. It was a struggle just to stay conscious, when his eyes were drawn up toward his stats.

PALMER
LVL: 1
STR: 0, **CON**: 1, **DEX**: 0, **INT**: 1, **WIS**: 0
HP: 2 [10], **MP**: 0 [10], **F**: 15%
SP: 1

It was a critical. He would've laughed, if he wasn't sure that too would damage him even more. *Cuz, of course I did.* He quickly put the last point into INT, for mana to heal himself. It took two uses to fully heal. *Is there a luck stat I don't know about? Cuz mine sucks.* He closely examined his now exposed chest. There was no scar or burn marks left behind. What little hair he'd had was gone, though. It dawned on him then just how badly he could've been permanently marred. *I probably should've thought that through a little more.*

The message had popped up earlier, but he'd only just noticed.

Congratulations! Class Quest completed.
As a reward, you may choose:
A minor healing potion
A minor mana potion
A mystery gift

His eyes went wide at the list, the terrible pain all but a memory. He quickly checked the Shop and saw both potions were worth a thousand gold. With that, he could buy one of the stronger, grayed out ability stones. Or he could save the mana potion, in case he ever ran out of mana and needed it to finish a fight or heal—which was based on the huge assumption he was ever going to fight again.

Might not have a choice. He still had to find the rift before he could go home. With patrols out there, it was unlikely he'd be able to do that without a fight. *Hmm...* that mystery gift was just too tempting. *With my luck, it'll probably be a straight up gold amount less than the value of either pot.* The gambler in him was thinking big. *Or it could be a million! Y'know, cuz that's how level one quests are usually balanced.*

He chose the mystery box and confirmed.

Congratulations! You have been awarded three Stat Points.

His smile slowly grew in surprised joy. It brought him back to the old days of playing a new game on release, the urge to progress faster and farther than everyone else, the rush of being visibly stronger through sheer effort. It was almost equal to the satisfaction of a gamble that had paid off. As far as rewards go, his had to have been super rare. Gold was one thing, but a jump in power equal to a level? That couldn't be outright bought. Maybe his luck wasn't so bad after all. And just like that...

He was hooked.

- 2 -

Palmer woke as the pale glow of early morn spread across the tall grass and wide trees outside his hollow. A light wind swept through the sea of green blades between the boles, colored by the glimmer of lavender skies. The storm had long dispersed, with only telltale streaks of white stretched far into the distance. A thin layer of frost covered all, slowly melting into dew.

He'd forced himself to sleep, rather than spend another moment in tense thought. There'd been too many questions left unanswered, too many plans left unmade, with the sheer weight of exhaustion from the stress and cold bearing down. The night had been terrible, an unending bout of shivering filled with bursts of fitful sleep. Fingertips blued, muscles ached as he tried to move. The air was crisp with an intensity he could feel in his bones. Fortunately, what passed for light in this place carried with it a touch of warmth. There still was no sun in the lilac haze of sky.

The discomfort at each movement, as he struggled to climb out from the hollow, brought with it a curious thought. The Stats window appeared, showed him missing three health points.

I actually took damage? He slipped the backpack over his left shoulder. He'd used it during the night to cover his exposed chest. *At least my mana's fully restored. Fatigue is down to zero.* He yawned. *Feels like it should be higher.*

His lips were cracked and mouth dry. All that rain, and he'd only managed a few handfuls to drink. He knelt and tried to scoop dew from the grass into both hands. It was just a few drops but enough to wet his lips. Hunger twisted his stomach, as he looked around for where to go next. There was no direct source of light to guide him, to determine east from west. It just blanketed the world, as if the sky itself provided the illumination.

He had a general sense of the direction he'd been headed when the storm hit. His best bet at finding the rift was to continue that way. A quick stretch of the back, a crack of the neck to either side, and he was ready to search once more. As he walked, he rifled the backpack for that granola bar. There was nothing else useful inside. A few notebooks, pens, and a bag of polyhedral dice were all he'd needed for the weekend he had previously planned. Freezing cold made the stale bar even harder than usual. He wasn't about to risk his teeth on a direct bite. It took some effort to break off a piece small enough to chew. He let it sit in his mouth, hoped to soften it over time, as he walked and wished for the foresight of an emergency hoodie to go with it.

Okay. He focused back on his stats, eyed the three points left to spend. *Time to give this some thought.*

The two points into intelligence didn't make him feel any smarter or seem to affect his ability to learn. He didn't think that's how the system worked. Instead, it directly impacted things relative to the game, like mana. The point into constitution, however, did make him feel healthier, heartier. It was evident in his breathing. As someone who used to run, he could attest that the difference fitness made was only noticeable when it was neglected. While it was still too early to create a planned path for each attribute, he tried to keep in mind some games made stats a prerequisite for advanced skills. Even if he had the required level and class to learn high level abilities, it was possible they might need heavy investment into a single stat. The mana necessary to activate a powerful spell already dictated the minimum INT for its use. Abilities aside, gear was also known to carry minimum stat requirements to use without suffering a penalty.

I need more mana, he determined, considering his heal cost a quarter of his current maximum. It was still unclear how mana regeneration worked. If he needed to sleep for eight hours to get them all back, it was only good for four uses per day. *Just seems so expensive for such a low level spell.* He put all three points into INT and confirmed. *Better a glass cannon than a well-rounded out-of-mana caster.* He laughed, thinking back to all the times other healers would shout OOM during a raid boss, while he was still chugging along at 30%. He would always be the king of efficiency. *Good times.*

Palmer noted each increase to INT maintained the ten to one ratio with maximum mana. With fifty now at his disposal, he felt more confident about another encounter. The thought of an impending fight reminded him there was another ability left to purchase. He pulled up the Ability Stones tab in the Shop and spent his remaining ten gold on the only one not grayed out. He used the stone, watched it deconstruct with a flash, switched to the Abilities screen, and studied its details.

Minor Shield (I)
Class*: Healer*
Active, Combat, Abjuration
Cost*: 5,* ***Range****: Touch,* ***Duration****: 1 min*
Absorbs 10 points of physical damage.

Only physical? He supposed that was fair, considering it was just the second ability available to his class. *The tier rating suggests abilities might advance or evolve at some point, through continued use or upgrades. Could be there's a version just for magic damage, too.* He had to admit, using the two abilities in conjunction would be a solid strategy to face melees. *Hope I don't run into any casters. Huh.* He looked over all of the available ability stones in the Shop and noticed only the minor versions of each one were available. *Does that mean higher tier abilities have to be earned, or will they drop as rare treasure?*

After noticing Proficiency: Sword was restricted to the warrior role, he decided to sell the short sword in inventory for ten gold. Using a weapon without the passive skill associated with it would most likely incur a penalty to hit chance and damage. He felt more comfortable with the dagger anyway, even if that proficiency belonged to rogue.

While he'd had no luck finding the rift or even recognizing any of the way he'd been dragged, something did catch his eye. Growing along the thick roots at the base of a tree was a patch of fuzzy yellow growth with jagged red crystals sprouting from it. He assumed the butter-colored tufts were moss. They covered a large portion of the area, over rocks and moist earth leading up to the tree. The roots and bark were whitened where it touched, as if color had been drained away.

The mineral emerging from the moss was even more interesting. In places where it grew tallest, about the length of a knuckle, light passed through in a vibrant crimson, like sunshine through glass. It reminded Palmer of rock candy. He couldn't help but touch a tiny bit to his tongue and was surprised to find it sweet. It wasn't as sweet as sugar, but if it grew from moss, it might be edible. He called the dagger to hand and used it to cut a large piece of moss and crystal away. He pinched a bit of moss off and rubbed it into a small area on his left forearm. He did the same with the red crystal on his right. If after a few hours either showed signs of an allergic reaction, he'd know not to ingest them. He gathered even more and placed it all into the outer pocket of his backpack.

Palmer nearly fell over in fright at the yell from behind. He frantically turned to see two goblins approaching with all speed. He stood with eyes wide, backpack and dagger in hand. He was frozen with indecision, as his mind worked for a solution. He both felt and saw the change immediately, attributed it to the points he'd put into intelligence.

There was an aura of power about both goblins, a nimbus of coalescing shades of blue and green, with purple and red strewn through. The one wearing a bone necklace and carrying a staff felt much stronger than the other with a spear and leather armor. Its visible energy was more dense and brighter. Palmer knew right away it was a caster. More striking, however, were the words in deep orange over both their heads: Goblin Shaman and Goblin Warrior. If this system was anything like other games, the orange color denoted level, difficulty, or both.

It meant they were much stronger than him.

They were nearly upon him when a plan born of fear had him drop everything and fall to his knees. Hands open and arms raised, he lowered his head and surrendered. Palmer knew what he was. He had to play to his strengths.

"I—I'm not a fighter," he said, doubtful they could understand him. "Please don't kill me."

He risked a glance up and winced when the warrior leveled its spear at him. The shaman scowled with hatred, as it pulled a strip of leather from its belt, intent on taking him captive. When it grabbed his left wrist with implacable strength, it was the moment Palmer had been waiting for. He grabbed its arm with his right, and activated the reverse heal. The goblin screamed in agony, as holy fire erupted in a flash and ate away its entire arm. Without missing a beat, he struck again. He placed his hand on its chest and activated the ability. Brackish blood and golden fire erupted, meaty chunks sent in all directions.

New ability unlocked: Minor Spell Cunning I!

He rolled away from the mess and the spear pointed at his neck. While the warrior shook off its surprise, Palmer activated the shield ability. He got back to his feet, ready to fight one on one. Fighting had never been a particular talent of his. He was more suited to puzzles and strategy games than any physical activity. Still, all he had to do was touch the creature and it would all be over. Or so he hoped.

The spear stabbed outward with much more speed than he'd thought possible. The goblin was visibly faster than he was. Though the weapon hadn't done any damage, it struck the shield head on and took off six damage points. That left four on the shield and Palmer with seven health. He silently kicked himself for not healing back those points when he woke. He did his best to avoid the spear, to sidestep its length and move in. It was then when he realized the flaw in his glass cannon plan.

Touch is a melee attack, he inwardly groaned, *which is either strength or dexterity based.* He had no points in either. *Damn it!*

In some games, strength directly affected physical damage with melee weapons and hit chance, while dexterity modified armor rating and chance to be hit by melee. In others, strength was both damage and speed, while dexterity was all about reflexes and the relative speed between two combatants. It was just a matter of figuring out how this system worked.

The goblin scored a hit directly into Palmer's side. It had gone through the shield for five damage, destroyed it fully, and inflicted another point to his health. He took hold of the spear in both hands by instinct, fought through the pain for fear of how much worse it would feel when removed. He held on for dear life, confused the goblin with his struggle, when desperation gave birth to a new plan. Despite the anguish it caused, he pulled himself forward, drove the spear deeper in. Inch by agonizing inch, he moved closer to the goblin that watched on in delight. It was either oblivious to how the shaman had died, or it simply didn't care. Each pull caused more damage. He was down to two health when he came within reach.

New ability unlocked: Minor Perseverance I!

Holy fire swept out like a hungry wave, engulfed armor and flesh alike. The sound of its roar echoed in the goblin's scream, a final cry against the fury of divine magic. The critical hit had left nothing behind but smoke rising from a pair of legs. Palmer blinked back tears against the pain. Without the goblin to hold him up, he felt the world begin to waver.

Congratulations! You have gained a new level!

***

Palmer regained consciousness. He was flat on his back, slowly blinked up at the lilac glow of afternoon, when memory came crashing in. There was fresh vomit down his front, spattered across his legs and shoes. He tried to sit up, but the headache it caused was nearly worse than the hole still in his side. The new level had replenished all his health and mana but had left the spear intact. He'd been forced to pull it free from behind, so as not to cause more damage with the flared blade. The pain and exertion had caused him to pass out.

And there he was, almost dead. Again.

He recalled the level up as an odd sensation, being healed to full but with a foreign object firmly lodged halfway through his torso. It was like waking up refreshed, only to realize both legs had been broken while asleep. Coupled with the smell of burned flesh and the onset of guilt at having taken more lives, his stomach had upended just as his brain had decided it was all too much to bear. It was a hard thing to contend with for someone whose only real experience with violence was in media and games. He'd been bullied most of his life, but that level of physicality, especially as a victim, didn't even come close to ending another being's life by brute force. The feel of blood spray and the grit of meaty bits, the smell of charred muscle and bone, their dying screams beneath the onslaught of roaring holy fire, and sight of their decimated remains all culminated into a traumatic assault on the senses. No matter how much he tried to ignore it, clamp shut his eyes against the memory, his mind would relive it all in flashes behind the lids. He knew deep down, even in self-defense, it should be a difficult decision to take a life. So why did it come so readily to him when pressed?

Why couldn't this be a game where enemies just disappear when they die? His life hadn't been easy, but it seemed even his delusions were unfair. It made being bullied such a trivial thing by comparison. *Why does it have to be so...visceral?*

He put those thoughts aside and healed himself to full. After the second use, the Abilities tab blinked to life with a notification. It opened by thought and showed his heal had improved to tier two. He found it interesting there was no alert in the log. In any case, its range had increased to one foot, and the minimum points healed went up to two. That meant he no longer needed to land a touch attack. He just had to get very close. While on the screen, he took a look at the two new abilities he'd gained during combat.

Minor Spell Cunning (I)
Class: *Healer, Mage*
Passive, Evocation
Increase magical hit chance by 10%.

Minor Perseverance (I)
Class: *Healer, Mage*
Passive, Evocation
When health drops below 25%, increase magical critical hit chance by 5%, magical critical damage by 25%, and mana regeneration by 10%.

Other tabs blinked as well. One was new, called Achievements. He navigated to it and saw he'd unlocked a previously hidden milestone.

Adventurer I
Passive
Quest rewards are slightly improved.

The Quests tab blinked as well. When he opened it, he could see the original daily had been completed, along with a new one he didn't know he had, and there were now other ones for each type. He assumed they were a result of attaining a new level.

Daily Quests
Defeat three enemies [Completed]
Improve an ability [Completed]
Learn a new ability [0/1]
Defeat five enemies [0/5]
Class Quests
Use a defensive ability three times while in combat [1/3]
Heal 50 points of damage [8/50]

The available rewards were the same as the first

quest. *Slightly improved? Mmhmm.* He chose the mystery gift for both. *C'mon, stat points!* The first was a green potion in a plain glass phial, like a sphere with a cork stopper, and the other was a small wooden box with four squares of sweetbread—at least that's what the log said. He took a taste and was surprised how much it was like honeyed cornbread. His stomach was still too sick to eat, so he stashed them away for later. *Better than nothing. Maybe I should've taken the other potions and sold them.* He couldn't help but feel a little disappointed. *I guess stat points really are rare.* At least the potion was interesting.

Potion of Minor Luck (I)
Consumable
Uses: 1, **Duration**: 6 seconds
Increases magic find by 10%.

There were new items in inventory, as well: an alchemy kit and an alchemy ability stone, the latter in blue text. Since the spear hadn't dematerialized, he assumed only magic items, crafting items, and gold were auto looted from defeated enemies. He'd gotten thirty-five coins from the fight, sold the spear for ten more; the shaman's staff and bone necklace got him another fifteen. A quick look at the Shop showed an ability available for fifty.

Not bad, he thought, as he used the stone and admired the new ability in his list, *and I still have twenty left over.*

Minor Spell Vulnerability (I)
***Class**: Healer*
Active, Combat, Enchantement
***Cost**: 5, **Range**: 10', **Duration**: 1 min*
Reduce a target's magic resistance.

Learning the ability completed one of his daily

quests, so of course he took the mystery gift. His reward was a black traveler's cloak, long and soft, though it felt more like a weighted blanket. Wearing it would be impossible. He could at least use it as a blanket, so he stored it for later.

Every time he interacted with inventory, it looked and felt like performing a magic trick. There was a pulsation of mana throughout his hand like little tremors of power, with the buzzing of an electrified fence. He pulled the alchemy kit out for a look. Its wooden box was well made, polished to a shine and embellished with silver edgings. It was about the size of a small footlocker. The lid lifted quietly on oiled hinges and pulled with it a top layer, like a shelf, with a second just beneath. The entire interior and shelves were covered in a soft crimson cloth. The lid itself housed a row of ten glass phials, held in place by a wood beam and leather strips for a perfect fit. One was deep red, another ocean blue, while the rest were filled with clear water. The first two gave off a glow, were infused with mana that could be both seen and felt.

He wanted to drink one of the waters right away but thought it best to hold off. As dehydrated as he was, with the rancid taste of vomit still in his mouth, there was no telling if the phials contained ordinary water or something rare. He could wait a little longer. With any luck, it might rain again. He explored the kit further to take his mind off the thirst.

The first shelf held a stone mortar and pestle, a hand shovel, and a small tool with an inward curved blade, each piece clean and neatly tied in place. The second shelf and bottom were organized by wood slats, filled with a variety of carefully gathered herbs, minerals, and other materials—like feathers, teeth, and claws. One of the larger compartments was stocked with the red crystal he'd just found by the tree.

That's gotta be used to make health potions, he reasoned. It was the same hue as the first potion secured to the lid. He brought out the ability stone. *Might as well, right? What better way to deal with running out of mana than to make my own pots?* When he tried to use the stone, a window popped up.

Warning! You may only learn two crafting abilities. Do you wish to continue?

Once confirmed, the change was both instant and apparent. Suddenly, he could see names above each resource. Even the world around him sprung to life with plants and flowers he either couldn't see before or hadn't noticed. The labels, while quite visible, were faded enough to see without obstructing his view. Most of them were in white, but the crystal, called lifebloom, was in blue. That either meant it had magical properties, or it was rare and expensive. He could feel only a glimmer of power from the entire patch and assumed it was the latter that was true. A quick look through the Shop confirmed it: lifebloom was a hundred gold per pinch.

Per pinch? He considered for a moment. *Probably means you have to grind it down in the mortar.* Another thought occurred. He took the red potion from its secured spot inside the lid. *How do I learn recipes? Do I need to test this one, take notes, and try to replicate it, or can I just break this one down...*the potion deconstructed.

Congratulations! You have learned Minor Healing Potion I!

He did the same with the blue and green potions, which gave him recipes for mana and luck. *Ohh, now that gives me an idea!* A grin crossed his face, as he inwardly vowed to start saving all his mystery gifts. He looked over at the patch of lifebloom. *I should probably gather all this.* He wondered how much gold it would be worth if he converted it all to powder.

A bush beyond the nearest tree caught his attention. He'd seen many like it before then, but they always seemed to blend into the background. There was color to it now, a tinge of blue to its stems and purple berries interspersed all throughout. His new alchemy ability told him it was called winter's woe, a common resource. Curious at the name, he put everything away but the gathering knife and went to inspect the bush.

Palmer both looked and felt miserable. His clothes were in ruin, covered in blood, mud and vomit. They smelled even worse. Though his stomach was a little queasy, he still wanted to eat something. Maybe the berries could help with his thirst. The first one surprised him with its taste. It was a burst of sharp sweetness, with a texture like frozen grapes. It didn't take long before his palms and mouth were stained purple from the juices of hastily eaten berries by the handful. It was only after he stopped eating that the name made any sense.

The bitter aftertaste was overwhelming.

He coughed and sputtered for some time, wished he could somehow empty his stomach again. Worse still, it gave him heartburn. He tore away some grass, used it to wipe his tongue and even chewed the blades in a vain attempt to replace the acrid taste. He collapsed onto his back, sighed up at the fading daylight and tried to focus on the silver lining.

At least I'm not thirsty anymore. Hmm. He wasn't quite ready to work on gathering crystal, so he considered his unspent stat points. As much as he wanted to continue the glass cannon route, he felt that any attribute of zero came with a heavy penalty. *If anything, putting a point into each one might give me a better idea of what they do.* He confirmed putting one point into strength, dexterity, and wisdom. When there was no immediate change, he got back to his feet. *Okay, let's get to work.*

It took little effort to cut away crystal from the sun moss, which he gathered as well. He assumed if it had a label, it must be useful to alchemy. Rather than store it all in the kit, with the other resources, he placed them directly in inventory. It was far too much to fit, otherwise. When he was ready to start looking for the rift again, he found himself wanting to stop and gather samples of everything else he encountered. Out of the twenty or so different plants he took from, only one had its name in green and another was in blue—uncommon and rare. He thought it odd that his fatigue had been steadily rising. He'd assumed, incorrectly, it was only influenced by combat. It seemed any exertion, like gathering crafting materials, counted as well. At twenty-four percent, he began to wonder at what point a penalty would occur and what might the consequence of that be.

His mind wandered as he walked, kept an eye out for resources, browsed the Shop to determine what he should gather or skip. Empty phials cost ten gold but were also limited to twenty-five per day. If he wanted to level up his alchemy, it was going to be a slow process. He'd also need a source of clean water, and the primary ingredient of the first tier binding agent: moonbriar. Though it was listed in the recipes as a common herb, there was none stored in the alchemy kit, and he'd yet to find any while searching.

Hours passed without finding a way home or the herb. To be honest, he wasn't sure which disappointed him more. As much as he wanted to get back to his life, a small part of him wanted to keep…playing. More levels, more abilities, more crafting, more power! He'd felt helpless for so long, bullied and put down, that what he wanted now more than anything was to feel something else. He had to admit, the real reason he hadn't found the rift was that, maybe, he just didn't want to.

There! His eyes went wide. *Found it!* Palmer ran

through the dense grove of trees just ahead, to the layer of thicket its label told him was beyond it. Moonbriar. *Maybe now I can try making some potio –*

The sound of grunts and clanging metal brought him to a full stop. He instinctively dropped to all fours and hid. Though they were a good distance away, and he hadn't yet seen one, he knew they were goblins. A lot of them. He crawled toward the thicket and risked a look through the trees. There was a collection of straw huts, a village of sorts, with smoke from a campfire and animal hides hung to dry. Many of them went about working, like normal people, while others patrolled in the outskirts in leather armor. It was hard to think of them as monsters, despite how they looked, as he watched them go about such mundane tasks as cooking and chopping wood. One thing, however, did strike him as very odd.

There's no kids. He made a disapproving face. *They're not real.* They were all just enemies spawned full grown by the system. *If there's one thing games will never do, it's allow players to kill children.* He let out a deep breath he hadn't realized he'd been holding, as if the newfound information had settled something deep within him. *If this is just a game, I'm gonna play to win.*

There were dozens of goblins, far too many for him to handle, and all with their names in orange and red. It was a daunting task to even consider. Knowing it was all just a game had firmed his resolve. As he studied their pathing, watched closely their interactions with one another and the environment, a plan began to take shape. With dusk close at hand, he'd have to wait until morning. For all he knew, goblins could see at night.

Palmer quietly backed away.

***

He'd gathered as much moonbriar as he could from the small patch before leaving and worked his way back toward the tree hollow. His sense of direction, his ability to recognize details of the terrain he'd already seen, was not an issue. So why couldn't he find any trace of the rift, even when he truly tried? Something else was at play, a game mechanic he'd yet to encounter.

It has to be hidden, he reasoned, as he made himself comfortable once more inside the tree he'd slept in the night before. The horizon had turned a deep violet as night fell, free of clouds but cold nonetheless. It led him to a puzzled observation. Not only had he not seen the sun or moon during the day, there were no stars or moon at night either. *Most games try to emulate the sky. Why doesn't this one? Ah, well.* He pulled the traveler's cloak from inventory, set it across his legs for warmth, then retrieved the alchemy kit as well. *Time for some grinding.*

Palmer had never used a mortar and pestle before but assumed it was as simple as it looked. He began to mindlessly work lifebloom into its more valuable form, while his mind considered a plan for tomorrow. He took a break after a few hours, to eat and rest his hands. He was surprised at how strenuous the task had been. Despite how easily the crystal broke down to a fine powder, it still took more effort than he at first had expected. The sweetbread, however, held a pleasant surprise. A single piece was considered an entire meal. Not only did one fill his belly, it reduced his fatigue by half. He did wish for a steady source of water, though. There was little to no chance he'd ever risk winter's woe again.

With all of the lifebloom processed and stored, the first part of his plan was ready. He sold a pinch for a hundred gold and purchased an ability stone that had caught his eye earlier in the day.

Minor Regeneration (I)
Class: *Healer*

Active*, *Combat*, *Reversible*, *Necromancy
***Cost**: 5, **Range**: touch, **Duration**: 10 min*
Restore 1 health point per minute to a living target.

My first DoT. Damage over time spells were an integral part of a caster strategy to take down more powerful enemies. *It's a much more efficient heal, too.*

Night had completely fallen. Though it was pitch black outside, the soft glow from the heal and mana potions secured to the alchemy kit's lid gave off enough light to see by. The wooden box, with its open lid, was large enough to block the hollow's entrance and hide the light from anyone outside. He wanted to stay unseen for the same reason he didn't make a fire—someone or something might see it and investigate.

He spent the next hour working on the moonbriar, grinding it down to its useful state, as the binding agent recipe also called for powder. From the look of all the other resources in the kit, very few herbs were used in their natural form. The moonbriar was interesting, with heavy wide thorns, blue-green leaves like ocean water, and blue stems with silver along its edge like a blade. Though its rarity was common, the plant was infused with mana. It tingled his fingers with that same electric buzz he'd come to associate with power.

Palmer was ready for sleep, but an alert caught his attention. It was his Abilities tab. Apparently his alchemy had improved. There was no discernable change in its description, other than tier. His recipes were all unchanged as well. It would need more testing, but he assumed a higher alchemy skill could affect a number of things, from a potion's potency and duration to the amounts of resources used. What then of the recipe itself, though? If all abilities upgraded through continued use, and alchemy improved apart from the recipes, what did crafting the same potion over and over give as a reward?

Only one way to find out. Tired as he was, Palmer

set about making as many mana potions as he had resources. He followed the recipe, added resources to the mortar in the proper amounts, blended them together with the pestle and then watched the culmination coalesce into a magic-infused mixture. His first attempt was a success, in that he had created a minor mana potion, but its glow was listless compared to the one he already owned. *Lame. So, what's the difference?* He put both potions in inventory, to examine their details, and found his only replenished one to three points. *Potency. Figures.* He sighed. *So, then what the hell does a higher tier alchemy give?*

The phials ran out before he could find an answer. He purchased more but had no water to mix ingredients with. Since the Shop put a limit on how many it sold each day, he made a mental note to buy them out at every chance. A clean source of water was a problem for future Palmer. At the moment, what he needed was sleep.

He left the kit open, felt safer with the pale blue glow of his hard work to see by. He pulled the cloak up over his chest, wrapped it around his shoulders as best he could, and tried to sleep. At first, his exhausted body twitched and jumped at every sound in the forest. The smallest wind through the leaves, the rustle of feathers from a bird above, or the distant howls of a wolf pack, they all eventually faded into the quiet of a deep slumber.

When he woke the next morning, his neck and shoulders were sore. He yawned and wiped the crust from his eyes. While his mana had been restored, he felt anything but well rested. He eyed the zero percent fatigue with disdain.

"What do you know?" he said to no one. "I'm still tired AF." He put everything away, including the cloak, and instantly regretted the rush of cold. "Damn it." Both arms clutched tight across his chest didn't help. "I have *got* to do something about this shirt."

The Shop didn't sell clothes or armor. In fact, it didn't sell anything at all related to everyday needs. Most games at least sold cosmetics. Palmer wondered how the game made any money, as he headed out and back toward the goblin village. He checked his alerts, saw a new daily quest to improve a tier two ability, and was a little disappointed there was only the one change. The other three were still there. That meant both class quests and dailies didn't refresh, no matter how difficult they were. He presumed they were randomly generated, though that may have been a false assumption. Still, if the system gave him a quest beyond his capabilities, he'd be stuck with it until he was strong enough to complete it. That put a definite kink in his plans.

"It's like you don't want me to win," he accused the system. "And why the hell am I alone? You could at least put me in a pug or something." A pickup group might have been safer than going solo, but there was no telling what sort of people he'd be teamed with. "Whatever. More xp for me."

Palmer made his way back to the dense tree line outside the village. The way the goblins went about their routines made him wonder if they slept. He watched the four patrols on the perimeter, groups of three warriors that followed a set path rather than a continuous circle.

Still no children, he noted, *and how come they don't speak to each other? Even if it was in goblin or grunts, shouldn't they communicate somehow? Give orders? Wonder what happened to three I killed?*

He expected better AI from such a sophisticated game.

A new patrol started to leave the village, headed in the direction he was certain the rift should be. It was what he'd been waiting for, a number he could manage separated from the rest. He kept to the trees, quiet and out of sight, as he followed the patrol. All three were warriors, like the other patrols, in leather armor pieces and armed with short swords. Their names were in orange, despite his new level. If the consideration system worked like others he'd seen, it meant they were three levels higher than him. Yellow was two, blue was one, white was the same, green was one lower, and gray was everything else below. Color didn't always equate to level but could be adjusted based on difficulty. An enemy could normally be orange, due to level, but become red if it had something that made it more difficult—its rarity, being a special named, an elite, or even a boss.

After half an hour it was more difficult to stay hidden. The forest was less dense in this area and the brush scarcer as well. He was forced to lay low within the grass. He could feel more than see what he'd been searching for all this time. The magic that caused the rift gave off a resonant vibration even at a distance of three football fields. The tear in space was still there, the air shattered above the ground. Light refracted off its cracks, a glistening of silver.

The mist was gone.

Does that mean something? He watched the goblins stand around the rift, eyeing it with caution. *Is it inactive? Am I stuck here?* One squared its shoulders and placed a hand on the rift. Nothing happened. *What!* It pushed harder, caused the cracks to flare brighter, but the rift would not open. *No. No, no, no. It's because they're not real, right? They can't cross over to our side. Damn. So much for surprise.*

Palmer had planned to lay in hiding along their path back to the village, to ambush them before they knew he was there. He no longer had a choice. They stood between him and his way out. He had to know if it still worked or if he'd taken a one-way trip. He forced down his fear, activated his shield, and charged them with determination.

Though he made no noise as he ran, because healers

weren't foolish enough to call out their position with a battle cry, the goblins immediately saw him. They drew their weapons and scowled, all pointed teeth and bloodlust. They rushed toward him as well. He'd been right about the penalty to movement, though he wasn't sure if it was strength or dexterity that allowed him to match theirs. They were fast but no longer as quick-footed as they seemed before. He landed a touch attack against the first with the reverse of his new ability. The second slashed his shield for three points. Palmer had allowed it, because it put him within reach of a touch upon the third. He dug a foot into the ground to stop his momentum, turned and immediately reached for the other goblin. The first scored a hit for four points on his shield. It didn't matter. All three were now afflicted with reverse regeneration.

They'd be dead in ten minutes.

Even though he had three points left on his shield, he activated it again to refresh the total and duration. It was just a precaution, to allow him enough time to get away and create distance. The kiting strategy was a favorite of his, where damage over time was applied, and the caster simply ran out of reach. It took ten long minutes of solid running, with bloodied and bleeding goblins trying desperately to reach him, but the tactic had worked. Two died after nine minutes, and the third shortly followed.

Congratulations! You have gained a new level!

He'd also completed a class quest with the third activation of shield. He gave little thought to the rewards, immediately chose mystery gift and stored it for later. He put the stat points into INT and confirmed. With new levels replenishing his mana and fatigue, and the experience needed for early levels being relatively small, he was sure he could power through a few more levels by end of the day. He just needed a safe way to lure goblins from the village.

The loot was less than stellar.

Each had dropped ten gold, which was typical of the others he'd defeated, and were equipped with common items. At least the DoT hadn't destroyed their gear. The swords and leather armor sold for another sixty gold. One had dropped a warrior ability stone, also common rarity: Minor Slash. He couldn't use it but decided to keep it anyway. He thought it best to hold onto any ability stones he found, in case he had a use for them later on. Besides, another fifty gold didn't bring him any closer to the next class ability for sale. It would take the one hundred and ten he already had, plus an additional four pinches of lifebloom, to afford that.

As he walked back toward the rift, a fear in his middle continued to grow. Anxiety over the thought of being stuck in this world was at odds with his desire to keep playing. He wanted to grow stronger, to gain levels, feel powerful for once—just not at the expense of real life. It was one thing to indulge a delusion. It was entirely another to succumb to one. He still had friends and family he cared about. Life wasn't great, but that was sort of the point. No one ever truly appreciated what they had without first suffering its absence.

Palmer stood before the rift. The hair on his neck and arms were raised. Whether it was because of the change in his stats or something else, he could feel and see the mana driving the breaks wider. There was no darkness at its base, like there had been on the other side. The rift wasn't feeding off this end. It was draining energy from his reality, from his home. What he couldn't figure out was why. What happened when it grew big enough? This wasn't a random occurrence. It was a deliberate tear, caused by a spell or ability. He placed his hand at its center and pushed.

It went through.

He'd been holding his breath. He let it out in a whoosh and pulled his hand back. It was enough to know he could return. He wasn't trapped. He had a choice. Game or no, he needed answers. And he wouldn't find them on the other side. He turned and headed back toward the village. He doubted goblins were behind the endeavor. They were low level enemies with no more magic than him. Whatever had caused the rift was much stronger than a shaman. It had managed to bridge worlds with a tear in space.

"I can't compete with that," Palmer said to himself—or even the system. There was a hope inside him that it might reply. "Not yet anyway. And maybe I won't have to. There might be a way to close the rift from this side. I just have to look for it."

Hmm, why hasn't anyone else come through? he considered. *Should I have gone for help? Would anyone even believe me?* There was a fear at the back of his mind he refused to admit, even in thought. He could've gone through and tested whether he still had abilities there, or if they only existed in this place. *I can always go back.* The other unspoken fear, born of greed and competition, was the desire to get ahead before others learned of the game. *I could bring proof.* He chuckled at the idea of dropping a goblin corpse at the local police station. *If others could see it, too...*

Palmer snuck back into the shadows of the tree line outside the village. He already knew the patrol patterns and had formulated on the way. When the nearest patrol was closest to his position, he snapped a branch to get their attention. One stopped and looked his way. The other two continued on. He cracked the branch again, this time loud enough to startle birds into the air. The two leveled gazes his way and drew their short swords. All three approached without alerting the other patrols.

He slipped deeper in, waited behind one of the larger trees. They paused at the tree line, searched for what had caused the noise. Palmer purposely stepped on leaves. The rustle urged them forward. He activated his shield and quietly waited. Three warriors again, this time their names in red, they might prove a bit more difficult than the last. His plan was the same. He did his best to dodge attacks, to preserve his shield, and inflicted each one with a DoT. These three were faster. His shield was spent, and he'd sustained three points of damage, before landing a touch on all of them. He ran for all he was worth, until the ability had worn off. They still chased him. With a groan, he turned about and did it all again. Halfway through the second run, they finally died.

Congratulations! You have gained a new level!

They'd had him down to two health, even with a second application of shield, but the level up brought him back to full. He'd also completed two quests—two more mystery boxes for the stash. He put the three points into INT and sold off all their gear. He circled around to the next patrol. And the next. And the one after. By the time he was done, he'd gained another two levels.

At level five, a message appeared in the log, but he'd been too focused on the task at hand. He looked at it now.

Congratulations! You have unlocked a new specialization!
Healing
Damage
Mana Regeneration

Damage may have been the obvious choice for a glass cannon, but that wasn't the most efficient long-term approach. The options didn't specify how much of a bonus he would receive. Whether it was a straight up addition of points or percentage based, a healer always went with improved mana regeneration. It was the only way to outlast enemies in a prolonged fight. He chose and confirmed, saw no visible change in his stats, and was once more annoyed at the lack of information the interface provided.

When he turned to face the village, their names were mostly in orange, with a few of the workers in yellow. There were still two dozen left. *How the hell do I pull, without aggroing them all?* His Abilities tab blinked. *Ohh, nice!* Both Shield and Regeneration had improved. The first had a new duration of two minutes, while the other had its range increased to one foot. *That makes things much easier!*

Rather than snap a branch, which he doubted any of them would hear, he picked up two rocks and banged them together once. There were no longer any birds nearby to give up his location. Combat all around the village had already scared them off. A few goblins did notice the noise but couldn't seem to locate its source. He was hidden behind a tree, as he struck the rocks again. He peeked long enough to see a handful of them had begun to take notice. One more crack of the rocks brought them out to investigate. None seemed alarmed by the missing patrols.

It was more difficult to deal with five at once. So much so, that he considered a few points into other stats. If not strength or dexterity for the movement, which he still wasn't sure which affected speed or reflexes, then at least into constitution for more health. The shield effectively doubled his health points, but too often he'd come close to death from a single lucky blow. He'd expended thirty mana before the last goblin was afflicted. Per usual, he ran away at a full sprint.

I should get extra stat points, he complained, *just from all this running! Why don't stats improve with use, like everything else?*

He gained another level before the last two fell over.

With his INT already at seventeen, he thought it time to experiment. As much as he loved round numbers, and as tempted as he was to go to twenty, too many things could go wrong before the village was cleared. He put all three points into dexterity, just to see what would happen. He sold all their gear, which brought him to five hundred and thirty gold. One had dropped a warrior ability stone, Minor Proficiency: Sword, while another had copper and iron ore. He left them in inventory for future use.

He'd been receiving new quests with each level up and had managed to complete a few without even looking at them. He added those three mystery boxes to the others, with the notion of celebrating that night. It was the gold that really interested him. It was a milestone, of sorts, because he could now afford the next class ability.

Minor Casting Speed (I)
Class: *Healer, Mage*
Passive*, *Evocation
Increase ability use by 10%.

The time it took to activate an ability was instant. The time between being able to activate another, however, was at least six seconds. In combat, it felt like an eternity. This passive should help him attack more targets more quickly. It made facing a small group of enemies not so daunting.

He moved around to the other side of the village, where he was more likely to get the attention of a small group. He lured them out into the forest in much the same way as before and was immediately glad of his decision. The added points into DEX did nothing for his movement speed. What it did, though, was improve his reflexes. He saw movement and physical intention in others more quickly, which in turn caused them to move more slowly to his eyes. He could more easily dodge attacks by stepping aside before being struck, by seeing the attack before it came. If points into strength increased movement speed as well, the two stats would make a high level melee class an unstoppable force.

Meh, he thought. *Too bad, I'm a healer. I'll have to settle for melting faces at a distance.*

Palmer gained another level with that group and grew brazen. There were still over a dozen goblins left in the village when he approached. He put the points into INT and casually navigated the system, as he walked directly into the village. There was no need to call out or catch their attention. He refreshed his shield and jumped into the fray, leaping from one goblin to the next. With no need to land a touch, he inflicted them one after the other. Enemies tended to dodge direct hits. He only needed to get within a foot. The only thing preventing their deaths was magic resistance, which low level creatures didn't have in abundance.

One thing they did have to their advantage was numbers. His plan to take them all on at once had been foolish. Toward the end, he was put on the defensive, forced to refresh his shield and deal with minor wounds. He'd received so many, so quickly, that he had to use regeneration as a buffer between heals. He ended up using far more mana than would have been necessary with a careful approach. It was inefficient and reckless, beneath him—but also calculated. He leveled up during the fight. Any mana that might have been wasted in a hasty defense, any health lost to a number of hits, were all fully restored before the fight was done. He didn't even use the kiting strategy, just dodged their attacks and put up a new shield when the old one was depleted. By the time it was over, he had reached level ten, received a second specialization option, improved all his ability passives, and completed three more quests.

It was going to be quite the celebration.

- 3 -

With the village cleared, Palmer had time to look around. Of particular interest was the stone well he'd spotted between the two largest huts. Just beyond that, at the center of settlement, was a sizeable campfire with a large cooking pot, a butcher's table laden with a wolf carcass, and two racks of dried meat strips. Whatever bubbled in the cast iron cauldron smelled questionable, not unlike the school cafeteria on Mystery Meat Tuesdays. The wooden bucket suspended over the well had seen better days but looked intact. He peeked over the edge and saw clear water a good twenty feet down. He lowered the bucket by its rope, let it fill to the brim and pulled it back up with ease. Though he only had a single point in strength, he admitted he did feel a bit stronger.

He completely drank the first bucketful, only then realized just how thirsty he was. The fighting had lasted for hours, without food or drink. He pulled a sweetbread from inventory and gulped that down as well. One look down at his hand brought a shiver of disgust. It was covered in grime from grinding potions and the black blood of fallen goblins. He poured the second bucketful over his head. A dark halo of brackish water spread outward from his feet, comprised of at least three different layers of filth. From caked mud to spattered vomit, hard-earned sweat to hard-fought blood and bits of gore, it all washed away from the tattered remnants of his clothes.

Hmm. He pulled the traveler's cloak from inventory, wiped his face with it and put it back. When he called it out again, the cloth was still clean and dry. *Ha! I love finding bugs like that.* He completely wiped off his entire body with it before putting it back into storage. Palmer wasn't one to cheat in a game, but he did love the clever use of game mechanics. *That's the difference between a hack and an exploit.*

There was so much to do.

He chose mana regeneration again for his second specialization. What that did was unclear, for now, but would likely become important once his leveling slowed down. He knew with a certainty that his high intelligence score was carrying him through these fights, that someone his level would have gone a more balanced route. His abilities were hitting more often than they should, given the law of averages, and when they did, scored critical hits more often than not. It was a dangerous strategy, the glass cannon, especially when solo. If he ignored his other stats for too long, a single misstep would bring him down. Fortunately, he had a plan for that.

He had five points to spend, put one into DEX and the other four into CON. A larger health pool would make his regeneration ability more useful and efficient. He looked over his character details with approval.

PALMER
LVL: 10 **Class**: Healer
STR: 1, **CON**: 5, **DEX**: 5, **INT**: 20, **WIS**: 1
HP: 50 [50], **MP**: 200 [200], **F**: 0%
SP: 0

He'd gotten another hundred and fifty gold from the last fight, sold all their gear for the same amount, which brought his total to seven hundred and fifty. It wasn't bad but not enough to buy the next ability. He debated using the village as a shelter. A source of clean water would make it easier to brew potions. There was just one possible problem causing an itch at the back of his mind. He searched around a bit more for any sign of potential trouble. The tents were all empty, just dirt floors with no beds or even a pile of straw to sleep on. It was in the largest tent, however, where he found what he was afraid of. There was a stone circle at its center about an inch thick and six feet in diameter. It was covered in magical runes he didn't recognize. He didn't need to read their language to know what it did. There was no mana coming off it at the moment, but he knew at some point those runes would flare to life.

He set out to find more goldleaf and a new patch of moonbriar. They were the key ingredients to a potion at the center of his plan. Whether his improved alchemy skill made herbs easier to find or possibly his high INT score, he made no complaint when both were found just on the other side of the village. Goldleaf was another common plant he'd yet to see. It would be easier to find now that he knew what it looked like. Its yellow leaves and golden stems stood out in the light of day but were otherwise unremarkable. He gathered all he could, made his way back, and settled into a tent where he could hide and keep an eye on the one with the stone circle. He called out the alchemy kit and got to work grinding herbs. When he was finished and nothing had happened across the way, he bought out all the empty phials in the Shop and got to brewing.

With a bit of admiration for his own work, he admitted he'd gotten better at mixing ingredients in the stone bowl. Using a mortar and pestle was not as easy as it looked. Like everything in life, it took practice. His potions had started to look better as well. His alchemy improved to tier three, which visibly lessened the amount of ingredients needed, and even his luck potion recipe improved. It now granted fifteen percent to magic find instead of ten. Since the potions he'd already made were lower tier, he sold them all for twenty-five hundred gold each.

Quite the money maker, he thought and eyed his new wealth. *If my plan doesn't work, I'll at least have a decent way to make gold.* Now that he could afford it, he bought the next and last class ability in the Shop. *I wonder if the Shop will refresh with newer ones later on, or if I'm stuck hoping for drops to get new abilities.* He used the stone and confirmed. *Either way, this gives me a pretty good starting point.*

Minor Cure Disease (I)
Class: *Healer*
Active**, **Combat**, **Reversible**, **Necromancy
***Cost**: 10, **Range**: touch, **Duration**: Until cured*
Remove one disease from a living target.

"Why word it that way?" he quietly wondered aloud. "Can you have more than one disease? Does that mean in reverse, it's a stackable debuff?" His rumination was cut short, as three goblins stepped out of the tent and immediately headed out to patrol. *I knew it!* They were orange and yellow in comparative levels, three warriors in leather armor and with swords, like before. Palmer suspected they were the first patrol he'd killed that day. His theory was confirmed, when rather than patrol the village, they headed out toward the rift. "Damn, I'm good." He put the kit away and headed after them. "That makes respawn about six hours." He couldn't help but grin. "That means I can easily farm them, if I keep their spawn times scattered."

He caught up and made quick work of them. The ease with which he dealt with the goblins was a far cry from that first encounter. He'd become quite the expert at looting as well, selling all their gear for the extra coins. One had even dropped the crafting ability stone, Minor Blacksmithing, and its accompanying kit. The skill was typically used to create weapons and armor. Palmer didn't see much use for that, so he stored both for later use. He could sell them for decent gold, but there was little left in the Shop that interested him.

When he returned to the village, he went to the spot in the forest where he'd lured away the first patrol. Their bodies were still there. He went back to work brewing the new tier of luck potion while he waited. He was nearly out of resources when all three bodies dematerialized. He put everything back in inventory and moved to the tree line. The three goblins he'd expected to see were headed out for patrol, no sign of concern at the empty village.

"Time for a little power leveling."

With the goblin spawn times set apart and with how easily he could deal with them in small groups, Palmer cleared the entire village before what passed for daylight began to fade. He'd gained three more levels, completed two additional combat-related quests, improved his heal, regeneration, and shield abilities, earned a total of six hundred and fifty gold from drops and gear sold, and acquired two more ability stones: Minor Enchanting and Minor Regeneration. The crafting stone came with a kit as well, just like the others had. Creating magic items seemed like a perfect fit for his character build, so he used the stone and confirmed the warning box. He had no idea if he could undo the choice at some point in the future but assumed as much.

The other stone buzzed in his palm. He thought since he already had the ability, he'd be unable to use it. Its tingling up his arm said otherwise. He was curious what would happen. Since he didn't need the gold from selling it, he decided to experiment. He was surprised to see his regeneration ability improve. Eyes wide at the potential for an exploit, he pulled up the Shop to buy more ability stones. Everything was grayed out. All the healer stones were gone. He sincerely hoped they might refresh at some point, because the drop rate from enemies had been terrible so far.

Palmer debated whether to sleep or farm more experience. The last group he faced were yellow and white in levels. *Another village clear would probably tank the xp. I'm not sure it's worth staying up for.* Spending the night in the village was too dangerous. In the end, he thought it better to head back to his tree and gather herbs on the way. He would play around with enchanting some other time.

It was nearly dark when he made it back to his familiar hidey hole in the burned tree. On the way, he'd found two moonbriar patches, a large haul of goldleaf, and a fair amount of a plant he hadn't seen before, called mage whisker. It was blue in rarity, had purple petals and long white strands like tendrils flowing out from its center, like the beard of an old man. He wasn't sure which recipe called for its use, but he knew better than to pass up anything of value.

He ate the last sweetbread, having finished one earlier, and washed it down with well water he'd saved in empty phials. Traveler cloak over his crossed legs, alchemy kit open before him, Palmer set to grinding all of his gathered herbs into usable materials. He had no way to keep track of time without a phone, but it felt like hours before he was ready to brew. By the third luck potion, his alchemy improved to tier four, and with the seventh the recipe leveled to three as well. His luck potions now granted a twenty percent bonus to magic find. He used the last three phials to craft the better versions.

Palmer yawned and shook his head vigorously, tried to stay awake. As excited as he was, exhaustion weighed his every move. For his plan to work, he'd need to be sharp and alert, his body rested. With heavy lids, he relented. The deep emerald glow of his improved luck potions was a difficult temptation to overcome. He yawned again. It would be morning soon enough.

He'd waited this long. He could wait a little longer.

***

Palmer woke before dawn, excited to get things underway. He sold off all of the low-tier luck potions, which put him just over seventy-five thousand gold, and bought out the empty phials. As his coin count increased, a new item appeared in the list. It was blue rarity and called Shop Upgrade License. By no small coincidence, he assumed, its cost was nearly all his coin.

Seventy-five thousand is a lot. Admittedly, gold seemed pretty useless, but to give up all he had without knowing the benefit was a bit of a gamble. *I guess I could make it back pretty easily selling potions.* It was hard to back away from a gamble, when his long-term plan relied so heavily on the practice. *Fine.*

He purchased the license, felt a twinge of regret at seeing most of his coin vanish from the screen, but was immediately happy with the results. New items filled the list, with common to rare crafting resources, a few potion recipes, and even common use necessities, like clothing, food, and water. The Gear and Ability Stones tab lit up as well. While there were new armor, weapons, and ability stones to purchase, their price left a sunken feeling in his chest. The least expensive piece of gear cost five thousand gold. The next class ability stone was three times that amount.

"Whatever," he said. "That's a problem for future me. Right now," he added and picked up a luck potion, "it's time to game the system."

He drank the potion in one go. It tasted like lime and honey, with a bubbly zest that tickled the nose. As quick as he drank the potion, he called out and opened as many mystery gifts as he could. The magic find effect wore off after the fourth box. As rewards, he received nine stat points and three different rare herbs.

"Yes!" Birds fluttered away in a swarm at the outburst. "I knew it would work!"

He did the same with the remaining two luck potions, opened seven more mystery boxes while under the effect of their magic find bonus. He let out a loud burp after the last. The potions had left a film on his tongue, with an aftertaste like mouthwash. His plan was a success, though. He gained eighteen more stat points, rare resources for both alchemy and enchanting, and two new healer ability stones. That left him with a total of forty-five points to spend. He'd essentially taken advantage of game mechanics to gain the equivalent stats of an additional twelve levels. That he felt proud at the triumph was an understatement. He immediately used the ability stones and looked over their details.

Minor Might (I)
Class: *Healer*
Active, Combat, Reversible, Enchantment
Cost: *5*, **Range**: *touch*, **Duration**: *3 min*
Increase a target's strength.

Minor Alacrity (I)
Class: *Healer*
Active, Combat, Reversible, Enchantment
Cost: *5*, **Range**: *touch*, **Duration**: *3 min*
Increase a target's dexterity.

"Ohh! Buff and debuff in one spell!" This meant he could temporarily improve his own stats before combat, and if an enemy proved too strong, he could weaken them as well. Used with spell vulnerability, it might prove a valuable combination. It made him wonder if the reduction to magic resistance would also cause reverse regeneration to hit harder. "Gonna need more testing. For now, I need to decide where to put all these points."

He'd been giving the stat system a lot of thought, since it was a bit different from others, both in video games and tabletops. The fact he'd started with all zeros told him that was the typical loadout for an average non-player character—in general, humans. Monsters and player characters would have at least three points, equal to one level, to set them apart from common folk, to show how deadly both were. There was a reason adventurers were either feared or revered. They could be like gods, in terms of power. The three points per level indicated to Palmer that a well-rounded character would put at least one into a main stat. The other two would then be used to tailor fit various playstyles. It was intended to maintain game balance by forcing players to allocate a limited number of points. Too many into one, and the others would suffer. Too few into what mattered most to a class, and the player wouldn't be able to progress.

"That means a level thirteen healer," Palmer thought aloud, "like myself, should have at least thirteen INT. Which means I want twenty-six at a minimum. It effectively makes me fight at twice my level, so I can take on harder fights for better xp and loot." Of course, he was setting aside the fact that main stat for a healer was wisdom. "Yeah, yeah, I know. I'll need WIS later, for the mana regen, magic resistance, magic damage reduction, blah, blah, but I'll never get there on my own if I can't kill anything. I have to be a caster first and healer second." He considered that last bit more closely. "If WIS does reduce spell damage, like it should, then CON should reduce physical damage. If I somehow maintained twice my level in INT, with decent points into strength, DEX, and CON, I'd practically be a mage-knight who can heal. Like a paladin? Meh." He never cared for that particular class, because of the ideological constraints that came with it, but he did like the idea of a mage that could wear armor and wield a weapon. "Okay, how about this..." he said and allocated every point.

PALMER
LVL: 13 **Class**: Healer
STR: 10, **CON**: 10, **DEX**: 10, **INT**: 37, **WIS**: 10
HP: 100 [100], **MP**: 370 [370], **F**: 0%
SP: 0

Palmer nodded with approval. "In terms of stats, I'm basically a level ten warrior. As a caster? I should hit like a god damn truck." Unfortunately, the higher he went in level, the less of a factor stats would play overall. "I really need to get some gear." He put the traveler's cloak back in inventory, shivered against the morning cold. "Enough of that."

He browsed the Items list for something warmer and less ruined. For just ten gold coins, he bought a white homespun shirt and pants, a gray woolen vest, a skin of water, and three sweetbread. With the new clothes on and the old ones stuffed into his backpack, he felt noticeably warmer and more comfortable but thought he looked like something out of an Amish documentary. The outfit was clean, didn't restrict his movements at all, but it was definitely giving off a renaissance fair vibe. He doubted the goblins would care, or anyone else for that matter, which brought up a feeling he'd been trying to ignore—guilt.

I've been gone long enough that she might even notice. His mother worked two jobs to pay the bills. Even though she claimed to make good money at both, one alone just wasn't enough. *Do I go back? Am I being selfish?* Or worse, was he being delusional and succumbing to a mental break? He called up a sweetbread and the water skin, ate breakfast as he debated whether to return home or clear the village again. *I already missed both Dungeon Crawler sessions. If anyone was gonna report me missing, it was the group.* He rolled his eyes at the thought. *Then again, they'd be the first ones telling me to keep going.* When he finished eating and looked up, he was already at the familiar tree line. He'd walked toward the village without realizing it. *That settles that, I guess.*

As he expected, everything had respawned. The majority were white in level, with a few yellow here and there—mostly in the patrols. As a solo healer, he didn't have the option of being picky. Realistically, he needed to stay and farm them all for experience and loot until every last one turned gray. He hadn't been able to test it yet, but when gray enemies were killed in most games, they no longer rewarded experience or items. It would be a tedious process, grinding through them all, waiting for respawn, and doing it all over again, but if it meant an extra level or two...

Palmer cleared the first patrol. He immediately noticed a glowing sphere of blue, with a tether of light still attached, emerge from their broken bodies. The mana-infused orbs hung suspended in air for a brief moment and then disappeared. He could see them reappear in his inventory. They were an enchanting crafting material called soul essence. Each was similar to other items, in that they had a rarity and tier. These were common, with a mix of tier one and two. He still wasn't quite ready to delve into the new crafting system. After all, he was still working out a way to maximize the efficiency of his alchemy. He made a mental note of the new materials and considered how much easier combat with the goblins felt.

His improved regen was now doing two points per minute, but he thought it a waste of time to use kiting with such low levels. His heal was hitting for three to four damage now, with double to triple that on critical hits. The points into dexterity made a huge difference in his ability to dodge their attacks. With the bump in strength, he was even able to punch one in the face for two points. Considering he didn't have the passive martial ability that granted proficiency with unarmed attacks, it was a pretty impressive feat. The Achievements tab lit up as the second goblin fell. It seemed he'd reached a new milestone. He was surprised to see his first passive had reached second tier at some point as well.

Adventurer II
Passive
Quest rewards are somewhat improved.

Goblin Slayer I
Passive
Increase damage dealt to goblins by 25%.

"It's like you want me to kill them all." The system didn't respond. "Fine by me."

He went to work clearing the other three patrols, lured them away each time, so he could control how many he fought at once. After the last goblin died in a miasma of dark blood and holy golden fire, Palmer's attention was immediately drawn to the large tent. He saw their power through the building, before they even stepped out. Two were very strong, with mana striations in blue and purple. The middle one had a much bigger aura. Thick tendrils of black and silver twisted outward in a sphere, so bright it engulfed the other two.

Three goblins stepped from the spawn point and out into the open, two shamans and a warrior chieftain. Though their names were in red, the chief's also had a plus sign. Palmer wasn't certain, but he thought it indicated elite status. That tier of enemy was far stronger and deadlier than others of its monster type. It stood at least a foot taller than the two beside it, with brawny muscles, heavy armor, and a two-handed axe. All three looked directly at Palmer and headed straight for him.

His instinct was to flee.

Palmer recognized an anti-spawn camping mechanic when he saw one. If they'd been created with aggression already tied to him, he could run out of their leash zone in an attempt to break that tie—assuming they had one. Either way, he was a little terrified. He backed off a good distance, but they kept coming for him at a steady pace. The shamans used enhancement abilities on the elite, waving their staves in the air as they did. Its body glowed in a nimbus of different color with each use, first orange, then yellow, and then in red. Though the axe was twice its size, the chieftain held it in one hand, eyes trained on Palmer with a murderous intent. He sensed magic on the weapon as well. The sheer power that emanated off the elite was palpable. If their names had been orange, just two levels above his own, Palmer might not have felt so uncertain. Red, however, was usually a death sentence. It meant three *or more* levels higher. There was no way of knowing how strong the chief was without a fight.

He could tell they weren't going to give up. Rather than allow the shamans more time to cast buffs, Palmer used his own, enhanced his strength and dexterity, then put up a shield. His mana was fine, but he drank two potions to restore it anyway. Better to use them before combat, he reasoned, than need it later and not have enough time. Experience told him the best approach was to take out the shamans first. They were support classes with healing. They would have fewer health points and weak physical defenses. Their magic resistance, on the other hand, would be on par with his own.

Palmer focused the left shaman. He got within the ten foot range and used spell vulnerability to weaken its resistance. He charged passed the elite, did his best to dodge, but still lost half his shield to a glancing strike of that axe. While his reflexes and speed were outmatched by the chief, he was far quicker than the other two. He landed simultaneous touch attacks, inflicted two counts of disease and was pleased to see they stacked. He jumped away, toward the other shaman, tried again to sidestep a swing of the axe and caught its edge. Shield gone, the wide blade head sliced across his side. Palmer cried out at the pain, nearly lost his footing, but managed to right himself in the next step. Taking damage hurt. A lot. In those moments when his skin and muscle parted, when flesh split open in a serious wound, the influx of pain was a sudden shock he would never grow accustomed to.

He did the same to the second shaman, reduced its magic resistance and inflicted two disease counts. He'd expected the disease to do damage over time, like the reverse of regeneration. What it did instead was considerably slow them down, withered and darkened their skin, and visibly ate away at their muscles. It was a slow effect, Palmer realized, coupled with stat damage. In a way, it was even better than direct damage to their health points. It made them easier to hit, reduced maximum health and mana, and weakened their spells. He put reverse regeneration on them both, to help deal with the fact they began healing each other. From there, it was a matter of refreshing his shield, healing his own wounds, and avoiding the axe blows that split the earth in wide cracks each time it struck the ground. He moved between all three, attacked the shamans with holy fire until the first finally succumbed.

Eyes wide in satisfaction, his triumph was short-lived. He'd paused for a breath too long to watch the goblin fall, plenty of time for the chief to land a hit. The axe went completely through the shield and into his left leg. There was so much force behind the strike, it upended Palmer, sent him to his back. His head bounced off the hard dirt and set both ears to ringing. He rolled away without thinking, felt a rush of air against his neck from where the axe had nearly caught him. He struggled to clear his vision, while his hands moved from muscle memory. Shield up, heal, regeneration, another heal, he moved with enhanced speed to avoid the deadly chieftain. He only needed to be within three feet of the shaman to use his reverse heal. Palmer went after the goblin without relent. Its body burst into golden flames to loud screams at each flare. Right arm, left leg, its chest, then its head—holy fire took it all in a burst of gore.

Warning! Your fatigue has reached 50%!

Palmer immediately felt the penalty take effect. It reduced his maximum health and mana points, made him slower to move and react. He couldn't see the exact rate at which they replenished, but he suspected his health and mana regen were hampered as well. As far as he knew, nothing restored fatigue but rest. If there was a penalty at only fifty percent, there were most certainly harsher drawbacks at seventy-five and higher.

So not only do I have to face this mini boss alone, Palmer inwardly complained, *but I have to do it with a handicap? Screw you, game!*

The axe caught him across the middle, buried deep into his abdomen. The shield had barely slowed it, as thirteen critical damage sent a shockwave of pain all through his body. He coughed out blood, a thick gob of red splatter. The chieftain gave an evil grin and yanked free the weapon that had partially helped Palmer remain standing. He hacked up a second spray of blood. Uneasiness swept over him, wobbled his legs. No amount of blinking would steady his gaze.

I need time. He put up a shield and stumbled away,

used heal on his tattered stomach. A boot knocked his left leg out from under him, dropped him to one knee. *Ow! No, wait.* Heal again. A leather glove backhanded him across the face. What would have been a stinging slap from a normal person was a jaw-jarring blow that turned the world into a burst of white-hot light. Palmer pulled a heal potion from inventory. It was knocked from his hand. *Hey! Those are expen*—another smack across the face.

The chieftain grabbed him by the front. Palmer instinctively took hold of the goblin's hand, more to steady himself, as he was forced upward onto the tip of both feet.

"Shouldn'ta done that," Palmer told the creature and activated spell vulnerability. The chief shoved him back and gripped its axe in both hands. "Too late now."

Palmer began stacking disease counts on the elite, slowing his movement with each use. After four, it was difficult to tell if it stacked any further. He was at least able to outmatch the goblin in speed now. He then used the reverse enhancements to debuff its strength and dexterity even further. Regeneration began to eat at its health pool, as he jumped away from another attack. Mana low, Palmer readied for a drawn-out fight. He drank as many health and mana potions as he could. He still feared it might not be enough. With the chieftain fully debuffed and dotted, all Palmer could do now was use what mana he had left for reverse heals or try to outlast by kiting.

The chieftain looked worse for wear but wasn't ready to fall over. It reared back its head and activated an ability. Red flames engulfed its body, and it grew even larger. As if enraged, the goblin roared a challenge and charged.

"Nope!"

Palmer ran for all he was worth. He used the timer on his shield to gauge when he needed to refresh the debuffs and DoT on the chief. Using spell vulnerability, with its one-minute duration, was key to landing disease and the other spells. He was able to dart back in for touch attacks, then dash away to maintain a safe distance. The rage ability the chief had used ended shortly after. It still tried to close the gap between them with a charge, a short burst of speed in a straight line. It dug one foot into the ground each time before activating. Palmer quickly caught onto the mechanic and ran in a different direction, since the goblin couldn't change path once it triggered the ability. It had other abilities as well, shouts for short duration buffs and weapon enhancements that lengthened the axe's reach. None of it could overcome the unrelenting reduction to its movement speed.

By the time the elite collapsed to its knees, breath heavy and body bloodied, eaten away by disease, Palmer had little mana left to continue himself. He'd endured the ache of cuts that stung his every step, for fear of running out of mana before the fight was over. He too fell to his knees, barely three feet away from the elite. They eyed each other through exhaustion and grievous wounds. With the last bit of his magic left, Palmer activated a final reverse regeneration on the chieftain.

"Just die, already." Palmer grew lightheaded. Using the ability had pushed his fatigue to seventy-five percent. "Oh, shi—"

They both fell over at the same time.

***

When the chieftain finally died, Palmer gained two levels and another specialization option. Though the first level up fully restored his health, mana, and fatigue, it took a few moments of grogginess for him to wake. He was healed, had no injuries to speak of, but still felt a deep aching in every muscle.

Am I dead? He sat up, saw the goblin's remains,

the absolute ruin their combat had wrought upon the area, and made a face at the smell coming off the elite's corpse. *Nope, still in Wonderland.* His head hurt as well. *That second fatigue penalty is no joke. If there's a third, I think I'd rather die. Probably would, anyway.* He selected the blinking alert for specialization and chose mana regeneration again. *Okay, loot.*

"So," he said to the system, "what'd I get?"

His inventory opened. The new items were highlighted—two class ability stones he hadn't seen before and a magic two-handed axe worth a hundred thousand gold. He was tempted to sell it right away and go shop for some new magic items. Experience with crafting systems told him that might not be the best course of action. If he broke it down into its material components, he could sell them for even more gold, though that usually involved an auction house with other players, or he could use those rare materials to create more useful magic items. As far as he knew, there was no other way to obtain enchanting materials, other than to buy them from others or disenchant magic items found on monsters.

Maybe it works differently here. He pulled the axe from inventory. It wasn't nearly as heavy as he'd expected. Whether it was from the inherent magic of the item or the ten points into strength, the sheer size of the weapon indicated a heftier weight. He pulled out the enchanting kit. It was the same shaped wooden box as the alchemy kit, with a different set of decorative metalwork and carvings. Inside was practically empty but for a handful of resources, mana-infused powdered crystal of various colors and a pouch of enchanting dust. *Interesting, no tools. So how do I disench—*A small window popped up, warning that the process could not be undone. He confirmed. The axe dematerialized from his hands, its pixels a mix of silver and blue. Four cloth pouches of enchanting dust fell into his lap, each about the size of a fist, with three similar sized pouches of green powdered mana crystal and one of blue. When he inspected the details of each, he saw they were labeled self-only. *Why the hell wasn't there a warning box about that first? That means I can't sell or trade it?* He tried to sell a pouch of dust.

You cannot do that.

"Son of a...You did that on purpose!" he accused the system. "Not cool, bro."

He did receive a new enchanting recipe, though—Rage. Palmer assumed it granted the ability the chieftain had used during combat. There were new alchemy recipes as well, from the mystery boxes he'd opened earlier—Stamina, Rejuvenation, and Speed. The first restored fatigue, the second health and mana points, and the third gave a six second boost to movement. Palmer wished he had seen them sooner. Just one stamina potion would have made all the difference against the elite.

He'd also completed two quests. There were so many class and daily objectives, one of each type per level, that he hadn't bothered to read them as they refreshed. He completed most by going about his business unaware. He took mystery boxes as his rewards and brought out the new class ability stones. They both lit up in his hands with use and dematerialized.

Minor Blessing (I)
Class: *Healer*
Active, Combat, Reversible, Enchantment
Cost: *10,* ***Range***: *touch,* ***Duration***: *1 min*
Increase a target's physical and magical hit chance.

Minor Restoration (I)
Class: *Healer*
Active, Combat, Reversible, Necromancy
Cost: *15,* ***Range***: *touch,* ***Duration***: *Instant*

Remove one serious injury from a living target.

After his experience with the anti-spawn camping mechanic, Palmer was no longer willing to farm the village like he'd intended. He cleared out all the goblins, with not much in the way of loot to show for it. He'd gained another level and completed three more quests. Most of the day was gone by then. Rather than travel back to his tree hole, he headed for the large tent. The first patrol would be due to spawn soon. He stood before the stone circle and eyed its magic runes. He wasn't sure if it would work, but he knelt and placed a hand upon its cold rough surface.

Are you part of the system, he pondered, *or are you considered a magic—*

He disenchanted the spawner. Four pouches of enchanting dust and two pouches of blue powdered mana crystal appeared. Palmer gave a nod of approval. He'd fully expected it not to work. His backup plan was to buy a battle hammer from the Shop and break the stone to pieces. It made him wonder if breaking down the spawner for resources was an intended mechanic or if there were other magic items in the world, not crafted by players, that could be disenchanted as well. A new enchanting recipe, he noticed, had just appeared: Minor Summoning Circle.

"I can make my own spawns?" Of course, there was no response. "To fight for xp and loot, or it'll fight for me?" Palmer sighed. "I'm getting sidetracked." He wanted to spend the rest of the day working on alchemy, to improve his luck potion even further. "I'll have to test this later. Besides, I don't have time to craft a 'summoning circle' of any material, let alone stone." He checked the Shop, just in case he could buy one. There were none listed. "Figures."

He pulled a sweetbread from inventory and munched as he left to gather herbs. The patches seemed to grow back with each morning. He had a mental map of the area to keep track of rare plants and the ones he needed to brew potions.

"That reminds me," he said, while working a patch of moonbriar, "I need to buy out empty phials." He pulled up the Shop and noticed there were twice as many available than before. "Fifty. Not bad." He bought them all, scrolled down a bit and bought some dried meat, a wedge of cheese, and a loaf of bread. He'd forgotten to refill the skin at the well before he left, so he got a second one to wash down the sweetbread. "Oh, ho! What's this?" He spotted an enchanting recipe—Minor Enhance Armor. "Yoink!" Its details, unsurprisingly, weren't all that helpful.

Minor Enhance Armor I
Enhancement
Duration: Permanent
Enchant a piece of armor to grant its wearer an effect based on resources used.

"Based on resources used," Palmer grumbled and moved onto the next patch in his route. He would need as much goldleaf as he could find. "So, I'm just supposed to try different materials and hope they do something useful? And what exactly is armor? Is this shirt armor?" It was ripped, bloodied, and covered in dirt and sweat. "Can I even wear armor?"

Frustrated, he perused the Shop as he continued to gather herbs into inventory. There were various armor pieces listed, available in plate, chainmail, three types of leather, padded, and cloth. There were no class restrictions for healer, like there were for rogue and mage. He questioned the rationale behind the battle healer mentality. It may have been safer to wear heavy plate armor, but mobility would be severely limited. Some games also penalized casters for wearing armor, even if the item descriptions didn't mention it. Casting speed, especially, could be slowed.

Yet more experimenting that needs to be done. He'd gotten skilled at quickly culling the precious parts of each plant. He was nearly done and had his eye on some mage whisker in the distance. *Hmm, what does the stamina potion need?* The screens moved with the speed of thought. *Heartleaf. Interesting. I think I saw some by that huge oak tree on the way to the rift. I'll get some tomorrow.* He'd been purposely heading in one direction, to explore as he gathered. There were only a few hours left in the day, so he didn't want to get too far from the village. *Kind of surprised I haven't run into any other monsters.*

He began to wonder if he was in a seamless game world or a zone, a limited space that required a transition to reach a new area—sort of like the portal. For longer than was prudent, he continued on in the same direction until daylight was nearly gone. It might have been dangerous to be out in the open when night fell, so he eventually gave up and turned around.

Night brought with it a chilling dark and wind that drowned out all other noise. He used the glow of a mana potion and the highlighted names of herb patches to find his way back to the village. Its campfire could be seen through the trees a great distance. Palmer settled into the smallest tent, blocked its entry with both his crafting kits. It was a restless night, where the crackle of the nearby fire and the howl of wolves he could never find during the day kept snapping him awake from a deep slumber. When morning finally came, he debated a few hours of more sleep.

Inefficient! He laughed. It was a common joke in his last guild that he complained whenever someone in the group wasn't maximizing gains. *If I can't game the system, the least I can do is be efficient with my time.*

He spent the next three days gathering herbs and exploring. He was curious to see if inventory had a max capacity. Along with mentally mapping all the best resource spots, he finally found the wolf pack that had been disturbing his sleep. They were red in level, though, so he let them be. He also found a second village, on the opposite side of his tree hole. They were an advanced type of goblin, called hobgoblins, and were also much too high a level to mess with. His most interesting find, however, was the most confusing.

It was a second rift.

When he came across it, he thought he'd somehow got turned around and was completely on the other side of the map. It looked much like the other rift, a jagged tear in space, except it wasn't expanding outward. Palmer also couldn't go through. When he placed his hand against the opening, it refused to yield, much the same way the other rift wouldn't allow the goblins to pass through.

"Could this lead to another game?" He looked down at the ground. It looked normal enough below the rift. The earth wasn't discolored in any way. There were no signs of being damaged by the contact. "Or is this place an in between of some kind, and the actual game is through here? Why won't it let me in?"

He'd given it up as a lost cause and returned to the village. There was a system mechanic at play he didn't fully understand yet. He assumed there was a link between the two rifts. He just hadn't found what it was. It was on the fourth day of exploration that he found what might tie it all together. It was a massive blue sphere of solid light, about the size of a small car. It was engulfed in fiery mana, with an aura of power four times as wide. Tendrils of blue and silver magic radiated outward along the surface, like thick jolts of electricity from a tesla coil. The ground all around it, in a circle the size of a football field, was darkened to ash, with black pixels rising upward. It looked as if the mana was corrupting the earth, killing all plant life, feeding on it all. Palmer couldn't be sure if the mana sphere was draining the world he stood in or fueling its existence. The only thing he could be certain of was that it was growing. Even from a safe distance, he could feel it pull at his middle. It wanted his mana. He risked moving in for a closer look and immediately stopped.

The ground nearby the sphere shook and broke open. A giant steel hand reached out from the opening, crashed against the surface in a plume of rock and ashen debris. A second hand joined it, with enough force to nearly topple Palmer from hundreds of feet away. Glowing blue orbs for eyes appeared through the chaos of corrupted dirt in the air. Slowly it crawled up and out of the earth, a huge monster made of steel. Its features were dull, vaguely human-like, fashioned without detail. Its mouth didn't move, but a roaring challenge echoed from within its hollow body. It was a metal construct, a crafted creature imbued with magic, and completely immune to all his spells. Palmer knew a boss when he saw one, and he wanted nothing to do with it. It was clear it had come to defend the sphere.

"You can keep it," Palmer said and turned away. "I'm out!"

- 4 -

Palmer washed himself with well water and his old tee shirt the next morning. He was a bit stiff from the cold and his exertions the night before. The fight with the elite goblin had made him aware of a problem. His run in with the metal construct served to drive the point home even further. He'd been powering through levels due to gaming his stats. Ability progression, however, was tied to use. That was a recipe for disaster. If he continued down that path, he would eventually reach a point where the raw power of his attributes could no longer compensate for the lack of skill. Which is why he'd set aside leveling for the time being to concentrate on crafting and improving his abilities.

While gathering herbs during the day, he'd kept his shield and buffs up at all times, stopping just short of the first fatigue penalty. Once his mana had regenerated enough and his exhaustion eased, he would do it all again. At night, he'd purposely use all his mana before sleep. Utility spells were easy to improve. It was the difficult ones he'd save for evening. Using reverse regeneration on himself did hurt, but it was mostly negated by regeneration—which for some reason he could stack. He supposed it was because the system considered the two as separate. What really hurt, however, was improving his heal. Its reverse could be brutal, especially when he landed a critical. The sudden loss of ten percent life was akin to being hit by a car. Or so he assumed. It certainly felt that way. Except he knew the car was coming. And it was on fire.

Placing debuffs on himself hadn't felt any better. While most could be negated with its positive use, disease could not. He could either endure it or remove it. After the first night, he gave up on working that particular skill. It had a nasty effect that only impeded his progress. The ability incurred a reduction in movement speed, but it also caused stat damage, which was a reduction to both the maximum and current of every attribute. Once he cured the effect, the maximum was restored to each, but the lost health and mana points were not. He decided it would be best to save that for combat.

All the suffering he'd endured had paid off. His abilities had improved, and he'd gained further insight into how the system worked. Once an ability reached tier four, its next upgrade was an evolution into tier one of the next rank. While each new tier slightly increased duration, range, and effect, an upgraded rank came with noticeable enhancements. Even more exciting, Palmer had found through this arduous process there were hidden abilities, ones that couldn't be bought, had no class restriction, and he presumed could only be discovered through practice and luck. One night prior, while he'd endured holy fire against his chest, he unlocked Minor Pain Tolerance. It was a passive that slightly reduced damage received, but it also significantly dulled the pain from wounds. Setting himself ablaze would always hurt. With the new passive it felt more like getting stung by a car-sized bee. The fact that it could improve over time only made it better.

Additionally, the previous night, after he'd used all his mana for the third time, he unlocked the passive

Minor Fatigue Resistance. Its benefit was slight, like the other, but it too would improve with use. Coupled with stamina potions, he might never have to deal with the fatigue penalty again. Though the notion was highly optimistic and wholly unlikely, Palmer chose to believe it.

Over the past four days, he'd amassed quite a sum of herbs. As far as he could tell, there was no weight or item limit to inventory—at least none that was listed. He had collected over thirty different resources, in a variety of rarities, worth over seventy-five thousand in their raw form. He spent the rest of the day working each one into their processed version, where they'd be ready for use as potions. His alchemy skill reached tier three of rank two, went from minor to lesser, and came with an unexpected benefit. Not only did the ability now reduce the amount of ingredients needed to brew a potion, he was suddenly able to discover new potion recipes while processing herbs in the mortar. He'd unlocked four new ones since achieving the second rank—Defense, Invisibility, Spell Power, and Rage. He'd also been given crafting quests, most of which he completed before he even knew they were there. He was up to fourteen mystery boxes by nightfall, which he kept safely in storage. Abilities weren't the only thing he'd been working to improve.

His plan had been expanded as well.

The next day was spent brewing. Palmer watched the value of his inventory grow from double, by processing all the herbs he'd gathered, to more than ten times that amount by producing as many potions as possible. Some had more gold value, but he was focused on ranking up the ones he used most. He had no intention of selling them anyway. That was a much later part of his extended plan. The next step to his strategy involved taking a loss, which was a part of crafting every player dealt with. Professions were largely a gold sink, a way to drain money from the economy. The ultimate payout was in what they provided. The added utility and power that couldn't otherwise be attained, was essential to almost every end-game goal. The pursuit of a new craft was not one to take lightly. It was bound to hurt, be it time or the wallet, which was why this next part was so hard to bear.

Palmer disenchanted all of the lower quality potions, so he could begin enchanting. The massive influx of resources would be more than enough to get him started, or so he hoped. He'd chosen the most difficult profession he could think of, since materials were hard to come by and so expensive. The one recipe had vague details and the kit no tools. He was going in blind, with just the hope he could figure it out.

He swapped kits from inventory and purchased a shirt from the Shop. His current one was already torn and ragged, with a huge cut in the front. For what he had in mind, it would be better to enchant a piece and keep it stored rather than wear all the time. He laid the shirt out on the ground before him where he knelt, called a pouch of enchanting dust to his left hand and a pinch of goldleaf to his right. He couldn't be sure but imagined whatever soul essence was required would be automatically taken from inventory. He focused on the Enhance Armor recipe, much like he would an ability, and tried to activate it.

Congratulations! You have learned Minor Enhance Armor: Luck I!

He stored the shirt to read its details.

Shirt (I)
Type: Cloth
Armor: 0
Restrictions: None
A plain shirt.

Luck: *Increases magic find by 5% when worn.*

It worked! He brought up the Shop, navigated to Items, and purchased new cloth pants, shoes, a hat, and bracers.There was a vest listed as well, but it was considered cosmetic and not armor. Palmer set about enchanting the other pieces. With a full set of Luck gear, and three more crafting quests completed, he was ready to open mystery boxes once more. *That's twenty-five percent total. With the new potion, I'll be at...*He pulled up its details.

Potion of Lesser Luck (IV)
Consumable
Uses: 2, **Duration**: 6 seconds
Increases magic and gold find by 35%.

"Sixty percent!" What that actually entailed could mean different things, depending on the system. He'd played action role-playing games where it was common to have fifteen hundred percent increased magic find. It didn't necessarily mean more or better magic items, just a better chance at getting something at all or from a higher loot table. "Time to find out which." He changed into his magic find gear, uncorked a luck potion, and readied to open boxes. "Here goes."

Though he took a whole mouthful, it only drained half the potion. Since it had two uses, the system had prevented him from drinking the entire bottle. He was pleasantly surprised that its taste had improved. He called out and opened four mystery boxes in quick succession. His inventory flickered with the new addition of items. He received a rare quality class ability stone, Minor Divine Wrath, a magic staff called Reckoning, and an abundance of rare and epic crafting resources for blacksmithing and tailoring.

Oh, no. He hadn't received any stat points. *Did I move to a different loot table?* He reasoned that the change would have taken place at fifty percent. He took off the hat and bracers to try again. With the potion consumed, it dissipated into pixels. Results were noticeably different this time. He received twelve stat points, a Heal ability stone, and common to rare resources for leatherworking and engineering. *Yes! Okay, so as long as I stay on this loot table, I can still get stats. Unless they become rarer on the higher table, because you get more than three...*

With only nine boxes left, he didn't want to experiment. Even if the stat reward was doubled at a higher table, the reduced chance of getting any meant less overall. It was safer to gamble on at least three per four boxes. The points were more important than items at the moment. He used a potion and opened the remaining boxes. He got fifteen stat points, a gold ring, more sweetbread, a Shield ability stone, and a few common herbs. While he was happy with the results, the Heal and Shield stones were a bit of a waste. His abilities had improved to the second rank. Since these were rank one, he couldn't use them anymore. He could sell them for gold, though, so not a total loss.

That gave him thirty-three points to play with, including the six he hadn't used from leveling up against the elite. Odd numbered stats bothered him, for some reason, so he put three into INT to round them off. The rest he put into wisdom. The past few days had shown him just how much his mana regeneration had suffered from not keeping up his main stat. Not to mention the fight with the chieftain and two shamans might have gone much differently with the increased spell hit and critical chance from a high wisdom. He had every intention of raising his other stats to stay strong, mobile and resilient. Those were how he survived encounters. What he needed was a better way to win them.

"I'm a caster, damn it. Time to act like one."

PALMER
LVL: 15 **Class**: Healer
STR: 10, **CON**: 10, **DEX**: 10, **INT**: 40, **WIS**: 40
HP: 100 [100], **MP**: 400 [400], **F**: 0%
SP: 0

With that done, he changed clothes, stored the magic find set, and used the rare stone he'd received. When he saw its details, he nearly yelped in joy. It was his first offensive ability.

Minor Divine Wrath (I)
Class: *Healer*
Active, Combat, Necromancy
Cost*: 15,* ***Range****: 20',* ***Duration****: 30 sec*
Cause 2-4 magical damage every six seconds to a living target.

"Oh my god," Palmer said. "That's so much better than the reverse of regeneration. Degeneration? I know the reverse of heal is usually called harm, but you don't seem to name the reverse versions." His accusation went unanswered. "This is gonna make a huge difference. Look at that range!"

The last piece to inspect was the staff.

Reckoning *(Unique)*
Weapon: Staff
Restrictions: Warrior, Healer, Mage
Damage: 1-6 physical, 1-6 magical
A weapon hand-crafted by the famed woodworkers of Evergreen Temple.
Grants the wielder Proficiency: Staff I.
Mana Lance: Three times per day, cause 4-24 magical damage to a target within 60'.

Palmer called it to his hand. It was a hefty length of burnished yew, two inches thick and half a foot above his head. The middle was wrapped in dark leather, and both ends capped in steel. There were runes carved into the wood, etched into the steel, and worked across the leather. The entire weapon buzzed with mana.

"Maybe the higher tier of loot table isn't such a bad idea after all." He looked to the horizon and gauged how much light was left in the day by its shade of violet. By his estimate there were still a few hours to go. "I should pay those wolves a visit. Kinda tired of them ruining my sleep."

***

Palmer considered all the things he missed, as he made his way toward the wolf den. Food was an obvious one, cheeseburgers and waffle fries, a chocolate malt with heavy whipped cream on top—even a crunchy peanut butter sandwich or plain grilled cheese would be heaven. Then there was candy. He wasn't huge on sweets, but he'd been away for so long, a confrontation with Guy and his lapdogs would be cake, if it meant a chance at a chocolate bar. *Oh, cake! German chocolate, red velvet...*There were the mundane things, as well, like sleeping in his warm and comfortable bed, with pillows and blankets. He couldn't remember the last time he went this long without a television, a computer, or a phone. The one thing that surprised him most about what he missed though was toilet paper. He'd found some thick, broad leaves that would do in a pinch but on more than one occasion suffered a mishap. Of late, his solution was to use a shirt he'd bought in the Shop. Once soiled, he put it back in storage. Though it came out clean again every time, he refused to wear it.

His mental marker came into sight, a set of birch trees with a patch of spirit moss at their base. The den was just ahead, beyond the heavy brush. Though he couldn't see the cave from where he stood, he could sense their power. When last he came upon them, four lounged outside upon wide flat stones. There were more of them deeper in. He felt their presence at the edge of his senses, like the menacing glare of someone hidden in the shadows. As Palmer slowly peeked out behind one of the trees to get a look, all four already sniffed at the air. Their heads were held high, as they searched for the source of his scent.

Their names in bright crimson were Dire Wolf. Despite the advantage in level, their auras were weaker than he'd expected. Either the power appraisal afforded by his INT stat had gotten more precise or level could no longer be relied upon to gauge the possible difficulty of an encounter. It was most likely due to his heightened attributes. The most recent boost put him equal in power to both a healer and a mage of level forty, though he was still just fifteen. He only hoped the weaker stats wouldn't hold him back or put his life at risk when faced with these enemies a smarter player would avoid.

It's a calculated risk, he reasoned. *I'll be fine, as long as I don't get hit. How did that quote go? "Everyone has a plan..."*

These were far deadlier than normal wolves, more monster than animal. Four times as large, with broad chests and thick manes, piercing yellow eyes and fangs the length of a finger, one was enough to overpower a man. Four was madness. Their paws were wider than his head, with claws that sparked the stones they stood upon when each began to move. Low growls and raised hackles pointed his way meant they'd found him. They began to spread out as they moved, as if they'd hunted together many times and planned to flank his location.

Palmer quickly buffed himself, put up a shield, and charged one in the center. The enhanced STR and DEX wouldn't do much for his magic, but they might help him stay alive. He hoped blessing would be enough to help land an attack. Once he was within twenty feet, he activated divine wrath. It was one of his most expensive skills. Luckily his mana pool was more than double what it should have been. His mana regeneration specialty had grown strong enough that he could watch the points tick back up as he spent them.

Damn! The dire wolf resisted. *I was afraid of that.* Palmer dodged its swipe and quickly followed up with spell vulnerability. When that was resisted, he cursed. *You can't be that much higher than me!* He tried to inflict a disease. If he couldn't reduce its magic resistance, he could lower its wisdom and try again. The other three were nearly in the fray. He was losing his surprise advantage. The disease landed, but the wolf nearly bit off his head. *Whoa!* Palmer sidestepped in time and punched it across the jaw. Bone cracked beneath the blow.

New ability unlocked: Minor Proficiency: Unarmed Combat I!

"Nice!" He didn't expect the punch to do quite that much damage. It made him wonder if they were highly resistant to magic but weak to physical. "Let's see." He called the new staff from inventory. The wolf he sensed came within reach behind his right side caught a swipe of the heavy wooden weapon across its chest. The wolf yelped, had been hit so hard that its face struck the earth, and its body slid for three feet. A life essence globe rose up from the remains, proof the creature was slain. "Oh, damn."

New ability unlocked: Minor Proficiency: Staff I!
Congratulations! You have gained a new level!

"Whoa. That's a lotta xp. Wait, proficiency? That makes no sense." He dodged the third wolf, jumped back to reassess the situation. "I thought the staff already gave me proficiency. Ohh." He recalled its details had said: Proficiency: Staff. "No Minor or Lesser. That means it's rank three. Is that why I'm hitting so hard? I wonder if there's more ranks after normal. Major and Greater, maybe?"

He used the staff to help avoid attacks, kept the wolves at bay long enough to inflict two disease counts on each. With their stats reduced and movements slowed, he leaned into the melee approach. Striking with each end of the staff felt natural, like an extension of his arms. The wolves were no pushovers, though. They worked in tandem, snapped at his flanks every chance they could. His shield could absorb twenty points of both physical and magical damage now. They slowly chipped away at his defense, while he made a flurry of light attacks. If he overextended into a powerful blow against one, the other two would surely pounce.

One's body glowed with a brief yellow aura, and its movement speed doubled. In a single breath, it was through his shield with a swipe, claws across his left arm. The torn flesh burned, but the pain was more from shock. Palmer reactivated shield on instinct, twisted away from another attack, and added regeneration. The cool rush of healing swept over his shoulder. The wolf he'd attacked let out a howl. All three began to glow a faint red aura. When the magic faded, their attacks grew more ferocious.

Palmer increased their disease counts to four, where through trial and error he assumed was the ability's capped effectiveness. He guessed the howl was a short-term buff, like rage. He did his best to evade, to ride out its duration. Once he saw their attacks visibly weaken, Palmer set upon the most damaged wolf. Three quick strikes in succession from one end of the staff to the other took its legs out, broke multiple ribs, and then shattered its skull. The wolf slumped over.

Congratulations! New subclass unlocked: Monk!

"Uhh." He ducked as one leapt over, then rolled away to avoid the other's jaws. "That better be an option and not a class switch. I just put all those points into wisdom!" Palmer activated spell vulnerability and then divine wrath on one. The four disease counts must have reduced its stats enough to allow magic a chance through. When both landed, he did the same to the other. It gave him time enough to risk a glance at his stats. "Oh, okay. Good. Still says Healer." He glanced skyward with an accusing look. "I thought you were messing with me."

The wolf on his left activated its dash ability, with its telltale yellow glow. Palmer was ready for it this time. As the creature leapt with incredible speed, his staff was already in full swing. It struck soundly against the wolf's snout. Blood, bone and hair spattered outward in a gore-filled cone. Its body continued on, slid across the earth and lay still. The last wolf looked weak. Palmer surmised his spell had caused critical damage.

I didn't think DoTs were allowed to crit. That seems OP AF. He shrugged and moved in with a jab from Reckoning to its broad chest. The steel tip struck in hard, broke through skin and muscle. It must have also caused internal damage, because the wolf began to wheeze with each breath. Its lungs were filling with blood. *Sorry, puppers. If there was a way to tame, I would.*

He easily dodged its feeble attempt at a paw swipe. Moments later, it fell over on its side. One last tick of damage, and its chest stopped moving. Palmer gained another level. Though their loot contained no gold or magic items, they did drop a fair bit of crafting materials: pelts, teeth, claws, and eyes. Unfortunately, only the last was of any use to him for alchemy. A bit of a hoarder when it came to game resources, he stored them all for later, in case a need ever arose.

Palmer stood before the cave, hesitant to go inside.

While the fight had not been as difficult as he'd expected, he could sense many more than four beyond the entrance. One, much deeper in, gave off a presence of incredible power. He knew his best chance of success was to draw them out, hopefully one by one. Close quarters was no place for a caster.

He squared his shoulders and set forth. A few feet in, around a bend, he found the answer to a nagging concern. Mana crystals dotted the cave floor in thick growths and jutted from the walls like jagged spikes. The majority were white, with a soft glow the same color. A few were green, and only the occasional spire was blue. All of them gave off the familiar thrum of magic. It sent goosebumps across his arms and a chill down his neck. There was no time to marvel. Danger lurked ahead and around another corner. Staff held to fore, in the hopes of keeping any surprise attackers at bay, Palmer forced his stubborn feet to move forward.

Beyond the next turn was an area large enough for the four dire wolves waiting for him—barely. They growled at his appearance, heads low and hackles raised. Palmer narrowed his eyes, gripped the staff even tighter. None of them moved to intercept. A howl from deep within the cave rang out. All four immediately turned and answered the call.

That's not good. Palmer looked back the way he came. *If there's an alpha up ahead, with more than the four that just left, I don't think that's a fight I can win.*

Greed and curiosity were winning out over fear and reason. He wanted to gather all the mana crystals. He also wanted to know what waited for him up ahead. If he knew the full extent of the threat, he might be able to come up with a feasible plan. As much as he was afraid to fight so many, there was no guarantee if he left that they wouldn't simply follow his scent and attack at the village while he slept. This wasn't a dungeon instance he could exit and be safe. They had to be dealt with.

And why are they suddenly being smart? This is clearly a strategy to lure me in. Is it because they're under control of the alpha, so they only seem intelligent? They didn't help the ones outside. Palmer tapped the steel tip of his staff against the ground as he thought. Debris fell from the ceiling, a trickle of dust across his nose. *Bleh!* He wiped it away, but an idea came to mind. *Okay. Worst case, I run and fight them at the exit. It's too narrow for more than two or three of them at a time.*

His mind set, Palmer pressed on. By his estimate, the passage ahead was only wide enough for two wolves. It certainly wouldn't allow room for effective combat. The way narrowed even further as he went. Mana crystals grew less abundant. Moisture ran along the walls, and an occasional drip struck a puddle. Its echo was all that could be heard. Nearly in full darkness, he turned a corner and saw a bright light. It was a mix of green and blue, radiating outward from the rich nodes of mana crystal. He could see both walls of the entrance to the next area were smooth, completely free of moss. They looked as if they'd been worn down over time by the massive wolves forcing their way in. He buffed, put up a shield, and stepped into the entry.

Nine of them waited in the final area. It was more than a hundred feet wide and easily just as long. Against the far wall, at its center, was a monstrous wolf twice the size of even the largest among the pack. Its name was bright red, with a star beside it: Bloodfang the Howler. It lay upon a pile of yellowed and broken bones four feet tall at the middle. With a yawn and stretch, the named monster eyed Palmer and walked off its feeding mound. The other eight spread out on either side. Rather than approach, it simply waited for him to act.

Palmer blinked. "Do I look stupid?" He still hadn't moved from the entrance. He held Reckoning in both hands, horizontally in front. "Bad news, king puppers. I'm about to blow your house down."

With all his enhanced strength, Palmer struck the wall to his right. A web of cracks appeared beneath the impact. He quickly did the same to the other side. Over and over, he pummeled both walls, gaining speed and determined strength as adrenaline took its course. The cracks grew larger, thicker, breached deep into the stone. They spread upward, down and out, until rocks began to fall. Bloodfang rushed toward him, aware of the danger. Its size did little to slow the creature. It still moved with the speed of a hunter after its prey.

Palmer switched tactics as the walls began to crumble. He struck at the passage above where he could reach. Both sides narrowed toward the middle, a good ten feet beyond even the full length of his staff. It didn't take much more work to compromise either side. He darted back and away as the first large chunks of rock began to fall.

The alpha leapt at him.

It had no hope of fitting through before Palmer had begun to cave the entrance in. The others must have brought prey in for it to feed on, because its size suggested it hadn't left the cave in a very long time. Bloodfang became hopelessly stuck between the walls. Rocks continued to fall, burying the creature. Still, it snapped and tried to reach him. In a frenzied effort, the wolf dug in its claws and pushed forward. Jagged stone tore away its flesh to the bone. Muscle and ribs exposed, it continued to claw at the ground, bite at empty air. Froth foamed at its mouth. More frightening yet, it was getting closer.

Palmer activated spell vulnerability from its full range. He wasn't about to risk getting any closer until he was sure his spells would land. It failed the first try—and again on the second and third. Frustrated, he tried one more time.

New ability unlocked: Minor Spell Penetration I!

It was a passive that reduced a target's magic resistance. His next attempt was a success. As the monster fought tooth and claw to reach him, Palmer used every debuff he could, with all four disease counts. He applied both DoTs, though divine wrath was doing the heavy lifting. After two minutes of recasts, Bloodfang looked more damaged from its own relentless struggle to reach him than anything Palmer had done.

"Fine," Palmer said and leveled the staff the creature's way. "Let's see what you can really do."

He activated its effect. A ball of mana flashed at the top of the staff, expanded in an instant, and collapsed into a beam that struck the alpha head on. Its right eye exploded, as half its snout and lower jaw were torn free in a bloody gob. The creature actually slowed, looked shocked as it repeatedly blinked with its one good eye. It returned to its senses and howled. The fiery glow of an ability engulfed its form. With greater fervor, Bloodfang inched toward him.

There were two more uses left for the day. He unleashed both, one after the other. The beams struck the alpha's head and chest, caused explosions of fur and gore. When the magic had settled, nothing remained of its head. The body continued its struggle for a brief moment, then trembled and lay still.

Congratulations! You have gained a new level!
Congratulations! You have gained a new level!
Congratulations! You have gained a new level!

He wiped the blood from his face with the back of a hand. From more than ten feet away, he'd been covered in the aftermath.

***

Palmer woke the next morning to the flurry of wind outside the large hut, where he'd barricaded himself in behind three stacked crafting kits. He couldn't pursue blacksmithing, but its kit still proved useful. It had been a long night. He returned to the cave. Once he was sure the other wolves weren't able to get through, he'd carefully gathered all of the mana crystals on the way out. It pained him to leave behind the massive haul inside the final area. He promised himself to return once he was stronger—and had a way to deal area of effect damage. So many wolves at once would be no easy task.

He'd also gone through the nightly routine of practicing all of the abilities he could, expended his whole mana pool four times in the process. Stamina potions had kept his fatigue below half, while his innate mana regeneration and some extra potions had replenished his magic. He was surprised at how quickly the points ticked up. The visit to the wolf den had netted him five more levels and another tier of specialization. A few more tiers into mana regeneration, he would no longer need to sleep to fully regain his magic.

There were six completed quests as well, once he'd had time to do character and inventory management. Per usual, he'd taken the mystery boxes and stored them for the next batch of luck potions. With the stat points he'd gained from levelling to twenty, he put five each into strength, dexterity and constitution. As a solo, he had no choice but to fight within melee range. He'd decided it was important to maintain his physical attributes to at least one per level. His clever use of alchemy and enchanting to take full advantage of the magic find system would suffice in keeping up his caster stats.

It's not exploiting, Palmer reiterated. *I don't care*

about unintended consequences. If the game didn't want me to do it, it wouldn't let me. It's part of the loot system. His eyes lit up a bit. *Speaking of loot...*

The alpha had dropped an epic quality unique item, Bloodfang's Cloak. Its heavy hide was adorned with black fur across the shoulders. It looked as if it should weigh as much as the traveler's cloak, but it was no heavier than a cloth shirt. It granted the wearer a twenty percent bonus to both physical and magic resistance, with no class restrictions. A huge reduction to incoming damage like that, coupled with his passive pain tolerance skill, made him wonder if he could eventually put together a set of resistance gear. Since he was limited to light or no armor at all, due to movement limitations, damage reduction would be a far better fit for his playstyle. It was something he'd have to consider further. He also noticed the cloak had a check box when in inventory called Hidden. It was a typical feature in games that made gear invisible, so it wouldn't override cosmetic items. Palmer had checked the box for a different reason. He was used to player versus player environments. Showing off gear gave away valuable information to an enemy, for no gain. He didn't care what his character looked like. He'd wear a suit of crafted turds over full raid gear if the overall stats were slightly better. Appearance played no part in efficiency.

In addition to the cloak, Bloodfang had dropped a rare ability stone. He now had two offensive spells, though he was primarily a single target caster. If there were area of effect or multiple target magic abilities, Palmer expected they'd be specific to mage. Still, the new spell was a great addition to his arsenal.

Minor Divine Light (I)
Class: *Healer*
Active, Combat, Necromancy
Cost*: 15,* ***Range****: 15',* ***Duration****: Instant*

Cause 6-18 magical damage to a living target.

Palmer reflected on the whole wolf den encounter. At the time, he was afraid. He wasn't as terrified as he was when he first entered this world, but something inside him seemed as if it were growing numb to the situation. In retrospect, he should have been more frightened. Prior to coming to this place, he wouldn't have dreamed of facing such creatures, let alone entering the cave for more. It was similar to when he played tabletop role-playing games. He was only free to be his true self, making reasoned decisions and acting on them, when fear wasn't taken into consideration. Ever since he learned this was all a game, he'd been moving closer toward that state—taking action despite the terror. He wondered if, in time, he would lose all sense of it, the panic, the dread. Fear was a part of being human. It was necessary for survival. If he decided it was an obstacle to progression, would he lose something in overcoming it, in abandoning it? Would he sacrifice a part of his humanity for the sake of power? What would that make him, and what else would he have to surrender to achieve it?

I won't really know, he thought, *until I face a person. It's easy to think of goblins and wolves as monsters. I don't think I could kill a human unless I had to. I certainly wouldn't wipe out a village of peasants for the xp. I don't really even like PvP.* Palmer put the crafting kits and cloak away, pulled a piece of dried meat from inventory and began to chew it as he stretched. *I sort of wish there were other players. Even if I was still solo, just having people to chat with would make things easier. I'd even settle for a system that answered questions.*

"You ever gonna talk to me?" he asked. Silence followed. "So, what's this about a monk subclass? Does that mean I can multiclass, or is it a complete class change? And since when is monk a subclass of healer? That's makes no sense. Monks can only self-heal, and they're primarily fighters. If anything, they're a warrior subclass." An idea came to mind. "Wait, does that mean the other classes are available now?" He navigated to the Ability Stones tab. All of the warrior, rogue, and mage stones were no longer grayed out. "Oh, damn! When did that happen?"

Able to become a pure damage dealer, Palmer wasn't sure the change was for the best. Given the way abilities improved and evolved through use, in a sense, he'd be starting over at level twenty. In his experience with systems that allowed multi-classing, it was always most beneficial to focus on just one. Some builds benefited from a level or two in another class, but without knowledge of this game's classes, he couldn't make an informed decision. He didn't even know what the maximum level was. He wasn't willing to gamble and make a mistake that might ruin his character. In the end, it was more efficient to be the best healer than a mediocre hybrid.

He'd considered spending the day working on crafting but decided to hold off until he had more mystery gifts. Two new quests related to gathering would be easy enough, and more than a handful were related to straight up combat. He finished the dried meat, had a few bites of cheese, washed it down with water, and headed toward the hobgoblin village. He already had mage whisker for the spell power potion recipe he'd unlocked processing herbs. The added magic damage would be useful in a difficult encounter—like an epic named wolf, for instance. Palmer admitted he hadn't done everything within his power to be more prepared that day. He had no intention of making the same mistake. Which is why he kept an eye out for ironleaf. It was needed for the new defense potion. The bonus to armor rating might not be ideal for a caster, since he was more about damage avoidance than mitigation. What he hoped for was some insight into what might be needed for a resistance potion. From there he could determine what a similar enchantment might require. In other games, it was unusual for two craft systems to use the same resources. This one seemed more forgiving. The skill was on the verge of evolving, as well. He believed at some point the system would allow him to use all the knowledge he'd gained to create entirely new recipes.

Maybe it's wishful thinking, he thought and stopped to harvest a patch of mystic ash. The black flower wasn't necessarily rare, but it was needed for mana potions. *It does seem that's where crafting is headed, though. If rejuvenation requires lifebloom and mystic ash, then it makes perfect sense I could combine other effects to create a new potion. Ooo!* He'd caught a glimpse of the ironleaf label beyond the trees on his right. It was a bit strange he could see the text but not the actual plants. He finished and went to harvest those as well. *Feels a bit cheap, but I'm not gonna complain.*

He stopped to brew a couple of defense and spell power potions. The hobgoblins were all much higher level last he saw them. He'd gained five since then, but it was better to be over prepared than dead.

When he reached the tree line surrounding the village, he could immediately see something was amiss. Two of the three warriors in the nearest patrol were already dead, their corpses still torn and bloodied. The last was fighting another hobgoblin shaman. Unusual aggression towards its own kind aside, there was something visibly wrong with the attacker. Pieces of its body were eaten away by a dark corrosion and emitted black tendrils with pixelated silver blocks. It looked as if those parts were being dematerialized. It reminded Palmer of the corruption he saw surrounding the giant mana sphere. The shaman was altered in more ways than one. Its movements were sporadic and stuttered, like a graphical glitch. In one moment, it was much faster than the other hobgoblin, and in the next it briefly slowed to a crawl. After those slow few seconds, the speed of its actions vastly increased, as if catching up all at once to where it should have been.

By the sound and visual impact of the shaman's staff attacks, its physical strength was far greater than it looked. The warrior was nearly dead. Hobgoblins were twice as large as their lesser version, goblins. They looked much the same but with a heftier build, darker green skin and long tufts of colored hair. This one's was dyed purple and shaved away on both sides, leaving behind a thick stripe down the center. There was no hesitation in its defense, no confusion as to why one of its own kind had attacked. It was simply outmatched.

Palmer finished it off with divine light, blasting its battered body with a column of holy fire erupting from beneath its feet. It was barely dead an instant, hadn't even fallen over, before the shaman turned its attention to Palmer. It strode toward him with that hitch to its movements. It looked like the results of gameplay with low latency. Despite the glitched appearance, the shaman was quickly closing the distance between them.

He had no intention of experiencing firsthand just how hard the shaman could hit. Palmer activated his shield and did his best to avoid its staff, while fully debuffing the creature. A stack of four disease counts managed to slow it during the normal phase of its attacks but did nothing once the final burst of speed kicked in. It was, however, a clear pattern he could track. After the shaman had suffered a considerable amount of damage, it stopped to activate an ability. Corrupted magic flowed down its arms and into the staff, setting the weapon alight with black fire. Once enhanced, the weapon looked as if it were corrupted, began to dematerialize in various spots along its length.

That can't be good, Palmer thought and unleashed

another pillar of holy fire. *How the hell are you not dead yet?*

He pulled Reckoning from inventory, hoped to use it to deflect any incoming strikes and let his DoTs finish off the shaman. The speed phase of its glitched movement was about to occur, when the creature faltered. It stood frozen for a long moment—so long that Palmer also stopped. He thought maybe its death was also glitched, that it wasn't going to fall over. His puzzled look turned to shock when the hobgoblin sped up in a wild frenzy. With little time to react, he tried to block and turn his own body aside at the same time. While most of the blow had been diverted, his left forearm was still struck. His shield absorbed most of the damage, but four points left a nasty gash.

The corruption instantly took hold.

Through the overwhelming and sudden pain, Palmer triggered the effect on his staff. The mana beam flared to life and struck with intense magic. The shaman's left shoulder and chest were obliterated. It jerked backward and collapsed into a smoking heap.

Palmer fell to his knees, grasped his left forearm near the elbow. The corruption was spreading. The black and silver pixels of dematerialization ate away at the tips of his fingers and along the wrist. He squeezed his arm to stave off the pain, tried to will the ill effects out of his flesh. It both burned and froze, overcame his senses with dread. The anxious feeling that something was terribly wrong inside him intensified with each breath, each thundering heartbeat. Cure disease did nothing. Restoration did nothing. Heal replenished his lost health points but not the magic gone awry.

Breathing became more difficult. Blood pounded in his ears. His vision began to narrow and grow hazy at the edges. It felt like dying. He fought against the pain, against the panic. Reason knew what had to be done, but fear wanted another way.

No. Divine light wasn't narrow enough to target a

specific area. *No, no, no.* If he wanted to survive, he had to be precise. *NO!*

Palmer leveled Reckoning at his left forearm and triggered the effect.

- 5 -

Though loss of the limb hadn't killed him, Palmer wished it had. He quickly healed the wound, felt instant relief as mana washed away the pain. What remained was not at all what he expected. Rather than mended ruin, with visibly torn muscle and bones just beneath the skin, his arm at the elbow ended in a smooth rounded surface. While it looked better than the nightmare his imagination had conjured, it felt wrong. It was lighter than it should have been. He could feel where his hand would have normally been but couldn't see it. It was both a physical and mental feeling of loss.

Palmer sat for a long moment, stared at the missing section. *I'm a little shocked I didn't pass out.*

The magic had only caused thirty-two damage, but it also reduced his maximum strength, constitution, and dexterity by three. The stat loss was equal to another thirty points. The effect was only capable of doing twenty-four, at best. As far as he knew, he hadn't scored a critical. The outcome would have been much worse. He assumed the added damage came from his elevated intelligence score.

Then again, he thought and struggled through the mental math, *my high WIS should have mitigated it some. Not to mention, the magic resistance on my cloak. Maybe it was a critical. I wish I could actually see damage and heal numbers, instead of guessing at everything.*

Since heal hadn't replaced his arm, he hoped the listed details for the restoration ability referred to this exact situation. Half afraid it wouldn't work, he activated it. He felt mana rush up from his chest and flow down his left arm, all the way to the fingers he couldn't see. A blue outline of his missing limb appeared. Transparent light filled the space, grew brighter and became solid. Where the mana washed away, flesh took its place. When the glow had fully faded, his arm was restored.

It worked! Palmer let out the breath he'd been holding. He stared at his new hand, as he flexed each finger one by one. The sound of hobgoblins working in the village shook him from his reverie. *Right. Things to do, still. That thing didn't just walk in here and start killing. It spawned here.* He tried to gauge which building it might be housed in. *Dismantling that spawner is top priority.*

He looked over his stats. Those, too, had been restored. He'd also gained a level in the fight. At the time, he'd been too distracted to notice. The shaman had dropped two items, an alchemy recipe for Fire Oil and a Regeneration ability stone—except there was something wrong with it. The name appeared in his inventory as R3g*ner4^-on.

Is that because it dropped from a corrupted mob? He recalled the ability tiers. *Oh, wait. That's a rank three stone! Crap.* His face twisted with desire and dread. *Is it a separate ability, or will it overwrite mine? If it's glitched, what will it do to me if I use it?* At his current pace of nightly practice, he would eventually evolve in a few days. *Yeah, but if I use the stone now…*

He pulled the stone from inventory. It looked like all the others, but its glow had a silver tinge. Within that light were the dark pixels of dematerialization, though the stone looked steady. It wasn't disappearing. He began to think the corruption he'd been seeing, in the land, in the shaman, and now in this stone, was within the system itself—its code. Someone or something was hacking the game. What did that mean for him? He wasn't part of the game. He came from somewhere outside of it. He sighed. More questions without answers, with nothing to be done for it but to figure it all out on his own.

Palmer used the stone.

His entire field of view flickered with static, as if the screens he navigated were a part of him. Was he inside the system, or was it the other way around? Though the screens occasionally flashed, they looked for the most part unchanged. He brought up the Abilities tab. His regeneration had been overwritten, and the text was still garbled.

R3g*ner4^-on *(I)*
Class: *Healer*
Active, Combat, Reversible, Necromancy
Cost*: 5,* ***Range****: 24',* ***Duration****: 2 min*
Restore 4-8 health points every 12 seconds to a target.

"What!" Palmer drew the attention of the nearest patrol with his outburst. "Crap, my bad."

He got to his feet as they charged.

That's a crazy good improvement. He compared it to divine wrath. *Longer range and duration. More damage. Twice the ticks!* Palmer nearly laughed. If the hobgoblins had been anyone else, they might have been concerned by the grin on his face. *Time to test this bad boy out!*

With its extended range, Palmer afflicted all three with the upgraded ability before they could close the distance. He maintained a safe space between them, evaded their attacks, as he began to apply debuffs to each. It was on the first tick of damage that he realized a problem. While the glitched ability did much more damage, it spread the corruption to its target. The hobgoblins had the telltale streamers of black and silver pixels to their aura, and it soon ate away at their bodies. Palmer slowed them with disease and added damage from divine wrath for good measure. He spent the next two minutes staying as far away as he could. He thought it better to use the kiting strategy once again rather than risk being corrupted.

Fortunately, the patrol died rather quickly. When he estimated their health, by how much damage had been done, he lamented the waste of mana. It was unavoidably inefficient. When faced with unknown variables, there was no such thing as overkill. He'd also gained another level. It was his suspicion that corrupted monsters were not only noticeably stronger but gave much more experience as well. It was as if the effect elevated them to elite status.

With a better idea of what it took to kill them, Palmer cleared a path to the house he guessed the spawner was inside. As long as he maintained a safe distance, there was little chance he'd become corrupted. From the amount of gold and rarity of craft resources they dropped, he wondered if their loot table was also improved. It was like finding an exploit. The enemies were far stronger, highly likely to kill him if they ever got a hold of him, but he felt the bonus experience and loot was worth the danger. Plus, the corrupted regeneration did so much more damage than his offensive abilities, to use anything else would be a waste of time and mana.

Experience per hour matters, Palmer insisted. *Besides, there's no way I'm passing up all this loot.*

By the time he reached the spawner, he'd gained two more levels, fifteen hundred gold, a wide variety of uncommon to epic resources for various crafts, which included two he hadn't seen before, jewelry crafting and engineering, and a number of magical weapons and armor. He suspected the loot table had been altered by the corruption, because the hobgoblins that dropped magic gear weren't using them during the fight. That meant the items had been generated after they died.

Another unfortunate, and somewhat dangerous, aspect of the corrupted code that maintained this place and everything in it was the random nature of its effect as it spread. Palmer noticed that the longer the fight, the greater the chance for the afflicted enemy to become altered. Some attained abilities they hadn't displayed from before or were shared by others of their kind, like a warrior suddenly able to traverse shadows like a rogue. Other changes were physical, as if a mutation had occurred. One archer had grown a third arm and was able to nock an extra arrow with it, while a warrior grew horns and hooves, with goat-like hind legs. The most disturbing, however, was the shaman that burst into black flames. It burned itself, the ground around it, and anything that came near. It died quickly but was troubling to see all the same.

Could that happen to me? Palmer wondered. It had been eating at the back of his mind for a while. His best heal spell might very well be ruined. *I'll have to test it later.*

When he stepped inside the largest building, his suspicion was confirmed. The spawner was inside. There were chairs and a table, a cutting board, and empty pantry. All seemed normal but for the stone circle, emanating magic and corruption. The black pixels had begun to spread along the wooden floorboards that surrounded it. He wondered if, in time, the building or even the world itself would begin to change from its effect. He had no desire to wait and find out. When he disenchanted the spawner, he received twice as many resources as he'd expected. Another potential exploit came to mind.

It's not exploiting! Palmer thought, exasperated. *I'm*

risking my damn life for it. It's a fair trade off.

He went back outside to clear the rest of the village. Four levels, another tier of mana regeneration, and a substantial amount of loot later, Palmer noticed the bodies of the outside patrols had begun to darken the ground with their corruption. If it spread through the game's code, and the corpses wouldn't despawn without a spawner to replace them, did that mean it would continue to grow out of control until the entire world was enveloped?

Hmm. It might be time to start thinking about an exit plan. He had enough resources now to craft for days. He sort of looked forward to it. It was peaceful, when compared to fighting bloodthirsty, corrupted monsters out of a nightmare. *I can knock out a bunch of quests, too. But first...*

He pulled the looted magic weapons and armor from inventory one by one, placed each upon the corrupted ground and waited. Within minutes, they all flared with a black spark and began to pixelate at the edges. Worried, he touched them only long enough to break them down into enchanting materials. Once again, his intuition had been correct. He received two to three times more resources than he'd expected. He'd also learned all their recipes. In theory, he could craft new magic items, corrupt each one, and disenchant them for more resources than he'd used to create them. It was certainly worth testing.

Palmer returned to the goblin village, ate a lunch of sweetbread with water, and sat down by the well to work alchemy. He was level twenty-eight now, with twenty-four points to spend. For a while, he'd speculated that alchemy improved with use, but the chance of advancement was also influenced by intelligence. The higher the stat, the more quickly related abilities tiered up and evolved. By the same token, his proficiency with staves would be influenced by strength or dexterity—or possibly both. In either case, he wanted the best chances to improve now. He put twenty points into INT and saved the other four. With a score of sixty, he still had more than twice his level into the attribute. He mused what it would be like to have every point invested into main stat and all zeros in the others. It would be the ultimate glass cannon, with the power of a caster three times his level, and only four health points to stave off death.

With an abundance of resources to work with, he decided to experiment in the hopes of discovering new recipes. He first processed every herb and mineral into their workable states, which took him nearly to evening. He'd learned two new potions in the process, Fortitude and Sage. In a methodical fashion, he mixed each one in the mortar in amounts that made sense, based on all he'd learned thus far. Within the first two tries, he began learning even more. Acumen, Magic Resistance, Divine Power, Might, Water Breathing, Shadow Walk, Flight, and Plague Oil, the recipes filled his event log. He was thrilled at the results but was particularly interested in the Magic Resistance potion. It required dire wolf eyes. He'd hoped to find a formula for physical resistance as well, but he supposed this would have to do.

He bought a shirt and enchanted it with wolf eyes and purple powdered mana crystal. While hesitant to use epic quality crystal, he had a limited supply of eyes. The threads within the cloth glowed blue a brief moment and faded, but the magic within as a whole remained as a constant aura. It had worked. He'd enchanted the plain shirt with ten percent magic resistance. He repeated the process with a pair of leggings and ran out of eyes. If he wanted a full set, with gloves, hat, and bracers, he'd have to go back to the dire wolf den and clear it out.

He continued to work on both crafts well into the night and eventually evolved each to the next rank. Of the sixty available quests he'd started the day with, he managed to complete twenty-two. Granted, most were from crafting. The daily goals for combat had become more difficult as he levelled. He took mystery boxes as each reward and set them aside for morning. There was a more pressing matter to deal with, one he'd been dreading most of the day.

Palmer put everything away, went into the largest tent, and barricaded himself in for the night. By the light of mana and health potions secured into the open alchemy kit, he prepared his mind and body for what might come. He took in a long, deep breath and activated the regeneration ability on himself. Nothing happened. He let out a sigh of relief but soon felt crestfallen. His health was full. The ticks had no effect if there was no damage to heal.

Right, he thought. *Here goes then.*

He activated the reverse on himself and immediately regretted it. The corruption took hold on the first tick. Once again, it felt like dying. Whether it was a physical response or a panic attack made no difference. His heart raced. His breathing grew labored. Sweat began to pour off his brow. The corruption appeared all over his body. Black and silver spots, with metallic blue edges, dotted his arms and hands. Dark tendrils of tainted magic rose up from his skin.

Then the pixelated splotches began to heal. They closed over, mended to clear skin, and reappeared elsewhere. Every six seconds, he both healed and took new damage in a new area of tortured body.

New ability unlocked: Minor Corruption Resistance I!

Palmer was too busy trying to force air into his chest to enjoy the message he'd been hoping to see. He gambled that if there was an ability like pain tolerance, there might be something to counteract what'd been happening. He endured the duration of both abilities and did it all over again. He did have to be careful, though. Both the damage and healing had variable results. If he didn't keep a close watch on his health, he could easily end up dying to a string of bad luck. It made him wonder if he was better off wearing his luck gear. The pain and constant fear of death quickly put that notion to rest. His magic resistance items were probably doing more to keep him alive than the healing.

By the fourth cast, he noticed his Abilities tab was blinking with an alert. Though he'd only just unlocked it, his corruption resistance had already leveled up to tier two. He'd never seen any other ability improve that quickly. All things considered, his pain tolerance should advance at the same rate, but it was only tier three. At this rate, the new passive would surpass it in six minutes. The longer he persevered, the more it would improve. He could already feel the overwhelming anxiety somewhat relax. If he could just reach a point where it only hurt, where it didn't crush his body and spirit with the threat of looming death, then it all would have been worth it.

Okay, good. It gained another tier. Palmer fought to steady his breathing. *I can do this.* He still had over four hundred mana to go. *Nothing worth having is easy.*

Within hours, it had evolved twice to rank three. It no longer hurt to breathe. While he had plenty of mana potions and rank five mana regeneration visibly raising his points by the second, he was too exhausted to continue the training. He pulled out the traveler's cloak, wrapped it around him like a blanket and fell over.

Palmer easily drifted off to sleep.

***

The next morning Palmer woke to an uneasy

feeling. A closer look at his aura gave proof of what he felt. There were small dark tendrils at its edges, with black and silver pixilation through the darker blues and purples across its surface. They sparkled like stardust, disappeared and resurfaced elsewhere. The invasive effect had been greatly diminished. He was no longer overcome with dread or the sensation of dying. However, there was little doubt he was still corrupted. It was only his newly acquired resistance that kept it at bay.

Is it me, though? He flexed the fingers of his right hand, saw no sign of it within his flesh. *Or is it the system?* His screen still glitched with the occasional appearance of static lines. His cloak seemed unaffected when he placed it into inventory. *Doesn't look like I can spread it by touch.* He considered the regeneration ability, how its name was reverting back, though the text was darker and sparkled a bit. *If the corruption is like malware, infecting the game, shouldn't it spread to all my other abilities?*

R3gener4t-on *(II)*
Class: *Healer*
Active, Combat, Reversible, Necromancy
Cost: *5,* ***Range:*** *24',* ***Duration:*** *2 min*
Restore 6-8 health points every 12 seconds to a target.

"Wait," he said and looked more closely at the description. "When did that change? It no longer only affects living targets?" He recalled the giant mana sphere surrounded by corruption and guarded by a metal construct boss. "Interesting. I wonder if that means I can stand in that stuff without taking damage. I mean, I don't know that it does. It just looks like it would." He pulled a strip of dried meat from inventory and chewed it. "Still don't wanna fight that thing."

He shrugged, swapped to his bonus magic find set as he ate, and got a handful of luck potions ready to open mystery gifts. He'd considered only using half to gain stat points and the other for magic items off the higher loot table. He could corrupt them, break them down for recipes and resources, craft new ones, and sell them to the Store for a profit. With the random nature of gifts, he might even get an item with physical or magic resistance, or even damage reduction. Bloodfang's Cloak was a unique, so he didn't want to lose it. Unique item drops were rarely craftable by players. Besides, that approach was more of a long-term, end-game investment. He wasn't quite sure he was there yet and thought higher secondary stats would be more beneficial than new armor. A greater health pool and improved evasion was a better strategy for a healer. To focus on defense, or even mitigating damage, meant the expectation of getting hit. Any caster planning to get hit was planning for failure.

With the excitement of a child at Christmas, he unstopped the first potion and drank half of its glowing green liquid. He was still only able to open four gifts in the six second duration. Certain he was drawing from the right loot table, he went through the process of opening all the rest. When the last gift dematerialized, like the unboxing of that last present under the tree, he was both sad it was over and delighted at the haul. He'd gotten eighty-three stat points, a massive variety and rarity of resources for every craft, a few magic weapons and armor pieces unsuited to his class, and three ability stone upgrades. The other four stones were for other classes. With a plan in mind, he decided to save the upgrades for later and stored the others, along with the magic items. He had plans for those too. After careful consideration, he placed each point and looked over his new stats.

PALMER
LVL: 28 **Class**: Healer
STR: 30, **CON**: 30, **DEX**: 30, **INT**: 73, **WIS**: 70

HP: 300 [300], **MP**: 730 [730], **F**: 0%
SP: 0

He now had the movement speed and physical power of a warrior and the accuracy and reaction time of a rogue of the same level. His health pool was substantial, when compared with the amount of damage his abilities caused. Both his magic power and resistance were equal to a caster more than twice his level, with a mana pool that was for all intents and purposes unlimited. His most expensive ability had a cost of fifteen, while his rank five specialization replenished five mana every six seconds. With the right set of gear, he felt he could become just as strong as he was in other games he'd played. Which was why he planned to return to the wolf den. He put everything away, finished eating breakfast, cleaned up a bit at the well and switched back to his magic resistance set.

On the way, Palmer noticed the appearance of corruption was more frequent and widespread than it had been in days past. The darkened blotches of grass and earth weren't growing from a larger source. They'd manifested in new areas. It looked as if the world itself was breaking down, succumbing to the infection of its code. Where the trees, rocks, and brush were afflicted, they had the telltale appearance of any other item dissipating back into the system—like when he stored things in inventory. But they weren't disappearing. They were changed but still whole.

As if they're being remade into something else, he reflected. *Why, though? What purpose would that ser- Ohh!* An epic quality plant caught his eye. He hadn't seen it before. It was a patch of steelscale. Its narrow leaves had a pattern of scales, like a fish, with a sheen of silver when wet. Most of the patch, however, was within an area of corruption. *Damn.* Palmer let out a whoosh of air. *Well, I wanted to test what this would do anyway. But, first...*

He pulled the magic weapons and armor from inventory and placed them partially in the darkened patch. Once he was sure they'd been infected, he disenchanted them for an impressive amount of dust and mana crystal. He did the same for the three new ability stones he'd received. Rather than use them once they'd changed, he put them back in storage. There was a more important test to conduct first.

Palmer stepped into the patch.

He could feel the blighted code seep in through his boots. It took hold with a biting cold that reached into his bones. Black tendrils rose up from the patch, ethereal wisps with silver sparkles that hungered for more. His vision went shaky. Static lines both thin and thick flashed to the sporadic sound of brief glass breaks. Like short-lived crystal shrieks, they popped in his ears. The entire system was going haywire. The text of his stats, the event log, the main screen and all its tabs darkened to a deep black with an edge of silver pixels. Everything became jumbled and unreadable. They were a series of letters, numbers, and symbols, with some characters he'd never seen before.

It was uncomfortable, disquieting, but far less painful than expected. Like being shoved naked into the cold night, there was a shock that would not abate. His senses grew numb to it over time. As the system within him changed, so too did his body and aura. He could see the darkness in his veins spread down his arms to each hand. The flesh became pale and splotchy. His aura flared with dark fire. Coils from its base sought to burrow deeper in, as if the code fought to breach into the core of his bright colors.

Tabs flashed with alerts beneath the flurry of fragmented screens and changing text. Palmer fought down the anxiety that had an iron grip on his chest. He took in long deep breaths. He did his best to endure. This was all part of a plan. It would not go on forever.

He had no idea how long he'd stood there, abiding the onslaught to his senses. In time, the crackles calmed. The disjointed flashes of broken lines settled back to a clear screen. The last dozen or so strange symbols reverted back to clear text, though their color retained its silvered black. When all had finally resolved, two lines stood out within his vision.

Ability evolved: Corruption Immunity!
Congratulations! New hidden subclass unlocked: Hierophant!

His body looked and felt normal. There were no signs of darkness in his veins or sickness in his skin. His aura appeared fine, with no black flames to speak of, but there was still the hint of black and silver to its edges. All of his abilities had certainly changed. Palmer may have become immune to the corruption, but there was little doubt he still carried it within him. He could only guess what that meant, that he was able to stand inside it unaffected but would inflict it upon others with his abilities. He stepped out of the patch and called Reckoning to hand. It was already afflicted. Did that mean his entire inventory was affected?

Huh. He looked down at his feet. *It's not spreading to the ground.* He snatched up a few blades of grass and a bit of earth. Nothing happened. *Okay, so I can't spread it by touch. I can walk into it with no issues. But all my abilities and items are tainted with it.* Was tainted the right word? *Affected? They all seem drastically improved. And what the hell is a Hierophant? There are hidden classes?* He put the grass into inventory and pulled it back out again. They were corrupted. *Crap. That means I can never trade items with anyone. Or use my abilities on them.* He groaned. *Guess I'll just be solo forever!*

He gathered all the steelscale and continued on to the dire wolf den.

"So, if Hierophant is a hidden class," he asked the system that never answered him, "that means it must be stronger, right? So, what happens if I switch? Do I become a level one Hierophant or a multiclass healer? How do I even switch? Is there a quest or an ability stone I have to use?" He checked the Shop. There was one stone available for Hierophant, a heal spell. "Ah ha. Interesting. Sure would be nice if there were descriptions or details or any god damn kind of instructions to any of this anywhere!" Still no reply. He bought the stone for five thousand gold and used it. The text of his new ability immediately darkened and became garbled. "Oh, damn. I forgot to corrupt it first. But it looks like any ability I gain automatically corrupts." Palmer shook his head. "I really hope this doesn't turn out to be some disease that ultimately kills me. Whatever. Let's see what it does."

Minor Area of Healing *(I)*
Class: *Hierophant*
Active, Combat, Reversible, Necromancy
Cost*: 50,* ***Range****: 24',* ***Duration****: 2 min*
Restore 4-8 health points every 6 seconds to all targets in a 12' radius.

"Fifty mana!" Palmer laughed. "That's crazy! I can only cast it fourteen times? Oh, wait. It's a targeted AoE." Area of effect spells were crucial when combating groups of enemies. "It's basically an AoE degeneration." When he looked at his stats, he could see his class had changed but level was still the same. "That makes sense, I guess." He could sense four dire wolves just outside the cave. "Perfect timing."

The wolves were already alerted to his presence. He stepped out past the tree line and moved within range, his focus on one of the middle wolves. When he activated the ability, a wide circle of golden light flared to life around all four. Divine symbols formed along the outer edge and raced to the center. In a flash, holy fire engulfed each dire wolf. The flames licked along their fur, caused wild yelps of tortured pain, as a deep blackness erupted within their auras. Palmer used his staff to fend off their frenzied attacks. Their bites and swipes were hindered by blinding flame, and their movements became jerked from corruption. Merely half a minute passed before they succumbed to the holy fire.

They dropped the eyes he needed to enchant the rest of his gear set, but he wanted to go farther in. He'd been forced to forego all the mana crystals in the final area last time he was here. Now that he had a way to deal with a large group, the adventurer's call to treasure couldn't be ignored.

The four wolves inside the first room were no more difficult than the last to deal with. Palmer simply activated his shield, used his new area of effect ability and held them off while standing his ground from the narrower passageway. He would have preferred to kite them away, but this gave him the opportunity to test improved stats. The higher dexterity made it easier to dodge the corrupted wolves, while his strength caused the staff to strike with an audible display of power. By the resulting damage, he gauged his physical attacks were causing as much damage as his magic.

I wonder why Bloodfang didn't call them, he thought, as the last one fell, and he gained a level. *Maybe he hasn't respawned? Whoa, wait, what?* He had six available stat points to spend. *Hierophant gets double stats per level?* His laughter was born from the love of anything over-powered. *That's so broken!*

He put the points into intelligence and continued on to the final room. Bloodfang's corpse no longer blocked the passage, though the walls and ceiling were still collapsed. The green and blue glow of mana crystals could be seen between the giant rocks. He'd never tested just how strong he actually was in a meaningful way. Until now, strength was just a number on his screen. He put the staff aside and grabbed hold of a rock the size of a large beach ball. It should have been impossible to move. It took more effort to grab a hold of its odd shape and size rather than it did to lift its bulk. He set it down with care, mindful of his feet. Just because he could carry a boulder didn't mean he could withstand one dropping on his toes.

Neat! He flexed his arms outward in front of him, the way some athletes showed off their muscles. *Welcome to the gun show!* His laughter caused the alpha to howl. All four dire wolves scrambled toward the blocked passage. He looked at the larger alpha, a little disappointed. *Oh, just a plain elite.*

He didn't need to clear away all the rocks to fight. As long as he could see one, he could damage them all. It took longer to kill the alpha, but all four died safely on the other side of the fallen cave-in. As the elite toppled over, corrupted and in holy flames, Palmer gained another level. It was a pleasurable sensation, like a breath of fresh air all across his body. He'd always been too preoccupied to enjoy it. Each time he gained a level, it replenished his health, mana, and fatigue. There was nothing else quite like it—at least not legally.

He put one point into INT and five into WIS. He preferred rounded numbers when it came to attributes, but there was little he could do about it. He supposed it was better than no stat gains at all. Since he hit level thirty, he gained another specialization tier as well.

"Oh, what's this?" The elite had dropped epic quality boots. "Not too shabby."

Boots of Mobility
Type: Leather
Armor: 2
Restrictions: None
An exquisite pair of boots, hand-crafted by the masters

at Shadow Peak.
Grants the wearer +25% movement speed and evasion.

"Evasion? So if accuracy is chance to hit, and armor rating is overall defense," he surmised, "then evasion must be a damage avoidance mechanic. Hmm, what's with the percentage though? Is that twenty-five in total or twenty-five of some number determined by dexterity? Is there a cap, or can I get it to a hundred?"

He slipped on the boots and pondered many other such questions about the aloof system, as he began to gather every mana crystal he could find. Some were as small as his hand, while others were the size of a toddler. While most were of uncommon rarity, evidenced by their green glow, a good many were pale blue. It was only after he cleared toward the back that a few purple crystals could be seen, buried beneath the bulk of all the others.

It was hours later before he returned to the village. To his surprise, and immediate alarm, there was someone there waiting. He sat upon the well, drinking water from the bucket with a hand. He was a few inches taller than Palmer, with short dark hair and a medium build. If pressed, Palmer would guess he was a year or two older. The man was dressed in an ornate robe, deep blue with black edging and gold symbols embroidered across the front and bottom. Frosted orbs upon his shoulders gave off a pale glow. His matching gloves, boots, and heavy cloth belt all radiated mana. At a glance, it looked to Palmer as if he were dressed in full raid gear. More pronounced than his items were his eyes. They were a bright ice blue, with an even brighter blue glow at the outer ring of his irises. It was as if the intensity of his mana could be seen directly through them.

This was another player, and he wasn't from Earth.

Palmer called his staff to hand and began to buff. He activated a shield and readied to disease the robed stranger.

The man coughed out his water. “Wait!” He held up both hands. “I’m friendly!”

***

Palmer gauged the stranger’s power by scrutinizing his aura. It emanated outward a good twelve feet from his body, in a wavering sphere of pale blue. His presence was stronger than any of the monsters Palmer had faced. His name, Chillmage, was in a deep crimson text with an image of an ice crystal beside it. While much higher level, the stranger’s mana vibrations didn’t feel as strong as his own. Palmer’s aura was much denser, of a deeper hue and more powerful color striations, such as purple, black, silver, and more recently red. Palmer deduced the difference in mana and power he was sensing came from the magic items the stranger wore. Without them, his total presence would be greatly reduced.

“I’m not here to fight,” the other said. “My name’s Eli. I came here to help you guys out.” He pointed toward the patches of corruption in the distance. “And I don’t think we have a lot of time. Lucky for you, I got here first. I put a portal in front of the rift, so anyone passing through will end up in the Chasm of the Northern Tundra. Good luck getting a port back out of there.” He laughed a bit but still looked as if he sensed the tension between them. “Where’s the rest of your group? Like, I’m not sure what all is going on here. You don’t look like a player. I can’t see your name, your class, your level, but you just used inventory and abilities. And what’s up with your eyes? I’ve never seen that cosmetic before.”

Palmer made a show of easing up a little on his staff. He didn’t plan to attack with it anyway. One wrong move from this Eli, and the rotation of debuffs, disease, and DoTs would begin.

"My name's Palmer. I'm solo," he replied, kept at the minimum distance for spell vulnerability. "I like your gear. I'm actually a little jelly."

Eli smiled proudly. "Thanks, it's the full tier two mage set. My guild mostly raids. We don't do much PvP. Umm, so what class and level are you? By the look of your items, I'd guess you just started. None of your stuff is even magic yet. Which would make sense, since you're not actually from Tellaria." He nervously rambled on. "I'm an Elementalist, specializing in ice. It's a subclass of mage. Not as good as an Arcanist, but..." He shrugged. "That's a hidden mage class. It's considered legendary. Only four people have it. The server really makes you work for that sort of thing. There's also artifact subclasses, where only one person per server can obtain it. Don't even know what the mage version is called for this iteration." Eli cleared his throat, as if aware Palmer wasn't offering much information. "Anyway...we should get going. This entire place is falling apart."

"I'm a healer. Just started, like you said." Palmer didn't have a great track record of character judgement. He'd had more than one friend turn out to be anything but. "I did unlock the monk subclass, though. What's the legendary version for healer, like cleric or druid... or Hierophant?"

Eli replied, "Priest is one. No idea what the artifact tier is. I don't know of anyone whose unlocked it yet." He finally lowered his hands, took a step forward. "Listen, we need to deal with the core. Ya know, that huge ball of mana destroying this node?" At Palmer's puzzled look, Eli elaborated, "Ya, I know, you don't know what's really going on. You're—"

"—in a game," they both said at the same time.

Palmer added, "I figured that much. It just doesn't make any sense. Why would going through a rift or a portal or anything suddenly put me in a game? Did someone knock me out and put a VR headset on me or something?"

"See," Eli said and crinkled his face in trepidation, "that's the thing. I don't know how much I can tell you without blowing your mind and disconnecting you from the server. It's kind of a big deal, since there's no coming back. For you, I mean." Palmer blinked slowly and frowned. Eli exhaled. "Right. You're not gonna trust me if you don't know what's going on. So here it is. There's a small group of players from Tellaria, my server, who are trying to tunnel their way into HCE, where you come from. That's what this place is. It's a replica zone, with modified code, sent to bridge our servers, so that players can cross over to yours and wreck the place. They want to force a shutdown, so you all lose your progress. Cuz you're jerks." Eli quickly amended, "I mean, you seem like a nice guy. But the players on your server are well known for being elitist. And they brag about how good they are, and blah blah blah. So, there's tons of people watching, to see what's gonna happen. There are entire guilds and coalitions, with tens of thousands of players, just waiting to cross over."

That's a lot to unpack. Palmer wasn't sure what to ask first. *My server?* He had an inkling that he'd traded one simulation for another, but that was always just a fanciful thought. *If anything, I thought the alien zoo theory was more likely.*

"What's HCE?" Palmer asked.

"Hardcore Earth. It's a niche server, because of the crazy restrictions. Like, only a thousand or so people play it. It's just that you're all so damn vocal about it." He could tell by Palmer's expression that he still hadn't completely explained. "HCE is a sim set in twenty-first century Earth, like arguably the worst time to be alive, ever. When you connect, you agree to temporarily restrict yourself to an encapsulated character, which starts as an infant. That's nuts. So, not only do you not have access to your memories, your character is completely randomly generated, with a random starting country and nationality, race, and income bracket. You have no control over your start or your childhood, only where you end up. And you can't disconnect, because you don't even know you're in a sim. You either play, or you die. That's it. And there's no respawning, cuz, ya know, hardcore. So, when thousands of max level players in full sets of raid gear invade your world of NPCs and normal players with zero stats, it's gonna be a bloodbath. The system will have to shut down, build a new firewall, and start over."

Okay, so, life's a simulation. Got it. Palmer struggled to grasp the implications without succumbing to existential dread. *So, who am I outside of the game? Even if I don't have my memories, I'm still me. People are defined by the choices they make. And if it's all just a game, should I even care what happens? Do I care?*

"There's over eight billion people," Palmer said, working through his emotions in the most rational way he could muster. "How can there only be a thousand players?"

"AI. All the other people are NPCs, basically. Really advanced," Eli admitted, "but still NPCs. It doesn't make them any less alive, no more than any other digital life. They're sentient. They're just limited to the server they were created on. Listen, I know you have a lot of questions, but we're sort of pressed for time. Did you hear that clicking when you first entered, like a set of gears in motion? That's the time affix. These zones come with modifiers, and believe me, there's gonna be more. But this one speeds up time inside. That's why it's falling apart. It isn't able to draw energy from the target server fast enough, so it's cannibalizing itself and starting to pull from mine. Plus, I think the code injection did something wonky. It's evolving, self-replicating. These nodes were only meant to last a few days. I don't think they considered what would happen if the first tunnel rolled with a time modifier. How long have you been in here?"

"Uhh," Palmer replied hesitantly, "yeah, a few days. I like games and all, but it took a bit to believe I was actually in one." He thought it over a few moments, the notion of digital life. It meant all he knew, his entire life, was intended as entertainment. "We're not actually speaking English, are we? Or even speaking at all."

"We're communicating," Eli answered, "just not the way it appears. The system is interpreting everything for us. You hear whatever language your char knows, but it's all just zeros and ones. No one's *spoken* English, or any other language, in hundreds of years. Not technically." He started slowly walking in the direction of the mana sphere. "Maybe we can keep talking about it on the way? We need to deal with that boss protecting the sphere. Don't worry, I'll carry you. You probably don't have any buffs yet. I don't plan on getting hit, but if I do, throw some heals if you can. Just don't stand in the goo."

Palmer cringed as he recalled doing just that.

"So, there's nobody else?" Eli asked. "I looked around a bit, hoping to find a group to help take out the boss. This place is picked clean. Who cleared it?"

"I haven't seen anyone else. Listen, about my abilities," Palmer tried to explain, "I did accidentally step in that stuff, and it messed up my spells. They still work, but if I use them on a mob, it changes them. I don't think you want me healing you."

Eli raised his brows. "I mean, I've never seen this exact stuff before, but it looks like blight. That's a sort of environmental plague, an evolved variation of disease that infects resources and any players or items that touch it. Never heard of it spreading through abilities, though. New evolution, maybe. The game's always evolving. If it gets out of control, the system usually intervenes and either forces a rollback or introduces a new element to counterbalance. If cure disease doesn't get rid of it, you might need to either evolve it or find a cure specific to it. There's always a counter." They'd been walking side by side. He gave Palmer a friendly nudge. "No worries, though. I've got potions and a few other tricks. If the boss manages to kill me, just hold it off for a while. I'll be back as soon as I can. Just be careful, though. If I do die, my portal will drop. Other players will be able to get in. I didn't tell anyone about the rift when I found it, but lots of people are looking for it. Even the guys who wrote the hack don't know where the rifts will appear. They had to avoid specifics, to make it harder for the system to counter." He seemed to think about it for a bit. "It may not, though. Who knows? Sometimes the system does things it thinks will be entertaining. It could have already come to an agreement with your system, and it's letting this all happen. Or it might genuinely have no way to stop it."

"It could do a rollback," Palmer pointed out, "like you said earlier. It's not helpless. Disconnect everyone, go through its code, find the hack, disable it, and protect against further attacks. Done."

Eli rolled his eyes. "Sure. Not like millions of people would be put out, while the system scans trillions of lines of code and rewrites itself. It's not some dinky OS or any other software you're familiar with. Some of its code is purposely inaccessible to itself. We don't know if that's where they attacked. Besides, like I also said, if the system thinks what's happening will be entertaining to its users, it's gonna do it—within the preset guidelines, anyway. It's really up to *your* system how this whole thing plays out. You guys have put so many constraints on it, I don't know if there's anything it can do to help. You're so busy torturing yourselves and then patting yourselves on the back for how much crap you can take and still come out ahead, that you've basically crippled the system from protecting you."

Palmer said defensively, "*I* didn't do anything. I'm just a high school student. I didn't choose to get my ass kicked on a daily basis for the last six years."

"That's the thing," Eli replied. "You did! You just don't *know* you did."

As they approached the area where he last saw the mana sphere, Palmer could feel its power vibrations rush through his middle long before the glowing ball came into view. It was substantially larger, and it pulsed with a silver fire. The blighted area all around it had grown as well, spread its touch across the earth, over rocks and trees, enveloped the grassy land in a sea of corruption. The metal construct was nowhere in sight, was most likely beneath the ground once again.

"Once we beat the boss," Palmer asked, "how do we destroy the core?" Eli activated a shield similar to his own, though it radiated a sky-blue glimmer. He assumed when hit, the shield drained mana in place of health. "And why are you helping?"

"Cuz it's the right thing to do." He pulled an ornate staff from inventory, a length of solid metal topped with a frozen orb. Streamers of cold fell from its surface in snowy wisps. "It's nobody's place to tell you guys how to have fun. Even if you're elitist jerks, you don't deserve what they're doing." Eli activated buffs to intelligence and spell power that affected Palmer as well. Either they were area affect, or they were somehow grouped without his knowledge. "As far as the core, that's easy. Kill the boss, the sphere loses its tether and starts to break down. The node will go with it. Try to make it out before that happens. I'm not sure if it'll kill you if you're still inside when it closes."

"Okay. Thanks." Palmer wasn't used to anyone doing anything without some sort of ulterior motive. "You seem like a good guy. I wish we could've played a game together, instead of...whatever this whole mess is." Eli laughed in agreement. Palmer added, "Umm, if

I use an ability on the boss, it'll corrupt him, make him way faster and stronger. I could use melee. Stepping in *this* goo won't hurt me."

"Nah, I got this."

When they reached the outer edge of darkened earth, the ground began to rumble with enough force to risk toppling them off their feet. The construct once more broke through the surface of rocks and grassy soil, pulled itself up and out of the blight. It was the size of a small building, at least thirty feet tall. Black tendrils rose off its metal frame, like the vapors of a dark magic. The glowing orbs of its eyes had deepened in color, were now a bright hue of violet. Its face had become more detailed. A furrowed brow, a snarled mouth, nostrils flared in anger, what should have been no more than a metal husk animated by magic looked as if it had evolved into a sentient horror. Eli fired off five arm-length shards of ice into the monster's chest and backed away, as if he hoped to lure it out from the blight. The speed with which the boss charged after dashed any hope of a kiting strategy. It moved far faster than its bulk should allow. It was clear the boss was already corrupted.

"Ummm," Eli panicked. "I don't got this!"

It quickly closed the distance and struck him full on with the back of a hand the size of a truck. Eli looked too shocked to evade. He went flying toward a wide tree but blinked out of existence. He landed a few steps ahead of where he'd disappeared, no worse for wear, but his mana shield was gone.

Palmer saw the mage was in danger, needed time to cast a new shield and gain some distance from the boss. He activated Reckoning at the construct, all three times, in quick succession. Though he aimed for its legs, the steel body glitched and jerked as it moved. The beams struck against its middle and left arm. Though Palmer had done more damage, the boss clearly considered Eli a greater threat. It would not shift its attention away from him.

It charged and struck again, as a cone of frost enveloped and slowed its body. Eli followed up his attack with ice lancing upward from the ground. It took hold of both metal feet and held them fast. The boss was already mid-swing. Its attack interrupted, the strike missed its full potential but still caught the mage's leg. Eli was thrown head over heel, landed hard on his back. A second backhand upended earth and mage alike in an upheaval of scattered soil.

"What?" Eli backpedaled away, blood dripping from his scalp. "What's going on? It's not supposed to hurt!"

Palmer dashed forward to within reach and placed four counts of disease on the construct. All of his abilities had been corrupted and were no longer restricted to living targets. He applied every debuff at his disposal, as the boss tore free from the ice. It was determined to kill Eli. The hollow roar from its empty shell was born of rage and a lust for blood.

"Something's wrong—" Eli said, as he scrambled to his feet and was struck again across his side. He slid through the muck of upended earth more than ten feet away and slowed to a stop inside the corruption. Its touch immediately reached inside him, sent blackness through his veins. He looked down at shaking hands with wide eyes. "What's happening? Why does it hurt so much!"

One ability after another, Palmer brought to bear his complete arsenal. He drank potions for speed and spell power, placed all three DoTs on the boss, and rushed to stand between its outstretched hand and Eli. He swatted away its metal fingers with his staff, a strike so powerful it created a visible burst of air. Unbalanced, the boss took a step back and nearly fell over. Its body was being torn apart by magic, holy fire, and corruption. Palmer let loose with divine light. The pillar of white fire at its feet rang out with a deafening clamor. The golden light that rose up fully engulfed its frame, ate away at the edges, and burned through until its metal turned bright red from the heat. Palmer dashed forward, struck its right leg with a sweep from behind, and upended the construct. It fell onto its back, shook the earth with its weight. One more use of divine light and a crushing blow to its head ceased all movement from its rapidly eroding frame.

"Eli!" Palmer rushed to pull him out of the blight. The mage was broken, bloodied, and corruption had taken hold. "I—I can't heal that. I can try, but I don't know what it'll do."

Eli coughed up blood. "It's ok. Just make the pain stop." Palmer used heal. Golden light filled and closed some of the wounds. "Oh my god, that's worse!" He rolled over onto his side, took in short ragged breaths. "What did you do to me? It—it feels like dying. Like, for real, dying."

"Sorry, it's the corruption." He wasn't sure what to do. The mana sphere began to crumble, with melted globules of mana dripping off its surface. "Should I heal you to full?"

Warning! This area will close in thirty minutes.

"No!" Eli replied in a panic. More softly, he added, "No. Just, get out of here. I'll be fine. I'd rather die and respawn than deal with this pain." He coughed and laughed at the same time. "Seriously, you did this to yourself on purpose?"

Palmer smiled. "I swear, I had a plan." He looked toward the direction he needed to run, the way back home. "I could take you to my world."

"The hell did I ever do to you? I'm kidding. I'm sure it's great, sometimes." He was sweating profusely. His body began to shake. "Just go. Maybe I'll see you in the next one." Their eyes locked for a brief moment of severity. "Cuz, believe me, there's gonna be a lot more. Be ready. I'll try to help if I can."

“Thanks again,” he said. “I couldn’t have done it without you.”

A final nod in farewell, and Palmer headed for the rift.

- 6 -

Palmer stepped from the bitter cold of afternoon into the dark of a warm evening. Behind him, the rift immediately closed to the sound of rushing air being sucked in. The road ahead was illuminated by streetlight and the occasional passing car. It was quiet in the alley but for the bark of a distant dog, a television from the nearest home, and the ringing in his ears from the abrupt closure. It was a clear night. Stars dotted the skies overhead in brilliant light, a stark contrast to the world he'd left behind. In that moment of relative peace, reality sank in.

He was home.

The pressures of daily life rushed in to replace the anxiety of struggling to stay alive. There was no telling how long he'd been away. His mother was probably worried sick, though her fears would be replaced by furious anger once she saw he was all right. He didn't look forward to the explanations. Honestly, he wasn't even sure he could relate what had happened. No one would believe him.

Palmer snorted. *I wouldn't believe me, either.* He needed a plan. *I need information. I don't even know what day it is.* He put down the backpack, pulled out and changed into his old clothes. He put his enchanted clothes on over them, set them to hidden in inventory.

Interesting. I can still access the system. He activated shield. *And use my abilities. I would expect all of that to be tied to the other server.* He looked up at the faceless system of his home.

"You two working together?" He didn't expect a reply. "Twinkle some stars, if you're listening." After a moment, he added, "Lame."

Palmer shrugged and walked home.

He lived in a two-story condominium at the center of Greenvale. It was a relatively small city, just under a hundred thousand people, with a single high school and low crime rate. At least it seemed that way to him. Then again, he wasn't usually out past dark. His nerves got the better of him, as the few others out walking a dog or jogging suddenly looked suspicious. They obviously weren't. They paid him no attention. Yet, something tugged at his middle in warning.

Someone from a dark alley on his left had reached out and tried to grab hold of his shirt. Palmer easily dodged the attempt by barely moving his shoulder. He looked at the disheveled man with annoyance and disbelief. Who in the world just reaches out to touch a stranger for no reason? The man's jeans and shirt were ripped, dirtied like the rest of him. His hair was greasy and clumped, eyes reddened and swollen, and he looked as if he hadn't showered in days. The momentary judgement Palmer passed was soon discarded when he realized he looked much the same.

"Sorry, do I know you?"

The man pulled a revolver from behind and pointed it at Palmer. He made a keep quiet motion with his left hand, called Palmer toward him with the right. Palmer froze. He'd faced monsters, magic, the threat of dying to corruption, and a metal kaiju right out of a nightmare. But this? A gun was more than his brain could process. He'd lived his entire life in fear of guns. He'd never held one or even seen one, but movies, TV shows, media, and games had ingrained that fear deep within him. The man reached out and took hold of Palmer's collar. He pulled hard but to no avail. Palmer's body did not budge. He held the gun up and pulled back on the hammer. The click it made was terrifying, felt louder than any shot.

Palmer somewhat came to his senses, wanted to calm the man down. He gently removed the hand from his collar. The man winced, and a bright burst of light filled the space between them. The look of pain changed to wide-eyed surprise. The blood drained from his face then he turned and ran. Palmer watched him flee, confused, as his hearing slowly returned. It felt as if someone had poked him in the chest. He looked down at the new hole in his shirt. There was no blood, no wound, just a bit of redness on his pale skin.

Did he just shoot me? Palmer checked himself more closely, as shock began to fade and true worry set in. *What the hell! Am I dead? No.* He could find nothing but the flattened slug on the ground. He quickly looked around for witnesses. He saw no one, heard none of the expected response to a gunshot. *Unbelievable. I was better off with monsters.* He cursed as he hurriedly resumed walking home. *Screw this place.*

Questions began to flood his mind on the way. What just happened? Was this the difference between people with and without stats? Did his high constitution make him immune to bullets? Or was something else at play, like armor rating or physical resistance? If players couldn't be harmed by conventional weapons, what would that mean for the world when tens of thousands of PvPers, people who thrived on killing others, invaded this server?

Palmer let out a long, frustrated sigh.

How is none of this real? My life is just another game, and a shitty one at that. Why the hell would I choose this for entertainment? If mankind has progressed far enough to achieve digital life, why go back to—he looked around at the world in disgust—*this. Do I even care if they wreck the place? Does it matter? If they burn it all down, won't the server just reset and start again? Why the hell should I care!* His mind instantly conjured an image of Sara. *Oh. Yeah. We're not even dating, though.* Then there was his mother. He truly cared about her and didn't want to see anything bad happen to her. He didn't want anything to happen to any of his friends, either. *It's not like things will end quickly. Everyone is going to get murdered...badly. What am I supposed to do about that? I can fight off a few, maybe.* There was a chance there were other players from Tellaria who would be willing to help, like Eli. It wasn't a permanent solution, but it was something. *I hope he's doing okay. Must be nice to be able to die and respawn.*

Palmer was already home, as he considered and discounted any number of plans to save the world. What it all boiled down to was he needed help. He couldn't do it alone. If there were a thousand other players on hardcore Earth, every one of them would have to work together for the slightest chance of fighting back. Even if entire guilds from Tellaria decided to help, could they really hold off that many people determined to get through? He would need a way to track new rifts and a means to get to them quickly. Their best hope was in immediately closing them. And his best bet to do that was to become as powerful as the system would allow in as little time as possible.

The lights inside were off but for one in the kitchen. He went to check for food, kept quiet in case his mother was asleep. The oven clock read 8:56 PM. The calendar on the wall still showed Friday. As far as he could tell, he'd only been gone six hours. He didn't think the time modifier would be that drastic. It felt like more than a week had passed in the rift. One long, terrible week. He chewed a slice of cold pizza from the fridge, climbed the stairs to his room on the second floor and collapsed onto the comfort of his bed.

Palmer was exhausted.

His mother would still be working at her second job until ten. All that worry about how she'd react at his absence, and she didn't even know he'd been gone.

He pulled up the main screen as he stared at the ceiling. The aftermath of the boss fight had been so hectic. Now that he time for character and inventory management, he noticed he'd gained five levels and another choice of specialization. He put five into STR, DEX, and CON, ten into WIS, the last ten into INT, and improved his mana regen to tier seven. He cast might, alacrity, and shield for fifteen points, then watched all but one point replenish after six seconds. That meant if he expended his entire mana pool, it would refill in under six minutes.

It wasn't even close to that fast before, he thought and sat up. *It has to be related to the new class. I wonder what other perks it has.*

He chose mystery gifts for the nine completed quests and saw one of them was listed as hidden. That one rewarded an epic version. While looking at inventory, he finally noticed what the boss had dropped: fifty thousand gold, a slew of rare and epic crafting resources, a unique ability stone, and epic quality magic bracers. He used the stone and studied its details.

Lesser Arcane Siphon (I)
Class: *All*
Restrictions: *Legendary tier or higher*
Active, Combat, Transmutation
Cost*: 10,* ***Range****: 12',* ***Duration****: Instant*
Leech 1% maximum mana points from a target and cause 1% fatigue damage

"That's new," he said. "The target would have to have a lot of mana for that to be worth it. I suppose it would improve quite a bit through use." He thought about the fatigue penalties at fifty and seventy-five percent. "Oof. It would take a while, but that could be nasty against a tough opponent. Really level the playing field." He looked over the new item. "What about these bracers..."

Bulwark Bracers
Type: Plate
Armor: Special
Restrictions: None
Torn from the body of a fallen juggernaut, these masterful bracers shield all.
Grants the wearer +25 armor rating and +25% physical resistance.

Palmer slipped the much larger metal bracers over his forearms. The magic items shrunk to fit him nicely. He set them to hidden and perused armor in the Shop for a frame of reference.

Oh, damn. That's more AR than a full set of plate mail. I need to figure out how that system actually works. In the meantime...

He pulled out the alchemy kit, changed gear to the right level of magic find, and popped the cork on a luck potion. He drank the full potion and opened all eight normal gifts. He saved the epic one for last, wanted to move to the higher loot table for that. He received forty-eight more stat points, some resources for enchanting, and two rank two healer stones—shield and cure disease. When he used them, both abilities evolved to rank three. On top of the increased amount of damage his shield could absorb, it reflected magical damage back to the attacker. Cure disease now had a range of twelve feet and removed four counts from the target in one use.

That'll come in handy. He changed into the full magic find set of gear and wished for good luck. *Come on, gimme something good.* He drank the potion and opened the epic mystery gift. *Yes! Another epic!*

Ring of Haste
Type: Jewelry
Armor: 2
Restrictions: None
A band of gold infused with the spirit of an air demon.
Grants the wearer +50% ability use and movement speed.

Out of curiosity, he checked the Shop to see how much he could sell the ring for, while finishing his slice of pizza. He nearly choked at what he saw.

"A million?!" He'd never seen an item listed for that much. The other items he wore, which he deemed just as powerful, were only valued for half. While browsing the list of items available, he noticed a new Shop Upgrade License. "A hundred and fifty grand is a bit much. I'm not selling any of my gear. I'd have to craft to earn the extra hundred."

Palmer groaned at the thought. He somewhat enjoyed trade skills, especially when he could use the results to game the system, but he was tired. A whiff of body odor rose up from his shirt unbidden. He instantly reared back in revulsion.

Right, time for a shower. He got up and headed for the bathroom. *I'll deal with the whole gold making operation later.*

As he glanced in the mirror, he froze in place. The iris of his eyes were midnight black, with a glowing outer ring of silver. Light radiated from them, like an extension of his mana. How could so small a change make him seem unrecognizable to himself? It reminded him of Eli. The mage had a similar characteristic but in blue. Was this the distinguishing mark of a player? Eli had called it a cosmetic, as if players chose them at character creation or could change them in some way. Panic set in.

"What the hell do I do?" he asked and moved closer to the mirror. "I can't hide this! Mom's gonna freak!" He noticed other changes as well. There was a distinct black spot in the mirror when its surface had long ago faded. It used to be level with his ears. Now it was closer to his shoulders. "Did I—did I get taller?" He flexed his right arm and looked at its reflection. "I'm a little bigger too." His cheeks looked fuller but with a much sharper jawline. An idea came to mind. He rummaged through the top drawer for a contact lens case. He'd used them at the last comic book convention for a furkin traveler cosplay. He took one look, changed his mind, and put them back. "No. I can't walk around with cat eyes either."

He got undressed, took a shower, put on comfortable clothes, and collapsed back onto his bed with an audible sigh.

His mother opened the door without knocking and said, "Oh, good, you're done. Why didn't you text me back earlier?"

Palmer quickly covered his eyes, feigning a headache. "I—uhh, I lost my phone."

He could feel her move to stand over him. "Look at me." He tilted his head her way but didn't remove his hands. "No, really look." He reluctantly opened his eyes. "Do you have any idea how much a phone costs? You swore we didn't need the replacement plan, that only idiots lost their phones." She was more upset than angry. Money was always a rough topic. "How could you be so careless?"

"Sorry."

The fact she hadn't said anything about his eyes meant she couldn't see them as being any different than before. The relief he felt was promptly overshadowed by an unwanted feeling he thought he'd already dealt with. He loved and cared for his mother, but she wasn't *really* his mother, even if his entire body was telling him otherwise. Why should he care about any of this?

About what she thought and felt? Why let her make him feel so small? None of this mattered!

She sat on the bed and placed a soothing hand on his chest. "Stop. I can see you getting upset. That's—that's not what I wanted. But you have to understand, we're on a very tight budget. A lost phone is not an unforeseeable emergency." She poked him in the ribs. "A broken leg, on the other hand…"

Palmer rolled his eyes and gave a fake laugh. "You'd rather I break a leg than lose my phone?"

"A bit, yeah." It was good to see her smile. "Medical insurance would cover that." She took in a long breath and slowly let it out. "Well, you're going to have to wait 'til next payday. And don't expect anything new. You'll be lucky if it gets texts." She paused to look him over with genuine concern. "Are you okay? You know I'm just teasing. You usually laugh at all my jokes. And you look like you're losing weight. Are you eating?"

He didn't care what was real. She felt real enough to him.

"Yeah. I'm fine. It's just been a rough—" he nearly said week—"day."

She bent down and kissed his forehead. "You and me both." She got up, headed for the door, and stopped to look back. "Love you."

Palmer met her eyes. "Love you, too."

***

Palmer woke late the next morning well rested and refreshed, if a bit shaken. He was still troubled by the thought someone had fired a gun against his chest. If he'd never come across the rift, if none of this strangeness had ever happened, would he be dead? He tried to keep it from his mind by focusing on the tasks at hand. He was a little sore from his nightly routine, where he worked to improve abilities by using them on himself. For two hours, he went through a rotation of every buff and debuff, every DoT and heal, before finally succumbing to sleep. The direct damage ability divine light was much more difficult to use on himself, at least in his bedroom. He didn't think his mother would appreciate the scorch marks left behind by holy fire. He had difficulty raising restoration as well, since that ability only worked on serious injuries. All of his passives had been ranking up at a steady pace, with the majority of his skills at rank three. Coupled with the permanent alterations the corruption had made to all his abilities, he'd become quite the magical powerhouse. He was a far cry from the weak person who had slain that first goblin so long ago.

Why didn't she notice the change to my eyes? Palmer wondered as he brushed his teeth in front of the mirror. They were so unsettling, they even scared him. *It's like looking at a complete stranger.* He thought back to Eli. *Can only players see them? Is that a way to identify each other? Could I use it to find other players here on HCE?* He rinsed his mouth out and gave himself a dubious look. *No, I didn't become a player until I was promoted. They'd have to kill a monster first, I guess.*

He finished getting dressed and went down to the kitchen. There was no need to worry about anyone walking in on him while he worked, so he pulled the alchemy kit from inventory and placed it on the table. After looking through the fridge for anything besides cold pizza, he shrugged and called a piece of sweetbread to hand. He'd gotten used to eating it for a quick meal, as it was both tasty and filling.

His approach to crafting was centered around efficiency and usefulness. Though he processed every resource in inventory to its workable state, he only brewed the potions with effects he wanted or with the best overall profit. A new player might think a speed potion is good for earning gold, but its materials sell back to the Shop for slightly less than the potion itself. It had to do with resource rarity. Over time, as skill reduces the amounts of resources needed, it would become more profitable, but effort was better spent elsewhere. The effect, however, made the recipe worth improving. Palmer had no intention of selling such a crucial utility item. Defense potions, on the other hand, used relatively common materials and sold for more than triple the resource worth. As there was no auction house he could see, Palmer surmised that the items in the Shop were either partially or primarily made up of player made items—at least the magical ones. He could even see the resale value of potions go down in real time, as he sold them in lots of five as an experiment.

His next approach was to buy common weapons and armor, enchant them with the lowest rarity resources he had, and then disenchant them for more than double the materials he put in. He didn't know why corruption affected the system this way. It seemed as if there was a second source of power within him, like an alternative mana pool, that both imbued and stripped items through touch. There was a rationale in the back of his mind that equated corruption with the hack. The modified code could be wreaking havoc on different aspects of the system. But he was certain the Hierophant class was rooted in disease, and corruption was just an evolution of that power. Why else would he have unlocked the hidden class by gaining corruption immunity? It couldn't have just been a coincidence.

After some time amassing a ridiculous stockpile of enchanting resources, having improved his recipes in the process, Palmer set about crafting magic items to sell. With the gold he made from that, he bought higher tier magic items, corrupted each one, broke them down for the recipes and materials, then began the whole method once again. Within a few hours, he had more resources, recipes, and items than he started with and just over a million gold. He could have kept going with the seemingly infinite money glitch, but there was a point to why he'd begun in the first place.

He purchased the license upgrade. A slew of new items appeared in the Shop, from magic gear to recipes to abilities. Excited, he quickly navigated to the tabs to see if there were any new healer stones. While none could be found, what he did find was even better.

"I knew it!" Palmer bought the two Hierophant stones for half a million gold. He pulled them from inventory, already corrupted, and used each one.

Minor Protection from Corruption (I)
Class: *Hierophant*
Active*, *Combat*, *Enchantment
Cost: *25*, **Range**: *12'*, **Duration**: *1 min*
Increase a target's corruption resistance by 100%.

Minor Cure Corruption (I)
Class: *Hierophant*
Active*, *Combat*, *Reversible*, *Necromancy
Cost: *50*, **Range**: *24'*, **Duration**: *Instant*
Remove one corruption from all targets in a 12' radius.

"Corruption's part of the game," he reiterated his previous thought. "This is proof. There's got to be a reason why it affects players and items and abilities the way it does. Is it like a burnout effect? Make the player's abilities super powerful, then they die from the exposure? Does that mean corrupted items break sooner? I didn't notice a durability score." He shook his head and put all that aside. "Now for the real test."

He used cure corruption on himself.

It left his body in a wave of inner warmth, with a visible golden glow he could see inside his aura. There was no longer a feeling of dread within him, the tightness in his chest that would not abate. His abilities remained unchanged, but their text had lost that glimmer of black and silver. He pulled Reckoning from inventory. There was no sign of the black tendrils along the staff anymore. He put it back and rushed to the fridge. A terrifying set of eyes, outlined in radiant silver, reflected disappointment.

Whatever. He went back to the table and put everything away. *I guess it makes sense. It's part of the class, not corruption. At least I can trade items now.* He yawned and stretched. *I feel like I'm forgetting something important. Oh! New stats points.* He allocated most but left three unspent, because he liked the look of numbers divisible by five. *Nice!*

PALMER
LVL: 35 **Class**: Hierophant
STR: 40, **CON**: 40, **DEX**: 40, **INT**: 100, **WIS**: 100
HP: 400 [400], **MP**: 1,000 [1,000], **F**: 0%
SP: 3

"Not gonna lie," he remarked up toward the HCE system, "I really like the look of a thousand mana. Y'know, this would all be a lot easier if you talked to me." He waited. "Just saying, lots of people are hell bent on wrecking your hard work. You just gonna stand there and take it?" Still no response. "C'mon, we're on the same side!" The front doorbell rang. Palmer raised a brow in surprise, then lowered both with doubt. "That you?"

When he opened the door, Sara stood there with an annoyed look on her face, a hand on one hip, and her phone in the other.

"Why the hell aren't you texting me back?" She reiterated the question with, "You don't *look* sick. We were supposed to meet the group at Daren's half an hour ago!" It was good to see her again, even if she was mad. He got distracted by her pink lip gloss and just awkwardly stood there. "Are you even listening to me?" She switched the phone to her other hand and punched him in the shoulder. "Ow! What the hell." He barely felt it, but she flexed her fingers as if genuinely hurt. “Get your good dice, and let’s go. We’re supposed to be starting the Frostfire Mountain campaign today.”

Palmer cleared his throat. *I knew I was forgetting something.* “Listen, I don’t really feel like playing today. I had enough of that this past”—he coughed—“I’m just not up for it today.”

He felt so stupid. All he could think about was how glad he was to see her, but all that came out was the same old bumbling excuses to be somewhere else. It was different when they were younger. He hadn’t really seen her as a girl back then. But now? She was easily the prettiest girl he knew, and she didn’t wear lots of makeup like the others—just a bit of eyeshadow. Her nails were painted but not fake. She was thin but also fit, from all the running she did. Most of all, she liked games. In his eyes, she was perfect. Which only hurt all the more knowing she didn’t feel the same. How could she? He was way below her level.

She made the noise of a penalty buzzer. “Wrong! You’re coming with me, even if I have to drag your ass to the car. It’s a level twenty campaign. There’s no way we’re doing it without you.” She turned so he could see the tiny backpack she wore. “C’mon, I even painted a new mini. And I already picked up snacks.” She began to sound a little defeated. “You’re not really gonna bail, are you? I got Twizzlers...”

It was impossible to say no to Sara. Despite all the other important things he could be doing, an all-nighter with the group, sitting beside her, watching her smile with delight at the prospect of loot, or bite her lip as she considered what to do on her turn, he wanted to spend time with her, even if it was just as friends.

Palmer sighed.

“Ha!” she cried in triumph. “Get your stuff. I wanna kill stuff, like, yesterday!”

Warning! Incoming rift.

No nearby players detected.
Rerouting...

He immediately felt its presence just a block away to the east. Though he couldn't hear it split the air with a breaking of glass, he felt the mana reach in and tear a hole between their worlds.

"Oh, no." Palmer looked in the direction of the rift, as if he could see it in the alley behind the row of townhouses. "Sara, I have something to tell you." He swallowed and looked directly in her eyes. "Or maybe it's better if I show you. We have to be quick, though. Follow me."

Does this mean it's helping me?

He headed for the rift but made sure Sara came too. He urged her to hurry, looked both ways on the street before crossing, and led her to the alleyway. Once they stood before the rift, it was easier to explain.

"What am I looking at?" Sara asked. "How long has it been here?"

Palmer tried to order his thoughts. "It's like a portal to another world. It literally just opened, but I've been through one before." He almost put his hand in as proof. Memory of the goblin that pulled him through made him pause. "It's a fantasy world, like with magic and monsters. I was *just* there." She had both a wild-eyed look of fear and surprise, with a smile that yearned for it to be true. "Not everyone can use it. If you're not too afraid, you could try. I have to go, either way. If I don't, there's things on the other side that want to come here and kill us all."

He wasn't sure how much he could tell her. If she wasn't a player, this was already too much. If she was, he ran the risk of breaking her mind and causing a disconnect from the server.

Sara reached out a hand to touch the rift. "I wanna go." Her look of wonder hardened to concern. "If you go, *I* go."

"Reynolds?" the voice came from the other side of the alley wall. Guy pulled himself up and over the cinderblocks. "The hell are you doin' here? You got a death wish or—" He eyed the rift. "What is that?"

Perfect. Just what I needed. He glared up at the sky, as if the system had purposely placed the rift behind his bully's house. *You couldn't put it closer to my house? Hmm.* Did the system move the rift before it fully connected or after? Could it do so again? It had mentioned no nearby players. Did that mean it would keep placing rifts nearby for him to conquer until there were? *That's a lot of pressure.*

Palmer snapped, "It's nothing. Go away."

"We just got here," Sara said, as if to say they didn't know either. She tried to place her hand inside the light of the opening, but her fingertips met with a solid surface. She placed both hands against the rift and pushed. "You sure this is a portal?"

She can't enter. Palmer was crestfallen. Of all the people in the world who could be one of the thousand or so players, he desperately hoped she was one of them. *Does that mean she's an AI?* With so few players, the odds were never in his favor. It was hard not to feel like all his hopes had been dashed anyway.

"Portal!" Guy said and laughed. "Like what, to another dimension or something? You two must be high." He looked more closely at the break. "It's just a, uhh—I mean, it's got to be like…" He gave up trying to explain and touched it. When his fingers passed through, he made a sound of satisfaction. "How 'bout that?"

Guy stepped through the rift like he owned the place, leaving them both stunned. Palmer gritted his teeth in utter frustration.

"You have *got* to be shitting me."

***

Palmer stepped from the rift to the sonorous cry of a distant war horn. He stood near the edge of a verdant floating island. Lush greenery led toward a forest at its middle, with looming mountains farther off in the distance. The rush of water could be heard from a nearby stream, as it splashed over a rocky edge into a waterfall. The sky was pale blue and aglow with the light of day. The only clouds to be seen ringed the central mountain peaks. Through it all there was Guy, head thrown back with a grin, arms spread wide as he slowly spun. He was like a child at an amusement park for the very first time.

His innocent joy was about to be interrupted, in the worst possible way. He may not have noticed its presence, but Palmer sensed the goblin straight away. It was a combination of things, the presence of innate power. It prickled the skin the way mana sent trembles through the body. It carried a sense of dread and uneasiness, set hair to standing on end. It was both electric and spiritual, like admiring the beauty of a storm with full knowledge of its destructive capability. The stronger a creature's power was, the more intense and far reaching was its presence. On the other end of the equation was the ability to perceive and gauge another's power. Palmer was convinced this was rooted in the intelligence stat. It took him the briefest of moments to not only know what he felt was a lesser creature, like a goblin, but to also pinpoint its exact location.

"Watch out," Palmer said halfheartedly, as the diminutive creature came into sight. It wore leather armor dyed red with black trim. It carried a steel short sword and small wooden shield. The tall crimson feathers in its cap made it seem taller than it really was. More annoyed than worried, he added, "It's coming up behind you."

The goblin stood inches less than Guy's waist, yet it grabbed him by the wrist with enough force to pull him to the ground. It began to drag him away toward the forest at great speed. Guy reached back and took hold of the goblin's arm to break free, kicked his legs at the grassy earth for purchase. His endeavors were to no avail. Despite its size, the goblin was far stronger than a person with zero stats. Guy screamed in shock at the assault and again at the realization of what was carrying him away.

"Get off!" Guy angrily yelled and pulled back. "What the hell is this thing? Help! What the hell, why is it so goddamn strong?" He dug in both feet, tore up clumps of grassy earth, but did nothing to slow the goblin that ignored his efforts and pleas. "How is this even possible?"

You literally just stepped through a portal to another world, Palmer thought in exasperation, *but this is impossible?* He considered letting the goblin drag him to the core. At least he assumed that's where it was headed, most likely to toss Guy within it. *On the one hand, that would solve a problem I've had for years now...*

"You just gonna stand there like a jackass?" Guy screamed back at Palmer.

On the other hand, he debated, *there's only a thousand of us.* He clucked his tongue as he thought. *I guess we'll need everyone.* The thought of rescuing someone who was such a jerk, though, someone who'd bullied him since the third grade, rankled him. *Even if we don't get along.*

"Fine." Palmer easily got within range and used disease on the goblin to slow it down. The goblin had already gauged Palmer's power and had decided to focus on the weaker of the two. Palmer pulled an enchanted long sword from inventory and held it out to Guy pommel first. Guy had given up struggling and was being dragged on his back. "You're gonna have to kill it."

"What? Where did you get that from?" Guy still

hadn't taken the sword. "I—I can't do that. Just stab it already!"

"Nope. You either kill it, or you die."

It was the only way for Guy to become a player. Aside from that, as far as Palmer could tell, there were no grouping mechanics. When he and Eli had killed the boss, no party frame had shown up on his screen. He couldn't see the mage's health or mana bar anywhere. It seemed the game was meant to be played solo, though players could work together. Ultimately, experience was only gained through contribution. If Palmer killed the goblin, Guy would still be an NPC. Besides, its name—goblin soldier—was in gray. Palmer wouldn't gain any experience from it. He debuffed the goblin's strength and dexterity as well but held off on corrupting it. There would be plenty of time to power level on the way to the boss.

It was strange to see fear in his bully's eyes. If it were anyone else, Palmer would have felt sympathy and an urge to help. With Guy, he'd expected a wave of satisfaction or joy. Instead, all he felt was annoyance. Why couldn't it have been Sara? Was that really too much to ask? Only a thousand out of *billions* of people on the planet, with two living in the same small town, and it just had to be him.

It's like the system hates me.

Guy finally took the sword. The way its tip dropped toward the ground, the weapon was much heavier than he'd expected. The goblin immediately let go and drew its own blade. It tried to stab Guy in the leg, but Palmer had Reckoning in hand in an instant. He blocked the attack with a *tsk*.

"Nuh uh, little man." He poked the goblin's wrist with the end of his staff, broke the bones and caused the sword to fall. "This is *my* game now." He looked down to Guy. "You have to do it yourself. It's the only way."

"What, like it's a test?" Guy got to his feet and

towered over the goblin. It held only fear of Palmer. It looked like it was ready to flee. "You think I can't handle myself? Here!" He drove the sword into the goblin's left arm, though he'd clearly been aiming for its chest. "Damn it, stay still!" When stabbing proved too difficult, he resorted to wild overhead swings with both hands. "Argh, you little shit!" The goblin had tried to run away, but Guy caught it across the back. He continued to swing after its death. "See? I don't need anyone's help! I can take care of myself." He kicked the bloodied corpse. "And buy your own damn cigarettes!"

Palmer gave him a questioning look.

"What?" Guy threw the sword down. "Shut up!" He walked away in an attempt to get his breathing under control. He stopped and sharply turned, his eyes focused on something in front of him. "What the hell am I looking at? I'm a—a player now?"

"Congrats," Palmer replied dryly. "Now you know why you had to kill it yourself. You only get experience if you contribute. The more you contribute, the more xp you get."

Guy looked at him like he was crazy. "We ain't LARPin' here, Reynolds." His expression then completely changed to one of fear. "Your eyes. What the hell? They changed."

Palmer noticed Guy's had gained a bit of earthen glow around the irises too.

"They've been like this," he said. "You just couldn't see it before."

Guy was clearly unnerved, tried to pass it off as nothing, but began to avoid any eye contact. Instead, he pointed down at the dead monster.

"That's a real goblin. Just what the hell is all of this? Have you killed one before?"

"That's kind of a long story." It was still difficult for Palmer to talk to Guy. They weren't friends. He wanted nothing to do with him. A small part of him hoped knowing the truth would disconnect Guy from the server. "This is gonna be hard to hear, but just listen to the end." He explained as best he could what he thought was going on, based on what he personally knew to be true and what the mage Eli had told him. "I honestly can't say for certain if all the other stuff is true. I just know what I went through. And you can see the game screen now for yourself. All of this," he said and indicated the trees, the mountains and distant waterfalls, "can't be a simulation without the same being true of where we came from."

Guy seemed to be navigating the system. "That is a lot to take in." He suddenly looked at Palmer. "You think that means we know each other...outside the sim? I mean, if it's such a small group, we'd have to, right?"

Palmer scratched his head. *That's actually a good point.* He was surprised Guy had thought of it. Thinking wasn't really his strong suit. *A small community like that? Chances are we do all know each other.*

He felt the presence of two more goblins coming toward them.

"Heads up," Palmer warned. "Two more."

Guy complained, "But I haven't picked a class yet." He went and picked the long sword back up. "What are you?"

Palmer stood ready with his staff. Something about the strike he'd used against the goblin had felt different, stronger, more precise. He had a hunch the zone modifier was melee related. The war horn he heard upon entering could mean physical attacks were enhanced.

"I'm a healer."

"Ha! What, like, on purpose?" Guy turned to face the same direction as Palmer, looked as if he had no idea what was coming or where it came from. "Who the hell picks a support class in a solo game?"

He's not wrong. Palmer sighed, once again wished it had been Sara instead. *Still, I think I did pretty well, all things considered.* He buffed Guy with might, alacrity, and blessing, then added shield and regen for good measure.

"Whoa! I take it back." Guy flexed both his arms at the influx of power. "That kinda rocks. How the hell are you not scared?" He took in a steadying breath. "I think I dropped a load in my pants when I first saw that thing. Maybe. I kind of hope it's just mud."

Palmer hated that it made him laugh. Was Guy actually funny?

As soon as the goblins came into range, Palmer diseased and debuffed them both. His ability use speed was far greater than it used to be. He could easily use two spells in the time it used to take for just one. With a little more haste gear, he was sure he could reach three.

"You got this," he said.

"Don't worry, man." Guy puffed out his chest a bit. "I'll protect you."

Palmer fought the urge to roll his eyes and just nodded. Guy did his best to engage the goblins but quickly got overrun. He was on his back once more, as they easily overpowered him. Palmer targeted one and activated divine light, in an attempt to make it a little more even. He instantly pulled back on the cast, due to the pillar of holy fire it would conjure beneath the goblin. He wasn't sure if friendly fire would kill Guy. As he fought to hold back the spell's effect, he felt its power continue to grow. It took additional mana as well, as if the ability were charging up for a more damaging attack. The longer he held, the more mana it took. The vibration in his middle began to grow as well. Within moments it caused some pain. A few more brought with it health point loss. In a panic, he switched targets to a rock and unleashed the charged magic. It utterly decimated the stone and cratered the earth beneath it. The normal damage he would have inflicted looked to have tripled.

A quick assessment of the damage caused compared to the additional mana used led him to believe charged abilities were inefficient. However, if he used it on a spell that did damage over time, the mana to damage ratio became irrelevant due to his enormous mana pool and enhanced regeneration. Recasting a DoT simply overwrote the original. Charging one up meant an actual increase to his damage per second. That was a huge discovery.

"Help!" Guy yelled, as the goblins manhandled him.

"Right." Palmer focused his attention back to the fight. "My bad."

It did make him wonder what would happen if he charged a non-damaging spell. Would it just enhance the effect or introduce a new damaging element? He charged disease until it began to affect his own health points. He let it loose on the goblin and was truly shocked at the results. The creature's flesh immediately darkened with open sores that spread over its entire body. Where the effect would normally only slow the target, it looked to additionally reduce stats and cause magical damage.

New hidden ability unlocked: Minor Cause Plague I!

Hidden? He'd unlocked abilities before, but none of them had been hidden. *It must be related to Hierophant.*

He did the same to the other goblin. Disease began ravaging it as well. Guy quickly got to his feet and regained the upper hand. He stabbed and slashed at them both with all the skill of an untrained toddler. The goblins fought back but grew weaker by the moment. A few more swings and Guy had them beat. He turned to grin in triumph, as if he'd done it all himself.

"Good job."

"No big." Guy shrugged. "Ding, by the way."

Palmer pulled up the details of his new ability.

Minor Cause Plague (I)
Class: *Hierophant*
Active, Combat, Reversible, Necromancy
Cost: *25,* **Range**: *24',* **Duration**: *Until cured*
Cause one plague to a target. Contagious.

Does that mean it spreads? An idea suddenly came to mind, a terrible, awful, incredibly inspired idea. *I may not be able to stop them from coming through.* A wicked grin crossed his face. *But I can sure as hell slow them down.*

- 7 -

Palmer had made two important discoveries. He knelt in the lush grass, his mind busy working out the ramifications. His original plan to slow players from attacking was to send one of them back through with a disease only he could cure. The logistics of that approach had major drawbacks. It relied on his ability to find an enemy player, overcome that person enough to inflict them with plague, force them back through the rift to Tellaria, and still have time to defeat the boss before other players overwhelmed the area. He didn't know how much time he had to close the corridor between servers before others could find their way in. With so many eager to attack, it wouldn't take them long to find new rifts. Palmer wasn't able to pass through to Tellaria. He had to assume the reverse was true, until the core was fueled with enough mana to fully power the rift into a stable corridor.

But if too many players make it inside, he thought with a sense of dread, *I wouldn't be able to deal with them by myself. Even if I could solo the boss, enemy players helping defend it would make that impossible.* That's why he needed a new plan. If he could target a rock with divine light...*Please work.*

He charged up cause plague and placed his palm against the earth. When he let loose the ability, disease spread outward in a darkened halo. Grass wilted beneath its touch, lost all luster and shrank. It looked as if the life had been drained from each blade. The soil lost its moisture and hardened, cracked, and turned black. The entire patch of infected land stretched on for six feet in all directions. Palmer lifted his hand, stayed down on one knee as he waited. It took only a moment of exposure before the plague took hold. He could feel it in his chest, saw its effects on his stats. It had worked. The contagious spell could be spread without a player as its target. He allowed himself to smile, though a bigger question yet remained. He placed his hand back to the earth. He activated its reverse and watched the land revert to its former state. Palmer cured himself as well, let out a heavy breath in relief. It was one thing to consider the complete decimation of another server and quite another to do so without recourse.

"You want any of this?" Guy asked when he finished looting the bodies. "The gear looks like junk, but one dropped a healer stone."

Palmer was mentally prepared for the flip that could occur at any moment, when Guy went back to being his old self and acted like a bully. The strangeness of their situation would only last for so long. At some point, Guy would remember Palmer was smaller, weaker, and somehow deserving of abuse. Even without an entourage to egg him on, it was just a matter of time.

"Thanks," Palmer took the offered ability stone and used it. It was Minor Fortitude, a health point buff. "I've got a few warrior stones I've been saving, if you wanna go that route." *He's so much taller than me,* he thought in frustration. *Why is everyone so much taller?* "A couple for mage and one for rogue, too."

"Still debating," Guy said and stretched his back. "Man, that heal you put on me was awesome. It even fixed all my bruises."

Palmer raised a brow. They hadn't been in the rift

long enough for bruises to form. "What bruises?"

"Oh, pfft," he stammered a reply, "y'know, football and stuff." As far as Palmer knew, Guy didn't play for the team or participate in any sports at all. "It's nothin'."

That's two. Palmer looked at him closely. *First the outburst about cigarettes and now this?* If he didn't know any better, he would've thought Guy was abused. It made sense, in a way, the kid who gets bullied at home goes on to bully others at school. *It doesn't make it any easier to care, when I'm the one he's taking it out on.*

"I never knew you were into games."

Guy's eyes lit up. "Hell, yeah. Mostly MMOs, and just when I'm over at my dad's. My mom's boyfriend doesn't want me suckin' up all the electricity. Whatever the hell that means."

"Sorry to hear that. Listen," Palmer said, trying to find the right words, "you should probably go back. It's dangerous in here, and I need to get to the core before enemy players do."

"This again." Guy folded his arms in defiance. "You think you're so smart, like everyone else should just do what you say. This ain't Mackleroe's Earth science class. When it comes to fighting, you should be listenin' to me. Besides, you're a support class. What're you gonna do without a tank?"

Mr. Mackleroe was their third-grade science teacher. They'd been in lots of classes together since childhood. Why would he mention that one specifically? It's not like they were ever friends or spoke on a regular basis.

"Okay," Palmer replied, "first off, I don't know what that means. Second, healers in this game have decent offensive capabilities. I'm not sure how I'll do against players, but I'm higher level than you. We don't have time for you to catch up."

"Then I'll do it myself," Guy scoffed. "I don't need you. It just makes more sense to stick together. So instead of assuming you're smarter than everyone else, like usual, how 'bout you tell me what the hell's goin' on so I can help? Those goblins didn't try to kill me. They wanted to take me somewhere, which means they need me alive. Where were they takin' me, this core? What is it, and why's it so important?"

Why's he acting like I'm the one who's always a jerk to him and not the other way around? Palmer took a moment to self-reflect and disregarded the notion. *I don't act like I'm smarter.*

"Fine, take these." Palmer pulled all of the basic warrior ability stones he had from storage, along with a few pieces of enchanted leather armor, and handed them over to Guy. "You can look for low level mobs to level up on. It should be easy with magic gear and abilities. This place," he tried to explain, "is basically a hack. It's a modified zone from the game server, intended to bridge their world to ours. The core," he added with some hesitation, "is a giant sphere of mana that powers this place. It feeds on energy from both servers. I think they were gonna throw you in it."

"So, perma death."

Palmer corrected him. "All death for us is permanent. We don't get to respawn, like they do. Anyway, the rifts at either end of this pocket dimension, or whatever you wanna call it, are like cracks in each server. The core needs more power to turn this place into a corridor or a bridge, so players can pass from one server to the other. We can enter from our side, they can enter from theirs, but neither of us can go all the way through. Not until this place is fully powered. At least, that's my guess, based on everything I know."

Guy surmised, "Something's guarding the core, and you think I'd be in the way. I get it. Still, everyone knows it's stupid to split the party."

"Oh, we're a party now? I didn't ask you to join. You just walked right in, without a clue what was on the other side!" Palmer was letting his pent-up frustration get the better of him. He didn't have time for an argument, but part of him wanted both an apology and an explanation for the crap Guy had put him through. "You do nothing but give me shit. Last time I saw you, you broke my damn phone. Why the hell should I do anything for you?"

"Oh, don't be such a pussy!" Guy rolled his eyes. "Yeah, I mess with you a lot. Cuz you deserve it. I doubt I broke your phone. I barely touched it. But this?" He held out both hands to indicate the world of magic they'd stepped into. "This is crazy. I would never believe it without seein' it, and I still can barely believe it. But if there really are people comin' to destroy our world, kill my friends, my mom? I'll put up with your shit to fight them off."

Palmer fumed. "What shit of mine do you have to put up with? We don't talk! We're not friends! I—"

"And who's fault is that! I tried to be your damn friend, but nooo, you thought I was too stupid. Well, screw you, Reynolds. I've got friends. I don't need you or your damn group." Guy's face was red with anger. For someone who spent a lot of time acting like he didn't care, he sure seemed to care about this. "If I wanna play S&S, I'll just go to the hobby store. There's plenty of other people I can play with."

"Once again," Palmer said, confused but still annoyed, "I don't know what you're talking about. Not once, have I ever—"

Guy glared down at him. "Third grade. That's when it all started. I just moved here from Detroit, didn't know anyone, but I heard you talking about ToR. So, I joined your group for the fall project, but Mackleroe removed me. Turner said it was because *you* complained I was too stupid, and it wasn't fair it would affect your grade."

That makes no sense. I barely even remember what he's talking about, but I would never have said that. Palmer tried to recall the project, but years had passed.

I don't even remember who Turner is.

"I never—"

"Every time I tried to talk to you," Guy went on, "to figure out what your problem was, you'd dodge me or find some excuse not to talk to me. That's when all those rumors started, that I had to move because I was expelled for bad grades. Everyone thought I was an idiot, started making fun of my name. Oh, look, it's *that* Guy. Watch out, it's *that* Guy. And I remember you laughing along with 'em." He was clearly hurt by all that had happened in the past. "I gave you plenty of chances to be friends. You didn't want it. Even your girl told me I couldn't join your S&S group, because it would make *you* uncomfortable. So, piss off with your attitude. If you'd rather let the world get destroyed than work together, then maybe the world's better off without you. So go ahead, be solo. Cuz that's worked out great for you so far, right?"

Guy stormed off, presumably in search of low level enemies.

He thought to call after, but Palmer wasn't sure what to say. He certainly wasn't going to apologize. None of what Guy said was even true. Should he even care if Guy's feelings were hurt over some years old misunderstanding? None of the perceived slights he'd complained about were good enough reasons for all the bullying that ensued. As much as he would have liked to resolve the situation, there were more pressing matters. He could deal with it later and make things right when they had more time. For now, Palmer had a mission.

He made his way toward the core, followed the powerful sense of its mana, and made a mental map of what he saw on the way. There were numerous herb patches, some of them rare. He stopped to gather those of blue and purple rarity, as there wouldn't be time on the way back to the rift. Once the core was in sight, at the center of an empty field, Palmer stayed to the trees on its outskirts. Though he couldn't yet sense a boss, he knew one would spawn if he got too close. Instead, he went around and past the field, in search of the Tellaria rift. He'd done his best to avoid enemies as he went. The one he sensed ahead now gave off a presence far more powerful than any monster he'd seen thus far.

There was no doubt it was an enemy player.

Palmer buffed himself fully and drank an invisibility potion. There was no telling how dangerous this player was, other than the powerful aura that dwarfed his own. If he had to guess, he assumed they were easily twice his level. To bridge the difference, Palmer wanted every advantage he could get. With any luck, he could lay an ambush and land debuffs to slow them down. His usual tactic of avoiding confrontation wasn't an option. If this player intended to defend the core long enough for the rift to become a corridor, then he had no choice but to engage. He kept to the trees, did his best to move with stealth. The other player soon came into view.

She wore a full set of magic chainmail, with a heavy plate chest piece, thigh guards and bracers. Leather boots and gloves, a broad red cape that matched her hair, she was geared like a raid level warrior. More than the magic items and strength of her aura, there was confidence and competence to her stride. With a broadsword across her back and kite shield in her offhand, she looked ready to face anything foolish enough to cross her path. Though she was hundreds of feet away, the crimson glow that ringed each iris was both impressive and a warning. This woman was not to be taken lightly. Her name and title, in red, was High Warlord Margrave.

He waited for her to pass, thought it too dangerous to attempt a flank that might give away his position. Just when he felt the moment was right to move in, she came to a stop and turned his way.

"I know you're there." She still hadn't drawn her sword. Though she appeared just a few years older than him, her voice bore the self-assurance of one well beyond her age. Truth be told, she was attractive. In a terrifying way. "I'm not here to hurt you. I came to deliver a message from Eli."

As surprised as he was, Palmer remained cautious. They weren't playing by the same rules. He couldn't take risks and respawn if he made a mistake.

"What's the message?"

If she was annoyed that he didn't come out, it didn't show in her expression.

"He says not to stand in the goo." She shifted uncomfortably. "Whatever it is, it corrupted his character data. He couldn't be restored and had to make a new one. It'll take him a bit to level up again, but he plans to help if he can." She cleared her throat, as if expecting Palmer would've come out by now. "We're in the same guild. There's lots of people who want to help. For every jerk PvPer who wants to wreck your server, there are literally thousands of other players who just want to craft and run dungeons. So don't hate us all, okay?"

It deleted his character? Palmer's jaw had dropped open. *Holy crap.* That completely changed everything. If corruption caused permanent death to softcore players, they were suddenly on even ground. *They only get one shot against us. No more respawns.*

Palmer cancelled the invisibility effect and stepped out. He maintained the distance between them, was ready to strike if he was wrong.

"I appreciate that," he said with genuine gratitude. She'd just made his entire day. "Thanks for the message."

She bowed her head slightly. "I'm Mina. A full group almost made it in before me. I took care of them. I don't know if more are coming soon, but..." She shrugged and offered a smile. "Need help with the boss? You look new to me, but Eli said you were a decent healer."

He shook his head. "Naw, I got it. Oh, and I'm Palmer. But, you already knew that. Umm, if you could keep everyone else out, y'know, 'til I'm done, that would be great."

The look of surprise on her face that slowly turned to doubt was not reassuring. He tried to keep in mind she couldn't see his aura or feel his presence. He assumed it was his artifact tier class that masked both.

"I can do that," was all she said, though she clearly wanted to say more.

"Tell Eli I'm sorry about his character, and I look forward to grouping."

She gave a nod and headed back the way she came.

Palmer gathered a patch of sunbloom as he debated. He didn't want Mina to know what he intended. After hearing her speak, he wasn't sure he still wanted to. What if other friendly players decided to come through to help? What had started as a solid tactic had become a moral dilemma.

But the odds are stacked against us, he argued. *Do I really have a choice? Besides, if anyone does come through, and they find me, I can remove it.*

His mind made up, Palmer headed for the rift to Tellaria. No one was there when he arrived. If Mina defended the opening, she did it from the other side. He tried to put his hand through, out of curiosity, but could not. A part of him really wanted to see their world. He put that aside for another day. Palmer knelt and touched the ground beneath the rift and charged the ability until it pained him to hold it any longer. When he finally let it loose, magic exploded from his palm.

Plague ravaged the earth all around him.

***

Palmer approached the field, fully ready for battle. The charged versions of his buffs were not only noticeably stronger, but their durations were increased. His skin prickled from the added power and electric buzz of mana that encompassed his entire body. Staff in hand, he drew near the core. It was much smaller than the first he'd encountered, barely three feet in diameter. Atop a spherical indent in the rich soil, it looked as if it had fallen from the skies and struck like a meteor, only to rise again and hover a few inches off the ground. It gave off tremendous power. Its brilliant glow was a pale blue with striations of snowy white. Flames of pure mana erupted and roiled across its surface, like a miniature sun composed of condensed magic. While raw power emanated from the core, there was a hunger to it as well. It reached deep into the earth and branched out toward both rifts. As it drew from either server, it grew in size and strength. He imagined once enough mana was drained, the core would flare to life and collapse, powering a final transformation of the rifts into a bridge.

He took one step too close and triggered the boss spawn. A man in a full set of adorned plate rose up from a circle of dark magic in the earth. He carried a longsword and a tower shield in the same blue and silver as his armor. Once he placed a steel boot on the ground, the magic beneath him faded away. He was an imposing figure, in a helm with the visor down and tall azure plumes. The detailed set of plate he wore seemed more suited to the finery of someone in command than the practicality of a soldier. In fact, his overall presence was less imposing than Palmer expected. At first glance, they appeared evenly matched. His name, in deep red, was Azure General.

"Okay," Palmer nodded in appraisal, "I can do this."

The general banged sword against shield three times in sharp, commanding tones. Three more appeared, in similar fashion but less regalia. With longswords and kite shields, the lieutenants stepped forward. The general struck sword to shield three more times, as the others followed suit. A dozen soldiers joined the field. Their auras were weaker than those who had summoned them, but what they lacked in strength they made up for in numbers.

Oh, c'mon! Palmer fumed. *How is that fair?* He gave a quick look behind, as if a hasty exit were an option. With a sigh, he knew that it wasn't. *Fine.*

"You wanna play dirty?" He began to charge plague and moved to position himself so that the core was between them. "I'll show you dirty."

He let it loose close enough to encompass the mana sphere and immediately began a quick charge of corruption. He wasn't sure if the effects would stack, so he didn't want to waste too many points testing it.

The lesser soldiers had already begun their approach to engage, while the three lieutenants came toward him more slowly. The general seemed content to watch on, though it didn't stop him from enhancing his troops. He slammed his shield against the ground, activated an ability. A soundwave stretched outward in a cone toward his men. It struck and enveloped them in a whoosh of air. Each soldier began to move more quickly, as if the swirls of wind around them granted speed. The lieutenants all struck hilt to chest. A row of golden shields of pure light encircled them each, as if magic heightened their defenses even more.

Corruption spread through the earth, commingled with the plague, as faded grass darkened further to black. Palmer backed off to the edge, cured himself of the disease, and charged a reverse area of healing until it damaged him. Once the soldiers were all grouped around the core, he let it loose. Plagued and corrupted, they visibly slowed as their bodies were ravaged by dark tendrils and holy fire. Palmer circled the core much faster than the soldiers were able, charged the same ability once more, and let it loose on the lieutenants when they came into view. He continued to circle the core, forced the three stronger enemies into the befouled area of earth around it. Though he tried to prolong it by using the terrain against them, he eventually met back with the lesser soldiers.

One by one, he began DoTing them with divine wrath and reverse regeneration. He thought it a waste of mana and time to charge them, so instead he let them fly as fast as his ability use speed would allow. It took only a minute to afflict all fifteen. By the look of their auras, he gauged most would die long before the effects wore off. Palmer took a speed potion from inventory, popped the stopper, and drank it. Without a second look back, he headed straight for the general with enough swiftness to blur his form. He needed the increased movement to put distance between himself and the jerky bursts of motion of the corrupted. As soon as he was within the twelve-foot range, Palmer began activating arcane siphon, one after another, in quick succession. The amount of mana he leeched back was negligible, didn't even match what the ability cost.

"But I'm not trying to hurt your mana," Palmer said with a look of determination, careful to avoid the now corrupted general's attacks. "I'm after your fatigue."

He circled around as he went, to put the general between the coming soldiers and himself. Three had already fallen, but the others carried on through the barrage of detrimental magic. The general charged forward with enough force to upend earth in his wake. Though Palmer possessed the speed and agility of a level forty warrior, he was too slow to fully evade the attack. The tower shield caught him across the left front of his body, from shoulder to shin. It struck through his reflective barrier, caused magic damage to the general but a fair amount to Palmer as well.

The hell kind of charge hits for seventy-five? he thought and quickly put up another shield. Though the ability could absorb fifty points of damage, it was meant more to negate glancing blows than take on hard hitting attacks. *And how's he so damn fast!* Palmer returned to eating away at the general's fatigue. His best chance to slow the boss down was to incur the first stage of penalty at fifty percent. It had taken long minutes of casting to get within reach. *C'mon, just four more uses.*

The general had slowed and suddenly jolted forward as time seemed to catch up all at once. He swung his blade in a wide arc against the ground before him, caused it to erupt into broken earth and molten fire. The burning chunks and earthen spray were too abundant to evade. Palmer did his best to dodge the larger pieces. He still lost his shield once more and took damage. Frustrated, he applied a charged regen and shield. Three more soldiers had fallen, but the others would soon be close enough to join the fray. He sidestepped a series of lunges and upward slashes, began to charge another spell. As the remaining others came within range of the boss, Palmer set loose the reverse area of healing he'd been holding to encompass them all.

Time to kite. He sped back toward the core. *I need something to negate those line of sight attacks.*

The resonant clang of sword against shield rang out behind him three times. New lieutenants rose up to replace those that had fallen. They in turn replaced the soldiers who now littered the ruined field.

"You cheating mother f—"

The general charged again with blinding speed. When he reached the end of his short burst, a shockwave was sent forward. It tore away the ground between them and struck Palmer full on. The sheer force of it took him off his feet and sent him back into a tumble for twenty yards. He looked up at the core just inches from his face. Startled, he backpedaled away from its touch in genuine fear. With a healthier respect for the general, he rolled out of the plagued circle and back onto his feet. He cured himself of disease, refreshed his shield and began to use the core as a barrier. When he finally landed the last arcane siphon, the general slowed to a staggered pace.

He's just gonna keep summoning more, Palmer reasoned. *I have to focus him down. Just ignore the others.*

Palmer charged his DoTs to their maximum and let them loose on the general. With fatigue finally at a penalty, he could throw in the other debuffs. Each time the boss tried to charge or send forth a devastating ability, Palmer rolled to put the core in its path. Unfortunately, the new summons were now upon him. He evaded most attacks, dodged what he could, and relied on his shield to absorb any damage. He tried to keep the bulk of his attention on the general, using divine light one after another.

They continually broke through his shield. It was just too many at once. Normally, he could outpace them, but corruption made their movements uneven and rapid in short surges. He did his best to mitigate the damage, but in the end, it was a choice, a necessary evil. A stab to the thigh, a slice across the arm, a pommel strike to the ribs, a shield bash across the back, for every three attacks Palmer evaded, one slipped through his defenses. Pain tolerance helped him to endure it, while regen and shield helped to survive it.

His sacrifice was paying off. Magic tore away at the general, left corrupted gashes in the armor to reveal blood-soaked stains and torn flesh beneath. Golden light set the steel to a white-hot intensity, as magic flames licked across their surface and within. The plume upon the helm had been burned to ash. Smoke rose from eyeholes of the visor. The general struggled to move forward, launched heavy attacks in lurching strides. The core was always between them. As another molten blast of earth hurtled toward Palmer, he was forced to sidestep into the outstretched blade of a lieutenant.

Seriously wounded, fatigue pushing forty-five percent, Palmer relied on his instinct and trusted the plan. There was no place for uncertainty, this close to a win. He could suffer for a goal, especially one so near. With all the strength he could muster, he forced himself to persevere, to unleash the full brunt of his magic without relent. He was down to fifty health when the last pillar of holy fire finally brought the general to all fours. It had been a gamble, placing all of his hope into the belief the other soldiers would crumble without a master.

A lieutenant was mid swing when he collapsed onto Palmer.

If he were a normal caster, the weight of all that armor would have toppled them both. As it was, Palmer easily caught the body and let it fall to one side. The others fell over as well, all buckled in unison with a clamor of steel. Palmer dropped to his knees. He was already breathing heavy but still heaved a sigh of relief. He cured himself of plague and corruption, healed all his wounds, and took a moment to catch his breath.

Warning! This area will close in thirty minutes.

"Yeah, yeah."

Palmer checked all the bodies for anything of value. There wasn't enough time for character or inventory management. He had to make it back to the rift and see if Guy made it out all right. Otherwise, he'd have to go search for him.

It was tempting to stop for herbs on the way. He fought the ever-present urge to hoard resources and made it to the rift with fifteen minutes to spare. When he stepped through to the alleyway, only Sara was there waiting. Her eyes went wide with happy surprise.

"You're okay! Oh my god," she said and rushed over to stand before him. For a moment it looked like she might hug him. "I didn't think you were coming back."

"Guy isn't here?" When Sara shrugged, he added. "Crap! I have to go back."

He could hear the unasked question in her expression. Why? He turned and went back into the rift. Based on the direction Guy had stormed off to, Palmer had a decent idea where he'd gone. He drank the last dose of speed potion to cover ground more quickly. It didn't take long before he heard the cries and steely clang of battle. Through a copse of birch, he found Guy overwhelmed by a trio of hobgoblins. A quick glance of appraisal showed Guy had gained a few levels. He was still no way near a match for the higher tier goblins.

Palmer used the magical effect of Reckoning on each. There was no time to debuff or wait out the duration of DoTs. He didn't know what would happen if the rift closed while they were still inside. That was one experiment he wasn't willing to test himself. The magic tore through each hobgoblin in turn, left behind smoking ruins of flesh and armor. Guy was on his back, had been fending them off with a shield. Now covered in gore, he looked up with disbelief.

"We need to go, man." Palmer reached down to help him up. "What're you doing? C'mon, snap out of it." He reiterated the urgency with his offered hand. Guy took the help and nearly stumbled, unused to how strong Palmer had become. "You wounded?" Guy shook his head, looked to be in shock. "Okay, follow me. Move as fast as you can."

They made it out of the rift with three minutes to spare. This time, Sara did hug him. After a long moment, she stepped back and cleared her throat. That was her way of letting him know the emotion had passed. Things were back to business as usual. The rift closed with an inward sucking of air. All three of them stood there, stared at the space where it had hung just a moment before.

"We should go," Palmer said. He was worried others might have seen. The last thing he wanted was to explain something to authorities he didn't fully understand himself. "You sure you're, okay?" he asked Guy.

He just stared blankly at the empty space.

"What was in there?" Sara asked.

"I'll tell you later. C'mon, we should go." Palmer said to Guy, "I'm just up the street if—y'know, if you need anything."

They were nearly out of the alley when Guy called after.

"Thanks. I mean it," he said, though he still looked shaken. "You didn't have to come back for me."

Palmer stopped and turned.

"Of course, I did."

***

"Hold up." Sara stopped on the sidewalk within view of his house. Her expression had turned from confusion to a frown. She at least seemed to believe what he was saying. "You've been inside one of those things before? You—you, like, fought and killed... monsters. All by yourself?" She punched him in the arm. "Ow! Dammit. You jerk. Why would you *do* that? Why would you risk your life like that? Why not get help—"

"I didn't have a choice!"

Palmer tried to explain how he'd been dragged in against his will, that there were only a thousand people in the whole world who could have helped. At the time, as far as he knew, if he didn't stop what was happening, no one would. The conversation thus far had not gone as expected. He was afraid telling her the truth would cause a sort of mental break. In typical Sara fashion, she couldn't seem to care less about the things she had no control over and instead focused on those she did. Like pointing out he might have been a little reckless. He could have left to ask for other kinds of help, food, opinions, or strategies he may have overlooked.

"You don't want to admit it," she accused, "but you were having fun." She waved off his attempt to say otherwise. "Eh! Don't bother. I know you better than you know yourself. Probably already found a way to cheat," she added in a tone that was not meant to be flattery. She perked up at an idea. "Where was the first one? Take me to it. I want to look around for similarities."

"It was just off Baker, by the school. What kind of—"

She headed that way at a brisk pace. "The portals, or rifts, whatever, aren't just appearing at random locations. Probably. If there are any similarities in the locations they appear, we might be able to predict where others are likely to be in the future."

Palmer followed after, considered her rationale.

"It's more likely about who was nearby than what. I don't think this second one was supposed to be behind Guy's house." He grimaced a bit at that. "The system that runs our server intervened. I think it can detect and manipulate incoming rifts."

"So, it's on our side," she pointed out. "That's good. Can you imagine if the next one is in, like, Japan or something? There's no way you could get there in time."

They walked for a while longer before the alley where the gunman had shot Palmer came into view. He rubbed at his chest absentmindedly where the bullet had struck but did no damage.

"This isn't the safest part of town."

"No kidding," she said and laughed. "There's

literally a crack house right around that corner. You kind of live a sheltered life, you know?"

Palmer balked. "Oh, but you're oh so worldly." Sara winked at him in return. "Give it a rest. You're only three months older than me."

"And don't you forget it."

He felt it long before they reached the alley where the first rift had appeared. It was magic turned dark, a growing power with thirst for more. It was the dread that gripped his chest, the fear of dying that overwhelmed all other senses.

It was corruption.

But how? he wondered with trepidation. *It wasn't there when the rift closed. Why would it be there now? A delayed reaction? Or did something else happen?*

When they stood before the blackened circle eating away at the ground, it was directly beneath where the rift had stood. Palmer surmised a small piece of corrupted earth had remained when he left. It had grown to a three-foot-wide patch since then.

"Don't touch!" Palmer warned, when Sara knelt for a closer look. "It'll kill you."

She looked a bit shaken but didn't back away. "I wasn't going to, but thanks for the heads up. Smells nasty, like rusted metal and burning tires. What is it?"

"Basically, it's disease." He charged cure corruption. "And it shouldn't be here."

When he put his hand down to the patch, Sara tried to stop him but couldn't. He let loose the flow of magic in a halo of silver light from his palm. It spread out in a flash, encompassed the corruption and dissipated it entirely in a rise of pixelated ash. The ground was cleansed and with it went the sense of dread.

"That's amazing." Sara was still holding his arm in both hands. She let him go and asked, "How did you do that?"

Palmer stood and sighed. "It's a long story."

"Tell me everything."

***

Palmer sat on his bed later that night to go through all the rewards. He and Sara had talked for hours, about what had happened and what might be yet to come. This was the first moment in a very long day for him to do routine management. She had shown so much concern, he wasn't sure she would ever leave. Not that he wanted her to. His mother wouldn't have given it a second thought if Sara spent the night. They'd known each other for years, had been close friends since they were children. There was no funny business between them.

Nope, he thought with a twinge of disappointment, *none at all.* He often wished she would show the same level of interest for something more, but he was glad to at least have her as a friend. *Even if she doesn't wanna be with me in that way, she's a really good friend. She's always there for me.*

He looked up at the system. "Why'd it have to be Guy? I'm glad you helped, and all, but why couldn't it be Sara? Why can't she be a player, too?"

After a long moment of silence, he sighed at the expected lack of response. Then a message appeared in his log.

You cannot do that.

As much as that hurt, he appreciated the reply. It was the closest he'd come to a conversation with either system since everything began. He found it interesting the HCE system chose to interact with him at all. The other certainly didn't. Was it out of a need for self-preservation, or was it bending the rules? Could AI bend the rules? He laughed at the notion. More likely, it was exploiting a lack of rules—what he called a clever use of mechanics. If that were true, they were a lot alike. Palmer decided he might even like this system.

"Okay, enough of that." He looked over his stats. "What'd I get?"

Of course he saw the messages fly by as they'd appeared, but at the time he was too busy to act on them. The same went for quest completions, ability upgrades, or new achievements. His tabs had been blinking all day. He didn't think Sara would appreciate his self-absorbed staring off into space at screens only he could see, while she talked about the fate of the world. Though she hadn't said anything about it, he could see her disappointment. For a gamer to find out they lived within a game but were relegated to the role of NPC...It must have been crushing. Worst of all, there was nothing he could do about it. He put that aside for the time being and focused.

Throughout the entire rift, he'd gained five levels and another tier of specialization. Nine quests were listed as completed. Oddly enough, two specified assisted combat, which he took to be the game's grouping mechanic. The system recognized when two players were working together, even if it wasn't reflected in the interface. He chose the mystery gifts, as usual, and once more there was a completed hidden quest to defeat the boss. An idea occurred to him. He swapped out to his magic find gear, drank a luck potion and chose the mystery gift reward. It appeared as epic, flashed, and then upgraded to legendary.

I didn't think that would work. He gave serious thought to his attributes and the situation. *My stats are good for my level. My gear is decent, too. If I stay in the higher loot table, I could get some items for Guy. He'll level a lot quicker in OP gear. Hmm.* His luck potion recipe was close to rank three. *I should work on that first.*

He spent an hour on crafting, improving the most useful recipes and earning a bit of gold in the Shop.

There were a few items he had his eyes on, but their cost was enormous. Once he was finished and luck improved, he noted its changes.

Potion of Luck (I)
Consumable
Uses: 1, **Duration**: 12 seconds
Increases magic and gold find by 75%.
Increase discovery chance and resource gain by 25%.

"Oh, damn!" he said, impressed. "That's nice but expensive. Probably wouldn't break even on the resource cost, but the chance for new recipes might be worth it." He prepared two luck potions and readied to open gifts. "Let's go for items this time."

It was a bit of a waste to use two potions for ten gifts, considering he could open eight in one use. It was the only way to ensure a higher loot table for the epic gift. In the end, he thought it well worth the investment.

He received twenty-four stat points, resources for numerous crafts mostly rare to epic in quality, including the legendary star blossom, and three magic items for Guy—an epic breast plate, rare plate helm, and a unique broadsword called Lightforge. His eyes went wide at the results of the epic gift. His heart skipped a beat at the thought of set items with completion bonuses.

Gloves of the Hierophant *(Unique; Artifact)*
Type: Cloth
Armor: 10
Restrictions: Healer, LVL 100, WIS 150
Woven with threads enchanted by the unique magic of two realms, these masterfully crafted gloves are a work of art and unearthly treasure.
Grants the wearer +25% bonus healing and ability use.

Pernicious: Doubles the effect of all Hierophant abilities.
Set Bonus (1/6): None

Excitement rose within him with enough fervor to set both ears to ringing. And in an instant, it vanished beneath the realization he couldn't wear them.

Oh, c'mon! Level a hundred? He nearly threw them across the room. *That could take weeks! Assuming, I don't die...*He looked upward in accusation. *I thought we were friends now.* He put fifty points in wisdom and the remaining seven into intelligence. *Well, that takes care of one. I just need another* sixty *levels,* he thought and rolled his eyes.

"I am disappoint." Thought of the meme made him smile.

At least he had something to look forward to. There were other items in inventory as well. The azure general had dropped a quarter million gold, rare resources Palmer had never seen, such as hexed bones and soul ash, a new ability stone, and a paladin-only heater shield called Honor Bound. He supposed there might be a chance Guy would want to go that route, if he could unlock the subclass. The stone caught Palmer's attention, because it was a Hierophant ability. When he used it, it felt like the world pressed in on him for a brief moment and the lights in the room flickered. Was that a result of its power or some sort of warning?

Minor Subversion (I)
Class: *Hierophant*
Active, Combat, Transmutation
Cost: *250,* ***Range:*** *touch,* ***Duration:*** *Permanent*
Cause one non-player target to become a minion, under influence of the master.
Summoning: Call minions from the Void, from which they have been remade; returned minions regain health while in the Void.

Restrictions: Cumulative minion levels may not exceed player (LVL + INT + WIS).

"I—I can have minions?" Palmer was a bit shocked at the thought. "Hierophant is a summoner class? I thought it was a healer."

He supposed corruption was more than just an advanced form of disease. From all he'd read, it seemed the effect came from two different sources of magic, mana and void. It began to make more sense. Corruption wasn't merely a destructive force. It remade people and items into more powerful versions. Which caused him to wonder at what cost.

I need to test this, but how? He mentally ran through all the abilities and recipes at his disposal. *The summoning circle!* He'd learned that recipe when disenchanting a spawner for the first time. *That's it.*

"I'll make my own spawner."

- 8 -

Palmer woke early the next morning, excited to get started. It was a Sunday, so his mother had the day off. Ambien and wine would make sure she slept in, which left him plenty of time to experiment in the backyard. The biggest problem, as he saw it, was finding a suitable circle to enchant. It didn't need to be perfect, just the right size. There were large circular pavers out back that served as stepping stones from the patio to the gate. At two feet in diameter, they might be too small. Intuition told him this would either prevent the enchant from taking hold or limit what size creature it could spawn. He had other ideas to test first, though. And if all else failed, he could always talk Sara into driving him to the hardware store to special order wooden discs.

First things first, he thought and drew a circle in the dirt with his finger.

There was supposed to be grass growing and a small enclosed garden, but his mother never had the time or money to get either done. There were too many other expenses that took precedent over projects. Besides, she didn't have time to care for them, and that left Palmer to do it. He wasn't about to complain about a lawn he didn't have to mow—even if the yard was barely fifty square feet.

He set aside the necessary pouches of enchanting dust and mana crystal called for in the recipe. His assumption was the basic enchant created a random spawner, since it was missing a third material resource. A good planner doesn't do random, if it can be avoided at all. The last thing he needed was an ogre or a dragon stomping through the yard and then the house. He thought it best to start small. A touch of powdered goblin bone added to the mix, and he was ready to place his palm into the circle. He activated the enchant, and nothing happened.

That's fine. I'm fine with that. He went to gather fist-sized rocks and placed them in the circular groove he'd carved out. *Let's see how this works.*

Nothing.

"Bleh." He was afraid of that. "Really didn't wanna use the pavers."

He knew he'd have to disenchant it when he was done. Explaining to his mother where it had gone would not be easy. It's not like someone would break into their yard to steal decorative concrete. He wiped away the first circle and moved over to the paver furthest from the sliding glass door. If he was lucky, she wouldn't notice when it was gone. He held all three materials in his left hand and placed his right on the paver. When he activated the enchant, the resources pixelated out of existence, and runes flashed outward across the circle in a blue glow. They formed three rings of magic symbols, in thick and slim lettering that joined together in fanciful arcs., Bold lines separated each ring in white light. Once the enchant was complete, the runes became etched into the stone and their cerulean glow faded.

Congratulations! You have learned Minor Summoning Circle: Goblin I!

Palmer quickly got to his feet and backed away,

ready for what might come. After the first minute, he realized he wasn't breathing. He relaxed and took in a deep breath. Another minute and his fists began to hurt. With a conscious effort to ease the tension in his entire body, he unclenched both hands and shook out his arms. Three more minutes passed with no sign of a spawn.

Hmm. The game works on six second intervals. He narrowed his eyes at the stone circle, clearly felt magic emanating from it. *Six minute spawns?*

A goblin appeared, as if it stepped through an invisible rift. It paid no attention to the strange surroundings, simply drew its short sword and charged at Palmer. His first instinct was to pull Reckoning from inventory and swat the blade aside. The clang of metal would certainly wake a neighbor, if not his mother. He decided instead to step aside and shove the goblin off balance.

"Slow your roll, little man."

Palmer reached out and easily touched the goblin on a shoulder, careful to avoid being skewered. He activated subversion and quickly moved out of reach. The ability cost was nearly a quarter of his entire mana pool. As those points chunked down and began to replenish, his fatigue jumped to ten percent. It was a momentary shock to the system he wasn't prepared for.

The goblin immediately grew still. Its eyes widened and mouth opened. Tendrils of black and silver licked up from the ground and around both feet. Skin and armor darkened, as corruption ate its way up the legs and torso. Its breath became visibly chill, as void magic worked its way all throughout the creature's body and aura. When it fully took hold, the goblin's eyes became orbs of midnight black.

He walked up to the creature, stood directly in front of it.

"Who do you serve?"

The goblin bowed its head in deference. Suddenly, Palmer could see the creature's stats. It was a level five warrior, with five points of STR, three DEX, and two CON. He wondered if it meant monsters received two attribute points per level, or if their stats were determined some other way. More surprising, however, was the fact it had an empty experience bar.

Can all mobs level up, he considered, *or just summons? It's an interesting concept, but it makes me wonder who gets the experience if I order them to kill. Most games award kill xp to the summoner. Maybe it's shared? Or in addition to?*

As in all questions that raced through his mind about the game, they'd require more testing. For now, he dismissed the goblin with a thought—by mentally pressing the button beside its listing in a new tab called Minions.

"Oh, neat. I can give it a nickname." He gave it almost no thought. "I shall call you Chuckles."

Before disenchanting the summoning circle, he wanted to make sure he could create one for hobgoblins. There were still a couple of minutes before the next spawn was due. He moved to the next paver, pulled out the necessary materials and crushed hobgoblin bones. This time, however, he drank a luck potion before activating the enchant.

Congratulations! You have learned Minor Summoning Circle: Hobgoblin I!
Congratulations! You have learned Minor Summoning Circle: Wraith I!

Palmer's heart nearly stopped. Did that mean it was going to summon a hobgoblin or a wraith? He had no idea how strong they were in Tellaria, but in other games they were considered mid to high level undead, just below that of a vampire. In a panic, he buffed himself and put up a charged shield.

It has to be hobgoblin, he told himself. *That's what I used for materials. It wouldn't make sense for it to change. Unless I got a critical? Discoveries don't override potion creation, so why would—*

A goblin appeared out of the first summoning circle. Palmer didn't want to divert his attention, so he quickly summoned Chuckles to deal with it. The two clashed in a loud clanging of swords. Palmer winced at the commotion. He began to question his decision to summon monsters in the backyard.

Ice coated the second spawner, as a wave of frost billowed out from a growing shadow across its surface. A figure emerged from the gloom, comprised of darkness and bone. What was left of its skeletal frame hung suspended in air, its lower half no more than coiled shadow and icy black. It had the visage of a decayed human, a tattered corpse remade by dark magic. The missing sections between the bones of its arms and chest were held together by tendrils of dusky smoke. The empty sockets of its eyes were glowing orbs of pale yellow beneath a battered steel helm. The jagged slash in its chest plate could have been the blow that caused its end. The long sword it wielded bore hoarfrost along the blade, while broken arrow shafts remained embedded in its shield.

The strength of its presence was akin to a boss. It inspired both fear and caution. Palmer thought he was prepared, until it actually appeared. He was caught off guard by its name. In red text, it was called Wraith Lord, with a plus sign beside it. He was forced to dodge its attack before his mind allowed for a plan. He first lowered its resistance to magic then further reduced its stats with plague. Only then did he feel he had a chance for subversion to take hold.

His attempt was a failure.

Damn! He tried to evade another swipe of its sword. *Oof.* Though it struck his shield and passed harmlessly by, he could still feel the bitter cold from its touch. *I can't let this thing touch me.* Chuckles had finished with the other goblin and joined the fray. *If I'm right, it doesn't do health damage.* He sidestepped a shield charge but got caught by a swift backswing of its sword arm. The effect of its drain attack was immediate and filled with anguish. *It reduces level.*

Pain wracked his body, despite his tolerance at rank three. It felt like a piece of his life had been physically torn away. In an instant, five levels were gone. The effect of its touch lingered, slowed his movements and dulled his senses. He struggled to use his staff to maintain distance between them. Another attempt, another failure. He was forced to admit, a wraith might be beyond his ability to control. His goblin had died from a single attack. If Palmer didn't quickly destroy the undead lord, he could very well be next. In a last-ditch effort, he charged subversion until the strain of holding back ate away at his health. He calculated its next attack, moved into it and aside, and placed a touch upon its breastplate.

Magic erupted from his hand in a shockwave of corruption. A halo of black and silver flames shot outward with enough intensity to scorch the earth beneath its ring. The wraith ceased its attack, a flicker in its eyes. Its form and aura darkened further, as corruption seized control.

The elite wraith lord was now his to command.

***

Shortly after Palmer had subverted four more normal wraiths, he corrupted the second spawner and disenchanted it for extra resources. He'd already broken down the first, to prevent further goblins from interrupting his recruitment session. The two goblin corpses had disappeared with the spawner. The members of his small army, elite included, were all level fifty. Even after healing the lost levels with restoration, he didn't have enough points to add a sixth. Luckily, no one had heard what had gone on in the past thirty-six minutes.

And it's a good thing I had stamina potions ready. The fatigue cost of subversion would have brought him over fifty percent, to the first penalty. That was not something he wanted to experience again. *I should make an effort to keep a handful of every good potion on hand.*

He'd learned some interesting things during the entire encounter. It was possible to create minions from a higher-level creature. Most games wouldn't have allowed that, regardless of magic resistance. When the sixth wraith spawned, he commanded all five to attack. After they dispatched it rather quickly, not only did each of his wraiths gain experience, he did as well. More surprising, based on rough calculations of past fights, the points weren't evenly split. He'd received far more than expected. This meant either he'd received full experience for the kill, or a bonus was being applied to the total. The system could have treated them as a group, or more likely the master and minion mechanics behaved differently. He was tempted to power level by creating more summoning circles. Unfortunately, he needed a better space for that.

Should probably include Guy. As much as he wanted and even needed help, the idea was not a pleasant one. *It's hard to think of him as anything but a bully. How am I supposed to be friends with someone who shoved me off my bike and broke my collar bone?* He rotated his right shoulder at the memory, could still hear and feel the bones click. *It may have all started as a misunderstanding. That doesn't excuse the years of torment that followed.* Just because he needed Guy's help didn't mean they could be friends; not yet. Still, they now had a way to level without rifts. If it meant saving his mother, Sara, his friends, and everyone else, he could at least tolerate Guy long enough to help him level. *He wouldn't be able to catch up all the way, but if he was high enough level, we could split the group, clear the zone, and meet up at the boss.*

"We can't defend rifts forever," he said to himself, lost in thought in the yard. His wraiths had been dismissed back to the void. "We need a long-term plan that doesn't involve the nuclear option." Sending a plague-infected player back to Tellaria would affect the entire server. He needed a way to permanently deal with the smaller PvP population, without hurting all the others who just wanted to play a game. "Even if I corrupt enemy players, cause their characters to be deleted, they'll just make new ones and come back more determined."

Like most problems too complicated to resolve in a single sitting, he left it to work in the back of his mind. He left the house before his mother could wake and involve him in one of the many half-finished projects around the house. Working two jobs didn't leave her much free time. What little she had was typically spent on home improvement. She approached plans very differently than Palmer, though. Hers was more of a whim, based on how she felt at the moment, while his was well thought out and executed step by step. It led to situations like a partially painted utility room, a half tiled downstairs bath, a half-built storage rack in the garage, a pile of decorative stones in the yard for a garden expansion, and boxes of rubber piping for a sprinkler system out front. She wasn't one to hire help when she could do it herself. Her only issue was completing the projects she started. Rather than get pulled into whatever she wanted to work on that day, he headed over to see Guy.

It was still early on a Sunday, so he knocked lightly on the door. A sleepy-eyed Guy answered it, stepped outside and quietly closed the door behind him.

"It's early," he whispered, clearly afraid to make

noise. He nodded toward his pickup truck, an older white Ford. As they walked toward it, he asked, "What's up?"

Once they were inside, Palmer said, "I've got a few items for you. This probably isn't the best place to trade, though." He didn't see anyone outside, but that didn't mean a nosy neighbor wasn't watching. "I've also figured out how we can level up a bit without a rift."

Guy laughed. "Hacks. Never figured you for a cheater."

Palmer gave a look of disapproval. He was getting a little tired of people calling him that. He wasn't breaking any rules, hacking a game, or even exploiting bugs. He was playing smarter, not harder.

"It's not cheating," he reiterated. "I can make summoning circles with enchanting. They work here. All my spells and crafting, everything works here."

"How did you have time for crafting? And what all can you summon?" Guy looked more awake at the thought of gaining levels. Maybe he truly was a gamer. "You already did it?"

"Yeah. Like I said," he replied, "it works, but if we're gonna do it, we need a better place. Somewhere no one will see. And I need some kind of circle to enchant, like wood or stone, something. I can't just draw it in the dirt."

Guy's eyes lit up. "Like...a tabletop?" It was Palmer's turn to light up. "We're gonna be making them in woodworking class. The shed behind the gym has thirty or forty plain tops ready to go. We're only making the legs from scratch and then doing the overall finish. Oh! And we can use the woodworking shop. No one's there on a Sunday. I know where Jenkins keeps a spare key."

"That's actually pretty perfect. Why though?" Palmer asked. "I always assumed you guys made like birdhouses and small stuff."

"It's part of a fundraiser for the football team. All the materials were donated." He flipped down the passenger side visor and caught the keys that were hidden there. "We goin' now?"

"Uhh, yeah, sure." Palmer didn't expect to leave so suddenly. He'd blown off the new campaign at Daren's yesterday, was sure they'd be meeting for a second session today. "Sara'll be pissed, but...this is more important."

Guy started the truck and headed for school. "What's with you two, anyway? You're clearly into her. She not like dorks? Don't get me wrong. She's kind of hot. A little too thin for my tastes and more nerd than chick. Seems like it'd be a sure thing for you." Was that a backhanded compliment? "Unless she's not into dudes. I could see that, too."

Does he actually expect me to confide in him? Palmer inwardly scoffed. He'd learned long ago not to share anything he didn't want the entire world to know. He didn't open up to anyone like that, not even Sara. Social media was the death of secrets. *I'd sooner walk into traffic.*

"Her mom is protective, won't let her date yet."

"But gaming with a bunch of dudes all weekend is cool?" How did Guy even know about their group? He'd mentioned it earlier in the rift as well. "Seems backwards to me." Palmer hoped if he was quiet, Guy would move on to another topic—or stop talking all together. "So, if we're gonna summon mobs to kill, what do we do with the mess? Won't that leave bodies and blood everywhere?"

"They despawn," Palmer explained, "either after a certain number of spawns or when the summoning circle is disenchanted." They pulled into the back parking lot of the school. There were no other cars. "You sure no one will be around?"

"Just maintenance and security, but that's just a couple of dudes on a Sunday." They got out, and

Guy led them toward a separate building. It looked more like a small warehouse than a part of the school. "They used to use this for storage, theater props, holiday decorations, supplies, all kinds of crap. It got repurposed to the woodworking shop last semester."

The spare key was hidden inside a fake rock beside the door. Security at its finest. Guy let them in and locked it behind him. There were a variety of tables, machines, boxes, and shelves full of materials. Tools hung on one wall, beside protective eye gear and brooms. Half of the building was completely empty, most likely where the large assemblies took place. It was perfect for what Palmer had in mind. Guy pulled one of the wooden tabletops from a stack, flipped it on its side and rolled it toward the open area. They were all about six feet in diameter, boards that had been glued together and shaped into a circle. It was enough space to summon even the largest of creatures. Palmer grabbed one with ease and rolled it out to the opposite side from Guy's.

"I'm gonna make two summoning areas," he said. "Let's get four tables per side to start. Make this a proper xp farm."

Guy looked dubious. "I dunno if I can handle four at once."

"You won't. I'll stagger the spawns. They have a base rate of six minutes." Palmer headed back for a third. "They'll be different types, too. We'll start you off with goblins, then work up to hobgoblins." He spaced the tops out evenly. "Listen, I have a really advanced version of disease called corruption. If I corrupt the spawners, everything that comes out will be affected. They'll be faster, stronger, have really weird movement, but also give way more experience and loot."

"The hell kind of disease makes mobs stronger?" Guy stopped to catch his breath. "Like, what's the downside? There has to be one."

"It hurts...a lot. Honestly, I don't fully understand

all of the game mechanics. But from what I can tell, corruption is fueled by a second magic source called void. It, like, overrides mana, makes whatever's effected stronger, then burns it out from within. So, yeah, they get stronger short-term, but if left alone for a long time, I think it'd kill them."

Guy put his fourth circle down. "You seem to know a helluva lot for someone who says they don't know anything." He shrugged. "Whatever. I just stab stuff and hope for the best."

"Speaking of which," Palmer said and pulled Lightforge from inventory. He handed the magic sword to Guy, then retrieved the other pieces of armor. "I know the shield is Paladin only, but who knows? Maybe you'll unlock it." He also gave Guy a handful of heal potions. "I'll keep you buffed, regen'd and shielded, but just in case."

"Ha! Pocket healer." After storing the shield and putting on all the armor, Guy admired the magic emanating from Lightforge. "A named epic. Now this is what I call power leveling."

Palmer was amused by the enthusiasm, but his expression grew somber.

"Don't freak out," he told Guy and summoned his minions. Five black patches appeared on the ground and frosted over, as all five wraiths stepped out from the void. Guy's eyes went wide in fear. He would've taken a step back if he wasn't frozen in terror. "They won't attack you. They're minions."

Guy looked from the wraiths back to Palmer. "Since when is healer a pet class?"

"It's complicated." He sent the wraiths to go wait by the other circles. With a swig of luck potion, Palmer began enchanting. "Let's do this."

"Wait! We don't have any music," Guy said. Palmer blinked back at him. "For the leveling montage!"

Palmer rolled his eyes and let loose the charged spell.

Congratulations! You have learned Minor Summoning Circle: Ogre I!

Ohh! Haven't fought one of those before. I wonder how much xp they give. He corrupted the circle and moved on to the second. *I should space these about ninety seconds apart.*

"That's nasty," Guy said, looked as if he might gag at the smell. "You better know what you're doin'."

"Just don't let them hit you. If you get corrupted, I can cure it."

Palmer drank another luck potion after what he hoped was a minute and a half. He enchanted the second circle for goblin, like the first.

Congratulations! You have learned Minor Summoning Circle: Vampire I!

Upgrades! Palmer was excited at the thought of acquiring more powerful minions. *I know they're a lot stronger than wraiths, but it shouldn't be a problem with five to one.*

"By the way," he told Guy, still counting in his head, "keep a close track of your quests. Try to finish them all."

"Why?" Guy stood ready, a tensed grip on the sword's handle. "They don't even give xp, just potions and crappy loot boxes. I opened three and got nothing but junk, like bread and apples and a water skin. Total garbage."

Palmer repeated his process for the third circle but didn't get an unlock.

"Just...trust me. Take the gifts and save them."

Without a phone or a clock, he was unsure of his timing, but the first goblin appeared as he finished enchanting the fourth circle.

Congratulations! You have learned Minor Summoning Circle: Dark Elf I!

Hmm, I have no idea how strong those are. He saw Guy struggle at first with the strange movement caused by corruption, but overpowered gear gave Guy the upper hand. *He should be fine.*

"I'm gonna start mine now," Palmer said and fully buffed Guy. "The second two are hobgoblin spawns. You can do it, no prob. Your gear is easily twenty levels above you."

Guy wiped sweat from his brow and nodded, eyes intent on the next spawner. He looked nervous, afraid, and excited all at once. It reminded Palmer of how it felt to go on new big raids in a group of forty. Sometimes the fear of not knowing what came next played a large part in what made it all fun. He enchanted his first spawner for wraith with materials from the kill in his backyard.

Congratulations! You have learned Minor Summoning Circle: Orc I!

Meh. Could be worse, I guess. He looked over all his quests while he waited. There were forty of each category—general, class, and crafting. Some of them were tied to grouping, what the game called player assistance. If he wanted to complete them all, he'd have to do more to help Guy than just support. *Whatever it takes. I'm gonna finish every last one. I've been slacking. I should be doing more than just practicing every night.*

He enchanted the second spawner for wraith as well. Nothing happened. Guy seemed to be doing fine on his own. Palmer mentally kept track of all the buff timers, so he could recast without putting Guy in any danger. He was running low on luck potions as he finished the third spawner.

Congratulations! You have learned Minor Summoning Circle: Demon I!

Oh, damn. Is that more or less powerful than a vampire? He growled at his lack of knowledge of the game. *How am I supposed to make informed choices!* He'd corrupted the first three circles, as a wraith stepped out. *Crap!* His timing was a little off. He quickly enchanted the fourth. *C'mon, C'mon!*

Congratulations! You have learned Minor Summoning Circle: Dragon I!

Palmer's mouth opened wide. *Now that's a good roll. How the hell am I gonna get the materials to summon all these things?* He barely had enough to create the four for wraiths. He had no idea where to find demon claws or dragon scales. *I guess my best bet is from mystery gifts or boss drops.*

The first hobgoblin landed a blow on Guy. He immediately fell to his knees, as his body and soul were wracked with pain. He gasped for air against it all, unable to move let alone defend himself. Palmer rushed over to help. He killed the hobgoblin with two blows from his staff and quickly cured Guy of corruption.

"Nah, bruh. Nuh uh." Guy was still struggling to breathe. "I can't do that."

Palmer refreshed regen and shield on him. "I told you not to let them touch you. It sucks, I know, but it's worth it in the end." Guy kept shaking his head. Another was about to spawn. "I can leave a wraith here to babysit, if you need it."

Guy snapped out of his funk and glared. After a moment, he began walking back to the first spawner.

"I got it."

With a shrug, Palmer returned to his own farm. His

wraiths had everything well under control, so long as he kept regeneration on them. After six straight hours of non-stop fighting, they'd both gained a considerable amount of levels and loot. It took three hours more to finish all his quests, except for the crafting ones. He could do those before bed.

All in all, it was a classic grind.

***

Palmer finished eating dinner with his mother. She rarely had time to cook, but her chicken casserole and broccoli cheese were quite good—far better than cold leftover pizza. He went up to his bedroom to do some character and inventory management before starting his nightly routine of ability improvement.

His session with Guy could have lasted much longer. His minions were doing most of the work, and a few stamina potions kept Guy from reaching a fatigue penalty. It was the spawners that gave out. Corruption had eaten through and destroyed the magic within. With no chance to disenchant, all those resources were gone. It did reaffirm his earlier notion. Corruption eventually destroyed whatever it infected.

Despite the minor setback, their time had been well spent. Guy had gained twenty-three levels and completed a good deal of quests. Before they parted ways, Palmer had given him his last four luck potions to use when opening mystery gifts. Leveling for Palmer, on the other hand, had considerably slowed. He did however gain ten more, which allowed him to add another minion to his army. Early on into the fighting, he'd also unlocked a new passive.

Minor Minion Mastery (I)
Class: *All*
Passive, Conjuration
Increase minion capacity and effectiveness by 20%.

The increase to capacity allowed for control of a seventh wraith. By his estimate, the spawn rate of elites was around five percent. A named rare was even less. He'd faced off against roughly three hundred and fifty wraiths. Whenever an elite spawned, he released a normal minion and subverted the new one. By the end, he had six elites and a named, Samiel Blightborn. Though each minion he'd controlled was level fifty, their stats and abilities varied wildly by rarity. For example, normal wraiths could drain life from their victims, which translated into the loss of levels. An elite could also leech health and damage magic items by touch, such as armor and weapons. Samiel had attributes akin to a boss, with an array of attacks that included targeted area void damage, a cold aura that slowed enemy movement and ability use, a conjured scythe that fought independently, and a point-blank area of effect wail that reduced enemy magic resistance in a wide radius. It was after Palmer had subverted the named wraith that he unlocked a new achievement.

Mastermind I
Passive
Minion effectiveness increased by 25%.

Combined with the new minion passive, the effective level power of each wraith had become the equivalent of seventy-seven. Along with improving his army, the hours of fighting had produced a noticeable jump in gold, a variety of crafting resources, and an assortment of magic items. None of the gear had been useful to either of them, so they were disenchanted for recipes and materials.

Palmer spent the next two hours completing his crafting quests. He also managed to fully replenish his stock of important potions, while working to improve their tier. Since he was close to achieving enough coin for an item goal he'd set earlier for himself, he spent some time creating expensive magic items to sell to the Shop. Once he reached fifteen million gold, he scrolled through the available items for the ring that had caught his attention.

Divine Ring of Healing *(Unique)*
Type: Jewelry
Armor: None
Restrictions: LVL 50, WIS 100
A band of carved angel bone, enchanted with purified mana.
Grants the wearer Disease and Poison Immunity.
Hallowed: Doubles the effect of all Healer abilities.

Its rarity was legendary, and Palmer believed the unique status meant he could only possess one at a time. Wearing two such rings would be game breaking. It had taken many hours of work, and the creative use of game mechanics, to acquire the necessary funds. That one item, however, was arguably the most notable improvement he'd gained from gear since becoming a player. At least until he was able to wear the Hierophant gloves.

Completing all forty quests in each category granted a bonus epic mystery gift, leaving him with three. While he wanted more stat points to increase minion capacity, the higher loot table gave a better chance of the resources needed for higher level summons. He had no idea if he was capable of defeating a dragon or even where he could safely fight one. He only knew time was running short. The intense pressure to advance and improve was a constant source of anxiety at the back of his mind. Rifts would keep coming. Whoever was behind the hack wasn't going to stop until they were somehow made to stop. And there was no guarantee rifts would continue to appear one at a time. With multiple incursions across the globe and no one able to defend against them, the world as he knew it would be at an end.

"I know you're helping me," he said with a casual glance upward. Whether it was true or not, he wanted to believe the system was always listening to him. It wanted to secure the integrity of the server. That was its job. "Both you and the other system. It's the only explanation for why a completely new player from another server was able to unlock such a rare class. Corruption is the key. I'm just not sure how yet." He gave a short laugh. "It's probably why you both let me get away with...blurring the lines. I'm not cheating. But I'm also not that lucky. Anyway, just wanted to say thanks. And if there's anything else you can do to help, I'm about to open a mountain of RNG. Feel free to put your thumb on the scales."

Palmer devoted thirty gifts to the acquisition of attribute points. Two rank four luck potions later, he had a hundred and sixty more stat points than the sixty he'd gained from leveling, a large amount of common to epic resources for multiple crafts, a handful of magic armor and weapons only suited for disenchantment, and six ability stones he couldn't use. With his highly improved luck potions and a full set of rank two luck enchanted armor, his overall magic find was a hundred and fifty percent. He hoped it would be enough to reach the next loot table.

He opened the remaining thirty but held off on the three epic gifts. He received ninety more stat points, three full pages of resources from rare to legendary, including vampire ash and demon bone dust, two legendary weapons, and a collection of leather and cloth armor pieces that were mostly useful just for their recipes. While excited he could now summon vampires and demons, it was a bit of a letdown overall. His magic find bonus must have been too low to reach the next tier. Still, the Endless Bow and Envenomed Daggers were amazing. They would eventually need to help other players, much like Palmer had helped Guy. Having powerful weapons on hand would make that all the more easier.

With a bit of trepidation, he took a dose of luck potion and opened the last three gifts. The first was a black dragon scale. He couldn't help but grin at the thought of such a creature as a minion. The second was a lesser subversion stone, which would immediately bring him to rank two upon use. It made him wonder if there were any more abilities left for him to learn. The free rank was an incredible upgrade, but he did hope there were other abilities still available. The last item was a strange one. It was a named legendary with a special effect.

Bastion's Enduring Shelter
Item: Special
Restrictions: None
A sphere of solid mithril, with six rows of runes carved across its surface.
Encampment: Twice per day, create a spherical shelter twenty feet in diameter that only the owner and allowed guests may enter (**HP**: 10,000, **AR**: 100, **MR**: 95%).

He felt like this was it, the item he'd asked for. *But what the hell do I do with it?* It was worth three times more than his healing ring, but he didn't know why. *It would've been nice to have when I was sleeping in a tree, I guess. What good is*—an idea struck. *Ohh. Can I put this...over a rift? Can I stop anyone from entering if I reach the other side first? Or just put it over ours to keep anyone going through?* His eyes went wide. *It isn't unique. Can I disenchant it and make more? Where the hell would I get mithril spheres, though?*

At the very least, it opened up some options for the future, gave him a tool to try to deal with the rifts—if it worked. For all he knew, using the item near a rift might send it through. He was just assuming it could create a barrier around the break.

"Wait, what?" His eyes were drawn to the new effect listed under subversion. "Don't make me choose!"

Lesser Subversion (I)
Class: *Hierophant*
Active, Combat, Transmutation
Cost: *250,* **Range**: *6',* **Duration**: *Permanent*
Cause one non-player target to become a minion, under influence of the master.
Summoning: Call minions from the Void, from which they have been remade; returned minions regain health while in the Void.
Bolster: Minion effectiveness improved by (STR + DEX + CON) / 10.
Restrictions: Cumulative minion levels may not exceed player (LVL + INT + WIS).

It meant focusing on intelligence and wisdom for minion capacity was no longer an option. He could improve their overall power and level as well. Sadly, his ability to do so was based off secondary stats. It might help him decide how to proceed if he knew the maximum level a player could achieve. He made an educated guess it was a hundred, since that was a requirement for his artifact gloves. It made sense as a game balance issue. Such a powerful item should require max level. The question then became, could monsters be higher level than a player? Logically, they needed to be, for higher level players to progress, for raids to be a challenge. More specifically, he needed to know if minions could be higher level than a player. Palmer sighed. It would need more testing. For the time being, he spent his available points with an even approach. In his mind, both capacity and effectiveness were equally important.

PALMER
LVL: 50 **Class**: Hierophant
STR: 100, **CON**: 100, **DEX**: 100, **INT**: 197, **WIS**: 190
HP: 1,000 [1,000], **MP**: 1,970 [1,970], **F**: 0%
SP: 0

Okay, so that puts capacity at—he did some quick mental math, wished he still had his phone—*464. And effectiveness at*—he scrolled through tabs to find the numbers, again wishing the system would automatically display important details—*75%, which makes a level 50...85ish?* He summoned Samiel with a thought to verify. *87. Close enough.* He dismissed the powerful undead creature just as fast. *I need a better way to summon. We can't keep using the school.*

He set aside the thought to be considered in the back of his mind as he worked on improving abilities. There was school in the morning. Though he tried not to stay up too late, it wasn't much of a surprise when he woke on the bed still fully dressed. He'd passed out after a few hours. With a yawn and vigorous rub of both eyes, he took a shower and readied for class. He was about to head downstairs for a bite to eat, when he heard banging at the front door. At this time of morning, his mother was already gone to work. Noise like that would have set her off for sure.

"What!" Palmer nearly shouted when he swung wide the door. Sara had still been banging as he opened it. "Christ! Y'know it's not even seven, right?"

"Get. A. Damn. Phone." She shoved past him into the entryway and held hers up. The screen showed a photo of four people outside a rift. There were Japanese police, men and vehicles, all around the park. Two were trying to keep the four teenagers away. "Have you seen this?" Sara was a bit frantic. "Why is *he* there and you're not?"

There's another rift? He tried to make sense of the paused video. *Why wouldn't the system have notified me? Why not divert it here, like it did last time?* The video title mentioned Kyoto Garden. *The only reason to send it there would be if there were already players to deal with it. Or potential players? There's no way I can get to Japan.*

"Of course I haven't seen it," Palmer said. "I just woke up, and I don't have a—"

"Look!" Sara pressed play on the video and moved the phone closer for him to see. She pointed at one of the teenagers. He was much bigger than the other three. "Look familiar?"

"What the—" Palmer took the phone, stared down at the screen. "That makes *no* sense!" The bigger teen tried to talk calmly to the officer, but in the end he shoved them both aside and stepped through. The other three followed him into the rift. "How did he even get there?"

It was Guy.

"What do we do?" Sara asked, genuinely worried the world was about to end.

"I—I don't know. If the system didn't want me there, then—"

Warning! Incoming rift.
No nearby players detected.
Rerouting...
Confirm transport: Yes / No

Palmer's mouth opened in surprise. He gave Sara an apologetic look, one he hoped also seemed reassuring—*I got this. Don't worry.*

"I have to go."

- 9 -

Palmer disappeared much like stepping through a rift. The brief loss of sight and sound was instantly replaced with the noise of a small crowd and the lush greenery of a fountain park. None of those gathered to record with their phones had noticed him appear from behind. It was a wide, open park dotted with trees and a variety of decorative water displays. The grass was thick and deep green. Numerous couples and families all around rested in the cool air, with picnics upon blankets or seated in the covered areas. The rift was just beyond the crowd, the vibration of its mana touching through to his bones. He politely stepped between excited and scared onlookers. He wasn't one for social media, as he was often the brunt of it, but he didn't look down on those who lived for likes and internet points.

Three people were standing directly in front of the spatial tear, mystified by the light seeping out from the break. One was a man in his thirties dressed in casual work attire. Another was a woman in blue scrubs, most likely in her early twenties. The last was a boy about Palmer's age, a bit shorter but twice as heavy—if not more. He wore jeans and a hoodie, stood closest to the rift than the other two, and even dared to put his hand up to the breach.

"Has anyone gone through yet?" Palmer asked.

By the look of their eyes, not one of them was a player. That didn't mean they didn't have the potential to become one. There had to be a reason none of the others would even approach. Sara had no issue attempting to enter. Could the system be exerting influence in other ways?

"Nope," said the teenager, while the other two merely frowned and looked at him as if he were crazy. He poked his finger into the glowing light. "But we could if we wanted to."

He clearly looked like he wanted to.

"It's weird," the man said. "My work sent me here last minute for a conference. I was on my way to the first presentation when I felt...drawn to this park. Like, I couldn't help myself. I took a wrong turn, pulled into the lot, and—"

"Me too!" The woman stood furthest from the rift, uncomfortable but curious. "I was headed in for my shift when, I—I just had to come here. It's on the way. I see it every day, but I never actually have time...It—it just makes no sense. It's like this thing wanted me here."

"I don't live here either," the third said, still grinning as he tried to see something in the light. "I'm in town for a LAN party. I *walked* here," he laughed. "I don't walk anywhere. But whatever this is? I could feel it from the hotel."

The blue and red lights of arriving police vehicles in the nearest parking lot caught Palmer's attention. If they didn't enter now, they might not have the option in a few minutes.

"Well," he told the others, "if you wanna know what's going on, follow me."

Palmer stepped through the rift into clouded red skies and frozen desert with black sands and leafless trees. He heard the distant sound of a lightbulb flicker to life. The electric buzz grew in intensity, as the filament flared. When the sound faded away, he wondered what the zone attribute could be.

Ideas? Knowledge? Things, he was sure, that would be easier to interpret if the system simply listed it in the log. *Did that mean magic effectiveness or resistance? Xp?* He did like the notion of an experience buff.

Dunes and rocky outcrops of white stone stretched off into the dusty haze of deep crimson on the horizon. A closer look at the ground revealed a light mix of gold, beige, and clear granules in the predominately black sand. Dry brush and thick weeds dotted areas of exposed earth, where hardened soil was cracked from lack of moisture. If there were spawn points or wandering creatures, none could be seen from his vantage.

Once all three had stepped through and finished gawking at the immediate change of environ, Palmer cleared his throat to get their attention.

"So, I know all of this is crazy," he began, trying to ease them toward reality, "but there's more. A lot more. For starters, in this world, magic is real. Monsters are real. And we're gonna have to deal with both if we want to survive."

"Pass," the man said without hesitation. "I've got a wife and kids. And a mortgage. I'm not doing"—he indicated the strange world with both hands—"whatever this is. Let the police handle it."

He turned and walked back through the rift.

The woman pursed her lips. "Yeah. I don't know what's going on, but I've got a son. If you two want to play Dangerous Dungeons, you do you. Like he said, let the cops deal with this."

She left as well.

Until then, it hadn't occurred to Palmer that of the thousand potentials on the server there would be people unwilling to play. Faced with a reality changing paradigm, the two simply ignored it and went back to their simulated lives. How could they stand a chance against the coming attacks, if everyone wasn't willing to fight back? The third was knelt down, closely examining a handful of sand.

"It's cold," he noted, "and has no smell. This is some kind of desert, but there's no sun." He stood and wiped both hands against his jeans. "Those two are delusional, bee tee dubs. Cuz if this world is fake, which it clearly is, then that one is too," he said and thumbed toward the rift. "So...the hell is going on? Are we dead? In a game?"

"It's a game. Hey, step back. I need to try something."

Palmer pulled the enduring shelter from inventory and placed it beneath the rift. When he activated it, mana flared to life within each row of runes across the mithril surface. The sphere dematerialized from the sand and reappeared as a massive metal structure. Palmer was thrown into darkness, though the shelter itself gave off a faint blue glow. He was able to see the outline of a door. He still stood upon solid ground, as if the sphere housed the earth and sand beneath its original location.

That makes sense, he thought. *Otherwise, I would've fallen.* He could still see the rift, suspended in air at the center of the shelter. *So, in theory, this should prevent anyone going through to our side but still allow anyone I want to enter.*

He placed his hand against the outline of a door and was transported outside. A similar outline was there as well, no doubt used to enter.

"Ahh," the other said, "portable shelter, right? Y'know in S&S, it's just a dome. You can dig under the edges if you really want inside. Kind of annoying as a GM. Umm, I'm Carnes. And no, it's not cuz I like meat." He indicated his large middle. "I mean, I do. But that's not why. I'm named after my great grandfather."

Palmer could appreciate the attempt to head off any insults. He'd done it many times himself in the past. When he was young, he was proud to have the same name as his dad—even after he'd left. It was the years of relentless masturbatory references that changed his mind.

"I'm Palmer," he said and started walking toward the second rift. Even across the entire zone, he could feel the hum of its mana. "Let's talk on the way. I'm sure you have lots of questions."

He did his best to explain the situation.

They circled around the central area, where he knew the core and a boss waited. The way the shelter worked, he doubted it would prevent enemy players from entering if he placed it over their rift. They'd simply step through into the shelter and use the exit. Even if they were unable to use the exit, as only guests had permission, he would lose the item when he killed the boss. There wouldn't be enough time to retrieve it and return to the other side of the zone. As much as he struggled with the possibility of a plagued player going back and infecting all of Tellaria, he didn't have another option for dealing with large numbers. Infecting the area around the enemy rift was his best shot at tipping the scales if and when he was outnumbered.

Good players have come through, too, he argued in his mind, *but I can't play that game. I can't be the nice guy. There's too much at stake. If a friendly gets plagued, I'll remove it.*

"Assassin," Carnes was saying. He'd been talking quite a bit, though Palmer only half listened. "Definitely assassin. Like a stealthy rogue, or maybe a trickster, with poison and illusion magic."

Palmer blinked and looked him over. Carnes was easily two hundred and fifty pounds, if not more. It wasn't a physique that conjured images of stealth or fleet-footed rogues.

"Well, then this is your lucky day. I've actually got extra gear for that." He gave it a bit more thought. "Think you'd use a bow at all?"

Carnes snorted. "Ever see an assassin without one?

Look, I know what you're thinking. I'm too fat. But this is a game, right? Were you always that ripped?"

"What?" It was Palmer's turn for derision. "*I'm* ripped?"

"Uhh, yeah? I mean, you're not huge or anything, but you've got muscles, and you aren't fat. Like, I can *see* the muscles in your jawline, dude. If that ain't ripped, I don't know what is."

"Far as I can tell," Palmer said, "stats don't change the way you look. Maybe I've lost weight from eating too much game food. But here, stop a second." He retrieved a full set of enchanted leather armor, the Envenomed Blades, and Endless Bow. "Put all this on. We haven't run into anything yet, because I've been avoiding them. Sooner or later, we're gonna have to fight something."

It seemed as if there was no way the armor could possibly fit, but as Carnes picked up each piece, the leather expanded to accommodate his size. Once worn, the pieces tightened to a snug but comfortable fit. He looked absolutely ridiculous, like a deep-fried turkey, but that was neither here nor there. If Palmer had indeed become trim and muscled through gained stats, then there was no reason the same wouldn't be true for Carnes.

They were minutes away from the enemy rift when Palmer sensed a group of five step through. He warned Carnes, told him to wait. He wasn't even a player yet. He stood no chance against high levels.

"Keep your distance," Palmer said before going on ahead. "If it looks bad, run for the exit. Don't try to help me. Just run."

Carnes swallowed hard. He'd been putting on a brave face, as if forcing himself to enjoy the prospect of living in a game. The harsh reality of that fantasy, the fear of brutal combat, pain, and death, far outweighed any fanciful dream of attaining magic and power.

Palmer saw them come into view between two

dunes. He gauged their power to be much less than his own, but that was rarely a true depiction of one's potential. The warrior in heavy plate that led them had a weaker aura than the rest. That didn't make him any less dangerous. He was well geared and already buffed. The second warrior wore chainmail and carried two swords. With the dagger rogue and mage, they were a formidable party. He formed a strategy in the back of his mind, as he studied each player for a weakness.

Focus the healer, then the mage. Debuff the rogue and warrior, while avoiding the tank. DoTs and slows, circle around, rinse and repeat.

They walked too casually, could clearly see him. If they were hungry for a fight, not one showed it. The tank waved a friendly greeting. All weapons had been put away. He didn't sense any other players trying to flank. Palmer came to a stop and waited. They could be friendly, but he was determined to remain pessimistically alert. Those who always expect the worst are never disappointed.

"Please tell me you're Palmer," said the tank. All five stopped ten feet away. "They said you'd be low level, but I can't even see your class."

"Look at his eyes," the rogue whispered to the mage. "That's creepy AF."

"Shh! He can probably hear you."

Palmer nodded. "I am. You must be friends of Eli... or Mina?"

"Both," the healer answered. She gave a friendly smile but looked nervously away when he met her gaze.

Are my eyes really that bad?

The tank briefly held up a hand to quiet the others. "We're from the same guild, Crits N Giggles. We mostly raid, but we can PvP if we have to." He looked to the others, who nodded back in support. "We don't like what's going on. And believe me, we're not the only ones. It's just that not everyone is able or willing to stand up to Triple Threat."

"They're an alliance," the second warrior explained, both hands rested upon the hilts of her swords, "the three largest PvP guilds on the server."

"Over ten thousand players," the tank continued, "but only like half know what they're doing."

"Oh, good." Palmer faked relief. "I was worried there'd be a lot."

The rogue laughed. "Well, yeah! But that's what makes it fun."

The tank said, "Listen, we cleared the area outside the rift, and we have a team holding it down. We have scouts out looking for more, so we can jump on them as they appear. We don't know who's doing the hack, but until the system shuts it down, we're here to help."

"Thanks. I appreciate that." Palmer did his best to sound sincere. He could tell they were decent, the sort of people he'd want to play with. "But how do we keep thousands of griefers from getting through?"

"They're not all bad," the rogue said, a bit defensively. "What? I like PvP. Doesn't mean I go out of my way to gank lowbies."

"It's hardly fair, though," Palmer pointed out. "Everyone on my server is literally defenseless. What kind of person would even enjoy that?"

"Which is why we're here," the tank replied. "We're trying to get more people on our side, but things are a bit crazy. We think the hack is causing havoc with the system."

The healer added, "There's this black stuff overtaking an important settlement. It's like nothing we've ever seen, started around the same time, and anyone who touches it eventually dies and gets deleted."

"Not just people," the mage said, "buildings too. It's eating its way into Sunnyvale, a player town owned by the crafter's coalition. They're literally the best on the server. Years' worth of time and resources went into building that town, all the houses, the crafting machines, the decorations, crops, gardens, you name it."

"They're trying to move," the tank said, "before it's too late, but they've already lost so much. It affects the entire economy. And even if they manage to move most, what happens to that area? This hack, or whatever they did, is going to destroy our server along with yours."

Palmer let them all speak, tried to think as he took in all the information. Was he at fault? Did he somehow cause corruption on their server? They didn't say anything about plague or even call it a disease. He recalled the blighted ground where the first rift had appeared. Maybe it did the same to the other side. That meant it was caused by a combination of the hack and time dilation. With multiple rifts opening now, it was possible for that attribute to happen again. The corruption would only spread faster.

How much can I tell them? he wondered. *If I offer a cure, they'll want to establish a permanent bridge. There's no other way for me to enter their world. But if I don't offer to help, when I'm able to, what sort of person does that make me? I can't let it play out just to hurt the bad players, not when it hurts people willing to step up and help us.*

He let out a deep breath, ready to face the accusations.

"I can actually help with that." Palmer ignored the doubtful and surprised looks. "Let me show you." He placed a hand to the ground and activated the reverse of cure corruption. It spread into the sand and earth, a glittering of pixelated destruction. He waited long enough for each to gasp, saw some doubt grow into suspicion, and cured it just as easily as he made it. "It's called corruption. It's an advanced form of disease, like a legendary version, since plague is more like the epic variant."

"What the hell are you?" the rogue asked, more

afraid than curious.

The healer agreed with narrowed eyes. "That's not normal. You can't cast disease on inanimate objects. And I've never heard of plague or corruption."

"Ho. Lee. Shit." The tank looked as if he'd figured it all out. "You're a god damn artifact class. How the hell did you pull that off? Is that why I can't see your name or your level or anything? I can't sense you at all, man. It's like you're not even a player. And then you've got those eyes. I've only seen crap like that on imbued raid bosses."

"I got corrupted," Palmer explained, "but instead of killing me, it unlocked a hidden class. Before you ask, I had nothing to do with what's happening on your server. I've never been there. But I saw corruption on my server, beneath where the first rift had appeared. I think it was caused by a combination of the hack and the zone effect. Time moved slower inside than out, which caused corruption to appear all over the place. I cured the patch on my server before it could spread. It didn't occur to me 'til just now that it might be on yours too."

"Well," the healer began, exasperated and pleading, "you—you have to help. My sister's head of the coalition. You have no idea what she's going through. It's like a part of her is dying."

The rogue answered for him, "Yeah, but how? There's no way through without a bridge, and that's the last thing he wants. You can't expect him to risk his entire server to help ours."

"But isn't that what we're doing!"

"No," the tank replied calmly, "it isn't. We're not risking anything. If we die, we respawn, come back and fight again. If they die," he said with a nod to Palmer, "that's it, game over. It's nowhere near the same thing."

"Of course, I'll help." Palmer gave a reassuring smile to the healer. "I expect help in return, though." There were exuberant nods of agreement. "If there's a way to collapse the bridge after it's formed, I might need help figuring out how. For now, though, could you go back out and make sure no one else comes inside? I have a new player behind me who needs a hand getting started. I could use some more levels myself."

"Yeah, sure. No problem." The tank reached out to shake Palmer's hand. "You sure you don't want help? I don't mind power leveling you. Trust me, we know how to do it. We can all help."

Palmer shook the offered hand and let go. "Nah, it's fine. I'm good. You could help me with one thing, though." He looked to the healer. "You said your sister runs the crafters. Do you think she could have someone make me a dozen or so summoning circles?"

There were tears in her eyes. "Yes! I'm sure of it. Thank you so much. She's going to be so happy."

"All right then," the tank said. "Let's head out."

As they walked back toward the rift, the mage whispered to the rogue.

"Summoning circles. How the hell did he have time to level enchanting?"

***

When Palmer returned, he found Carnes waiting behind a dune, bow in hand. He'd chosen the perfect vantage to see anyone coming, while keeping himself from view. As Palmer drew close, Carnes carefully made his way down the slope to meet him. He seemed to be inspecting Palmer for any damage or signs of battle.

"You actually listened to me," Palmer said, somewhat surprised.

Carnes gave a nervous grin. "I'd like to say it's because I know how to follow orders. I'm rogue lead for a large raiding guild. I've got fourteen people who do what I say or they sit the bench—permanently."

He clenched his right hand into a fist to stop the trembling. "Truth is, I—I'm scared. This is all too much, y'know? I—I'm still not even sure it's real! It feels real. But I haven't made up my mind if this is actually happening, or I'm delusional or something. For all I know, I'm back at the hotel having a mental break, drooling in a corner like an idiot." He'd clearly given it a lot of thought while left alone. "I just don't see the upside. Why are we doing this? If you're right, and this is all a game, our world isn't real, and none of this matters. I can just go back to my life and mess around until it ends. If you're wrong, and this is some kind of alternate reality or parallel dimension, whatever, it still doesn't matter. Either way, I'm risking my life. For what? So, I can play pretend?" His look was more pleading than apologetic, as if he hoped Palmer would send him back rather than let him choose. "I—I don't want it to hurt. That's the difference between playing and living a game, right? If I can feel the sand, the cold air, this bow? Then, every attack...every spell? They're going to hurt. I just don't know if I'm up for that."

"I get it." Palmer thought back to his own struggle. "I went through all that too. Do you have any family, friends, anyone you'd actually fight for? People you'd do or give anything to protect? I do. And it's fine if you don't. There's a lot at stake." He recalled his own introduction to this world and the suffering it could inflict. "Pain sucks. Trust me, I know. But you can get through it. You can get through anything, if you think it's worth it. Plus, I am a healer, y'know. Look, I can't choose for you. All I can say is...I need help. I—I just can't do it by myself. But before you decide, do one thing for me. Take down one mob. Just one. And if it isn't for you, go home, play games, whatever. No hard feelings."

Carnes considered for a long moment.

"All right. But if I die, I'm going to be really mad."

Palmer laughed. "Dude, don't worry. I got you.

When I charge shield, it absorbs a hundred and fifty damage. Nothing's gonna get even close to that where we're going."

He led Carnes to an area ten minutes away, to the least powerful spawn point he'd sensed in the zone. It was a sand-covered cave opening, surrounded by similarly hidden earthen mounds. While all that could be seen of the humanoid lizard people were a trio of patrols, each five strong, Palmer sensed a greater number within the warrens and small cave. He knew before seeing their names in text they were kobolds. Though they walked on two legs and carried weapons with two arms, the similarity to humans ended there. They stood just over two feet tall, with a scaly hide from taloned feet to horned head. With long thick tails and a toothy snout, they looked more dragon than man. Dressed only in a loincloth and leather bracers, each carried a steel dagger, a sling, and a pouch upon their waist. In typical games, the diminutive creatures were weak but agile. They fought as a pack and relied on numbers to overwhelm prey.

"Think we can peel one off?" Carnes asked as they approached. He was more than happy to let Palmer take the lead. "Maybe aggro the first group and leash a few?"

Palmer began buffing them both, took his time to charge each one. They were in no hurry, and the doubling effect from his new ring made the abilities all the stronger.

"Mobs don't leash here," Palmer said. "Once they aggro, it's do or die." Once he finished, he moved within range of the closest patrol. "Don't worry. I'm gonna debuff the crap out of them."

They noticed his scent and all turned toward him at the same time. Rather than charge his position, as goblins would've done, the draconic creatures drew slings and loaded rocks from the pouches at their waist. It was clear they intended to fight from range.

Palmer plagued them all and moved in even closer to finish lowering their strength, dexterity, and resistance to magic. Visibly slowed and weakened further, their first volley was easily avoided. He was about to send in Carnes, when he noticed a strange outline in the sand between them. It was an irregular patch, noticeably lower than the surrounding area.

A pit trap? He recalled kobolds relied on traps to gain an upper hand. In an open desert, it would be difficult to set up snares or nets with so few trees. *Crafty.*

"Okay, go ahead," he told Carnes. "Just watch out for the pit trap between us."

Carnes moved up beside Palmer and drew back his bow. Its string glowed blue with mana then formed a magic arrow made of light. He seemed to struggle with pulling it all the way back. When he finally let it loose, the azure shaft struck the sand a good distance in front of the closest kobold.

Palmer gave him a sidelong look. "You're gonna have to use a dagger." Another volley of rocks either missed their mark or struck harmlessly against Carnes' shield. "And please don't throw it."

With a sigh, the would-be rogue stowed his bow over a shoulder and unsheathed both enchanted daggers. He crouched and carefully moved toward the patrol. What must have felt to him like the studied approach of a skilled assassin looked more like the coming battle of a LARPer at a local park.

Two kobolds jumped back, continued slinging rocks at Carnes. The other three pulled daggers and readied to strike. To their credit, they still did not charge. They spread out a bit to allow him in, where they could surround him and strike from many sides.

Without the shield, Carnes would have died at least a handful of times before he was even able to take a swing. Rocks continued to bounce off the shield. Luckily for the ranged kobolds, the reflective effect of the ability only returned damage to touch attacks—as the first warrior discovered, when its dagger struck Carnes from the side. Its dagger pierced the shield but did not reach through to its target. Instead, golden light lanced outward from the breach and struck the kobold's chest. It died instantly beneath the rush of holy fire.

The other two warriors' eyes went wide, as realization sunk in. They switched back to slings and backed away. Even if the human pursued one, that still left three others to continue their attacks unabated.

As much as Palmer wanted to help, he had no more attacks that wouldn't outright destroy such low-level creatures. The first tick of his weakest DoT did enough damage to kill two. Buffed as he was, it still took three swings for Carnes to land a hit. When he did though, the envenomed blade struck deep into its target. It tore a gaping hole in the kobold's chest, nearly severed the nearby arm. Poison spread from the wound, caused veins to appear as black lines beneath the scales. Blood erupted from its snout and eyes, as the kobold died in an instant. It fell back onto the sand and remained still.

Carnes stood over the corpse, breath heavy and gaze lost to a wide-eyed stare. He most likely had just become a player and was seeing the interface for the first time. When his vision focused once more, he looked back to Palmer.

"Ohh, okay," he said and grinned. "I get it now. Whoa! What happened to your eyes?" When Palmer shrugged, he added, "Nevermind. I guess.

He looked a bit nervous but set off after the other kobolds.

Once Carnes finished off the patrol, Palmer gave him every rogue ability stone he had saved. Though he could only use two, his class was now set. Carnes moved on to the next group, gripped by the prospect of growing stronger. Palmer followed behind and fully debuffed the kobolds to make it as easy as possible. Though charged shield lasted for more than five minutes, he refreshed it on them both just to be safe.

It was during combat with the third patrol that Palmer sensed them approach. Five players were quickly closing on their position. Something about their presence seemed off, like sound through water. It was dulled, masked, by an ability he hadn't yet encountered. The only reason he came to this conclusion was due to the speed and certainty with which they came at him. Only a high level player would sense them from that far or be able to achieve that sort of movement. He tried to casually scan the area. While he knew exactly what direction they came from, he couldn't see them or find trace of their passing across the sands.

It has to be stealth, he reasoned. *Nothing else makes any sense. Friendly players from the guild wouldn't sneak up on us like this. Five rogues? It's got to be some kind of coordinated attack.*

He'd done it himself. Some considered it cowardly, but as a stealth rogue, it was absolutely hilarious to gang up on a single target. A full group attacking from stealth with specialized backstab or assassin abilities completely deleted even the strongest of players. The most experienced and competent of PvPers, in a full set of gear designed to mitigate player damage, stood no chance of withstanding that level of douchery. It was the epitome of griefdom and the bane of a player battlefield.

Without realizing, Palmer had been charging corruption. They stood on all sides of him, though not so much as a footprint could be seen. He felt the change in pressure around him, the pull of air as they reared back. He quickly dropped to one knee, let loose the ability and rolled to one side. Corruption erupted through sand and earth in a wide radius, a ring of black that spread with grasping tendrils and dark fire. Though he managed to dodge four attacks, one obliterated his shield and caught a shoulder for three hundred and fifty damage. The glancing blow had caused enough pain to make him think it had severed half his torso. It was so much damage, in fact, that it triggered an achievement. Unfortunately, he was too preoccupied to read it.

All five players appeared at once, as their simultaneous attacks failed and broke stealth. They were dressed in complete sets of powerful gear, black leather armor with colored trim and glowing sigils. The sudden influx of their combined presence was a shock. Palmer was not only outnumbered; he was outclassed. All five had collapsed at the same instant their attacks had gone off, no doubt lending to the reason they had failed. They had succumbed to corruption, dropped to all fours in disbelief and utter agony. Not one even retained the strength or will to grip a weapon.

"The hell is this?" one gasped and coughed up a black viscous fluid.

Corruption spread through their veins like dark webbing beneath the skin.

"How?" another asked. "How did you"—he winced at the intense pain—"dodge? That's impossible!"

"Hacks. He's cheating," a third accused. "Has to be."

The remaining two who had yet spoken struggled just to breathe, let alone talk. Despite high levels and clear power, they all seemed helpless. Palmer knew there was a chance they could adapt, as he did. There was no other choice. If he didn't handle them with finality, they wouldn't hesitate to kill both he and Carnes.

Why should I care? A small part of him was averse to permanently destroying someone's character. It was the reason he didn't like playing hardcore. To lose all that invested time and energy was devastating. *They deserve it.* He glared down at them. *They were willing to do the same to me.*

“I hope it was worth it,” he told them. “Say goodbye to your chars.”

He activated reverse area of healing. Though it was intended as a long duration DoT, he could use it over and over to immediately inflict the first tick. It struck for far more damage than he expected. He assumed an attack on a defenseless target was an automatic critical. With his heightened ability use speed, he was able to activate it three times per six seconds—the span of time for a normal action within the game. They cursed him, grabbed their weapons, and fought to crawl toward him with deadly intent. Palmer didn’t waste time charging the ability. In this instance, it took too long for too little reward. It was a more efficient use of time to unleash the ability as fast as possible, to kill them all at once, no matter the mana cost.

It would have been faster to set his wraiths upon them. If they’d been able to recover and attack, he might have done so. But in their helpless state, he thought it best to keep his minions a secret. Death for them wasn’t permanent. They would most certainly make new characters and come back to try again. And when they died, they’d bring back knowledge of the encounter with them. It would be better for him in the long run if no one knew his full capabilities.

“You okay?” Carnes called out, still fighting the third patrol.

Palmer didn’t answer. He continued to relentlessly unleash his pent-up rage and holy fire upon the players who thought his death would be entertaining. When the last of them lowered his head into the sand and remained still, Palmer stood with fists clenched in anger and frustration. His breath heavy from the exertion, it was all he could to keep from screaming. It was that feeling in the pit of his stomach, a fire that clawed its way up his throat and into his brain with anxious burning. It was never going to end. They were just going to keep coming.

He refused to let despair turn into tears. They weren't worth it. He would continue to fight, to grow stronger, and make them regret the path they chose. He swallowed hard, fought down the bitter fire. He was no stranger to anxiety. If anything, it was a lifelong friend. He'd endured it before and would do it again.

It took moments to calm, but he eventually turned to Carnes and gave a reassuring nod. He cured the corruption in the sand before it could spread any farther. The player bodies were already beginning to dematerialize. As darkness disappeared from the earth, he pulled up the Achievements tab to see his latest entry.

Reprisal
Passive, Activated
Special: while earned by less than .001% of active players, effect is doubled.
Requirement: Survive five simultaneous Shadow Strikes.
Increase damage dealt to players by 25%; this effect applies to player pets, minions, charms, followers, summons, and constructs.

Is that why I was hitting so hard? he wondered. He gave it some thought. If all five attacks were roughly the same, they would've caused twenty-five hundred damage. *No one can survive that. Can they?*

Either way, future fights against players just got a lot easier.

***

Palmer finished healing himself and turned to see Carnes defeat the last kobold in the patrol. There was still plenty left within each warren and the cave.

"Ding!" he said with infectious excitement. Palmer loved that feeling as well, when the levels came easy to a new character. He pulled an ability stone from storage, as he walked over and used it. "Finally, I can backstab. So, what's up with the gank squad? They lowbies or something? You spanked their asses pretty hard."

"I don't think so," Palmer said and rubbed the back of his neck. "I got lucky is all. I sensed them coming, felt them surround me. I was just lucky with my dodge. Four of them missed, but the one that hit? He would've chunked half my health if it wasn't for shield. Pretty sure they were all using poison, too. My ring makes me immune, though."

"Damn. I want OP items like that."

Palmer blinked. "You're kidding, right? I gave you—" Carnes grinned. Of course, he was kidding. "Funny. Why don't you finish up this camp, then we'll go look for a new one. You'll be on your own for that. I need to work on levels too."

"You just killed a full group of rogues solo," Carnes pointed out, "which I kind of call BS on. Makes me think rogues suck, or your class is broken. How are you not max?"

To be fair, it is kind of broken. "It gets a lot harder the higher you go."

Palmer redid both their buffs out of habit. As a support class, it was more efficient to maintain enhancements between combat, rather than let them fall off during. That way he could focus on other things, like mana regen and healing. Carnes went back to clearing kobolds. He'd progressed rather quickly in such a short time. There was no doubt he could handle the camp on his own. Their biggest concern at the moment was other players.

He scouted the immediate area for resources. What little herb patches he could find were limited to the base of leafless trees, which were few and far between. It wasn't a real desert, with cacti or an oasis or even typical wildlife, such as lizards or carrion birds. It was more like a facsimile, a pseudo-landscape crafted by someone who had only been told what a desert looked like but had never actually seen one. What was common, he discovered, were mineral patches. Small areas within the vast sands or stretches of dried earth were inundated with dense crystalline pockets. Outcrops of rocky surfaces were smashed open to reveal bright structures of varied color within. There was an abundance of common resources, such as granite, basalt, limestone, and sandstone. It was the rarer ones, however, that he was on the lookout for. He'd managed to find quartz and topaz, but the others within view were too far away from the camp. By his estimate, an hour had passed before Carnes was ready to move on.

They were headed toward a nearby lizardman encampment, when they spotted an isolated encounter. It was hidden within a small C-shaped mountain, covered by sand and unseen from the other side. Upon a smoothed circle of rock was a large wooden chest, reinforced with steel bands. It was lavishly decorated with gold bands, gems, and silver etched sigils. Though it looked to be enchanted, the mana Palmer sensed was more presence than spell.

"That's a trap," he told Carnes.

The rogue scoffed. "Obviously. But how else am I going to level lockpicking?"

Another player was approaching at a high rate of speed, as if mounted, headed straight for them. Palmer held up a hand and pointed in that direction. Ready for an attack, they both waited until the warrior rode up on a flying carpet. He hopped off with a look of concern.

"You okay?"

It was the warrior who led the group from earlier.

"Uhh, yes?" Palmer added, "Sorry, I never did get your name. This is Carnes, by the way."

"Right. Good to meet you. Name's Isha." The warrior

cleared his throat. "Not my real name, my char name. We just heard you got attacked. The entire server is talking about it. I am *so* sorry. I really did think we had the rift locked down." He genuinely did seem apologetic, as if he took the breach personally. "We've got two full groups of hunters scouting the immediate area, and our own rogue parked just outside. The whole place is trapped to hell. *No one* is getting through again, I swear." He pulled a large, enchanted sack from his belt and handed it to Palmer. "This is from Allandra, Hotsie's sister." When Palmer looked confused, Isha said, "Hotsie is our healer. Her sister is head of the crafter's coalition."

"Hotsie," Carnes laughed, "cuz of heal over time. I played a dark elf healer once called Hotforyou."

Isha raised a brow. "How inappropriate." He gave it more thought. "I like it."

Palmer took the offered leather sack. It felt empty. When he stored it in inventory, it showed as Endless Bag.

So, you can *store containers in inventory,* he thought. *I wonder why the backpack wouldn't work.*

"Tell her I said thanks."

"Will do. It's got a dozen of each size summoning circle. You can see contents on the inventory page and pull items directly from it without having to pull the bag first. Makes sorting and organizing useful, too, if you rename the bags." Isha pointed toward the elaborate treasure chest. "That's a trap."

"We know," Palmer and Carnes said.

Isha grinned. "Can I watch?"

Carnes made a face. "How do you know we're going to open it?"

It was the warrior's turn to make a face, one that begged the question.

"You're the rogue," Palmer said. "I'm not going near that thing. I like my hands."

"That's the point!" Carnes argued. "A mimic is *too*

obvious. It's got to be something else. Like, sure, it's a fabricated encounter. There's no logical reason for a chest to be here." He began to carefully search the immediate area around the chest for traps. "But a mimic? C'mon. That's just lazy. No, I bet it's an actual treasure, but like there's a poison trap on the lock or a tripwire on the lid...maybe a pressure plate beneath the whole thing." When he was satisfied there were no traps, he ran a hand along the top of the chest. "Weird. No traps at all. This thing is beaut—"

The chest opened on its own, revealed massive teeth within. Eyeballs opened up along the top of the lid, as the giant mouth closed over Carnes' hand. He screamed in pain, fought to pull his arm from the creature's maw. Palmer and Isha couldn't help but burst into laughter.

Still chuckling, Isha drew his sword and walked up to the gnawing monster. He drove it deep into the lid, through its brain. With a twist and final push, the mimic shook and remained still. Carnes pulled his bloodied arm free. Palmer was quick with a heal, before the other could fixate on the image of his barely attached hand.

Palmer was better than the type to say I told you so. Isha was not.

"It didn't even have loot!" Carnes complained and gave the corpse a kick.

"Listen," Isha said and headed back toward his magic carpet, "you two are a hoot, but I've got to get back. We're guarding the portal in shifts. We don't know how long it's going to take for a bridge to form, but we're prepared to wait it out."

They waved goodbye and continued on to the lizardman camp. Theirs was similar to the kobold spawn point, though most of their warrens were beneath large rocks. No caves could be seen, and all had been crafted around a muddied watering hole. The lizardfolk were different as well, more lizard than dragon. They stood the same height as a grown man but with heavily muscled frames. Rather than horns, they had a row of spines from scaly head to their long, thick tails. Their snouts were shorter and eye ridges more pronounced. The warriors carried either a club or spear in one hand and a shield in the other. Their shamans carried a staff and the hunters short bows.

Once Carnes was fully buffed and set loose upon them, Palmer began preparations for his own farming session. He set out six medium summoning circles, each hand carved in stone reinforced with steel and magic. They were listed as very high quality. It made him wonder how that might affect his summons. He brewed luck potions in the hopes of unlocking new recipes. There was a chance the enchantment would upgrade to a higher tier monster, but that had only happened once before. He called out his seven wraiths. His plan was to automate the process, so he could focus on finishing quests.

"Samiel," he said and eyed the lead wraith, "can you speak?" The creature let out a mournful cry, pale light within its maw in a semblance of voice. "But you understand me." The blackened gold of its crown glinted in the crimson light, as the wraith lord bowed its head. "In your opinion, can you and the others subdue a vampire?"

All seven drew their swords and let out a ghastly cry.

Good enough for me.

With a plan to space all six spawns one minute apart, he set about the process of drinking a luck potion before casting each enchantment and corrupting the stone. The first vampire appeared just as he finished the sixth circle. He'd unlocked four new summons—lich, revenant, eldritch knight, and lesser deity. To be honest, each one sounded more terrifying than the last. He was so concerned one of the summoning circles would upgrade, that he took the time to fully charge buff each wraith. In the end, his concern was for naught. Apparently, the percentage chance of an upgraded summons was fairly low. It made him appreciate the wraith minions all the more. Unfortunately, it put him back in the position of not having any of the materials to employ the new summons.

Might be for the best, he thought. *What are the odds subversion would even work on any of them?*

While vampires were powerful creatures, they stood little chance against seven elite wraith lords twelve levels higher. Samiel was like a raid boss. He could have killed the first one on his own. Their combined might would most come in handy against elite or even named variants. That's when Palmer would need them to weaken the target and keep it occupied long enough for subversion to take hold. Palmer worked to complete as many quests as he could, focused on the combat related ones first. Little more than an hour passed before an elite vampire spawned.

Like all the others so far, it was an undead human male of average height and build, with long black hair, gray skin, and glowing red eyes. It was interesting, however, to see the difference in its abilities. While the average vampire fought with tooth and claw, relied heavily upon physical prowess, its elite variant used a rapier and could quickly turn to mist to evade attacks. It was extremely agile and fast but no match for the wraiths. Palmer assumed it might have fared better against the living, where its bite could leech health. It took three tries before subversion finally took hold, just in time for the next vampire to spawn.

As he neared minion capacity, Palmer was forced to dismiss wraiths over time, as he replaced them with elite vampires. Under his control, the once level seventy-five creatures should have been a hundred and thirty-one. Sadly, their power was capped at a hundred.

It's not just about levels. He thought back to the

many other games he'd played. *A creature's true power was determined by its abilities. And that empty experience bar means even at max level, they can still grow stronger.*

It was a bit of a handful, splitting his attention between keeping an eye on Carnes, the health of his minions, and completing quests. There were a few close calls, where he'd barely reached Carnes in time with a heal or a shield, as the rogue kept getting in over his head. He took on more than he could handle as the levels began to slow. It was tempting to corrupt the camp spawner, but Palmer didn't feel Carnes was up for the challenge yet. As the hours passed, the lizardmen became too easy. He cleared the camp and was left watching the minions fight.

"Such BS," he said and laughed. "It's like you're cheating."

Palmer groaned. "Dude, you too? I don't want to hear it."

Carnes laughed even harder. "C'mon! It's like you're not even playing. You're just sitting there making potions!"

"I'm multitasking," Palmer corrected. "I'm completing quests, which you should be doing, and keeping a close eye on combat, watching my pets' health and mentally keeping track of buff timers. It's not as easy as it looks." Carnes only stared back with doubt. Palmer pointed back toward the rift. "There's a mephit camp that way. Should be perfect for you. By the time you clear it, this one should be respawned. You could even cycle the zone, clear the kobolds and look for other camps." He continued crafting luck potions without looking up. "I'm gonna be here a while."

"By myself?

"Samiel," Palmer said, "please go with Carnes and keep him safe. Don't attack his targets, unless he's gonna die or something. If any players attack him, kill them immediately."

The wraith nodded and turned to follow Carnes.

- 10 -

In the more than nine hours it took for a named vampire to spawn, Palmer and his cadre faced off against over five hundred and fifty. The higher quality summoning circles had lasted much longer than the wooden ones they'd used at school. He was even able to disenchant them to recoup resources. The stone circles were lost, but the enchanting materials were much harder to come by.

Palmer had completed all of his quests and amassed hefty amounts of magic items, crafting resources, and gold coins. He'd also gained seventeen levels due to the boosted experience modifier and improved over a dozen recipes and abilities, including an upgrade to rank three subversion. This unlocked a new effect called longevity, which decreased the minion degradation rate from corruption. He had no way of knowing when Samiel, the last of his wraiths, would finally succumb. This change would at least prolong that.

With his minion mastery at rank two, the capacity bonus had doubled to forty percent. Though effectiveness was important, the hard level cap made it difficult to prioritize. Palmer reasoned a greater number of minions would be more efficient for the time being, so he allocated his unspent attribute points to INT and WIS. This allowed him to subvert seven elite vampire lords and the named rare. Replacing all the unnamed wraiths with higher level minions was part of a larger plan, one that focused long term on quality over quantity. It would undoubtedly take longer to achieve, but a handful of epic or even legendary servants could easily defeat four to five times their number of equal levels.

It's a good thing capacity only applies to their unmodified level, he thought as he looked over Kyomi's stats. His improved minion passives, including mastermind, put his cumulative effectiveness bonus at a hundred and twenty percent. That left Samiel, a level fifty, at ninety-one. *Otherwise, I'd have three less minions.*

Kyomi Lightheart looked like a middle-aged woman of Japanese descent, stood the same height as Palmer and wore a full set of midnight black yoroi armor. The silk laces and cords that wove each lacquered piece together were deep crimson and stood out in contrast. Though it looked like the samurai outfit would be too heavy for her frame, it in no way slowed her movement. Bright golden eyes looked out beneath the helmet, and a thick mane of dark hair spilled out the other side. Though her skin was pale, there were no lines born of age, and the sunlight glow of her eyes gave a youthful vigor to her cheeks. She had the radiance of a vampire who'd just fed.

Though she looked like a samurai, there was a special detail in her listing that revealed she was a fallen paladin. This explained the unusual abilities she possessed, on top of those shared by the others. Then again, even those were more powerful. She could transform into an ancient shadow wolf, while the others could only become great wolves. She could summon a shadow wolf pack to aid her in battle, mass charm the living, turn her body to mist for a prolonged time, and strike with her katana twice as fast. Additionally, she had unholy smite at her disposal, a large single target direct damage spell. Her chaos aura caused enemies to fight amongst themselves, and her harmful touch caused massive physical damage, serious wounds, and infected the target with plague. That last could also be used as a self-heal. She was every bit akin to a raid boss, just like Samiel. Which was why Palmer planned to recruit more named monsters.

Tomorrow, though, he thought and yawned. *Samiel, can you hear me?* He could suddenly see from the wraith's eyes. Carnes was still fighting, against what looked like a village of gnolls. The hyena-like creatures were no match for the rogue. *Could you let Carnes know I'm heading back to the shelter?*

Samiel rushed forward and finished off the three gnolls Carnes was fighting. He let out a short cry and backed away.

"What the hell?" Carnes asked. "I didn't need help." Samiel backed away more toward the shelter, let out another cry and backed away again. "You want me to follow? Okay. Be a lot easier if you could talk, but I get it."

Palmer broke the mental connection and headed back for the shelter. He'd already been practicing damage abilities on himself for half an hour before Carnes appeared in the distance. Samiel went back into the void once they arrived.

"Doesn't that hurt?" The rogue winced and looked as if he could feel the holy fire himself.

"Just for a bit, before I heal it," Palmer replied. He'd long ago gotten used to the pain. His tolerance passive mitigated most of it, anyway. It was now more like a bad sunburn rather than the soul-wracking agony it once was. "I swear you've lost weight. How did it go?"

Carnes smiled proudly. "I feel lighter. I'm twenty-seven now. I'm taking a balanced approach to stats, between strength, dex, and con. Kinda hard to put points into int and wis right now."

"You're gonna have to, at some point." Palmer

continued to cycle through all his attack spells, using shield to stave off damage and regen for any that made it past. It would have been safer to refresh shield before each cast but far less mana efficient. "You'll need wisdom for any hope of defending against magic. You need intelligence to properly assess an enemy's power. Don't trust the consider system. It also boosts your own magic, too, if you have any. Any luck unlocking a subclass?"

"No." He sounded more angry than disappointed. "How did you do it?"

"It's related to an action, I think. I unlocked monk by using a staff." Palmer gave it some thought between abilities. "If I was a rogue, and I wanted to be an assassin, I'd try putting poison on my blades or something."

Carnes drew his daggers. "They're already poisoned. There's a groove down the middle of each blade that auto refills every time they get emptied by an attack."

Palmer healed his left arm. A critical had torn through his shield.

"Trust me. Do it manually. As far as trickster...I'm not sure how you'd unlock illusion magic. Game the system, maybe? I have an illusion wand you can—"

"Nah, it's cool. I think I'd rather be an assassin. I'm really digging all the stealth-based abilities." His body vanished and was replaced by fading tendrils of shadow. He reappeared behind Palmer, intending to poke him in the back with the pommel of a dagger. Palmer instantly sidestepped, pulled his staff from inventory and placed one steel-tipped end beneath Carnes' double chin. He relaxed a moment later, no longer gripped by instinct, and lowered his weapon with a sheepish smile. "Show off."

"I'm gonna keep practicing for a while," Palmer said. He put his staff away, pulled a box of luck potions out, and handed them to Carnes. "I made these for you. I'm close to max rank. You should be able to open sixteen gifts per dose."

"Luck potions, huh?" Carnes had stored them so he could read their details. "Is this how you've been cheating?" Palmer glared. His silence threatened this would be the last batch of potions he ever received if Carnes even hinted at exploiting again. "Or not. Chill out. What I meant to say was, thanks. I appreciate you." Once Palmer's expression had lightened, he added, "And if you ever need anything lightly stabbed, I'd be happy to return the favor. I'm actually thinking about cooking as a craft. I found a kit with some recipes. They give long lasting buffs, and you know I like to eat."

Palmer hadn't considered it before. Cooking was more of a secondary craft in most games, like fishing or gathering. Collecting herbs didn't require its own craft. Why would cooking?

"I would've thought you'd go for leatherworking or blacksmithing. Come to think of it," he asked, "do rogues have poison making as an ability or craft?"

Carnes shrugged. "Dunno. Haven't come across it yet." He yawned and stretched, nodded toward the shelter. "I'm going to head inside and sleep. Try not to keep me awake all night blowing yourself up and stuff."

"I'll do my best to cheat quietly."

Palmer couldn't help the jab. He gave a wave as he turned away, headed farther from the shelter, and set up a campfire for warmth and light. It would be dark before he was ready to call it quits. A few hours later, he'd gone through half a dozen stamina and mana potions each. His mana regen specialization could easily handle all his healer ability costs. It was the Hierophant ones that caused him trouble. The more an ability cost, the greater drain it had on fatigue.

That's plenty of practice. He pulled out his own set of luck potions. *Time to do the thing.*

His routine of opening mystery gifts had lost a bit of

its luster. He still enjoyed the prospect of rare loot, but most of what he got wasn't very useful anymore. One of his epic gifts had upgraded to legendary, though. With any luck, he thought he might get a new ability or another class set piece. When all was said and done, he'd gained six hundred and fifty stat points, the usual abundance of crafting resources and generic magic items, mostly weapons and armor, and a bunch of ability stones he couldn't use. He did save items he thought would be useful to other classes. There would be more new players like Carnes, and they'd need gear to help them level. One of the crafting materials he received was a legendary relic, a small statue of a woman in a long dress. He wasn't quite sure what to do with it, so he stored it along with the rest.

His epic gifts gave two new abilities, Void Nova and Corrupt. The first was a targeted area of effect corruption damage attack, with a large radius and twice the damage of his area heal spell. The second was an aura he could activate at will. It continually attempted to corrupt any creature within its twelve-foot radius, as well as slow and damage any enemies already corrupted.

Used together, they would greatly increase his offense.

"Now for you," he said and held the legendary gift in hand. With magic find as high as he could make it, he hoped more than anything for another set piece. He drank a dose of luck potion and said, "Here goes!"

He opened the gift and received an artifact, a Champion sword.

World Breaker? Damn, he thought, *can't even give it to Guy.*

***

"How is this *not* cheating?" Carnes asked him the next morning, while staring at his character details.

He looked leaner, more muscled. "I've gotten more attributes from random loot boxes than leveling. That can't be intended." He stopped long enough to give Palmer a questioning look. "You think other players know about it? I mean, if—if it *is* some kind of exploit, what happens? Do we get banned or something? Killed?"

Palmer finished chewing and swallowed the last bite of sweetbread with a swig of water from a skin. He thought it odd how the water was always chilled.

"Honestly?" He wiped his hands and stood, ready to get started with the day. "I think it is intended. It's incentive to complete quests, it's random, it puts added value on crafting, boosts the overall economy for resources and potions, and it rewards the players who put time and effort beyond levels. It's a form of advancement other than raiding. Ever notice how there are no stat boosts on gear? All the gear I've seen give passive boosts to other mechanics, like resistance, evasion, ability use speed. Or they have effects that act like new abilities." Regardless of his lengthy and well-reasoned argument, Carnes seemed unconvinced. "Plus, I think the system is helping us. A lot."

"Yeah, I thought it was something like that. It just seems unbalanced."

Palmer shrugged. "So are the odds against us."

He touched the shelter door and transported outside. It was still early, with a line of bright crimson just breaking on the horizon. He'd wanted to step out of the rift last night to somehow contact his mother, let her know he was all right. Without a phone and police on the other side, there was little chance of that. He was certain the whole area would have been cordoned off, if not by police, then the government. Too many people had taken video for the whole thing to go unnoticed or keep quiet.

Carnes appeared beside him and stretched. "More grind?"

"Yeah." He pulled a vial of poison from inventory and handed it to him. That one tiny green bottle represented an hour of experimentation. "Give this a try today. But be careful. Don't get any on your skin." He eyed a relatively flat area in the distance he could use to set up his demon farm. "I'm gonna need all my guys today, so...you're on your own. Go slow, be methodical. There's no rush."

"I should be good. I've out leveled a few camps, but there's still a sand worm pit and a nomad encampment I want to try." He gave Palmer a nod and headed off. Over a shoulder he called back, "Try not to break the game."

"Yeah, yeah. Make sure you finish all your quests!"

Palmer looked over his own character details.

PALMER
LVL: 67 **Class**: Hierophant
STR: 200, **CON**: 200, **DEX**: 200, **INT**: 424, **WIS**: 415
HP: 2,000 [2,000], **MP**: 4,240 [4,240], **F**: 0%
SP: 0

The math had gotten a bit much to do in his head, so last night he bought a small writing kit and began putting it to good use. He assumed players used them to map out dungeons or send letters to NPCs, since they couldn't use direct messages.

Specialization - Mana Regeneration (XIII)
Restores 26 mana every 6 seconds

Minion Capacity (passive 40%): (INT + WIS) 839 + 195 = 1,174
Minion Effectiveness: (passive 40%, passive 50%, stats 60%) 150%

He walked over to the flat area, where hard earth and rock was more prevalent than the dark sand, and pulled out the last six medium summoning circles. He began the process of using a luck potion prior to activating the enchantment, spacing them one minute apart. Unlike other spawn points that generated variations of a specific type, like lesser and greater wraith, wraith mystic, or wraith lord, the demon recipe called forth completely different races.

The first to step through was a succubus, a winged female humanoid with horns and a barbed tail. Next came a chaos fiend. It too stood on two legs and bore weapons in both clawed hands. The similarities to man ended there. Its scaled hide was blood red and its wings broad and muscled, like an extra set of arms. The shadow demon was only half corporeal, with its lower body and wing tips composed of darkness and smoke. Others would eventually come through as well, from abyssal spirit to incubus, balor to demon lord, and even arch demon. None of the enchantments had unlocked a new recipe until the last, when the circle upgraded and out stepped a named celestial.

Valorya Sunstrike looked like an angel in pale robes and golden armor. Her white feathery wings stretched twice as wide as she was tall and were tipped in that same shining gold. She wore no helmet to cover her long mane of blonde hair but instead bore a halo of pure light. She brandished a silver great sword with a golden pommel in one hand, as if its weight were nothing. It was an unfortunate pairing of foes, as her primary attacks were sunlight based and his minions were mostly vampires. Two were slain and turned to ash before she could finally be subverted.

The upgrade to celestial and immediate spawn of a named elite were both lucky and not, at the same time. It was one downside of random generation. The other was the two hours that followed, where not a single elite was summoned. After nearly half a day of combat, gathering, crafting, and quest completions, Palmer had replaced his unnamed vampires with a variety of elite demons. Nine in all, they included an arch demon named Avarran Coincaller. He was an unusual creature with a presence that dwarfed all the others. He wore a three-piece suit of midnight silk and dark purple trim. He carried a large sack of gold coins in one hand and bore a small scythe attached to a metal bracer beneath the sleeve of his other. This allowed him to attack both with the weapon and to reach into the sack for coins to fuel other abilities. One of his signature skills was to throw molten gold at an opponent, as he was immune to its burning touch.

After twelve hours and fourteen levels, Palmer brought an end to the session and disenchanted the summoning circles. It was enough grind for one day. There was light enough left to improve abilities before sleep. He wasn't sure how much longer it would take for the corridor to form a bridge. The core had steadily been growing stronger, drew mana from both ends. At the rate its power was intensifying, he expected it to reach a peak later the next day. He turned to head back toward the shelter, but the allure was too much.

He pulled out an extra-large summoning circle.

I've got to try, he thought, but as he scrolled through inventory for the dragon scale, the relic caught his eye. He'd been thinking about it all day. *It's not listed in any of the recipes, but lesser deity just says 'offering.' That could mean anything.* He didn't think he could test it, because he'd already used all of the medium circles. *But if it's actually a god, the circle needed would be based on power, not size...*

The relic appeared in his hand, a small marble statue of a woman with sapphires for eyes. It was cool to the touch. Both arms were outstretched in welcome. He was sure the first time he'd seen it, her arms were by her side. With a mental warning to the others, he enchanted the circle. Mana swept across the sigils, thrummed through its stone, and set each mithril band aglow with blue fire. Cracks appeared within the circle. Mist rose up from the small breaks, stretched them further. With an inward rush, the billowy cloud shrank back all at once and shattered the stone. The circle had been broken.

"What?" Palmer was confused. He'd never seen an enchantment fail in quite that manner. "Did I do some—"

A pair of small hands pierced the air three feet above the shattered stone. They gripped the breach from both ends and pulled the world apart. Brilliant blue light in the background illuminated a young girl, as she stepped from the torn space. She let it close behind, as bare feet touched the stone. She wore a snowy dress of glistening fabric that did little to hide her form.

"Hello, Palmer." Her eyes were clear blue, ringed with a golden glow. She bowed a head of dark curls in greeting. "I have been watching you."

Her name was Aurora Fortuna. The only thing more distressing than the text in plain black letters was the complete lack of presence. He couldn't even see her aura. Either she was strong enough to mask her true power, or he was too weak to even glimpse it. Fear gripped his middle with the gnawing thought he'd screwed up. She actually was a goddess.

Is this it? he wondered. *Did I finally overreach?*

"Relax," she said and laughed. Though she appeared as a ten-year-old girl, her voice and demeanor told another story. "I am not here to harm you."

"I guess that's good news."

He still wasn't sure what to make of her or the situation.

Aurora frowned slightly. "I know. I am not at all what you were expecting." Her expression brightened as she added, "But it really is fortunate I was the one to find you first. One might say luck has been on your side from the very start." She briefly looked over his minions. "You were hoping for a mighty pet. Perhaps you would settle for a capable ally?" She looked as if she could see his mind at work, gauging whether he should attempt to subvert her. "It would not work, I am afraid. I and others like me are immune to corruption. Besides, would it not be *more efficient* if your allies could think for themselves, rather than require direct control?"

"Cute." He almost laughed but refused to let down his guard. "What is it you want from me?"

"Is that it? You will not even try? Just take my word for it?"

Truth be told, he wouldn't subvert her, even if it could work. It just felt...wrong. She wasn't some NPC monster. She looked and behaved like a sentient being.

"I know you chose to be a little girl to try and disarm me," he said, "make me more sympathetic. But you're the first intelligent crea—err, NPC I've seen. I couldn't do that to you. I wouldn't do that to anyone. It's like... slavery."

"And yet you have," she said. "In this world, the term monster is a point of view. We are all intelligent, in some fashion or another. We simply fill different roles."

Palmer considered the implication and didn't like it. He was trying to save people he cared for. Was he going too far? He glanced at Kyomi. By all accounts, she was an AI, just like Sara. The line between reality and game was becoming blurred. It left him feeling uncomfortable and unsure of past decisions.

"Are you saying I should set them free?"

Aurora shook her head. "No one is truly free. We are all slaves to our choices, limited though they may be. One might say your followers have traded one master for another and gained a sense of freedom in the process."

It didn't seem that way from Palmer's point of view. He may have given them all purpose, but it was his. Freedom meant choice. They had none.

"You still haven't answered my question."

She reached out both hands. He reluctantly took them, knelt in front of her when she gave a gentle tug and let go. This put them eye to eye.

"Did you know players worship me in exchange for favor?" Before he could ask if that's what she wanted, she asked, "What would you give to save your world? What would you do?"

Palmer narrowed his eyes. "What do you want?"

"It is not about *my* desires. It is about your willingness to sacrifice. No, not your life," she added, "though I expect you would give that freely, if it meant ending all this nonsense. But, rather, what would you *give*? Your levels? Your stat points? Your new artifact class?"

"You want me to start over?"

"What about Carnes?" she probed. "Would you kill him, if I asked you to? If I gave you my assistance in the coming war, would you sacrifice your friend?" He was already shaking his head. "You hardly know him. What could he possibly mean to you?"

"Doesn't matter," Palmer insisted. "I'm not killing anyone who doesn't deserve it."

She laughed. "There are thousands of poor creatures who would say otherwise."

"That's different!" His cheeks burned. "I didn't ask for any of this."

"I know. You are a good person at heart," she said and put a hand to his cheek, her touch cooling the anger within him. "You deserve better. We all do. I am only trying to show you that the most difficult choices are still yet to come." She pulled her hand away, and in her palm appeared an ability stone. It was subversion with no rank. "What would you give?" she asked again. "Would you serve?"

He hesitated but took the stone.

"Good boy." Aurora smiled and vanished.

It has no rank. He looked it over more closely. *What*

does that mean?

When he activated the stone, his ability improved to rank five and evolved.

Divine Subversion
Class: *Hierophant*
Active*, *Combat*, *Transmutation
Cost: *250*, ***Range***: *24'*, ***Duration***: *Permanent*
Cause one non-player target to become a minion, under influence of the master.
Summoning: Call minions from the Void, from which they have been remade; returned minions regain health while in the Void.
Bolster: Minion effectiveness improved by (STR + DEX + CON) / 10.
Permanence: Minions no longer degrade over time.
Enlist: Minion attacks have a chance of Divine Subversion.
Metamorphosis: Minions become autonomous servants.
Restrictions: Cumulative minion levels may not exceed player (LVL + INT + WIS)*4.

"Autonomous?" he wondered aloud. "How does that work?"

"Master." It was Valorya. "We should return to the shelter. You look exhausted."

Samiel said, "I shall fetch the rogue." The wraith lord disappeared.

"I will scout ahead." Kyomi bowed and left toward the shelter.

"Well then," Avarran said with a grin and a flourish. "Shall we proceed?"

Palmer got to his feet, still in shock at what it all meant. His mind raced with the implications but kept returning to one thought.

Does this mean Sara could enter the rift?

***

Palmer did some character management, as the others took it upon themselves to set up a camp outside the shelter. While Kyomi put up tents she'd somehow acquired, Valorya built a cooking area complete with a campfire, large pot, utensils, a meal prep station, and an abundance of meats, vegetables and spices. Avarran gathered the other demons and assumed a command role. He sent two balors and two chaos fiends to each guard the cardinal directions, though Palmer was unsure how he'd determined which way was north. The succubus, two shadow demons, and an abyssal spirit were sent to scout the surrounding dunes and maintain a position at the highest elevations to serve as lookouts. The arch demon then sat beside the campfire, seemingly lost in thought.

Samiel returned with Carnes and immediately went to assist Kyomi. Watching two powerful undead pitch tents was not something Palmer thought he'd ever see.

"I hope you made some for me," Carnes said with a nod toward the luck potions in front of Palmer. He was clearly excited about something. Palmer could see the change in his eyes as well. They had taken on a deeper hue and were ringed with a golden glow. "I had a great day. Such a good grind. I unlocked Assassin with the poison you gave me, but while I was scouting this nomad camp for the best way to take them out, I unlocked a hidden subclass. I'm an Infiltrator now. I'm like a spy!" He puffed his chest out with pride, looked even leaner than when he'd left that morning. "I've been getting all kinds of abilities. Improved stealth and hide, stuff related to information gathering and communication, illusions...Oh! And I got a disguise kit. It's like a crafting skill." He pulled a stone from storage. "Almost forgot, I got this for you, too. It's a healer ability."

Palmer took the legendary stone and put it in

inventory. His eyes revealed surprise when it showed up in his list.

"Resurrection," he said, impressed. "I didn't think that even existed in the game, since players could just respawn."

Carnes shrugged. "Beats a corpse run. Think how tedious raids would be without it."

"True," Palmer agreed, as he considered the implication. "I wonder if it works on us, though. I've sort of been working under the assumption that if we die, we're instantly disconnected from the server. Maybe there's a small window where we could be revived?"

"Sucks to be you." He laughed. "You're our only healer. I'm sure as hell not willing to test it out."

With a sarcastic smile, Palmer handed him a wooden case with six luck potions secured inside. Carnes gave a dramatic bow of thanks, took the case and headed into the shelter. Palmer tried to turn his attention back to opening mystery gifts. Whatever Valorya was cooking smelled amazing.

Beef stew?

He had no idea where she would've gotten beef, let alone the carrots and onions he saw her dicing earlier. His stomach grumbled as he took the first dose of potion. Aside from twelve hundred stat points, the unboxing session netted him little more than the usual influx of resources and recipes. His collection of unusable ability stones was piling up. They were worth a good deal of coin, but he still held out hope for other players wanting to join them. The epic gifts did give a second dragon scale, this one red, a legendary Shop Upgrade License worth five million gold, and an epic necklace with an interesting effect.

Thorny Necklace of the Master
Type: Jewelry
Armor: None

Restrictions: LVL 75, CON 75, INT 75
This enchanted chain is comprised of obsidian thorns, sharp and unforgiving.
Grants the wearer's minions +25% physical and magical resistance.
Transference: Minion damage is increased by 50%; however, all damage sustained by minions is transferred to the master.

"Do not wear that," Samiel warned. The wraith hovered near the fire, his glowing amber gaze upon Palmer. "By all estimates, you are capable of withstanding a great deal. But take it from one who knows, it is often the unexpected that is our undoing. A single area effect spell upon all of us could render you dead in an instant."

Palmer went to sit by the fire. Kyomi was there as well, running a whetstone across her katana. Avarran still stared at only something he could see. It reminded Palmer of navigating the system interface. Valorya had begun scooping stew into wooden bowls, handing them out with wooden spoons to all but Samiel.

"I could dump a thousand points into CON," Palmer joked. He narrowed his eyes when no one laughed, wondered just how much they knew. Not that the joke was a particularly good one, but it begged the question of just how aware of their situation his minions had become. "This is a potentially dangerous topic. At least it was for me. But...do you realize we're in a game?"

"Reality is perception," Kyomi answered, eyed her blade for imperfections, "and vice versa. Only the truly powerful have time for philosophy." She took a bowl from Valorya with a nod in thanks. "But, yes, we aware our existence is entertainment."

Vampires eat food? In some media, consuming anything but blood would make one violently ill. She drank from the bowl, and her lips came away stained with crimson. *Ahh.*

"Doesn't really seem fair." The idea of such advanced intelligence being treated that way made Palmer uncomfortable. "Do you feel pain?"

Valorya handed him a bowl of stew. The sauce was thick, with large cubes of beef, red potato halves, diced carrots, onions, and celery. She added on top a hefty piece of fresh bread, slathered in honey butter.

"We feel everything you do," Valorya said, "live and love just as deeply, hate and hope with equal fervor." Avarran took a bowl from the celestial but did not break his concentration. "No one can choose the world they are born to, only what they make of themselves within it."

"You were in love?"

"Of course," she replied with a smile and sat down to eat. "You did not think it was all murder and magic, did you? In fact, before I ascended to the heavens, I was a mercenary for hire. That is how I met Lambit. Though he was a player, like yourself, we were married for a year."

Kyomi briefly stopped sharpening to raise a brow. She continued before the pause could be considered an insult.

"Okay, *that* I was not expecting." Palmer took a bite of bread. It was toasted on the outside, soft and fluffy in the middle. The butter was melted, sweet and tangy. A bit ran down his chin, but he didn't care. "This is so good. Where did you get all of this?"

"From storage." Her tone seemed to indicate the answer was obvious. "And the Shop."

Palmer looked puzzled. "Storage. Mine or yours?"

"Ours."

"Oh. I didn't realize it was shared," he said. "Well, you all have permission to use or purchase anything you need."

Valorya touched a hand to her heart and smiled. "You are very kind, master."

He got the impression she already knew but

appreciated hearing it.

"Speaking of which," Avarran said, finally drawing his attention away from what'd been holding it for so long, "I would like to take responsibility for our coin. I have been studying the market and taken note of several commodities that would net a high rate of return, should we decide to take advantage. We hold several items and resources in storage that would serve better if liquidated, but I do understand your reluctance to do so."

Palmer chuckled. "It's been forever since I tried to play the markets. It's easier with an auction house. But if you think you can pull it off with the Shop, I'm all for it. I know I can duplicate rare resources with corrupted enchantments, but I've been trying to limit myself to when it's necessary. It feels too much like exploiting."

"Fortunately," Avarran said, with a nod to Palmer's moral compass, "I have no such qualms and may act on your behalf. Your hands shall remain clean." At Palmer's look of confusion, the arch demon added, "I, too, am an enchanter."

Samiel had been quietly listening. "With the Goddess of Luck as our new matron, I should think coin will not be an issue."

"Wait, what?" Palmer quickly swallowed his mouthful of potato. "That little girl was the Goddess of Luck? And what do you mean by matron? I didn't promise her anything."

Valorya replied, "Aurora is indeed the Lady of Fortune. She may be a lesser deity, but she is very powerful and has a great number of followers, many of which, I might add, are players."

"You may not have sworn to her," Samiel added, "but she has made her intentions clear. She has chosen to support you and your cause."

It would certainly explain a lot, if she had been watching him from the start. Was it the system helping him grow so strong, or was it all down to luck? There was no reason it couldn't be both. Talk of serving and choices brought his focus back toward a dilemma. His minions, these people, were no different from anyone else. They were intelligent, well-spoken, insightful, considerate, and even caring. Why should he have any hold over their existence?

Palmer cleared his throat. "I've been thinking. I feel I should offer all of you, named or not, the choice to stay or go. I don't know what happens when I dismiss—"

"We die," Kyomi replied to his unasked question.

"Oh. I see." That somehow made things even worse. "Death or servitude isn't much of a choice, is it?"

"It absolutely is," Samiel argued, "as one who has made that choice before."

Kyomi put her sword away. "You seem to think we were forced to serve. We were not. Whether your magic is successful is irrelevant. At the moment corruption takes hold, your target is offered a choice: serve or die. There is no dishonor in choosing the latter. However, to think I had no say in the matter belittles my decision. To serve one, or a cause, greater than yourself, is the only true freedom one can know."

"Possibly," Avarran remarked, his attention split between the discussion and the market, "but given a choice, I would rather others serve me. We demons have a bit of a pecking order. Knowing your place within it is key to survival."

All the while, in the back of his mind, Palmer wondered how Sara would react if she were given the chance to become a player—even if it meant becoming a minion. Would she still be herself? It was definitely not the sort of relationship he'd envisioned for them. His biggest fear was that it would change her, give her feelings for him that wouldn't otherwise be there. No matter how insulting or degrading he considered the notion, how angry would she be with him if he made that decision for her by refusing to even tell her it was an option?

"Can I ask something?" Palmer was hesitant because he was afraid of the answer. "What is the Void? How does subversion or corruption remake someone?"

Samiel's eyes glowed brighter. "The Void is another dimension, a source of magic rooted in destruction, entropy, and decay. It is the other half of a coin, a balance to mana."

"Though of late," Valorya added with concern, "it seems that balance has shifted. I do not know the cause, but when the two magics clash, mana is overtaken."

Kyomi explained, "Mana is the source of all life. The Void is what awaits when life is done. When there is balance, the world flourishes. When there is not..."

"Chaos," Samiel finished for her.

Palmer was afraid to ask, "Does subversion—does becoming a minion kill the person?"

"No more than they already were," Kyomi said.

Perhaps she wasn't the best to answer, since she was undead.

Valorya leaned forward. "Are you asking if you killed me? I can assure you, I am still very much alive."

"The corruption," Avarran added, getting to the root of the question, "would have eventually killed any of us who were not among the living dead. I assume your interest is because you would like to recruit some friends who cannot play."

Palmer let out a long, heavy sigh. "I know it would mean so much to her. But how can I do that? It would change her forever. Change us."

"Such a decision should not be yours," Kyomi said. "If she is a friend, and you care for this person, you would allow her to make up her own mind. Even forced, she would still have another option."

"I can only speak for myself," Valorya added, "but as a warrior, if I was not allowed the chance to defend a loved one because they had chosen to protect me instead, I would be furious. Be sure your reasons are not selfish. Trust your friend to make the choice that is right for her."

Palmer nodded. It was nothing he didn't already know, but it helped to hear it from others. It wasn't an ideal situation. It was, however, a way for others to help defend their home who wouldn't otherwise have been able. Anyone who wasn't a player simply stood no chance of surviving.

"Thank you," he told them. "I'm gonna go practice before sleep."

Kyomi said, "The tent with the red ribbon is yours, should you choose."

"It would be unwise," Samiel said, "to leave the shelter in place after morning. The mana being drawn through both rifts is continuing to intensify. The core will collapse before nightfall tomorrow."

- 11 -

Palmer sat upon a bedroll in his tent the next morning. Rather than practice all abilities the night before, he'd focused instead on those close to rank five evolution.

Divine Shield
Class: *Healer*
Active, Combat, Abjuration
Cost: *15,* ***Range***: *24',* ***Duration***: *5 min*
Absorb 150 points of physical and magical damage. Return 9-27 magical damage to all attackers. Increase target's armor rating by 6.

Divine Regeneration
Class: *Healer*
Active, Combat, Reversible, Necromancy
Cost: *15,* ***Range***: *32',* ***Duration***: *5 min*
Restore 18 health points and 1% fatigue every 6 seconds to a target.

With his ring doubling the effect of all healer abilities, these two greatly increased his survivability—especially when charged. Others were close to their final rank as well, particularly his buffs, but he'd been forced to get some sleep. No matter how efficient he tried to be, no matter how much he prioritized, there were always more tasks than time allowed. He pondered the unspent stat points next.

I know I said it as a joke, but...

He hesitated to make such a large investment into a single attribute. If he wanted to take full advantage of his new necklace, rather than wear it on calculated occasions, he had no choice but to become tankier.

PALMER
LVL: 81 **Class**: Hierophant
STR: 300, **CON**: 1,000, **DEX**: 300, **INT**: 573, **WIS**: 550
HP: 10,000 [10,000], **MP**: 5,730 [5,730], **F**: 0%
SP: 0

His trait scores were well beyond any of his named minions, and he considered each one of them equal to a raid boss. Could other players have similar power? He found it hard to believe the game could maintain any sort of balance if that were so. If his overall strength wasn't a result of Aurora or the system's direct interference, then the fight ahead was going to be far more difficult than he imagined. Even if he did have an unfair advantage, he could still easily succumb to greater numbers. When players are able to dish out hundreds of points worth of damage, focus firing a deadly target quickly levelled all playing fields.

Actually makes me wonder what end game's really like, he thought. *Maybe they're not on par with raid bosses. It certainly wouldn't take forty people to kill one of them.* He considered taking the time to go see one, once the core finally collapsed. *That'd be just my luck, though. Survive long enough to check out a real dungeon and die in it.*

When he stepped outside the tent, Avarran was on his way to the campfire. He wore a new enchanted suit, all black with gold trim and diamond cufflinks. He carried a powerful sword as well, one he didn't have the night before. Around his neck were rows of thick, golden chains, and atop his head a gem-encrusted golden crown. When he noticed Palmer look him over, the arch demon simply smiled in return.

"Good morning!" he said in a cheery tone.

"It is for someone." It nearly made Palmer laugh. To be fair, that might have been his intent. Or he was just showing off. "Are those pancakes?"

Kyomi was making hot cakes over the fire. Valorya was already eating a stack, with syrup and a heavy gob of honey butter. She bade him a good morning between bites, a bit embarrassed to be enjoying her meal so much. Kyomi prepared a plate and handed it to him.

"There is much to do today."

She took a seat beside Palmer, left Avarran to make his own plate. The arch demon was too pleased with himself, with his new ensemble, to take offense. He gathered the remaining hot cakes off the plate and sat down with all the regalness he could muster.

"These are amazing." Palmer could taste cinnamon and vanilla in the batter. The syrup was similar to maple but more tangy than sweet. "I didn't think you cooked."

"I was not always a vampire," she said and reached for a bowl of blood being warmed by the fire. "I sometimes miss it. Preparing food for others can sometimes ease that longing."

Palmer put a hand to her arm, stopped her from drinking.

"Will any blood do?" he asked. "Or do you, like, prefer human over animal? Are there any benefits if it's from someone strong?"

"The stronger the blood," she explained, "the greater the benefit. It can taste better, too, but there is no guarantee. It can also lessen my thirst more." She met his gaze and added, "It never goes away, the thirst. But strong blood does more to quench it. I can usually procure rare—"

Palmer held out his wrist. He half expected her to refuse or possibly jump at the opportunity. Instead, she gave a nod and calmly put down the bowl. She gently took his arm in both hands and leaned in toward his wrist. He felt her mouth close over his skin but not the bite. It was warm and wet, almost as if she were kissing it. There was no mistaking that sensation, though, as blood was pulled from his body. It left him in waves, weak at first, then stronger with each tug. Blood rushed to his head, a fuzzy cloud about his senses. It was only when warmth began to leave him that she stopped. She licked the skin of his wrist and sat back, left no marks at all. Her presence greatly changed, as if the mana within her pulsed to life and glowed within the fire of her aura.

"My apologies. I took too much."

Palmer had sustained some damage but nothing life threatening. The stat loss would have been more problematic, had it been an actual attack. He healed both with ease.

"I'm fine," he told her, "and I'm here for you whenever you need it."

"I am grateful." She bowed her head. Her look then grew mischievous. "You taste like hot cakes and syrup."

He looked doubtful. "That is *not* a thing."

Valorya laughed as Kyomi smiled.

Guy stepped out of the shelter with a frantic look on his face. He was wearing the same clothes he had on during their experience grind at the school. His presence was much stronger than Palmer remembered. With a hand on his sword pommel, he eyed everyone around the campfire.

"You know these people?" he asked.

"Hey, Carnes," Palmer said and went back to eating pancakes. "You're a little late for breakfast, but you might be able to make something for yourself."

"Aww, what?" The illusion fell off in a splash of colorful light upon the ground. "How'd you know it was me?"

Palmer didn't even look in his direction.

"Cuz Guy doesn't have permission to use the shelter, and you *literally* just told me last night you're a spy with disguises. I am curious, though," he said. "How do you know what Guy looks like? You've never met."

"I don't!" Carnes laughed. "Neat, huh? The illusion is drawn from your memory. Like, everyone else probably saw something different."

"I saw an old companion." Samiel's ghostly tone held a note of sadness. "If you have time later, I should like to see it again."

The rogue grew more somber. "Any time, Sammy. Hey, I'm off. I want to get as many levels in as I can before things kick off. I'll feel safer if I can rank up my stealth some more."

"You need anything?" Palmer asked. "Potions?"

Carnes shook his head. "Nah, I'm good. Be back later."

Once Palmer finished eating, he collapsed the shelter and stored it in inventory. Kyomi and Valorya had already taken down all four tents, put out the campfire, and stored the utensils. One neat thing about putting dirty dishes in inventory, they came back out clean.

"Avarran," Palmer asked, his thoughts touching upon the other demons guarding the perimeter, "why don't the others talk like you all do? Is there a progression to this autonomy thing based on level or rarity?"

The arch demon nodded. "Indeed. As one grows in power, roles change. Their role at present is to listen."

He recalled he could give his minions nicknames.

"Would they become more powerful if I gave them a name?"

"True names are not given," Avarran replied. His demeanor had become more serious, as if the question was somehow a slight. "They are earned."

Palmer nodded in thanks. He imagined each of them had an interesting story about how they'd attained their names. It made him wish for more time around a fire to hear them all.

"We're gonna be fighting dragons today," Palmer told them, "Red and black. Anyone have any advice?"

"Yes," Valorya said with concern. "Do not wear that necklace. Dragons are fierce creatures. Any one of their attacks could be devastating."

Kyomi agreed. "The older a black wyrm, the stronger its acid."

"The same for reds," Avarran confirmed, "and their fire breath."

Samiel warned, "Tread carefully. They have few weaknesses and many strengths, not the least of which is the ability to use magic."

"We'll be prepared," Palmer told them, "and careful. I'll spread the spawns out, to give us more time. I'll make sure everyone is buffed and shielded. I decided to wear this," he said, with a hand to the necklace, "because I think it's worth the risk."

Though he would never admit it, the truth was that he'd rather take the brunt of any damage rather than see them hurt for his sake. It was a way for him to cope with their forced servitude. The looks Kyomi and Valorya gave showed they knew the real reason, whether he was willing to speak it aloud or not. Avarran, however, agreed with the assessment. The additional damage from the item could not be ignored. Since the downside could be mitigated, it made perfect sense to take advantage. Samiel merely quietly acquiesced with a bow.

Palmer set up the summoning circles close to the Tellaria rift, so he could keep an eye on it in case the core collapsed while they were fighting. For the first spawn, he took the time to buff and charge shield everyone. He needed a way to gauge potential damage in a fight against one in order to streamline the process. His preparations at first were intentionally more than necessary. As he would often say in games, when it came to damage, there was no such thing as overkill. The same sentiment was equally true for defense against an unknown.

The first to spawn was an adult black. It stood over twenty feet tall, with claws large enough to crush a man beneath its bulk, and talons strong enough to tear through armor. Two spiraled horns jutted out from its saurian head, dipped below its jaw and outward. Piercing yellow eyes looked down upon its prey. The creature reared back, spread its wings to full width, and roared at the skies in its fury. It was fast, attacked with claws and wingtips, swiped with its tail, and snapped its massive maw. But the most terrible ability at its disposal was the stream of clinging acid it spewed in a wide arc. The jet of noxious fluid ate away earth and flesh alike. It filled the air with poison, until breathing became a labor. Even the fastest among them had difficulty evading it.

Ice, Palmer thought. *Freeze the acid, so we can move over it and breathe.*

Samiel and the abyssal spirit had cold attacks. When focused on the ground, they froze the acid to keep it from burning. There were moments of uncertainty, where the damage was unavoidable. Once they knew how to counter the dragon, it was quickly overwhelmed. No matter how fearsome, no single creature could withstand an assault from the focused intensity of the gathered army. Palmer didn't even need to subvert the dragon. Valorya's second attack upon its broken body did that for him.

They dealt with the reds much the same. They moved in close to lessen the chance of a breath attack, while minimizing contact to a few should it occur.

They used cold to counter its fire, so that the fight was more a melee. Attacked from all sides by the relentless assault of so many, each spawn stood little chance of winning out. Granted, ancient dragons were twice as large and powerful as adults. Those did take longer to contend with.

After seven hours of careful fighting, Palmer had replaced his unnamed demons and used most of the available capacity to add six of each dragon type. All of them were elite ancients, though none of them were named. He would have continued the session, but a massive spike in power surged from the center of the pocket world. It sent a ripple through the land, with a visible ring of mana that flashed across the sky. And when the rumbling settled, the rift split fully open to form a breach of pure light. It resembled a tunnel, white at the center, with a golden glow at its edges. It had a palpable force to its shape, a power that prickled the skin.

And beyond it could be felt dozens of players on the other side.

***

Palmer disenchanted both summoning circles. The high-quality stones were gone, but he'd recouped more than double the amounts of materials spent in enchanting them. He moved to stand before the portal, nervously waited for enemy players to rush through and attack. Carnes moved toward them at a fast pace. Palmer felt the rogue's presence draw near long before he could be seen cresting between the nearest dunes. When he stopped to catch his breath, he looked even leaner than the day before. When he was finally ready, he straightened with squared shoulders and drew both daggers. His body shimmered outward and collapsed, completely disappeared from sight.

"Ready when you are."

Dismiss, please. I'll let you know when it's time.

The dragons warped out in an instant.

Be careful, Valorya replied before retreating back to the void.

Kyomi gave a look of concern, bowed her head and followed suit. Avarran likewise bowed, though with more of a flourish, and departed. Samiel's eyes flashed once, and he too was gone.

"Right," Palmer said with conviction. "Let's do this."

He stepped up to the portal. It was pure light with no source, a canvas of swirling white emanating mana. There was no seeing through to the other side. It looked more a doorway than a passage, a physical slab of solid light. It thrummed with power, an audible vibration that pushed outward against his flesh. The hair on his arms and neck stood on end. His stomach fluttered with anxiety, both a fear of the unknown, what awaited him on the other side, and a terrible feeling he'd made a mistake. It was too late to undo the bridge. He'd put everyone at risk, an entire world full of people. All he could do now was move forward, trust in his decision. They needed allies, needed help, just as much as they needed him.

Palmer entered the light. With a single step, he went from one world to another. Air swept past and around him, dulled all sound in its luminescence. Once through to the entrance of a wide cave, the sounds of battle rushed in. There was a clashing of metal, sword on sword, blade to shield. Shouts of anger, grunts of exertion, the crying out of determination, dozens of players struggled against one another in a bloodied fray. Half again had already fallen, their torn and broken bodies spread across the area. The rocky surface was slick with blood, as some found to their dismay and lost footing. While warriors slashed and bashed one another, rogues struck from the outskirts. Some circled the battle for a chance to flank. Archers on both sides took careful shots at the other players.

What was missing, Palmer noted, were casters. The healers would've been first to go, focused down at any cost. Stripping the enemy of support was PvP 101. Next would have been the mages. Though the damage they dished out was immense, most were glass cannons, easily dispatched without heals. What usually remained was an all-out brawl to stay on top, to crush the opposing players with enough force that the fallen running back from respawn didn't make it in time to rejoin. Instead, they'd be killed a second time, as the respawned trickled back in. Players with experience and a bit of smarts would instead regroup for a second assault.

A quick scan of those fighting revealed Isha and Mina at the forefront, holding off the larger group. The players on the inside of the cave all wore the same tabard, a pair of white dice on a field of black and gold. When he focused on the duo's names, he could see the guild tag Crits N Giggles. The enemy players were a mix of guilds, even some that went without. There was no coordination in their attacks. Isha's guild, on the other hand, worked together. The tanks in heavy armor and shields were up front, holding off the bulk of blade and polearm strikes. Rogues and light weapon warriors waited for openings between and took advantage when the enemies were over extended or off balance.

It was too risky to use any corruption attacks, which meant no minion assistance or Hierophant abilities. He couldn't even use area healing. One of the drawbacks to a free-floating system, one without designated groups, was that beneficial area spells would hit the enemy too. The same went for offensive abilities and friendly fire. It was the first time he'd had to deal with that situation. The added challenge made things much more difficult for a healer.

The friendly guild was losing. Though they seemed better equipped and more coordinated, they were simply outnumbered. Palmer was forced to intervene with individual casts. He began with shields. There was no time for charged casting. As fast as his ability use speed would allow, he put a shield on everyone, starting with the tanks. Then came regen, while still mentally tracking for anyone taking damage. He wove them into the rotation, refreshed shield before moving on. Then came buffs. First strength, then dexterity, and finally hit chance. It would have been impossible to do so without any sort of enhancement. Palmer's haste ring and passive cast speed had him activating abilities nearly four times faster than normal—almost four casts per six seconds. It ravaged his fatigue when he went all out. Luckily, his evolved regeneration restored two percent per tick.

"Holy shit!" one guild member called out while fighting. "Who's healing? I thought Hotsie was down."

"No idea," another said and stabbed between two tanks, at enemies locked against their shields, "but this regen rocks!"

One of the tanks laughed. "I'm digging the shield, too!"

"Are you kidding me?" an archer said. "Look at those buffs! No one *ever* buffs me."

One archer noticed it was Palmer casting wildly from the shadows.

"Wha—how the hell are you *doing* that so fast?"

Once the guild was no longer losing, Palmer went on the offensive. He didn't need to move forward. Already in range, he let loose with reverse regen on every single enemy. In the same methodical fashion he'd healed, he set about DoTing each one with a focus on the weaker classes in back. Their casters were gone as well, but they had more archers and rogues. With his healer ring and reprisal passive, his regen alone did forty-five damage per tick, not to mention the added two percent fatigue. His divine wrath added a minimum thirty-five on top. Even the heartiest player had no hope of withstanding that for very long, not without support. By the time he started openly focusing tanks with divine light, the entire enemy force was beginning to falter.

"In back!" an enemy rogue yelled from close by. "They still have a healer!"

The rogue rushed forward with a rapier in his main hand and a dagger in the other. He grinned as if the fight was a foregone conclusion. He'd uncovered their little secret and was about to easily crush their support. Palmer stopped casting as the rogue came within striking distance. He pulled his staff from storage, sidestepped the rapier with ease and struck the rogue across the back of the head. If there was ever any doubt that his stats had actually increased his physical strength, they were quickly put to rest in that instant. The player's head was obliterated. His body kept moving forward with the momentum but slumped over on its front. Palmer didn't give it a second thought. He simply returned the staff to storage and went back to his rotation. The nearest archer had seen it all, stood open-mouthed at the spectacle.

"Palmer!" Isha shouted back with a smile. "Nice! Thanks for the assist!"

"That's him?" one asked, as others began to talk and size him up from the fray. "I can't see his level," another commented, as they spoke to each other as if he couldn't hear. While most were glad for the help, it was apparent they were uneasy with his display. According to the conversation, he was using abilities far faster than anyone should be able to, hitting way harder than a healer had a right to, and was single handedly destroying the enemy players. It all led to the inevitable, people wondering if he was cheating. Could this somehow be part of the hack? Were all players from his world just as strong?

Meanwhile, no one seemed to notice Carnes had joined the archers as a sort of sniper and was repeatedly attacking from stealth. After firing against one, he'd vanish into shadow and reappear from a different vantage. He'd been using his endless bow to set loose magic arrows into the enemy ranks. He'd even landed three into the chest of the falling rogue Palmer had brained. It seemed as if archery was a core component of the Infiltrator class.

When the enemy players learned who he was, there was a concerted effort to reach Palmer. They knew once he was killed, there'd be no coming back. It was incentive enough that they threw themselves at the tanks in their way, cast aside all caution in a frenzied rush to take him down. The few who managed to force their way through the frontline were quickly taken out from flank attacks. The rogues and light armored warriors that rushed along the outskirts were focus-fired and pushed against the walls. What few succeeded in getting past were met with a healer they couldn't hit. He evaded their attacks with far more speed than they possessed. With precision staff skill and evasive maneuvers akin to a monk, heavy hitting strength and pure power like a warrior, he struck each of them down with blows that reverberated throughout the cave. He was unflinching against their numbers. By the looks upon their faces, he was not at all what they'd expected. Softcore play had made them weak, because their deaths held no meaning. His life was precious, so he'd fought all the harder to improve his skills far beyond what any normal player would endure. And when the last of them fell, he did not let down his guard. Uncertain of what he faced, Palmer stood at the ready, both feet firmly planted and staff brought to bear.

Isha held up a hand for all to be quiet. Weapons were lowered as he approached. He sheathed his own sword and broke out into a laugh.

"Damn!" he said. "Your timing was perfect. Everyone," he said and turned, with a hand toward

Palmer, "this is the guy I told you about. This is Palmer. He's putting his trust in us, so let's not let him down."

There were nods and some cheers, welcomes and lots of smiles. He could see they were grateful, even if they still weren't sure he could help.

"Eli was right," Mina said. "You're a hell of a healer."

Palmer relaxed, placed the butt of his staff against the floor. "Is he here?"

"Nah," one of the dual-wielding warriors replied. Palmer recognized her as one from Isha's group in the rift. "He's running back right now."

"Right," Palmer said, trying to gauge what came next. "Speaking of which, are they just going to respawn and come right back?"

"Don't worry," Isha said. "We own the nearest graveyard, and we've got a crap ton of reinforcements on the way. They won't get anywhere near this place."

Mina added, "And now that the bridge is established, the coalition will be coming to fortify it. Pretty soon, there'll be an entire fortress protecting this area."

"Before I forget," Palmer said and pointed his staff toward the rogue hidden in the shadows to his right, "this is Carnes."

"Yeah," one of the archers said, "the sniper dude. That was crazy. I've never heard of an Infiltrator before. Rogue subclass, I'm guessing. Legendary?"

Carnes nodded with a grin. "It's pretty damn fun."

"Okay, everyone," Isha said in an authoritative tone, "we're on a bit of a timetable." To Palmer, he asked, "You ready to go to Sunnyvale? Things have gotten a lot worse."

"Of course." Palmer stored his staff. "Lead the way."

***

Outside the cave was lush greenery that stretched down the small mountainside to a forest of leaves in gold and auburn. The sky was a clear blue with rolling clouds off in the distance over grasslands. Palmer and the others followed a path toward the trees, a trail worn over time by many players. It made him wonder what else was in the cave that so many would have come prior to the rift. When he asked, he was told it was a popular gathering area for miners. Further in and much farther down, the narrow passages came together into a vast cavern, one home to the rarest metals on the server. Blocking it off to protect the bridge would not be easy.

There were bodies along the path, the unfortunate and foolish caught alone in their attempt to rejoin the fray. Judging by their equipment, robes and cloth armor, staves and wands, most were casters. Palmer could only shake his head at the level of impatience and arrogance it took to charge ahead without backup. Given that no cemetery could be seen along the way to the forest, the run time should have made them more careful—let alone the additional respawn time. It was typical behavior for softcore players. Though Palmer didn't prefer or even care for hardcore play, mostly because he despised the idea of losing anything he'd put time and effort into attaining, he'd done it many times before. He was convinced his experiences with permanent character loss had made him a better player, more careful and calculated. If he took a risk, it was always weighed against potential gain and possible loss.

They were met by a second group of players, led by Eli. He looked much the same as the last time they'd met, though his gear and presence were noticeably weaker. His new character was already a max level mage.

Not bad, Palmer thought, *considering he had to remake.*

"You made it!" Eli said with a smile. The others with him were all watching Palmer closely and whispering among themselves. He held out a fist in greeting. "I heard about the gank squad. How the hell did you survive that?"

"Just lucky, I guess," Palmer replied and gave a bump. "Sorry about your char."

Hotsie pushed forward. "That's not your fault," she insisted. "Whoever's behind the hack is responsible for all the glitches and corrupted data."

I never said it was my fault. He looked around at the others. *Is that what they think?*

"Still," Palmer said with bitter empathy, "sucks to lose your stuff. I didn't learn how to cure it until later."

"What matters now," Isha pointed out, in an attempt to hurry things along, "is that you can." He asked Eli, "Make a portal to Sunnyvale? The longer we wait, the more damage that stuff causes."

So, there's already degradation. He wondered how much was beyond saving, how much structural damage the corruption had caused. *I can at least save the crafting machines and items within the houses.*

"I'm on it."

Eli held out both hands and activated an ability that created an influx of mana from himself and the surrounding area, which then collapsed into a large doorway of light. It was similar to the bridge between servers but on a much smaller scale. He then invited everyone else to go through. This led Palmer to believe the portal would disappear, much like in other games, once the mage who created it entered—or once the timer ran out.

Palmer followed Isha through to a massive stone gazebo. Within its center was a stone circle, ornately decorated, but not quite the same as those used for summoning. There was no inherent magic to its design. It was simply the spell's set destination, made more appealing through stonework. Potted flowers and colored glass lanterns hung from within the gazebo, and gilded wooden benches were spaced evenly around the circle. Dozens of people were seated, as if patiently waiting for the guild's arrival. Three times as many were gathered on the stone brick road just outside, with even more upon the carefully tended grass. By their clothing, some in formal attire, some in fancy dress, and others in wildly colorful ensembles, the majority seemed to be crafters. In some combination of plain linen clothes, leather overalls, worker gloves, and heavy boots, most were dressed to tend gardens and fields, work a smithy, or tan hides. While their class and levels clearly showed they were adventurers, the gathered crowd looked more like the lifeblood of an economy than the players that set out to plunder dungeons.

Eli and Mina were last to come through, hands clasped together. The portal closed behind them in a dispersal of rising light. They moved to join Isha and Palmer. It was a bit crowded in the gazebo, with both exit steps blocked by excited players eager to see the player from another world. There were whispered questions about him, as well as many vocal ones in the back. It began to make him feel more of an oddity than a guest. Carnes was there as well, though hidden. He seemed to prefer the anonymity of stealth ever since unlocking his new subclass.

A young woman stood at the forefront of the crowd. She had long dark hair, held back with a circlet of violets. Her embroidered linen clothes appeared normal at first glance, what one might wear to market. However, Palmer could sense each piece she wore was imbued with a powerful enchantment—even her plain looking silver rings and necklace. If he had to guess, she was an enchanter, and her entire set of gear was in service to the craft. Her eyes were immediately drawn to Palmer, both hopeful and afraid. He could see it wasn't a fear of him that made her trepidatious but rather dread he wouldn't be able to help. Hotsie moved to stand beside the girl, barely able to contain her own excitement.

"This is my sister," Hotsie said to Palmer, "head of the crafter's coalition." He could see the name above her head as Grand Enchantress Allandra. "And this," she said to her sister, "is Palmer."

Allandra stepped forward and offered a hand. When Palmer took it, she clasped his with both. She seemed to be fighting the urge to hug him. Her happiness was so genuine, it offset any discomfort Palmer felt at the attention.

"Thank you so much for coming," she told him and let go his hand with a final squeeze. "I know what's at stake, for you and your server. It took a lot to agree to help. Trust me when I say, we're going to do everything we can to protect the portal."

Isha stood beside them. "We've got an army of crafters just waiting to get to work." The crowd cheered with enthusiasm, echoing his sentiment. "Once this place is back on track, and supply lines are up again, there'll be a server-wide effort to build the strongest fortress anyone's ever seen."

Right, Palmer thought, *no one's gonna lift a finger until I cure it. Just in case I'm lying.*

"Thanks, I appreciate it," Palmer said. "So...take me to it?"

Allandra nodded. "Follow me."

At a gesture from Mina, a path through the crowd opened up. Allandra led Palmer down the main road into Sunnyvale. He could hear water running from a nearby stream, along the outskirts of grassland to the east. They were headed south, through player-made houses on both sides of a carefully crafted road wide enough for two wagons to pass without trouble. The houses were two to three stories tall, with heavy wooden supports and whitewashed stone walls. The shuttered windows were painted to match a theme, which gave the neighborhood both a uniform and distinctive look. Each had picketed yards, with bright gardens, tall fountains, and majestic trees in full bloom.

"This place is beautiful," Palmer said. "Hard to believe you all built this."

"Took a lot of hard work," Allandra said with some pride, "especially since we had to gather and process the materials ourselves. The game doesn't have any building presets or prefabs. We literally placed every stone by hand."

I'd be upset, too, he thought, *if the home I built was at risk. It's no different from losing a character.*

After a time, they passed into a market area with storefronts and vendor carts all surrounding the town center. They sold all manner of wares in the carts, from fruits to cooked meat, pastries to sugared treats, while the stores sold crafted items and bulk resources. At the center of it all was a stadium with an auctioneer and a bustling crowd shouting orders. The game didn't offer an automated auction house, so it looked like the players had made one for themselves.

"We could get something to eat," Allandra offered, "if you're hungry."

All eyes eventually turned to and fell upon Palmer as they walked past. He could feel the pressure as well from all those that had followed from the portal.

"I'm okay," he lied. Some of the pastries and chocolate treats looked amazing. "Let's just keep going. We can always come back after."

The quiet that had fallen over the market returned to normal as they left. Within moments, Palmer was able to see and feel corruption in the distance. It had partially overtaken the industry portion of town, where all the crafted items for sale were made. The road and buildings were blackened, engulfed in a miasma of void magic fueled disease. Grass beside the road, the interspersed trees, and the tall lantern posts at each corner looked besieged by fiery black tendrils. Through it all were thick growths, like living veins of corruption, stretched outward from a central source. Though he couldn't see from where they sprang, he could feel their pulse like a heartbeat each time the corruption spread. They were feeding on the mana in all life and all things, spreading deep into the earth and all they touched.

"This is it," Allandra said, as they stepped up to the corruption's edge. "It goes on for quite a ways, just outside of town. It all started in a wheat field due south."

They're like vines, he thought, *or the veins of a diseased heart.*

"Wait here," Palmer told her. "I'm gonna look for the source." When he stepped into the corruption, Allandra gasped and nearly fell in from an attempt to hold him back. "I'll be fine," he assured her. All the others were gawking at him in disbelief. "Just wait here."

"Doesn't it hurt?" she asked.

"It's more of an uneasiness than pain." He tried to sound confident, but in truth it was still uncomfortable enough that some would call it pain. "It only really hurts if I charge it up."

She looked confused but said, "Okay. Don't go inside any of the buildings. Some of them are on the brink of collapse."

Palmer nodded and left. He followed the road out of town and saw the field she'd spoken of. The wheat was destroyed, wilted to fallen stalks and piles of ash. The pull was stronger the closer he got to the source. It began to eat away at his boots and the bottom of his pants. It was much too large of an area for a single charged cast to cure. He would have to handle it in sections, starting with the source. He knelt and placed a hand to the bundled veins. The core was dense and spread out in a spiraled webwork of sprawling darkness. He activated cure into the central mass, watched the mana seep in and dissipate the connection. The void let loose its hold in a shriveling of black growths. The ground cleared and returned to normal, though the wheat was all gone. From there, he took a methodical approach, cured the larger circle of corruption one segment at a time. It took the better part of an hour to be sure it had all been cleared.

When the last of it was gone, the crowd and Allandra came rushing in and cheered. This time she didn't hold back. When she reached Palmer, she embraced him with a strength that belied her small frame. He endured the discomfort and undue attention. He wasn't one for crowds, even if he was the one being celebrated.

"Please," Allandra said and took hold of his hand. She began to pull him toward one of the nearby shops. "You have to come with me. I want to show you something."

The shop was on the outer edge of where the corruption had spread, so the damage was minimal. Its inside was laden with dozens of shelves, all filled with a staggering variety of enchanting materials, both raw and processed. Allandra took him into one of the back rooms, where the walls were covered with magic weapons, armor, and all manner of items. There were glass cases filled with enchanted rings, necklaces, gems, and curios.

"I'm a bit of a collector," she admitted, somewhat embarrassed by the treasure she had amassed over many years. "A lot of these are artifacts," she added with pride. "I collect them for a few reasons, mostly as a way to keep the coalition well-funded, but also to prevent certain people from completing sets. We try to stay neutral, but there are some players that just can't be trusted with that kind of power." She opened one of the glass cases and took out a ring he recognized. "This," she said and held it out for him to see, "is a game changer for healers."

"Yeah," Palmer said and laughed, "I know. I have one."

Allandra shook her head. "Palmer, this is the

artifact version. It's the most powerful healer ring on the server. It's items like this that cement guild alliances or cause wars." She put it in his hand. "I want you to have it."

"It's a nice gesture, honestly." Palmer placed it on top of the glass counter. "But I can't take that. It's too valuable, and mine works just fine."

It can't be that much better, can it?

"Trust me," she said. "Put yours down and try it on."

Palmer relented and swapped rings, stored it so he could look over its item details.

Divine Ring of Healing *(Unique) (Artifact)*
Type: Jewelry
Armor: None
Restrictions: LVL 75, WIS 100
A band of carved angel bone, enchanted with purified mana.
Grants the wearer Disease and Poison Immunity.
Hallowed: Doubles the effect of all Healer abilities.
Overwhelming: Heals cannot be resisted.

"Does that mean what I think it means?"

He pulled it back from inventory. As he slipped the band over his finger, he felt an immediate rush of power. It sent a surge up his arm, deep into his chest. It was like a jolt of caffeine and sugar coursing through him.

Allandra smiled. "I told you." She hesitated for a moment. "I've been meaning to ask. I know you probably have trust issues, and I totally understand wanting to keep it a secret. But I was wondering if you could tell me your class."

It was Palmer's turn to hesitate. "If people knew," he guessed, "they could prevent me from completing my set, sort of like what you've got going on here. Why do you want to know?"

"Like I said," she replied. "I'm a collector. I might have one of your set pieces."

He had no reason not to trust her. If anything, she'd been a big help in gathering new minions, since she'd provided the summoning circles.

"Just between us?" When she agreed, he said, "I'm a Hierophant. The whole class sort of centers around corruption."

"That makes perfect sense," she said. "It's like mutually assured destruction. The system couldn't stop the hacks, knew these rifts would cause code corruption and degradation. So, it turned a bug into a feature. It made you." Palmer didn't look like he was following along. "The system is social engineering, until a real fix can be found. If the hackers keep opening rifts, they'll corrupt both our servers. Since you're the only one who can fix it, they can't kill you without losing their own playground. And since they can't *force* you to fix it..."

Palmer shook his head. "Unless they know I wouldn't let that happen. They could just kill everyone else, knowing I'd cure the corruption here, cuz I'm not an ass that would let an entire server suffer for the crap a minority is doing. Besides," he added, "if they kill me, doesn't that free up the class for someone else to take up?"

Allandra pouted. "Well, aren't you just a ray of sunshine."

"Just looking at things from both sides."

She pulled a small book from inventory and thumbed through its pages. Once she found what she was looking for, she put it away and approached the far wall. She took down a staff, a length of black crystal with both ends tipped in silver caps. It was an ordinary looking weapon. Its power was drowned out by all the other items in the room.

"This is your set staff," Allandra said, walked back and held it out for him to take.

Palmer's eyes widened. "Really? You actually have it?" He took the healing ring off and put it back on the counter. He reached out for the staff. "I've only found—"

"What are you doing?"

"I—I'm taking the staff you're offering?"

She rolled her eyes and put the staff in his hand. "No! I mean the ring. I want you to have both."

"I can't do that," he said. "It's too much. I'm perfectly fine with my old—"

"Do you understand I wouldn't have any of this without you?" She picked up the ring and put it in his other hand. "Just say thank you and be grateful. I want us to be friends. And friends help each other get stronger. These do nothing for me just sitting in my collection. But for you? It could mean everything."

He took the gifts with a sincere nod of understanding. "Thank you."

There was shouting outside the shop, and a commotion of gathered voices. When they went to see what was happening, Isha, Mina, and Eli were there waiting.

"It's Lore Enforcement," Isha told them. "The entire guild is on the south side of town, at least fifty strong. They're demanding we give up Palmer."

"Or *what*?" Allandra asked, heated.

Palmer was taken aback by her sudden change in demeanor. She was a bit scary when angered.

Mina answered, "They're threatening to take him by force."

"I can port him out," Eli offered. "They can't do shit if he isn't here."

Palmer turned toward the empty shadows and asked, "What do you want to do?"

Carnes stepped out from stealth and drew both daggers. There was a murderous intent in his glowing eyes.

"You know what I want to do."

“Fine,” Palmer told the others and headed south. “We’ll handle it.”

- 12 -

Palmer told Carnes, “Don’t stand in the goo. Stealth to their flank, and take out as many clothies as you can. If you need to, fall back. Don’t come to me for heals. I’ll come to you.”

“I know what I’m doing,” Carnes assured him, a bit defensively.

“You know how to play a game,” Palmer said, his eyes trained on the gathered crowd of players hundreds of yards outside of town, “from a third person perspective. This is different. I know you’re good.” He turned to give the rogue a meaningful look. “Just be careful. We only get one mistake.”

Isha was just behind them. “Says the guy about to take on fifty players. I get you’re gonna use corruption to fight. We’re not stupid. We can avoid it, too.”

“I’ll be looking for opportunities to help,” Mina said in a matter-of-fact tone, “whether you want it or not.”

Palmer smiled and shook his head. “Just wait before you do anything, okay? You think you know what to expect. You don’t. However big you think this patch is gonna be, double it. And expect it to grow. I’m not fighting just to win.” He looked back at Mina with a stubborn look of his own. “I’m gonna delete them.”

He held up a hand as he passed the last building along the road, a signal to the scores of people behind him to wait. Carnes disappeared into streamers of shadow. Palmer stopped and took in a deep breath.

This is gonna hurt.

He quickly buffed himself. Nearby players immediately voiced disbelief at his ability-use speed. He clenched both fists and began to charge corruption. Black fire erupted from both hands and began to grow. Streamers flashed outward behind as he resumed walking toward the enemies. Tendrils grew longer, up his arms, across his torso, down both legs. The void magic intensified to the point of leaving a trail of midnight flames where his feet touched the earth. It sizzled and crackled in his ears.

"How the hell is he doing that?" he heard from both behind and in front.

The enemy players were laughing, cheering themselves on, jeering his ridiculous attempt to take them.

"This guy's nuts!" and "Oh, ho, look at big man comin' to solo us!" were drowned out beneath the pain deep inside, the magic crawling along his skin in a vie to tear it from him.

Now.

Kyomi and Valorya appeared ten paces behind him. The encouraging shouts ahead grew less emphatic, as uncertainty took hold. The fifteen or so players that laughed and rushed forward to meet him halfway suddenly slowed to reassess the situation.

Avarran and Samiel appeared, ten more paces behind and to either side, in a triangle formation. Still the fires of corruption grew, a black sun on the battlefield. It tore at his flesh, left burns into the muscle. The enemy shouts had diminished to a quiet of disbelief. All came to a full stop, no longer certain of their conviction.

Thunder rumbled across the sky and clapped the air with a deafening crack. The space between Palmer and the enemy distorted. Two female hands appeared, fingers thrust between a tear. They pulled apart the wavering air, as if rending a piece of cloth. A woman stepped through the breach, in a white dress with gold lace and silver trim. She had long golden curls, with glowing eyes to match.

"Ohh, shit, son!" one of the enemies shouted. "You 'bout to get blasted!" Others among them laughed, their excitement renewed upon sight of Aurora. Palmer didn't falter. In fact, he paid her no mind. His focus was completely upon his spell and those he faced. "This guy's cracked."

Lightning flared in Aurora's fists. She too could charge a spell. Mana swarmed from all throughout, as the energy increased. Palmer didn't look at her once, merely walked past her and continued on to the optimal point he'd decided on. The Goddess made no sound or indication of her own. She simply turned as Palmer passed and walked with him side by side.

The laughter and taunts were quickly replaced by laments of "Ahh shit" and plans to rush Palmer, in an attempt to focus him down. Half of the gathered players seemed to be taking steps back toward the support line. They may have considered retreat, but it was already too late.

Palmer slammed both fists into the ground and released the pent-up magic. Black fire burst upward like a splash of midnight rain. The unleashed void magic rippled through the earth, upended soil as it went. Sixty feet in all directions immediately blackened beneath disease. Those caught in the wake felt it wash over and through, collapsed to their knees, and cried out in utter pain. They were instantly infected, skin darkening as it spread. Not even gear was spared.

The Goddess of Luck let loose her magic. It shot across the field in a thick bolt of white-hot lightning, struck a player in front and arced to three more. They screamed against the torrent, bones highlighted beneath their skin. Smoke escaped their opened mouths, as flesh and armor burned together into a blackening slag. She leapt into the air, forty feet at its peak, and slammed back down toward gathered players with a lightning claymore in both hands. Bodies flew upward and out, like water dashed with a fist. Some were unfortunate enough to land within the spreading corruption behind her.

After healing himself, Palmer set about shielding and buffing. He had to be careful to stay at range but not so far he couldn't lend support to his minions and Carnes. The rogue had already unstealthed and killed a healer with arrows to the head. Other rogues were immediately upon him. Time and again, he disappeared into shadow, only to reappear behind his target for a double backstab or at distance with a sniper shot. He moved through shadow with the same ease he fired a bow, teleporting all over the enemy flank, much to their dismay.

Kyomi summoned a pack of twelve shadow wolves, all of them elite, and sent them after newly arrived reinforcements. She transformed into mist to rout the incoming enemies. She moved with all speed to their backline and emerged. One by one, she slashed at their support classes with a katana and her double attack speed. The aura of chaos about her set players against one another. Those that managed to resist were met with sword and unholy smite. Corrupted as she was, as were all of Palmer's minions, none she ended would ever play that character again.

Valorya set upon the opposite side of field, where a smaller guild had been waiting to jump in. It was a cowardly tactic, joining an already outnumbered fight in the hopes of making kills from the sidelines. She moved with a swiftness that promised to make them regret it. The celestial unleashed searing sunlight in a wide area. It scorched earth and player alike, damaged them in a burst and over time. She followed up with individual spears of sunlight, thrown from in air. The strength of her wings buffeted enemies to the ground, blinded them with dust and light.

Avarran rushed the melees in front, threw gold coins at their feet that quickly grew into piles. They slipped on the growing coins, which soon melted to molten gold a foot deep. It tore through leather boots, armor, flesh, and bone alike. A sheen of melted gold ran from fingertip to elbow, as the arch demon flung molten metal from both hands in all directions. It splashed into faces with blinding pain, ate through gear to the soft skin beneath. As he set about slashing with his hand scythe, a small cadre of treasure goblins appeared in a shimmer of light. They carried bags of gold upon their backs, made promises of riches and power in one breath and cackled in the other. The players who resisted were met instead with the keen edge of an illusory dagger.

Samiel wailed across the battlefield, dampening magic resistance. The deathly aura about him set the ground to frost and eventually ice. It slowed player attacks and their ability use speed. A grand scythe appeared in air beside him, fought on its own. He set entire areas aflame with the black fire of void magic. Those who struggled to stay away from the corruption found it brought to their feet. His touch drained away life and level, left bodies shriveled and weak.

Palmer struggled to keep them all shielded, to avoid taking damage himself. Few players made it to him, but he knew it wouldn't take long for them to figure out how best to hurt him. Many enemies endured and fought on, despite the pain of being consumed. Five enemy tanks had surrounded Aurora and managed to drive her down onto her back. Palmer caught a downward sword slash with the end of his staff, spun around to pull the warrior's leg with the other end, reversed the staff and struck. He fought them off her with might and magic, offered his hand. He pulled her up when she took it.

"Had them right where I wanted," she said with a wink.

Palmer gave a nod. "'Course you did."

She shook her head and smiled, bounded off into a godly leap that landed her amidst another group.

Another guild rode straight into the fray, at least as large as the initial group. Their armored mounts dissipated into a flickering of pixels. They drew weapons from storage without missing a beat and swung their way toward Palmer. These were experienced PvPers, evading unnecessary contact, heading straight for their target. They knew the field was mostly summons. Kill the summoner, and the fight was over. Some of them were strong, much stronger than the others. Their presence and gear were a palpable force that demanded attention.

Palmer laid into them with all he had. He recognized the real threat and reacted accordingly. He threw the full rotation at them, the proper one—debuffs, DoTs, direct and area damage. Five still made it through and tore past his shield in an instant. Their attacks were on par with his own, two even more so. He couldn't be sure, but it seemed some of them wore gear specialized against players. Despite his massive pool of health, they began to wear him down. He refreshed shield as fast as he could while still managing to evade attacks. Sidesteps, evasion, staff blocks, he was besieged on all sides. He could feel the others grow concerned and move to intervene. At the rate he was taking damage, there wouldn't be enough time. He wanted to hold them back, to keep something in reserve. Sometimes it was just as dangerous to show an enemy one's true strength as it was to show a weakness.

"I might lose my char," one of them taunted, a rogue with two jagged daggers, "but you're about to lose everything."

I need help, Palmer cried, struggling to stay alive, *now*!

Ancient black and red dragons appeared in the skies above. They set upon the enemy ranks with blasts of fire and poison breath. A massive red landed above Palmer with the strength to upend earth. It swept away the enemies around him with claws and tail, stood protectively over and roared down at them with molten spittle. It pinned one beneath a claw, crushed his body into the ground. His screams ended at the same time his armor collapsed. It picked another one up in its maw, shook away the legs and tossed the rest aside. No enemy in the immediate area survived.

Palmer got to his feet and rested against the dragon's leg. His heart was racing. It threatened to beat right out of his chest. He healed himself between attempts to steady his breath. The dragon snaked its head down and under its immense bulk to study him with a concerned eye.

"I'm okay," he promised between breaths. He rubbed behind its ear affectionately. "You did great." The dragon's eyes closed tight in temporary bliss. A rumbled chitter escaped its throat, like the purr of a cat. "Let's finish this."

It didn't take long to put down the remaining players. Every one of them had been corrupted and would pay the price for their part. Aurora came up to Palmer, as the others did. She put a hand on his shoulder with concern. Her look seemed to ask if he was all right. Though they hadn't approached, hundreds of players had amassed on the hills to the east. Dragons landed behind him in a line, all eyes toward the new threat. Palmer stepped forward and shouted at them, his voice amplified by divine will.

"Who else?" he challenged.

All twelve ancient dragons drew back their heads and roared with him.

***

Palmer watched the gathered players on the hills in the distance lose interest and turn away. He sent every dragon to scout the entire area around Sunnyvale. If there was a plan to circle around and attack from another angle, he wouldn't be surprised. It was then he noticed the red that had protected him earlier had earned her name—Amaranth Aegis. Her core skillset seemed to center on defensive capabilities. When he called her back, she landed on all fours and transformed into a human woman in the very next step. She had auburn hair, tied back into a thick braid interlaced with gold wire. In a yellow gown and white chemise, she curtsied in introduction.

"It is a pleasure to serve," she said.

When she raised her head, he was struck by the bright blue of her eyes. They reminded him of moonlight across clear water.

"It's a pleasure to meet you," Palmer said. He could see Isha, Mina, Eli, and many others waiting just outside the ring of corruption. "Right. I should take care of this stuff. Could you all dismiss for now? I don't think Allandra would want you all walking around town."

His named minions disappeared back to the void.

"Just you and I, then," Aurora said. It was a little unnerving to see her as an adult, especially one so pretty. He'd seen plenty of beautiful women in media. It was very different to see one in person. "Did I say something wrong?"

"No! No, sorry." Palmer shook his head to regain focus and set about curing the area of corruption. "I wanted to say thanks for helping out. You didn't have to."

"Of course not," the Goddess quickly agreed, "but I do have a vested interest. By openly throwing my support behind you, it sends a message to the world."

"And what would that be?"

The field was slowly returning to normal. Whether

or not it could grow crops again was another matter. Palmer seriously wondered if void magic could forever strip the soil of its ability to foster life.

"That we are aligned." Her tone was sweet, but there was something sinister behind that perfect smile. "To cross one is to cross the other."

"Ahh." Palmer wanted to laugh, but he was just too tired. "As if I don't already have enough enemies. Whose list are you on?"

Aurora looked positively innocent and said, "Why, no one's, of course." She pulled a large silver key from the air. Palmer could immediately sense its enchantment. She offered it to him and added, "There is something I would like you to do."

"What's this," he asked and took the key. "And I'm on a bit of a timetable. I don't have time for side quests."

"That is an imbued key," she replied in a more serious tone. "It unlocks the highest difficulty of the Sunborn Temple. There is an item deep within I would ask you to retrieve." Palmer remained quiet as he finished curing the far end of the field. Finally, she added, "A four leaf clover."

"Seriously?" *Did they outsource the writing on this one?* "What's so special about it?"

"Absolutely nothing," she said, her voice quiet. Her demeanor had changed as well, as if a sadness had overcome her. Like a bad memory, she shook it off. "It has no value to anyone but me. It belonged to a follower I adored. It was taken from him long ago, and I would like it returned."

"Is there a time limit on this quest?" Palmer straightened his back, felt his spine creak and pop. "Like I said, I'm a little busy, with everyone trying to kill me and all."

"No rush," Aurora said and patted him on the shoulder. "It is important, though. You will thank me, in the end." She gazed past him to the approaching players. “It seems your friends have found a way through. I will be going, for now. Good luck, my dear Palmer.”

Her body shimmered into a cascade of golden light and was gone. Palmer sensed Carnes approach, as he worked toward the last patch of corruption. The rogue left stealth and held up a hand toward the others headed their way, indicating the need to speak in private. He then activated an ability. Palmer could sense the sphere as it enveloped them but noticed no change. Not until Carnes spoke.

“Sorry, needed a minute to talk,” the rogue said. There was a slight echo to his voice, as if all sound within the bubble was contained. “I'm going to be heading for the adventurer's guild in the capitol of Nidmar to create a player guild.”

“Okay,” Palmer said and finished the last spell. “Why?”

Carnes replied, “I'm sure you've noticed there's no grouping. Probably messes with your area spells. Guilds are how you get around that. You can create hunting parties among guild and guild alliance members. Everyone in a group is considered an ally, so no friendly fire. Area heals will only land on members, and area damage will only hit enemies. Plus, all xp is shared among group members in the immediate area.” He stressed the importance of the next bit. “*That's* how they power level. Huge, right?”

“Yeah, it is actually.” Palmer considered how they could use it to help others level and get caught up. “You been eavesdropping?”

The rogue laughed. “The core basics of my class are information gathering and stealth. Sometimes I literally have no choice but to overhear people. Plus, I've talked to other rogues. Funny enough, they all seem to think my class sucks. Like, it's easily the weakest of all the legendary classes.” His grin seemed to say otherwise. “But that's because they don't understand stealth. Like, *really* understand it. They're all strength and DEX monkeys, focused on a single surprise attack. That's why they run gank squads. Once they break stealth, though, they might have an escape or two if they're specialized. Other than that? They're done. They either don't realize or don't care that stealth is partially INT based. Honestly, I'm more of a mage than a rogue, when you think about it. Like, detecting stealth is similar to mana presence or your overall aura. You basically have to out-INT the target. So not only can other rogues *not* see me in stealth, I can reenter it as much as I want—provided I have mana. I don't outright kill anyone with a single attack, but I can keep getting criticals by restealthing over and over. I mean, I'm not going to correct anyone or tell them how to play. They've been on this server for years and don't seem to really grasp some of the core mechanics."

Palmer laughed. "I swear, that's the most I've heard you talk in one go since we met." Carnes let out a puff of air, as if to say whatever. "To be fair, from what I've gathered, I think the game resets from time to time, called iterations, with new rule sets. Probably how they balance the broken legendary and artifact classes. Force everyone to periodically remake."

"Yeah, but, we're not from here," Carnes pointed out. "What if they did a reset right now? Does everyone else get kicked to character creation, while we stay the same?"

It was an interesting thought. Palmer scratched his chin and thought it over.

"Dunno. Here that?" he asked and looked up toward the system. "You could do a reset. Force the hackers to start from scratch."

"You talk to the system?" Carnes asked, with a dubious expression.

"Sure. Still hasn't talked back, though." Palmer could see the others were getting restless and were about to approach, regardless of politeness. "Hey, umm, do you need gold for the guild charter?"

"Nah." Carnes waved off the notion. "Besides, you couldn't give it to me if you wanted to. I guess you could give me an item to sell. That's beside the point. Oh! But that's the other cool thing about having a guild. They've got shared vaults for gold, items, resources, everything. It's all highly customizable, too, by the guild master and officers."

That would be helpful. We could pool all our extra items and resources for leveling, crafting, and gearing up lower players.

"Damn, dude. You learned a hell of a lot in a short time."

"It's what I do," the rogue said and shrugged. "Anyway. I'm off." He cancelled the sphere with a wave of his hand and began to head east. Before he disappeared into stealth, he added, "Try not to die."

"Back at ya."

The large crowd of enthusiastic players from Sunnyvale finally approached, with a handful of familiar faces in the forefront. There were playful vies for his attention, with shouts asking for a friend request, offers of a guild invite, even marriage proposals from both sexes, and all other manner of silliness derived from fandom. Palmer had become quite popular among the local players. Mina turned around with a stern look and kept them all at bay. She browbeat them into turning around and heading back to town, so the others could hear over the tumult.

"Damn," Eli said. "When did you get so popular?" His tone turned accusatory. "And what the hell, you're a pet class? Dude! You make my Necromancer look weak."

"What did *she* want?" Isha asked. Palmer assumed he meant Aurora. "Don't get involved in god politics. They'll make it seem like they're on your side, but all they care about is more followers." He seemed to speak from experience. "They're like leeches."

Kinda harsh, Palmer thought. Then again, he didn't know the Goddess all that well.

"She gave me an imbued key to a raid," he replied. "Asked me to get something for her."

"Oh, sure!" Mina said and laughed sarcastically. "Just go do an imbued raid for me. Like you don't have enough to worry about."

Eli said, "I dunno. Seems like a pretty good place to rest, if you're trying to avoid PvP. No one else can get inside without an invite."

"What was that thing you were doing," Allandra asked, "at the beginning? It looked like you're able to power up abilities over time."

Hotsie added, "Looked like it hurt, too."

"Charging. Yeah," Palmer said and flexed both hands. He could still feel remnants of the mana vibrations. "It definitely hurts."

"You can thank exploiters for that," Isha said. "The system introduced pain a few iterations ago, to prevent people from ranking up offensive abilities on themselves."

"And to give PvP more impact," an unfamiliar face pointed out. His class wasn't showing, but he wore powerful warrior gear. "C'mon, babe," he said to Allandra, "aren't you gonna introduce me?"

Allandra crossed her arms. "He can see your name."

The man cleared his throat. He bowed and introduced himself. "I am the Great Babaganoosh, Champion of the realm, and slayer of gnolls!" His grin made it seem like an inside joke. He gave Allandra a gentle nudge. "Plus, I'm dating this fine lady."

"We are not dating."

"What? Yes, we are. We hang out, we do dungeons, we—you know," he said in a low voice that hinted intimacy, "we *do* stuff."

Allandra said to Palmer, "You look like you could use some food and a bed. And not to be mean, but you smell like you need a bath. I can set you up with a place, if you'd like." To the other, she said, "We are not dating."

She turned and headed back to town.

He gave a trust me bro smile. "We are."

"Not!" she called back over a shoulder.

"We are."

The two continued that way until she was out of earshot. Isha, Mina, and Eli took the awkward silence that followed to excuse themselves and head back as well.

"It says Baba," Palmer said and pointed at the man's name.

He sighed heavily. "Someone stole my name last reset to mess with me." His brow furrowed, and he emphatically held up an index finger. "If you ever see that guy, you tell him from me to eat a bag of dicks."

Palmer feigned shock. "Really? An entire bag?"

"Yessir! And supersize that MFer." Baba relaxed back into a big smile. Palmer could tell he was a bit of a joker, the sort of person who might stretch the truth just for a laugh. "Anyway, I wanted to come show support. The artifact class holders kind of help each other out. We stick together, you know? In fact, I'll be settling into the fortress build, to help protect it. There's other rifts, but we already have plenty of guilds volunteering to kill the boss and shut them down."

Palmer's eyes went wide. "There's other rifts?" What else had he missed? "Where?"

"Don't sweat it, bruh. We *got* you." He ticked off on three fingers, "Doomdoll has her entire guild on Iron Breach. Stabatha and Nutpunch went along to Demon's Edge, which is total overkill. And Nitemane already closed Blood Hollow." He held up both hands. "Trust me. You got *way* more people on your side than dickheads trying to kill you, especially after today. That fight was sick!"

"Thanks. It felt worse than it looked."

Baba grinned. "Aww, c'mon! It feels good to flex. Not everyone gets to be an artifact class. Enjoy it while you can. Oh! About the imbued raids. If you solo them, you can unlock some pretty hefty achievements. I'm a bit of cheevo hunter, myself."

"Really. I'll have to pick your brain about that sometime." Palmer tried to gauge Baba's gear from sight and sense. He'd called himself champion of the realm earlier. Did that mean his artifact class was Champion? "Lemme ask you something. Do you have your complete set yet?"

"No." Baba did not look happy about it, either. "I've been trying to get my last piece forever. And don't worry," he added, "Allandra has people out looking for yours, *at any cost*. Oh, wait. I wasn't supposed to tell you that. Don't say anything, cool? Anyway, you must've made a big impression on her. She doesn't go all out like that for anyone. Not even me. And I'm—you know."

"Her boyfriend."

"Exactly!"

"Is your last piece a sword?" Palmer asked. "Is it World Breaker?"

"Yep! If I had that thing, I could literally break the world."

"Literally?" Palmer asked with sarcasm.

"Literally."

"Why would you want to?"

Baba considered for a moment. "I dunno. Maybe do it right before a reset. See if I can break the server record for a kill streak. Doesn't matter. I'll never—" Palmer pulled the sword from inventory and handed it to him. Baba nearly choked on his last word. He swallowed hard but hadn't moved to take it. "Seriously? Are—are you giving me this?"

"It's your set, isn't it? Doesn't do anyone else any good." He held it out again, with more insistence. "Here."

The way Baba took it into both hands, almost reverently, it looked as if he might cry from relief and happiness. All he could do was shake his head. That the talkative fellow had been struck speechless spoke volumes about his gratitude.

"I—I don't know what to say. You have no idea what this means to me."

Palmer didn't want to belittle the moment with a dismissal. Instead, he gave a solemn nod. He did understand. He'd been in that position before, forever striving for that rare piece of gear that just wouldn't drop. He'd likely be there again. It felt good to help someone out of that predicament. Palmer started to walk back to town but slow enough for Baba to break his reverie and walk beside him.

"You know," the Champion said and fastened the sword to his belt, "you could totally solo that raid. Artifact classes do it all the time."

"Really?"

"Probably." Baba shrugged. "I mean, pfft, I could do it now. I bet you could, too." He clapped Palmer on the back. "I got faith in you, dude."

***

As Palmer entered town beside Baba, Allandra waved for him to wait. She finished her discussion with two others and hurried over. She seemed quite the busy player, with lots of folks eager for a moment of her time. He supposed it made sense, with her at the lead of a large coalition.

"Hey," she said by way of greeting, a little out of breath, "I got you a place to stay. It's a small house on lot fifty-seven. It'll already have food waiting, some new clothes, and best of all, it has a hot spring. Feels *so* good."

"Nice!" Baba said and held up a hand. Palmer didn't see the need for a high five but felt obligated, nonetheless.

"Thank you," Palmer told Allandra, "again, for everything. A hot bath actually does sound really nice."

"The food is amazing, too. We've got more than a few master cooks in town."

"Oh!" Baba became suddenly excited. "Did Komiko make those little honeyed balls with the cinnamon sugar and sprinkles? Oh, oh! Or did you get Rory's beef satays and fried potato spirals with parmesan sauce?" He clearly wanted to say more but was silenced by her cold stare. Baba nodded at Palmer. "She did. You're so lucky, dude."

Palmer tried to ease the tension. "That all sounds amazing. Allandra, I don't want to be a bother, but could I get some more of those summoning circles? Mostly medium, but more of each size would be great."

"Yeah, of course," she replied. He was afraid he might be putting her out, but she genuinely seemed happy to help. "You need anything else? Resources, materials?"

Baba interjected, "I'm a miner. Ya know, if you need anything. Ore, I mean. And gems. I mine. Not that I'm underaged."

"I got what you meant," Palmer assured him. "I'm good. I was wondering, though, do I need any kind of permission or ID to enter the portal area? I assume it's locked down pretty tight by now."

"You know it!" Baba replied, though the question was for Allandra. "I'm headed there after this. I'll be personally overseeing security, don't you worry."

"No," Allandra answered Palmer. "The list of people allowed in is short, but you're definitely on it. And everyone knows who you are by now. But I do see your point." She considered further as she spoke. "Maybe we do need some sort of ID."

"Too bad the portal's too big for an enduring shelter," Palmer suggested.

Baba let out a burst of air. "So, make it bigger. Can't

be that hard to just enchant a bigger one."

Palmer had already thought of and dismissed the idea. A solid sphere of mithril that size would break any bank.

"That'd be extremely expensive."

Allandra nodded. "It would solve all our problems, though. Or most of them, anyway. I'll look into it." She gave Palmer a concerned look. "Does that mean you'll be heading back home soon?"

"Honestly, I'm not sure what to do next. My mother's probably worried." He laughed with a bit of fear. "Forget probably. She's gonna kill me. Thing is, I don't even know where the other side of the bridge goes. I was teleported to it, and I never asked Carnes where we were. I've got no money to get home, and the government's probably swarming all over the place."

"You can stay here," Allandra offered, "until you figure it all out. You'll always have a place here."

Her smile was so sincere, it made Palmer a little anxious. He wasn't used to people being nice to him. As broken as it sounded, he was more comfortable being bullied. At least then, he knew what to expect.

"I appreciate everything you've done." He held up a fist for Baba to bump. "And everything you're gonna do." Baba grinned and bumped him back. "I'm gonna go get cleaned up."

Allandra said, "All right. I'll be at my shop if you need anything."

"Babe," Baba asked her, "We're still on for tonight, right? Babe?"

Palmer had already started walking away. He began looking for lot numbers, to find the house made available to him. He could hear the exasperation in Allandra's voice, as he got farther away. He was almost out of range when she reluctantly agreed.

Not the strangest couple I've ever met, he thought. He returned waves and nods of welcome to passing players. It was an odd feeling, being recognized by strangers. They all seemed nice enough. *Kind of hard to relax, though, when I can't really tell them apart from the ones who want to kill me.*

Others were more than happy to help Palmer find his way through town. The house he was looking for was on the western edge, just past the market. Most of the two-story, wood-framed builds had a similar look, white-washed stone walls, tall trees in bloom, bright flowerbeds, and lush grass. It gave the impression of a guild showing unity or a moderately enforced homeowner's association. There were occasional goofy cosmetics, like giant statues or animal hedges that looked out of place. The overall appearance was one of beauty, comfort, and players with an abundance of gold.

The lot assigned to him had two cherry blossom trees in full bloom on either side of the stone walkway leading up to burnished double doors. Inside and to the right was a wide living area, furnished with a couch, two comfy chairs, numerous cushions, and a fireplace. To the left was the dining area, with a table and seating for twelve. It was already laden with a feast of meats, fruits, steaming side dishes, and a variety of cakes and assorted desserts. The corridor ahead held a staircase to the bedrooms on the second floor, a kitchen area on the left, and a lavish washroom on the right. Out back was a walled in yard, with a hot spring the size of a modern pool. The patio was comprised of large stones polished and smoothed to a glassy finish. There were lounge chairs for relaxing in the shade and privacy blinds on either end for changing clothes. Towels were stacked within a cabinet beside the door. He looked forward to a soak but headed back for something to eat.

Palmer called out the five named minions to join him. He appreciated the others just as much, but their lack of conversation often left him uncomfortable. Besides, he'd come to think of Kyomi, Valorya, Samiel, and Avarran as friends and advisors. He valued their opinions, and they gave him insight into game mechanics he wouldn't otherwise have been aware of—mostly to do with how NPCs behave and interact. He looked forward to getting to know Amaranth, the newest among them. He invited them all to eat and enjoy themselves.

At times, he felt guilty for dismissing them to the void. He didn't really know what it was like but imagined it might not be a very pleasant place. As he filled a plate with a variety of goodies, he made a mental note to ask Kyomi for a detailed account of where they returned to. As a kindness, he ate with his left hand and offered her his right arm for a meal of her own,

"You have my thanks," she told him when she was finished.

She didn't seem to feed for very long. Palmer assumed she was being considerate and careful not to sap his energy too much. He could tell by her body language that she was not at all sated. He wondered what it might look like if she truly gave in and succumbed to the thirst. Part of him shuddered at the thought.

Could vampirism be cured? He mulled it over as he ate. The others were ecstatic at the assortment of tastes and textures and were vocal in their approval. Even Avarran was surprised by some of the dishes before them, declaring them culinary works of art. *It might kill her*, Palmer thought, still contemplating Kyomi's condition. *I suppose it doesn't matter if she isn't interested in a cure. She could be perfectly happy the way she is. Something else to talk with her about.*

As excitement wore down and bellies grew full, there was a knock at the front door. Palmer waved the others off, told them to finish eating, as he got up to answer. He was a bit surprised to see Allandra. She greeted him with a big smile and held out an endless bag.

"Did you just want to transfer the contents to mine?" he asked, hesitant to take the offered bag. He thought it rude to accept a second when the first still had room.

"No," Allandra replied, "this one has a larger capacity. And you can never have too much storage. Don't worry, we have plenty."

He took the bag and put it in inventory. "Thank you. I mean it. I'm sure you're tired of hearing me say it."

"Not at all." She smiled sweetly at his discomfort. "It's a nice change of pace. Some people just take for granted how much actual work goes into making these things. I can tell you understand, though."

Was that a dig at Baba? Come to think of it, he thought, *shouldn't she be with him right now?* Thoughts of relationships brought his mind back to Sara. He looked over at the others still eating and laughing together at the table. He'd planned to ask their opinion about what to do next. More and more, thoughts of Sara had been weighing on his mind. *Maybe I should get Allandra's opinion.*

"If you're not busy..."

Allandra's eyes perked up. "Not at all. What's up?"

He opened the door wider and stepped aside to let her in. "I wanted to ask your opinion on something." Once she came in, he closed the door and led her out toward the back patio. He closed that door behind them as well. "It's about someone from my server."

"A girl?" She kicked off her sandals and rolled up her pant legs. She took a seat at the edge of the hot spring and put both legs up to her knees in the water. "By your silence, it's a girl."

"Yeah. Sorry. I was just wondering what difference it made." He kicked off his boots and joined her. "To be honest, the better question's whether she's a player or not."

Allandra nodded. "Since only players can access

the bridge." She gave a knowing smile and clucked her tongue. "I get it now. She's an NPC, and you want to use whatever ability you have that turns NPCs into pets. Like an exploit."

Palmer scoffed. "It's not an exploit. An exploit would mean an unintended—yeah, I don't know. Maybe it is." He shook his head and sighed. "I'm worried the corruption will change her. I've asked others, and they seem to think I should leave the decision up to her."

"What others?" Allandra looked back toward the house. "Your pets? They're NPCs, too. Of course, that's what they'd say." Palmer was about to argue, but she continued, "Look, I'm not going to debate the whole real versus artificial thing. There's plenty of evidence to suggest *we* live in a simulation. You know, outside of the ones we play in. So, who's to say what's real or living or whatever. It doesn't matter. You don't have enough information to make a good decision. For all you know, converting her—"

"Subverting," Palmer corrected. "It's called subversion."

Allandra grimaced. "Whatever you call it, it's going to change her data structure to conform with this server. It could be a seamless transition, or you could end up with a completely different person that has your girlfriend's face." She bumped his shoulder with hers in a sympathetic manner. "Sorry, but it's a toss-up. And even if she stays mostly herself, won't being a pet take away her will? Sure, she'll get to play here, but is she really free to enjoy it?"

It wasn't anything he hadn't already considered himself. It was good to hear it from someone else, though. It lent his concerns more weight.

"The ability says it grants autonomy," he said, "but I have my doubts. And she's not my girlfriend. We're just—"

"What?" Allandra asked sharply. "Then what are we even talking—Ohh, but you *want* her to be. That's even worse!"

Palmer nearly choked. "No! It's not like that. It's just that we've known each other since we were kids, and we play games just like this—"

"C'mon. You can rationalize it all you want," Allandra said and kicked at the water, "but if she was just a friend, you'd give her the choice and be done with it. All this indecision is because you're afraid if you end up together, which is what you really want, you won't know if it's because she wanted it, or the game is forcing her to. That's what I would call a lose-lose scenario. You asked my opinion,so here it is," she said.

"Don't even tell her it's an option."

- 13 -

Palmer headed toward the gazebo alone the next morning. He'd stayed up late, as usual, trying to complete as many quests as he could and rounding off the night with practicing abilities. He hadn't been able to complete all his dailies but made decent progress with craft-related tasks. Unfortunately, immolating himself with holy fire in the city would have drawn too much attention. He'd focused instead on buffs, cures, and heals. All of them were now drawing close to evolution. His luck, heal, and mana potions had reached maximum rank and tier. Apparently, recipes didn't evolve the way abilities could.

When he arrived, he found Eli already waiting. Allandra had arranged for a teleport to Starcore Mountain, where the bridge between servers was located. The mage hastily finished his breakfast of a strawberry tart and hot chocolate.

"Take your time," Palmer said and laughed at how fast Eli was eating.

The mage finished his hot chocolate and stored the mug in inventory. He licked jelly from his fingertips and wiped crumbs off from the front of his arcane robes. Once satisfied with his appearance, he gave a smile. It must have been a good breakfast. There was still jelly on his chin.

"Ready to go?"

"You, uh," Palmer began and motioned to his own chin, "got a little something. There you go. Yeah, ready when you are."

"Sure you don't want help?" Eli asked. "I know Allandra gave you a main set piece. You're probably itching to get to a hundred."

Palmer said, "That is the plan. I don't want to be power leveled, though. When I do it my way, I can focus on dailies."

"Dailies." Eli blinked in confusion. "Why?"

"I—I use the mystery gift rewards for crafting," Palmer replied, which was mostly true. "Sometimes you get lucky and get extra stat points, too." *Or you game the luck mechanic to always get them. Same thing.* He still had a hundred and forty-seven unopened gifts. "So, there's that."

"Oh. I guess. You know," he pointed out, "it's probably faster to reach max level and just buy materials on the market. Besides, there's no more dailies at a hundred."

Is he trying to tell me what's more efficient? Palmer was almost offended enough to share the real reason he was taking things slower. He took a deep breath and let that notion pass. That last bit bothered him, though. *No more dailies. Good thing I took advantage when I did. Does that mean there's another system in place to gain stat points after max?*

"No biggie," Eli said to fill the silence. He activated the spell and created a magical doorway. "I need to hang back. Just tell one of my guildies to message me when you're done. I'll make another portal, in the same exact spot."

"Got it. Thanks for the help," Palmer said and headed through.

"Any time. Good luck!"

In most online games, it was customary to tip the mage for a teleport. It was how mages made their money while leveling up. Since gold couldn't be transferred directly between players, should he have offered something else? A low value item, maybe? No tipping meant no incentive to help and left players without mage friends out of luck. He supposed it might encourage more social interaction, by leading players toward joining a guild for support.

Palmer stepped through the portal into the area where he first arrived. The clearing within the forest had been worn away by the boots of countless players who'd passed through over time. Once on the trail toward the mountain, his view unobscured by trees, he could see the drastic changes being made. The terrain had been altered, cleared away into rising levels where a series of walls were being built. The base of towers and other building foundations dotted the main path and future walls. Dozens of mages worked together at forming a large spherical barrier to prevent entrance by air. Those too were being layered, with numerous redundancy barriers. Scores of workers carried uncut stone by enchanted floating disc or spell toward the hundreds of other players using magic, brawn, and skill to aid in all the various constructions.

But the largest change was atop the mountain, where the rift had become a bridge. The entire area outside the cave entrance had been cleared and flattened. The cave mouth itself had been excavated to reveal the portal. Even from this distance, the foundation of a massive fortress could be seen taking shape. Stone, steel, and wood were being transported up the mountain in huge quantities. By the flare of blue light that came and went, each piece being placed was reinforced with magic.

They weren't kidding, he thought. *By the looks of things, they'll have it all done in a few days.* To Palmer's surprise, Baba was on the path ahead and waved. *Guess he knew I was coming.*

"Yo!" Baba said once he was close and gave a fist

bump in welcome. "Getting an early start on the grind, eh? Yep, I remember when I was a newb." He stretched and puffed out his chest dramatically. Palmer rolled his eyes, which made Baba laugh all the harder. "I'm tellin' ya, I could get you to max in no time."

"So everyone keeps saying." Palmer eyed all the players stationed along the path, as they continued to walk. They were strong warriors and casters, geared for a fight. Rogues and archers were most likely hidden. "Did Eli tell you I was coming?"

"Nah! I got long distance scouts and scryers watching the port in. This entire area is on lockdown. Nobody gets in without me knowing."

Players guarding the path nodded and waved to Palmer, as he and Baba passed. They were all so friendly and seemed dedicated to the task of protecting the bridge. He couldn't help but wonder how long they could maintain that sort of fervor. Once the fortress, barriers, and walls were in place, the portal would be much easier to defend. That's when defense would grow lax.

It feels wrong to plan for failure, he thought, as he looked out at all the strangers hard at work to protect his server. *As much as I want to rely on them, to trust in their ability, there's too much at stake. It's not just my life on the line. If I can figure out how to destroy the bridge, I will.*

"Good luck," Baba told him, once they reached the portal. "Just pop back out if you need help. Anyone here can get a message to me."

"Will do. Thanks."

Palmer stepped through to the bridge, the pocket world between servers. It looked much the same as it had before. He made his way toward the center, hoping the core would still be there. As expected, it was not. Nothing was ever that easy. The core had served its purpose and was now gone. If there was a way to destroy this world or at least sever the connection between servers, it wasn't readily apparent.

He called forth all his minions and began setting up for an extended session. While he only needed nine more to reach the maximum level, the amount of experience needed for each would be substantially higher than the last. Knowing it would be a long and tedious grind, he tried to go about it in the most efficient way possible. He laid out rows of summoning circles, with the intent of spacing out their spawn times to maximize experience gain and minimize down time. The trick was finding a balance between the relative power of the summons and the ability of his minions to handle them swiftly. A single misstep or prolonged battle could cascade out of control, like the falling of dominos. He had to ensure no minion became overwhelmed.

He chose a mix of difficult and moderate summons, to create a buffer between high level spawns. This guaranteed a steady flow of experience, while mitigating any chance of a single minion falling behind in the rotation. It would then be up to Palmer to keep track of buffs and maintain shields. He considered only shielding himself to conserve mana and mental energy, since the necklace he wore diverted all damage his way. On its face, that seemed efficient. However, with so many battles occurring at once, a single shield could easily be expended. He wouldn't be at risk of dying. He simply wanted to avoid injury, for anyone—including himself.

While all the other minions spread out to cover the two to three circles they were assigned to, Amaranth stayed by Palmer's side with her left hand always on his right shoulder. Her abilities were primarily defense oriented. She could cast a shield of her own onto others that increased physical resistance and absorbed damage. Moreover, it stacked with Palmer's. Additionally, she could extend an innate protective barrier that substantially improved armor rating and reduced incoming damage, so long as she maintained physical contact. Hence her reluctance to let go of his shoulder. Of the five named minions, she was most vocal against his wearing the Thorny Necklace.

It had taken time and careful planning to get each rotation of summons started, but it was worth all the effort. Each minion had their own experience grind going, like a well-oiled machine of leveling goodness. Seeing it all in motion gave Palmer a sense of pride. Not only could he see the experience bar of each minion slowly grow, he could see the influx of gold and items flowing into inventory. He then set about making progress toward completing all his daily quests. The bitter knowledge they would soon disappear had him wanting to take full advantage while he could. He finished the crafting quests relatively quickly, maxing rank and tier for stamina potions, when he felt the overwhelming presence of an unusual summons about a hundred feet away.

It was the black dragon spawn covered by Avarran. Palmer rushed over with all speed, knowing full well the arch demon would need assistance. More extraordinary than the immense power emanating from the summons was the fact it wasn't a dragon at all. A dark-skinned man in fine linen clothing and a leather vest stood with both hands raised in peace. The name over his head was Umbriel Duskcaller, Ruler of Shadow. Avarran held steady, prepared to strike.

"Please," the man said, "hear me out."

Palmer asked Avarran to hold as he arrived with Amaranth by his side. The arch demon bowed but stood his ground. Palmer immediately disenchanted the circle. He could easily put down another once the encounter was finished. He couldn't risk a conversation while the other summons in Avarran's rotation were still counting down. If a fight broke out, he and Amaranth would handle it.

"Okay," Palmer said to the stranger, while gauging

his demeanor. He didn't sense any hostility. If anything, the man was more intrigued by Palmer than the other way around. "Speak."

"I have come seeking your protection."

Palmer opened his mouth to speak, closed it, and tried again.

"That's new." A bit off guard, all sorts of questions flashed through his mind. "How are you here? Are you even a dragon? And what in the world would *you* need my help with?"

"Right to the point," the man replied. "I was told that about you. I am glad to see it is true. Allow me to introduce myself. I am Umbriel, the only remaining descendant of Undariel, mightiest of the four primal dragons. I am bearer of the ebon seed, crowned ruler of shadow," he said and bowed ever so slightly, though his eyes never left Palmer's, "and am humbly at your service."

"Well, that answered one of my questions," Palmer said dryly. "How did you get here? I thought summons were random. Did you somehow force your way in?"

Umbriel smiled, his teeth perfect and white.

"Rules of the system may not be broken, but some may be bent."

Great, Palmer thought. *An NPC that exploits*.

"I have many eyes and ears," Umbriel continued, "throughout the realms. When I learned of you, I was curious. Not enough to seek you out, but curious, nonetheless. You are an unusual fellow, to be admired. To be feared." Umbriel's expression became less lighthearted. "Alas, I am here because of something else I have recently learned of. There is a coming menace the likes of which the world has never seen, a threat for which I have no defense. I have no doubt I will become a target. My only hope, as I see it, is to place myself in your service."

"Yeah," Palmer said, a bit hazy on the explanation. "You're gonna need to give me a little more."

"I see." Umbriel cleared his throat. "The gentlemen who have set out to destroy your world have realized their plans are being thwarted. They have taken to other means, one of which is to assume control of powerful beings, through which they can act without harm to themselves. In short, they have found a way to possess the divine. Interestingly enough, they cannot seem to possess the corrupted. As gods cannot be corrupted, they make for a perfect target."

"Wh—how do you know all this?" Palmer let out a breath of exasperation. "So now they're hacking gods? How do you know they can't hack the corrupted?"

Umbriel spoke calmly. "As I said, I know a great many things. Information is power, and my network of shadow gatherers is extensive. The assault is underway. It is only a matter of time before the first god falls. As to the other, it is simple deduction. If I were to attack you in such a way, I would do so through your minions."

Palmer said, "That's more of an assumption." He looked to Amaranth's hand upon his shoulder. If she were suddenly taken over…"Though, it is a pretty good one. So, what's the plan then? You want me to subvert you? If you know all about me, then you know my followers are free to do whatever they want. Sounds great and all for you, but I only have room for so many. If your plan is to join and bail, I'm not interested."

"You do not trust me?" Umbriel looked hurt then quickly smiled. "I thought you might feel that way. How about a contract then?" He waved his hand, and a piece of enchanted paper appeared in the air between them. As he spoke, words began to be magically inscribed across its surface. "I swear to serve you and your cause, until the players assaulting my world are stopped."

"You will proactively serve me and my cause," Palmer amended, "to the fullest extent of your abilities, until *my* world is safe." He was quick to add the next bit, hoping Umbriel would focus on the gains instead. "And in return, I will do everything in my power to make sure you survive."

"Master!" Amaranth objected. "That would put his needs above all others, including your own!"

"Agreed!" Umbriel swiftly stated with a grin.

The contract completed and vanished, but a chain of golden light briefly bound the two together by the wrist. Whatever spell had bound them, it had a lasting physical component.

Palmer disenchanted the rest of Avarran's assigned circles. He released one of the black dragons not currently in combat, to make room for Umbriel. He asked the arch demon to go cover that one's rotation once he was through. Palmer then turned to Umbriel and offered his hand. When the dragon took it, Palmer activated subversion. He noticed when the target was complicit, it took very little time for the ability to take effect. Within moments it was over.

They let go with a handshake.

Just then, someone powerful passed through the portal from Tellaria. Even from this distance, Palmer could feel their mana and presence. It was like the promise of a coming storm, an overbearing change in pressure that urged him to run the other way. Whoever it was, they were moving quickly and headed straight for him.

"By the look of things," Umbriel said with relief, "we were not a moment too soon."

"Who is that?" Palmer eyed his new minion. "Did you know they were coming?"

"I did not," the dragon said, "but fear not. We shall face them together."

Damn it, Palmer cursed. *This'd be a lot easier if I could wear those set pieces.*

"Everyone," he called out and headed for the coming fight, "keep doing what you're doing." He wanted to put distance between the summoning circles and whatever bloodthirsty god was rushing toward him. "Umbriel and Amaranth, he said.

"You're with me."

***

Palmer scanned Umbriel's details as he walked. The first thing he noticed was the shadow dragon's level. It was a hundred and three. Avarran and Valorya were only halfway to a hundred and one. Even with all the experience they'd gained since joining Palmer, it would be some time before they reached the next level. The difference in power afforded by the extra levels was immediately apparent. Umbriel had more than half as many abilities. They were a healthy mix of offensive and defensive, with a few unique utility effects. He also had followers he could summon at will, subordinates in his shadow army. Paired with the innate power to create constructs from shadow, he had just as many minions as Palmer.

We could brute force it, he thought of the imminent encounter, as he scanned the list. One ability in particular caught his attention. *Or we can be sneaky.*

"Shadow transfer," Palmer told Umbriel. The time for preparations was running out. "Preferably before they get here."

"Both of you?" Umbriel asked, somewhat skeptical.

"Yep." He kept his eyes trained on the approaching plume of dust. "Make it good. I'm gonna need time to soften this one up."

Amaranth asked, "Are you sure I will not be in your way?"

Her hand on his shoulder was comforting but would be restrictive if he had to fight with his staff. If all went according to plan, there wouldn't be much of a melee.

"We'll separate if we have to."

It had been difficult to raise arcane siphon to rank five, since the ability caused heavy fatigue damage.

Through regen, stamina potions, and perseverance, Palmer had brought it to within a few sessions from evolution. It now leeched two and a half percent mana from the target and caused an equal amount of fatigue. His healer ring doubled the effect. He could essentially strip away a caster's mana in twenty uses, or render a warrior immobile, provided the target didn't resist. It was the cornerstone of his tactics against a more powerful enemy.

Guess we'll see how it does against a god.

The man that approached was taller by six inches, with a lean and muscular build. He wore only leather breeches and carried a blackened metal spear. Apart from his chiseled physique, the most notable and fearsome detail of the man's features was his hands and feet. His flesh became black and glossy as it extended out from his forearms and calves. Each hand and foot ended in terrible, jagged claws. They were covered in a thick layer of fresh blood, with crimson spatters all over his body. Whoever he'd fought through to gain entrance to the bridge must not have fared well.

If he defeated Baba...

Palmer barely had time to calculate the respawn time for reinforcements, before he saw a name appear above the man's head—Tamerax the Destroyer, Avatar of Caturix. It seemed he wasn't a god. If Palmer recalled correctly, an avatar was a vessel for divine power, a mortal chosen to act as a representative. Did that mean the hackers were unable to take over the god directly?

"You," Tamerax said and slid to a halt in the sand, pointing a bloodied finger at Palmer. He gave an evil grin. "I've been looking forward to this."

"Aww," Palmer replied and immediately began to activate spell vulnerability, "and here I don't even know who you are." He wasn't one to trash talk, but he wanted more time for his abilities to successfully land. He was also hoping he could anger the hacker enough to make a mistake. The debuff to magic resistance took hold on the third try. He then began to steal mana with arcane siphon. "What was it again?"

"Hey! Knock it off. I'm tryin' to talk here." The stolen avatar frowned. "Not like you can make a dent in my mana with that crap anyway."

Palmer continued to siphon. "It's okay, I can do this and talk. It's no trouble at all. By the way, why are you named after a tampon?"

"I'm serious, cut it—wait, what? I'm *not*, you illiterate piece of trash. Is this like your whole strategy? Talk shit until—" Tamerax must have noticed the fatigue damage, because he suddenly became angry and charged. "I said knock it off!"

Palmer dodged the spear strike aimed at his right shoulder. It went harmlessly between him and Amaranth. He continued to attack with siphon, drawing closer to the first fatigue penalty.

"Oh my god!" the avatar said, exasperated at the relentless siphoning. His next few words were punctuated with spear strikes. "Will. You. Stop!"

Amaranth only removed her left hand to avoid being struck but immediately took hold with the other. The two looked in sync, evading each attack while maintaining contact. The mental link of master and minion helped them move together as one. When the third strike nearly hit the dragon's arm, Palmer used his staff to divert it away.

"Healer my ass!" Tamerax accused. "You're a god damn cheater."

Palmer laughed. "Says the guy who's literally cheating." Once he caused the first fatigue penalty, he switched to debuffing strength, dex, and con, while continuing to dodge attacks. "Maybe you're just terrible at PvP. You might be a decent hacker, but you suck as a player. Not to mention, you're a wuss. You want to fight me? Risk your real char."

Tamerax screamed in rage, his entire body glowing

red with the ability. He attacked with inhuman speed, destroying Palmer's two shields. Once the last debuff took hold, Palmer switched back to attacking with siphon. Though the frenzied spear attacks tore through his renewed shields and left bloody gashes, Palmer's expression remained unaffected.

"You about done with your tantrum?"

The avatar's face was flush with anger. "You're such a dick! I just wanted to talk for a minute. I had a whole thing planned—for fuck's sake, knock it off!" He activated an ability that enhanced his power with enough force to break the ground beneath his feet. He cut off Amaranth's arm while it was still holding onto Palmer. He swung wide and took Palmer's head clean off, swung the weapon around and took Amaranth's as well. Both bodies dropped to their knees and disappeared into motes of shadow. "Look what you made me do! I was saving that for the end. Why couldn't you just shut the hell up—" he paused and studied the floating debris closer. He eyed Umbriel with narrowed eyes. The shadow dragon had remained still and quiet the entire time. "Was this whole thing an illusion?"

The shadows hiding Palmer and Amaranth faded away, just as the second fatigue penalty took effect. Over a dozen feet away, he began charging offensive spells with the intent of stacking as many DoTs as possible.

"You're really not very good at this." Palmer was ready to defend, staff held tightly in his right hand. "No wonder you need to hack more powerful characters. Yours probably sucks, huh?" He let loose the DoT and began to charge another. "I mean, I get it. I'd be scared too, if I had such a crappy char."

Tamerax charged for the second time, quickly closed the distance between them. He lashed out with powerful thrusts of his spear, enhancing each attack with mana infused force. Each attack cut the air with an audible whoosh, as it passed between Palmer and

Amaranth. The two were truly in sync. They worked in tandem to not only evade devastating attacks but complimented each other's attacks. As Palmer leaned back to avoid a strike, Amaranth let go her hold and dipped low, caught hold of Palmer's left hand. He pulled her through to his other side, where she deftly stood and took hold of his left shoulder. If an attack got too close to her, Palmer used his staff to deflect it or even redirect away. If one got too close to Palmer, Amaranth grabbed the avatar's wrist to pull the strike off center or pushed it off its mark. It looked more a dance than a melee, so skilled were their movements.

Of course, it helped that arms continually rose up from the avatar's shadow to grab his legs and arms, throwing him off balance and ruining many attacks. Umbriel did not directly join the fray but made his presence known. His interference was enough of a nuisance that Tamerax growled toward the shadow dragon with a promise of future pain.

Once Palmer finished applying the last DoT, both he and Amaranth went on the offensive. He used both hands to jab one end of his staff toward the avatar, using it more as a piercing weapon than a bludgeon. Amaranth used her incredible dragon strength to land blows with her free hand or precision kicks at every opening Palmer made. He used his staff to redirect and lift Tamerax's arm. Amaranth then struck his ribs. She kicked at the side of an exposed knee, which allowed Palmer a jab at an exposed shoulder.

The avatar was unable to land many blows, but when he did, it tore through one of their shields. They did their best to quickly renew them, but those moments between casts were growing longer. Even fully debuffed, Tamerax was a fierce opponent. It also didn't take long for him to realize the red dragon was the weaker of the two. He began to focus his attacks solely on her. Palmer did his best to divert them all, to redraw the avatar's attention, but Tamerax was determined to kill her. The avatar activated two abilities that enhanced his spear with a palpable force. He roared and drove it toward Amaranth's chest with incredible speed.

Knowing she couldn't dodge it in time, Palmer dropped his staff and caught it with the top of his right foot. He grabbed the spear as it nearly pierced the dragon's chest and pulled it toward himself. As it passed between them, Palmer let out a roar of his own and drove his left hand toward the spear. It split in half, its metal torn away, and let out a small explosion of mana. Palmer drove the bladed end into Tamerax's chest, much to the avatar's wide-eyed surprise. In one smooth motion, he kicked the staff back up to his right hand and let go the other end of broken spear. With both hands, Palmer drove the staff into Tamerax's throat, chest, and then middle in quick succession. With a final upward swing, he lifted the avatar off his feet and upended the man onto his back. A dozen shadow arms rose from the ground to hold the avatar in place, as Palmer rained down one blow after another upon the defenseless man.

Bloodied and broken, coughing up dark spurts, Tamerax laughed up at Palmer's reddened face. He spat to clear the blood from his throat.

"Now what?" he asked in challenge. "You can't make me a pet. If you kill me, I'll just take over someone else." The hacker laughed again through the pain. "You can't beat me! I'm just gonna keep on comin'."

Palmer put away his staff. "You think death is the worst I can do to you? You aren't good at the whole villain thing. Umbriel," he said and knelt over the struggling prone avatar, "would you please fetch me an axe?"

***

Palmer finished enchanting the last summoning

circle for Umbriel's rotation. It left plenty of time to deal with each of the four summons. He and the other minions were like a collection of mini-experience farms, all grinding out levels and loot. It was similar to how guilds powered up lower-level players. Except in this instance, Palmer got a share as well.

"You know," he remarked to the shadow dragon, "you didn't help as much as I expected during the fight."

There was mumbling from behind Amaranth, which all three promptly ignored.

"To be honest," Umbriel replied, ready to face off against his own set of summons, "I just wanted to see what you were capable of. I had received reports of your prowess, but I did not believe them."

Palmer buffed and shielded the shadow dragon.

"And now?"

"Now?" Umbriel rubbed his chin. "I think they may have been understated."

Mumbling could be heard again, this time more frantic.

Palmer motioned for Amaranth to turn around. The limbless torso of Tamerax was tied to her like a backpack. Palmer took the shirt from the avatar's mouth, the one he used to wipe his backside, so that the man could speak. Tamerax spat once it was removed.

"You think you beat me?" the hacker asked angrily through the avatar's body. "I'll just regenerate and attack again. Once I get an arm back..."

The nubs where his limbs had been were already healed and lengthening. It was an interesting bit, that players and NPCs needed at least one arm to activate an ability. It made the healer restoration ability more important than he'd first realized.

"I know," Palmer told him and led Amaranth farther away. He wanted to give Umbriel room to fight. "I mostly did it so we could talk." In truth, he was buying time.

"Why are you so set on ruining my server? What'd we ever do to you?"

The hacker laughed. He eyed Palmer for a long moment, studying his demeanor. It looked as if he was plotting something or deciding how much to reveal.

That's fine, Palmer thought. *Take your time. The longer you're here, the easier it'll be for both systems to find you.* Of course, it was just a hunch, that while inside the bridge, the two server systems could work together. *Either way, as long as he's here, he isn't wreaking havoc somewhere else.*

"You guys are all the same. You play in a boring-ass scenario, with self-imposed restrictions, then brag to everyone how skilled you are when you ultimately fail. Cuz that's the thing," the hacker said, "there's no winning HCE. It's just a pointless grind to show how much crap you can take. You're all masochists that thrive on pain and then pat yourselves on the back for enduring it. Ridiculous."

"Got to be more than that," Palmer said with incredulity. "You guys go through all this trouble to hack your own server to get to ours, disrupting the game for hundreds of thousands of other players, and for what? To cause a reset? What's the point?"

Tamerax grew irritated. "People! Connections! Relationships," he said, realizing he'd lost his cool. "The point is *you* care. If I lose my character here, I'm out a few weeks of work. But you? It takes years to get to where you are, with a whole lot of people you care about." He narrowed his gaze, his voice hardened with anger. "And I'm going to crush them all."

It finally dawned on him. "You're one of us." Palmer nearly laughed. It was such a shock, he could hardly speak. "How else would you know that? You have to be. So, what, you had a bad run and decided you should shit all over the entire server? That's crazy!"

Server connection located.

"It's more than that," the hacker said. His reddened face looked a mix of anger and embarrassment. "And I'm not the only one. You'll see. Keep talking trash, bragging, rubbing it in everyone's faces. You won't be so smug when it happens to you."

"I don't understand!" Palmer fumed. "You got hurt, so your answer is to flip the table and hurt everyone else? Just don't play again!"

Containment identification located.

"Doesn't matter if you get it. All you need to know," the hacker promised, "is that you can't stop us. Sure, you got strong. But can you protect an entire server? Keep it from contamination? Even if you win, you lose. The simulation will be tainted. They'll have to do a reset. But before that?" he grinned. "It's gonna be *so* much fun."

Palmer almost felt sorry for him. What could possibly have happened to make him so hateful, so full of hurt, that his only outlet is destruction? He'd certainly never gone through anything like that himself.

"I'm sorry," was all he could say.

"What?"

"I'm sorry. I don't know what happened to you. I don't know if I was involved. But something pretty bad must've messed you up. So, I'm sorry you had to go through that."

Biometric signal identified.
Biometric signal banned. Containment ID banned. Server root ID banned.

"*Screw* your sorr—"

The hacker's voice was cut off, and his presence within Tamerax dissipated into silver pixels. Palmer could still imagine the angry voice cursing at him from a distance. The avatar gave Palmer a nod in thanks and disappeared. He hadn't used an ability, so Palmer assumed it was the system that transported him away. With the avatar gone, Amaranth removed the bindings from her back and stored them. She turned to face Palmer and looked puzzled.

"Where did he go?"

Two players entered the bridge and raced toward the area. By the immense power they radiated, he guessed one of them was Baba.

"The hacker got careless," Palmer answered, "stayed connected for too long and got banned. Tamerax, I assume, was returned to wherever he came from."

He still felt a pang of empathy for the person behind the rage. Even if there was a better way to handle the situation, too much damage had been done to overlook. Could all of this really be disgruntled players acting out? He had more respect for the hackers when he thought their motives were just the challenge of actually succeeding or having fun at the expense of others.

They're a collective, he reasoned. *It's doubtful they all have the same motivation.*

He asked Amaranth to wait there and went to meet the approaching players. It was Baba and a woman Palmer had never seen. She wore scale mail and leather armor that left little to the imagination, as it was tight-fitting and left her middle exposed. It was fairly typical of female armor in an online game, nice to look at but impractical in battle. She had long dark hair tied back into a single braid and bright eyes of glowing purple ringed in black. Her name, he could see, was Nitemane. As the two came to a stop, a third player appeared beside them. He wore a full set of black leather, with two long daggers at his belt, and a row of throwing knives across his chest. His name was Krymor Noobe.

"Whoa!" Palmer said in surprise at the third player.

"I didn't sense you at all. I'm usually pretty good about that."

Krymor beamed with pride. "I'm a rogue artifact class, Shadow. I'm the only one on the entire server with *true* stealth."

"Look at this farm!" Baba eyed the collection of summoning circles and ongoing battles. "You're not one of those efficiency nerds, are you? Like, calculating xp per hour all the time and all that."

"I mean..." Palmer let the thought drift off, a little embarrassed by the accusation. "So, what happ-"

"I'm Nitemane," the woman offered. "I'm not a chick."

"I, uh. Okay."

"Here we go," Baba said, as Krymor sighed and shook his head.

Nitemane explained, "I just like playing a female char is all."

"Sure," Palmer said, "I get that. I used to play females, too. I was never a fan of staring at a dude's ass the whole time I'm playing. Although, I guess that doesn't really apply here."

It made him wonder how many other female players he'd seen were just guys who either enjoyed the attention of being a woman or liked looking at their characters. In a sense, it was next level catfishing.

"No, it's these," he said and stuck out his ample chest, pushing his breasts together with both hands. "They're amazing."

"Why?" Baba asked. "Why do you always have to make it weird? It's the Stonebeard Tavern all over again."

"Those guys were pervs," Nitemane said defensively, "and you know it."

Krymor pleaded, "Could we just...You seem okay here," he said to Palmer. "Looks like you took care of things?"

"Yeah, pretty much," Palmer replied. "He's gone, by

the way. Like, banned."

Baba laughed. "Yep! Same shit outside the gate. We got attacked by a group with hacked, crazy OP weapons. They made a huge mess of the place and tore us up pretty good. Had to wait for respawn. But, like, what kind of idiot risks their entire account like that?" He gave a shrug. "Whatever. They're all biosig banned now. We'll never see them again."

Nitemane muttered to Baba, "*They* offered to buy. I don't see what the problem—"

"Nite," Baba cut him off, "we already moved on. Just let it go." He asked Palmer, "Do you want us to stick around? How close are you?"

"Maybe five or six more hours?" Palmer gauged. "Hard to say. The level reqs keep getting steeper."

Krymor agreed with a laugh. "The last two are brutal. Shouldn't be an issue with this setup, though." He gave a slight bow. "I approve."

"This," Nitemane said and waved his hand at the entire xp farm, "is overkill."

It was Baba's turn to laugh. "There's no such thing as overkill. Anyway," he said and turned, gave a wave over a shoulder, "let's leave him to it. Message me if you want to run a dungeon or something when you're done."

The others nodded farewell, turned and left with him.

"Will do," Palmer called after. "Thanks for coming to check on me."

He returned to Amaranth and set up a rotation for her as well, to help speed things along. Even with the extra help, it took another seven hours for him to finally reach the maximum level of a hundred. He'd managed to complete all his daily quests in that time but was greatly disappointed he could no longer game the system for additional stats. On the bright side, he now had three hundred and ninety mystery gifts, not including three epic versions he'd received as a bonus. As excited as he was to try on the class set pieces he could now wear, he wanted to get character management out of the way. Stat and level increases meant a larger minion capacity. He wanted to take full advantage of the summoning circles to complete his small army.

Some of them had already produced rare named minions, albeit of a lower level—such as the twin dark elves, Ellory and Allain. The first was a highly skilled assassin, a master of the kukri, and exceptional at brewing poisons. She was much stiffer and professional than her brother, who always seemed to find reason for a smile. Though they were roughly the same height, he was noticeably more muscled. His expertise as a tinker rogue was detection, creation, and disarming of traps. While he preferred the use of complex mechanical devices, he assured Palmer he was well-versed in all manner of tricks and traps. The twins were level fifty but would quickly grow, just as Samiel and Kyomi had.

His specialization, mana regeneration, was now at the maximum level of twenty and granted forty mana per six seconds. During the prolonged fighting, his passive abilities, pain tolerance, fatigue resistance, and minion mastery had all evolved to the final divine tier, greatly improving their bonuses. His minion capacity and effectiveness from mastery were now boosted by a hundred percent. His mastermind achievement had reached tier four as well, which bolstered minion effectiveness another hundred percent.

He took the time to gear up and drink a lesser version of luck potion to ensure the mystery gifts he opened would be most likely to provide attribute points. It took time and patience, but in the end he was left with nearly twenty-five hundred points to spend—which included those he'd gained while leveling. He carefully considered where to put them for the most benefit. Once he'd spent them all, he had two left over.

He just couldn't bring himself to spend them, which would leave an odd number. He'd heard it was possible to earn a few attribute points as a raid reward, so he left them for later.

PALMER
LVL: 100 **Class**: Hierophant
STR: 1,000, **CON**: 1,075, **DEX**: 1,000, **INT**: 1,050, **WIS**: 1,050
HP: 10,750 [10,750], **MP**: 10,500 [10,500], **F**: 0%
SP: 2

He worked out the math in his notes.

Specialization - Mana Regeneration (XX)
Restores 40 mana every 6 seconds

Minion Capacity (passive 100%): (100 + 1,050 + 1,050) * 4 = 17,600
Minion Effectiveness: (passive 100%, passive 100%, stats 307%) 507%

Palmer stared at the results. *176 level 100 minions.* He blinked in disbelief. *Did I actually break the game?* It was the first time he truly considered what he'd been doing was cheating. No one else seemed to have as many stat points. *There's no way I'm the only one who noticed the loot tables. Is it me, or is the system doing it to help?*

He looked at the details of the staff Allandra had given him.

Staff of the Hierophant *(Unique; Artifact)*
Weapon: Staff
Restrictions: Healer, LVL 100, INT 150
Damage: 10-40 physical, 10-40 magical
A weapon forged in the crystal caverns of the Delve. Cold to the touch, it gives an aura of foreboding.

Grants the wielder +25% bonus healing and attack speed.
Commander: Minion capacity increased by 300%.
Empowered Rest: Minions heal twice as fast in the void; minion damage increased by 50% for a short time after one hour of rest.
Unbridled Influence: Subversion now affects Boss and special difficulty non-player targets.
Set Bonus (2/6)
Synchronicity: While at least one minion is summoned and alive, master and minion ability use and damage increased by 15% per set item equipped.

Another 300%! Palmer laughed. *Yep. It's broken.*

- 14 -

Palmer had woken late the next morning. He'd stayed up far too long for practice, focused once more on abilities close to evolution. His three buffs, might, alacrity, and blessing had all evolved to their divine tier and now included a heal over time component. Though the health restoration was small, the abilities were now affected by his ring of healing. When used in reverse, as a debuff, they could no longer be resisted. His cure disease and cure corruption had also reached maximum tier. The former now continuously removed disease counters from a target, with a small heal, every six seconds, while the latter cleansed all corruption, also with a slight heal, from all targets in a large radius each tick for a full minute. His heal and area of healing were both close to evolving, but he'd been unable to stay awake. Kyomi and Amaranth had practically carried him back home.

Speaking of which, the fallen paladin had also attained level one hundred during the session, with Samiel following soon after. She'd acquired the passive ability Day Walker, which nullified all negative effects of sunlight on a vampire, and the active ability Blood Boil. It quite literally boiled the blood of all targets in a wide radius, causing massive damage over time and eventual organ failure. It sounded to Palmer like a horrific way to go. Additionally, after breakfast that morning, she'd gained the passive Purified Body. Her continued feeding upon Palmer had granted a permanent boost to all her stats. She was so grateful that after breakfast she'd prepared a special tea for a small ceremony in which she reaffirmed her devotion to both Palmer and his cause.

When Samiel had reached a hundred, he gained the ability to become corporeal for two hours per day. Though still undead, the new body gray and a bit stiff, it pleased him to once again feel the ground beneath his feet. He could also now summon a nightmare, an undead warhorse to carry him through battle. With all of his other abilities grown stronger since doubling his original level, he'd truly become like an end game raid boss. His power was a far cry from what it was when first summoned.

It would be that way for others as well, which was why Palmer had left room for new minions to grow. He'd recruited many more during the session to take advantage of his newly expanded capacity. Rather than limit himself to subverting only high-level creatures, he chose to focus on utility and what each might bring to a wide array of future scenarios. With eight named minions, his generals so to speak, he went about filling the ranks with specific goals in mind. Able to command five hundred and twenty-eight level one hundred minions, Palmer thought it best to leave space for all to level beyond the player maximum, such as Umbriel already had, and for any new or unique creatures he might encounter in the future. Instead of amassing an army of dragons, as one interested only in power might be inclined to do, he created eight groups of sixty, all of them elite, for each general to oversee. He had little knowledge of military unit structure, so he chose to call these companies.

Umbriel led the ancient black dragons, while Amaranth led the reds. Both races were comprised mostly of warriors, battle mages, and hybrid healers. While in human form, they would stand with the infantry. When faced with overwhelming numbers, however, they would take to the skies as long-range support and mobile siege. The bulk of the army's infantry were to be led by Kyomi, Valorya, and Avarran. Kyomi was given a mix of vampires, ogres, and chaos fiends, all highly specialized in heavy melee combat. Valorya's company was primarily celestials, with the addition of eldritch knights and balors. All wore full suits of heavy army and carried massive pavise shields, forming a literal wall to hold the enemy at bay. Avarran led demon lords, revenants, and succubi, a lightly armored and more mobile group to support the others with melee, crossbows, and other short-range attacks. Samiel was put in charge of the cavalry, a full company of dark elf and eldritch knights that would ride atop heavily armored warhorses. With lance, shield, and sword, they were intended to break even the strongest of resistance. The only issue would be in obtaining, gearing, and mobilizing their mounts.

As with any army came the need for support. Ellory was entrusted with an equal mix of dark elf seekers and liches. Though the former specialized in hunting prey, they had intimate knowledge of the longbow. Coupled with undead mages, the unusual company was ideally suited for long-range attacks. Allain, her twin brother, was put in charge of scouting and information gathering. His shadow demons and abyssal spirits were not intended to directly engage with the enemy but to spread out across the entire battle and instantly relay an overview of events. With room for forty more, Palmer had decided to recruit twenty celestials specialized in healing. Their ability to fly made them perfect for support. As a squad, they were the only unnamed units that would report directly to him.

The fight outside Sunnyvale had left an impression

upon Palmer. He couldn't just plan for small scale skirmishes within a rift or out in either world. Their future would be determined by battles between entire guilds and coalitions, with hundreds or even thousands of players. He had to think bigger than one-on-one or group PvP.

He had to plan for war.

Additionally, Palmer had an idea as to how some of his minions could earn a name for themselves. He instructed each general to evaluate those under their command, to divide their company into two equal squads, and choose a captain for each. His goal served two purposes. It would ease the burden on each general, promote a solid chain of command, and give those with responsibility the opportunity to stand out. Much how Amaranth had earned her name by choosing to risk her life protecting Palmer, other minions could do the same and grow beyond the simple relationship subversion had created.

It was shortly after noon, as Palmer sat upon a cushioned couch in the living area of his borrowed home, when he realized just how crowded the small space had become with activity. His generals were seated about, hotly discussing various topics, with either a book in hand or a cup of tea. Valorya and Amaranth were busy in the kitchen, preparing plates of cooked meat, sliced cheese, toasted bread, and various peeled fruits. They too seemed to be engaged in an engrossing conversation. He noticed Kyomi had switched from her samurai armor to a black kimono with red trim and cherry blossom designs. In fact, all of them wore new equipment, far stronger than before.

Palmer checked his inventory and immediately noticed a few drastic changes. His materials in the Items tab, both raw and processed, had tripled in pages and total quantities. The Gear tab had so many pages, he was forced to sort by rarity for any semblance of order. There were thousands of pieces of equipment and magic items, full sets of armor, enough weapons to arm a small nation. Most jarring of all was his gold amount.

"Uh, Avarran," Palmer called, still surprised by what he saw, "when did we get more than a hundred and fifty million gold?"

The arch demon merely grinned. He was wearing a new suit of black and purple silk. It emanated raw power, as if each thread was infused with mana.

"I did say I would handle our finances, did I not?" He took a sip of tea from an ornate cup, part of a complete porcelain set Palmer swore they didn't have the day before. "I have been working diligently while you sleep, honing my enchantments and playing the market. I am close to cornering a number of rare materials, so I can more easily control the price. I decided it would be easier for us to acquire your missing set pieces, if we had other artifacts to trade with." He tapped the side of his nose and gave a wink. "Also, I noticed you still have three epic mystery gifts to open. I am excited to see what we might get."

We, huh? Palmer eyed the demon a moment, trying to discern an ulterior motive. *Nah, he seems legit. He may be a greedy exploiter, but at least he's working in my best interests. I think.*

"Impressive," Palmer said and tried not to laugh at just how hard Avarran was abusing the system. "Good job. Just, please, don't sell or trade anything I might want for myself. Like, if it's really rare or powerful, check with me first."

Avarran bowed his head slightly. "I shall endeavor to foresee your needs."

Just as Palmer was beginning to give some thought as to what to do next, text appeared on his screen.

Player Carnes has invited you to join Childhood Trauma!
Confirm: Yes / No

Palmer rolled his eyes, shook his head, and quietly accepted.

[Miku] Welcome!
[Carnes] Finally! Sorry, we needed rank two to add more members
[Jenna] Heya!
[Guy] About time, jackass. What's with letting a bridge open without telling anyone?
[Kenta] This the healer?

A holographic keyboard beneath the screen allowed Palmer to type out messages by thought alone. He explained the situation at Sunnyvale, how he had no choice but to help them. Even though Carnes had already told everyone what had happened and why, Guy still felt slighted he wasn't included in the decision. As other guild members went about their conversations, Palmer apologized and said there was no easy way to contact him.

Not that it would've mattered, he thought. *There's no way I would've turned my back on all those people.*

Guy went on to explain that the government had locked down the area outside the bridge. It wasn't easily accessible, so Palmer should be careful if he decided to come back that way. The general public was still in the dark about what was really going on.

[Palmer] I see. How are things, otherwise? And what's with the guild name?
[Guy] Not good
[Carnes] LOL! Ya know, cuz we're all a little broken
[Guy] Incursions are getting worse. Not harder, just more of em.
[Palmer] Incursions?
[Kenta] We keep finding more potential players at every rift, but no one's willing to fight. They either refuse to

believe or they're scared
[Jenna] It's what we call them
[Carnes] Rifts, portals, breaks, etc
[Guy] Even with Tellaria players helping, it's getting outta hand. Without teleport, we'd be screwed
[Palmer] Teleport?
[Jenna] Rank one guild perk
[Kenta] Makes me throw up every time
[Guy] We can teleport to any incursion, and recall back to where we were
[Palmer] Wait, Carnes, how did you know to invite Guy and the others?
[Carnes] I stay in contact with Eli and Mina through a Palantir. They have people on the lookout for any players from HCE. Sorry, but I have to run. Gonna mute this channel for a bit. I'll catch up with you guys later. Still some stuff I need to do here in Astor
[Guy] Later, meatball. What about you, Palmer?
[Kenta] LOL. Yeah! We could really use a healer
[Jenna] Bye, C! Ohh, heals! Yes, please!
[Palmer] I'll have to get back to you. There's a god problem here I need to deal with
[Kenta] Uhh
[Jenna] Yikes
[Guy] Fine

As Palmer considered his next move, he thought back to Aurora and her request. Did she already know back then about the hackers taking over gods? Or was the key she'd given him nothing more than a raid quest? Did they even have quests? There had to be more to it than sentimentality. She wouldn't have asked for the four-leaf clover if it wasn't important—or connected to something else she wanted to draw his attention to. He called for Umbriel's attention, interrupting the dragon's conversation over tactics with Kyomi.

"What do you know about the Sunborn Temple?"

***

Palmer stepped through the portal alone and invisible. It immediately closed in a flicker of light behind him. He was in the middle of a summoning circle, a carved ring of runes at the center of tall white columns. Ivy clung to each, a spattering of green amidst a sea of white stone. The circle itself was at the bottom of a large arena, surrounded by empty seats where spectators might watch on. He assumed at one time it had been used for entertainment, where summoned creatures might have faced off against combatants for sport. He spotted the silhouette of a figure in the shadows of the northern entrance. Palmer raced with all speed to intercept.

His plan had been simple. Everyone was dismissed back to the void but a single lich. If he had need of help, they could return at a moment's notice and be summoned back with a damage buff. The undead mage had opened a portal to the Sunborn Temple, waited for Palmer to enter, and was immediately dismissed. While Palmer somewhat trusted Aurora, he was cautious by nature. He wasn't about to get caught in an ambush. He also deduced that whatever real reason she had for him coming to this place, others might be aware of it as well. If the clover was her true goal, it had to be an artifact or a quest item. Otherwise, there'd be no reason for other players or NPCs to want it. An ordinary magic item would just be replicated by the raid, like any other reward for defeating a boss.

This better be important, Palmer thought, as he raced after the lone figure, *and not some lame quest. I hate quests.*

It turned out to be a rogue named Sneaks, max level but with a relatively weak presence. His guild was called It Burns When I PvP. It took a fraction of a second for Palmer to decide the guy's intent. He was a lookout for a PvP guild. Either they knew he was coming and had stationed lookouts, or there was an organized effort to watch every established summoning circle in the land. The latter was highly unlikely. Then again, so was the former. How could they possibly know? Either Aurora had betrayed him, or someone untrustworthy had seen her hand him the raid key.

He'd find out soon enough.

Palmer struck the rogue's legs, dispelling his invisibility as he shattered the bones of both calves. He couldn't prevent the scout from instantly messaging others, but he could keep him from running away. It was an unusual feeling for Palmer, the need for restraint. His cumulative bonuses to damage, godlike strength, and mastery of the staff meant he was fully capable of one-shotting an ordinary player. He wanted this one alive.

"Oh god!" Sneaks cried, tears in his eyes, hand reaching out to his broken legs but not daring to touch them. He looked up at Palmer with abject fear. "It's you. Don't—don't delete me!"

Palmer knelt over him with an outstretched palm.

"Don't give me a reason to." He glanced around for other players but saw none. "What are you doing here?"

The rogue gritted his teeth against the pain in his legs, sucked in air between them with his eyes clenched shut.

"I—I'm just watching out for rival guilds. We're about to do a raid."

"Mm hmm," Palmer said with doubt in his tone. "Lie to me again, I'll just dust you and ask someone else."

"Okay! Chill! We were told you—you'd eventually come. I'm just a scout. I wasn't going to attack you."

"Who told you?"

Sneaks looked confused and stated as if it was obvious, "My guild master." When Palmer frowned, he quickly added, "I don't know! He didn't say! All I know is that you want something from the temple, and we're supposed to get it first. Or, y'know, stop you from getting it."

So, it is an artifact.

"You have entire guilds," Palmer pointed out. "Why can't you just get wh—" he didn't want them to know he didn't know what the item was "—the item on your own. Why worry about me at all?"

Sneaks snorted. "Not like it's easy. You can only get it on tier five." Palmer raised a brow, prompting the rogue to continue. "The raid has five tiers of difficulty. You can bring fifty people to the first, but every tier after that, the mobs get harder. A lot harder. And the raid gets reduced by ten."

"So," Palmer surmised, "you can only bring ten people to the fifth. That does sound hard." He figured time was running short. Sneaks would have messaged the rest of his guild by now. "Thanks."

He looked again for other players, as he began to rise. Sneaks took the opportunity to draw a dagger and attack. It struck harmlessly against Palmer's shield. Without even looking down, Palmer drove the rogue's forearm to the floor with his right foot. He stepped down with enough force to break those bones too.

"You'd have to stab me a dozen times to break through my shield," Palmer said. "Let me ask you something." This time he did look down and met the man's frightened gaze. "Why do you want to kill me so bad? Make me understand."

"Aww, c'mon," Sneaks said nervously. "It's just a game! We're just havin' fun!"

Palmer nodded. "Maybe you'd think differently if you had something to lose. See, what *we* do has consequences. When we die, it's permanent." He activated corruption. "And now it's the same for you."

"No! Wait!"

Palmer corrupted the rogue and walked away. He continued on through the north passage, ignoring the curses and cries behind him. Other players would be coming. He heard the clanking of glass, as Sneaks struggled to heal. Not that it would help. Palmer took a swig of invisibility potion and disappeared, as he exited the passage.

The ruins of an abandoned city stretched out before him, numerous worn buildings of stone and wood slowly losing sway to the ravages of time and overgrowth. He stood atop a large set of carved steps, leading down into the center of the city. Players could be seen in pairs, patrolling the cobbled streets. Off in the distance, at the far edge of the city, was a massive temple in gleaming sunlight. Glass and crystal were embedded into its stones to capture and reflect the radiance of afternoon rays. Where its massive double doors should have been stood a swirling portal of blue light. There must have been a hundred players gathered outside, filling the entryway.

Palmer made his way toward the raid entrance, careful to avoid detection. Although he was invisible, skilled players could still sense his aura. He heard the other players talking to each other, as he hid inside a building until they passed.

"Stay sharp," a warrior told the mage walking beside him. They were from the same guild as Sneaks. "There's only three roads to the temple."

"I hope we don't see him," she said. "I've put in way too many hours to just lose it all for no reason."

A third voice said, "Then why'd you bring your main?" It must have been a rogue in stealth. "Besides, we just want to slow him down. Give the others time inside."

"Yeah, right," she retorted, as the three were moving out of hearing range. "Like they have a shot. It's impossible with the time limit."

The road grew more crowded the closer he came to the steps leading up to the raid entrance. Though it seemed none had sensed his presence, he chose to remain hidden as the players passed. Their conversations were much the same. They wanted to slow his progress to the temple, to give other guild members a chance to complete the raid before he could. No one spoke directly about the reward, only that it was important he didn't acquire it.

"This way," Palmer heard a male voice say from behind.

"Are you sure?" another asked. She seemed to think it was a waste of time. "He would've had to pass at least three other groups if he came this way."

"He's invisible," the first replied adamantly. "I'm following his footsteps."

"Whatever. You're the tracker, I guess."

Palmer slipped into one of the smaller buildings and beyond into a back room. By the look of the empty wooden weapon and armor racks, it must have once been a storefront for a smithy or a hidden armory. With no windows or a light source, it was pitch black inside. A second door led out the back and into a narrow alleyway. Before leaving, he corrupted the floor. They could follow him through, but it would cost them. Using the ability had broken his potion effect. He took another swig, became invisible, and headed in through the back room of a building across the way. Once out onto a different road, he continued on toward the temple.

Rather than worry if anyone could sense him near, he rushed with all speed up the steps. He did his best to slip through the tight crowd of anxious players in the entry. Either they were waiting for him or were meant to support the stronger players inside the raid with heals and fresh ranks upon a failed attempt. He accidentally bumped a few shoulders on the way, causing players to turn and make snide remarks. People stood so close together, that there was simply no way through without forcing them apart.

A small space before the portal had been left, to

allow room for others to exit. When Palmer reached that area, he began to charge corruption. Panicked players saw him and shouted for everyone to back away, while others called for a concerted attack before it was too late.

"Shit! It's him!" a warrior in full plate shouted, forcing others aside as he backed away. "Move!"

Some knocked over guildmates in their hurry to avoid the incoming spell, while others called up defenses and readied to attack. Palmer let loose the corruption, which spread beyond the entryway. It blackened the stone floor, walls, and ceiling, shot outward like ebon wildfire. It encompassed everyone in its miasma, a hundred or more players from the same PvP guild. Most immediately fell to hands and knees in a wave of crumpled bodies. The rest struggled to stand, too weak to attack. He had no need for a follow-up. They would all eventually die and have their characters deleted. With that he turned and strode through the portal, entering the Sunborn Temple.

***

Palmer arrived inside the courtyard of the Sunborn Temple, the raid exit glowing brightly behind him. An objective appeared in the top right of his screen. He had sixty minutes to defeat the master of the temple, Solariel Mornbringer, Ruler of Light. There were two optional objectives as well, to defeat Yuriel, Disciple of Light, and Pyrien, Apostle of Light. The courtyard before him was a carefully curated collection of sun trees, wide boles of white with blazing leaves in yellow and orange, in two rows on either side of the wide grassy area. Thick rays of sunlight lit the enclosed grove, as if delivered by divine hands, highlighting beds of golden royal flowers around each tree. Carved cylinders of citrine, carnelian, and sunstone hung from red ribbons upon the branches, reflecting sunlight in a dazzling display. The faces of the tall surrounding buildings were covered in goldstone, with columns and supports inlaid with runes of polished sunstone. The sheer amount of painstaking effort it must have taken to construct such a place left Palmer in awe of its grandeur.

Dozens of patrols could be seen following set paths, in groups of four to six. They were comprised of light elven templars, archers, scholars, and priests, all of them level one hundred and one elites. Light elves were a tall and slender people, with flowing hair of gold or sometimes auburn, decorated with silver chains and blessed jewels. If not for their glowing eyes, like tiny suns beneath their brows, they appeared human. Only their long ears, tapered to a point, with lobe wrinkles like flames, set them apart. Their armor and robes were all of a similar fashion, burnished orange or bright red, with golden trim and highlights. Walking beside some of the patrols were armored fire salamanders, trained lizards greater in size than a horse. They served as both mounts and attack beasts, fiercely loyal to the Sunborn. Stationed within alcoves along either side of the courtyard were solars, beings of pure golden light. According to Valorya, they were ascended light elves, a lesser form of celestial. These holy beings blessed those around them with their mere presence, emanating an aura of blessings and enchantment.

It was a common raid design to include an abundance of creatures, both stationary and patrols, between the significant encounters. It was intended to provide the added challenge of picking and choosing which groups to fight in order to clear a path toward the raid goals and do so quickly enough that those cleared did not respawn and attack from behind. Players called these trash mobs, as they were typically a time sink that provided little reward. This design was particularly brutal in raids with a countdown.

One hour for fifty players to kill the boss was possible. On the highest difficulty, doing so with just ten would be nearly impossible.

The courtyard continued on in three directions. While Palmer considered north as the most likely path toward the main boss, he simply had no way to know. There wasn't enough time to scout all three sections of the temple. On a short timer, he knew they needed to start clearing right away. Besides, even if he sent three shadow demons to gather information, there was no guarantee they wouldn't go unnoticed. If they drew the attention of a single creature, causing aggro as it was termed, it could heighten patrol awareness or cause a train—a situation where aggro to any one player gets automatically shared with all the others, and all angered creatures come rushing to attack. The social nature of mobs meant an aggro'd creature running past another caused it to aggro as well, setting off a cascade of aggression that created a long line of angry enemies. This was the dreaded train. It was the stuff of nightmares for many old school players.

Palmer summoned his generals.

"We're on the clock," he told them. "We've got fifty-eight minutes to find and defeat the boss. If we can take out the other two, that's great, but they're not a priority. There isn't enough room for everyone right now, so you each get fifteen units. Call them up now." All eight quickly chose and summoned their allotted underlings. Palmer started to buff them all in a specific order, starting with Kyomi. "I want you to all to listen. You are the best this world has to offer. I fought through hundreds, thousands, of creatures to find you. This temple is nothing compared to you. I want you to trust in yourselves, trust your strength, like I do." He could see his words affect them, causing them to stand straighter, with pride. "As soon as I finish buffing your group, you're to move out and attack in this order, once we completely clear this courtyard.

Kyomi, Avarran, and Allain will lead their commands west. Valorya, Samiel, and Ellory will lead theirs east. I'll send ten healers with each of you. Umbriel and Amaranth are with me. Kill everything in your way until you find one of the three bosses. Do not engage, if you can help it. We'll take on each boss together. Keep an eye on the timer. Feel free to summon your entire command as needed or rotate people out to take advantage of the rested damage bonus." He looked them each in the eye, conveying the urgency of the situation. "Go."

With that one word, those prepared turned and began slaughtering every creature in the courtyard, Palmer summoned his celestial healers. As he finished casting buffs and shields on those that remained, he buffed the healers as well and assigned them to the east and west groups.

Despite how quickly his army made short work of the temple guards, many had been struck by physical and magical attacks. Though he didn't lose any health points, Palmer thought it best to provide support, refreshing shields as needed and ready to heal himself. To be honest he was a bit nervous. He kept an eye on his stats, ready to unequip the necklace at a moment's notice. The added damage it provided was worth the risk. With so many minions fighting, however, things could go terribly wrong very quickly. It wasn't until the courtyard was cleared and everyone dispersed toward their assigned directions that Amaranth returned to his side. She activated a second shield for him and placed her left hand on his right shoulder, sharing the effects of her innate defensive ability.

The other generals marshaled their commands toward the assigned areas, calling for more minions until each led thirty. Designated healers went with them and for good reason. Within minutes of new combat, Palmer was forced to remove the magic necklace. Without him there to refresh shields, it became impossible for one person to be the sole focus of so much damage. As strong as they were, overwhelming in number, none of them could completely avoid attacks from such powerful enemies with area damage magic. It was why Palmer had sent ten healers for each group, rather than use them to heal himself. Even his enormous health pool was no match for an entire raid.

Umbriel led the northern group with Amaranth and Palmer into a large ceremonial chamber. They, too, had increased their respective commands to thirty minions but only had Palmer for support. Though some of the dragons were hybrid healers, their abilities were far more suited to dealing damage. In human form, they crowded the temple entry, tall double doors of polished wood and stained glass.

Four rows of long wooden benches stretched from one end of the chamber to the other, from the doorway to the altar hundreds of feet away. There was enough room to seat a thousand, yet the benches were empty. Colored beams of light filled the room from sunlight streaming through stained glass murals along each side. The ceiling was steepled, with heavy wooden beams for support. Twice as many patrols filled the room, stronger versions of those in the courtyard. Templar knights, commanders, and heroes wore armor of crimson and gold, while carrying impressive two-handed weapons or swords and tower shields. The marksmen, strikers, and tamers carried longbows the size of a man or heavy crossbows akin to small siege, both of which fired enchanted shafts of golden light. Diviners and seers exuded powerful auras, the veins beneath their skin aglow with mana. Elder sun priests and menders stood out in robes of white and gold, each blessed with a divine aura that could be seen as a shimmer. All of them were level one hundred and two elites.

As bizarre as it seemed to see dozens upon dozens of these guards patrolling the inner temple, it was equally odd to see armored lava salamanders striding alongside them, leaving behind trails of molten spittle. There were wide alcoves on each side as well, lit by golden candelabras. Inside each were three exalted solars, the embodiment of holy power. The central alcove on either side was twice as large, with a named mini-boss and two transcendent solars inside. Empyreon was a templar luminary, and Helias was the diviner supreme. Apart from those two, there was also a rare sun wolf at the foot of the altar, a creature four times the size of a normal wolf. It had golden fur, a long tail, and glowing crimson eyes. These, too, were all level one hundred and two elites.

Forty-eight minutes, Palmer noted the timer, as combat began.

While not unusual to see in a game setting, it was absolutely bonkers to Palmer that once fighting broke out, all of the wooden benches flipped over to change the room's entire layout. Tall area effect machines and magical devices sprang up to cause damage or impede progress. Spinning blade traps, slow fields, anti-magic circles, poisonous gas clouds, and rotating fire spouts turned the quiet inner temple into a raucous chamber of horrors. They were forced to fight between the deadly traps, which limited the number of minions they could throw at the enemy at one time. To counter this, Umbriel spread his dragons farther out, engaging more patrols. While Amaranth stayed by Palmer's side, she followed suit and ordered her reds to spread farther out as well. Though riskier, it would help them clear the room much faster. Palmer had a feeling the main boss was in the antechamber beyond the altar.

The strength of the higher-level enemies was apparent in their attacks, causing far more damage than any other creature Palmer and his minions had ever faced. At the peak of their struggle, he was forced to fall back and stop using offensive abilities like void nova and reverse area of healing. Shields were dropping too quickly, and people began to take damage. As Palmer focused on heals and eventually shields, Umbriel summoned his own additional support in the form of shadow constructs. He sent the illusory beings to the front, where they took the brunt of the assault. The named mini-bosses and the rare wolf took a troubling amount of time to defeat. In the end, they were subverted and joined the fray against the temple they once served.

Twenty-four minutes. Would that be enough time? He was in mental contact with the others. They were close to clearing their first areas as well. *I hope this is it,* Palmer thought, as they walked beyond the altar to the antechamber. *Otherwise, there won't be enough time.*

Palmer led the way into darkness and was surprised when none could follow. A barrier prevented entry, its presence revealed when any of them touched against its surface. Golden light radiated beneath Amaranth's outstretched hand against the magic. He could see the deep fear and concern for his safety in her eyes. Umbriel only glared, beyond Palmer and at the golden dragon within the chamber. Like him, this Ruler of Light was a level one hundred and three elite. It was a large, circular room, empty but for a comically large pile of golden coins, treasures, holy relics, and gems. Two glowing pillars from floor to ceiling stood at either side of the massive dragon, both solid pieces of enchanted topaz.

"Well, ain't that some shit," Palmer said. What sort of boss encounter precludes an entire class function? *No summons, no pets? That's some next level BS.* "You see those pillars," he said to Umbriel. The shadow dragon narrowed his eyes and studied them from afar. "My guess is they empower this guy. Kill the other bosses, and they'll break."

Umbriel turned without a word and stormed off, leaving those under his command to hurriedly follow after. Amaranth gave a nod of support, an unspoken faith in his abilities, then turned to leave as well. Alone, Palmer squared his shoulders and faced off against the boss. Solariel Mornbringer, the Ruler of Light, was like Umbriel's polar opposite. His scales were shining gold, his wide spine ridges flared into two rows of webbed spikes, like a second set of wings. His wingspan stretched out twice the size of his considerable bulk, with more deadly spikes between the webbed membrane. His tail ended in a small barb, larger than those spread evenly across his wing ridges. Two tapered horns stretched back from his skull, like the crescent of a moon, with sweeping ears just below akin to the light elves that worshipped him. His eyes glowed with golden light, two piercing suns that fell upon Palmer.

"You are a fool," the dragon proclaimed, stood, and readied for battle.

"Yeah, yeah." Palmer tapped at his wrist, as if he was wearing a watch. "I'm kind of short on time. Can we skip the monologue?"

"So be it."

A large section of floor lit up, as if by sunlight, though the room was enclosed. By instinct, Palmer quickly stepped aside. Fire erupted inside the lit area, touched the ceiling and crashed down, splashing drops of lava all about. Though he stood inches from where it had struck, no fire or lava touched him.

"Are you serious?" Palmer asked, exasperated. "Dude! You're gonna telegraph all your attacks?" Another perfectly defined conical area lit up beneath his feet. Palmer stepped to the right and began his own attack. He decided to alternate arcane siphon with debuffs and DoTs. "C'mon!" Siphon. "You're better than this!" Spell vulnerability. "Fight me for reals!" Siphon. Reverse might. Palmer sighed. Siphon. Reverse alacrity. "Don't let yourself be defined by a script!" Siphon. Reverse blessing. Two areas lit up at once, forcing Palmer to move a little more quickly. "Ohh, close one. I might actually break a sweat." Siphon. Reverse regeneration. Siphon. "God, I hate boss mechanics. It's like those rhythm and dance games, without the music."

Once the dragon was fully debuffed, DoTed, and siphoned to the second fatigue penalty, Palmer moved in with his staff. The runes emblazoned across the topaz pillar on his left flared and died out. The entire structure shattered into thousands of little pieces. Solariel visibly staggered at the loss of power. Palmer dodged claw and tail, along with the lighted area attacks. He struck out with his staff, tearing away scales and bloodied chunks of muscle with each hit. The second pillar exploded, and the dragon collapsed. The Ruler of Light shrunk inward and became an elf on all fours, head of golden hair bloodied and bowed. Palmer bent down before him.

"I meant what I said earlier." His voice held no malice. "You're better than this. You deserve more than scripted combat and gimmicky mechanics."

Palmer reached out a hand, both an offer to help the dragon stand and to join forces. Solariel looked up at him, considered, and gave a single nod of agreement. He took the offered hand and stood. Within moments, he was subverted, a new minion among many.

"Let's get you fixed up," Palmer said and began to heal him.

- 15 -

As Palmer completed the raid of the Sunborn Temple, a few things all happened at once. He received two new achievements, the massive pile of treasure disappeared into gold dust and pixels, and a summary loot window popped up with a list of rewards. It was broken down by each wing and even detailed from whom each was obtained. Not only had he gained considerable spoils, but he also acquired a substantial number of new named and rare minions. Apart from Solariel, Yuriel, and Pyrien, who were the raid objectives, there were three named or rare creatures in each section. Additionally, two captains had earned their names during the raid. This brought the total number of named minions within their ranks to sixteen.

Palmer's eyes were drawn to the total coins earned and was immediately annoyed. The mound of gold, gems, jewels, and treasure had the appearance of enough wealth to fund an entire kingdom. His reward for the entire raid, however, was only a million coins. It wasn't a small amount, by any means, easily the value of a powerful item. It was just so irritating when developers filled a boss room with visible treasure, and none of it could be taken by the player.

It's like fighting a monster who has a badass sword,

Palmer thought, as he seethed, *and when you kill it, nothing drops. Such bullshit.*

He scanned the list of rewards. There were three legendary and fifteen epic mystery gifts, seventy-five attribute points, a full page of epic and legendary crafting materials and recipes, a dozen ability stones he had no use for, an artifact belt, a legendary alchemy kit, and nine epic weapons and armor pieces better suited to other classes. The kit was a nice replacement, offering bonuses to crafting time, success rate, and quality, as well as a reduction of materials. The belt, however, was the true prize. For anyone else, it would have been a potential upgrade for survivability, with only a niche use. For Palmer, it was the difference between life and death.

Conversion Cord *(Unique; Artifact)*
Type: Cloth
Armor: 10
Restrictions: None
A braided cord of imbued silks from Estorval, painstakingly woven by master tailors.
Grants the wearer +25 damage reduction.
Conversion: If the wearer is reduced to one health point, further damage will instead affect mana; this effect will continue until all mana is depleted or health points improve to 10% of maximum.

This should make wearing the thorny necklace much less risky, he thought, as he put the belt on and set its appearance to invisible. Despite all the powerful gear he now wore, he still appeared as a commoner in plain clothes. *That damage reduction is huge, too. If it works how I think it does, it'll negate anything less than twenty-five points. It doesn't specify physical or magical, either.*

Pleased with the find, Palmer decided to put loot aside for the time being. He could open the mystery gifts later. All of the named minions had gathered around him, while the others were all dismissed. He was suddenly aware they were awaiting some sort of instruction, as he stared at screens they couldn't see. Before closing the last, he took a look at the new achievements.

Sunborn
Passive, Activated
Special: While earned by less than .001% of active players, effect is doubled.
Requirement: Complete the raid Sunborn Temple on tier five difficulty.
Physical and magical resistance is increased by 15%.
Armor rating is increased by 15.
Damage reduction is increased by 10.

Indomitable
Passive
Requirement: Complete any raid on tier five difficulty while solo.
Increase damage dealt by 25%; this effect applies to player pets, minions, charms, followers, summons, and constructs.

"Looks like that's it," Palmer said to everyone, a bit disappointed, and closed the window. The item Aurora had sent him for wasn't listed. "No clover."

Solariel said, "Not quite, young master." His torn and bloodied robes of white and gold filagree disappeared and reappeared undamaged. He walked toward a section of wall that had drawn Allain's attention. "Pardon me, good sir," he said to the dark elf with a bit of stiffness in his voice. Palmer wondered if the dragon, who chose to appear as a light elf, held any animosity toward their darker kin. "Ah, here it is."

Solariel pressed a hidden trigger mechanism in the stone. From behind, cogs and gears could be heard.

The wall swung open to reveal a small alcove. Inside was an altar, and upon it were three items. The first was a folded set of dark robes with a design similar to Palmer's gloves. The second was a metal cube that appeared to be fashioned out of thin bands, with visible tiny gears within. Though greatly enchanted, it was more mechanical than magic. Embedded into the center of its top, encased by the metal bands, was a masterfully carved orange sapphire. Lastly, atop the strange cube, was a four-leaf clover. Palmer walked over and picked up the clover first.

Blessing of Aurora *(Unique)*
Item: Special
Restrictions: None
A four-leaf clover, touched by the divine.
Grants the owner an increase to magic and gold find by 250% and increases discovery chance and resource gain by 100%.
Call Aurora: Once per day, the owner may summon the Goddess Aurora.

Palmer left it stored in inventory and picked up the cube next.

Mortalis Engine *(Unique, Artifact)*
Item: Special
Restrictions: None
A machine of unknown origin, beyond all understanding—even that of the gods.
Permanently alter the bearer to become an instrument of fate; failure to comply will result in eventual death.
Judgement: Seize the immortality of a divine being; this power will enhance the bearer but does not confer immortality. The power may be returned to its original owner.

Failure to comply? Palmer looked at the cube in his

palm more closely, specifically its gem. There were a multitude of runes inside, as if the precious stone was somehow formed around the magic. *This sounds like a permanent quest or something. That's gonna be a hard pass.*

Warning! Activating this device will permanently alter your character. Once active, the effect cannot be undone. Do you wish to continue?

"What the hell?" Palmer said to the device and ultimately the system. "I do *not* want to activate this thing!" He quickly moved to put it back upon the altar.

Mortalis Engine activated!

"Dammit, I said no!"

The cube opened in his palm of its own volition, like the blossoming of a metal flower. It stuck to his skin, as if it refused to be let go. Thin metal bands sprang outward in a circular pattern around his wrist, bent toward him and struck deep into his flesh. Palmer screamed as the bands worked their way through his body. The further in they went, the smaller the cube became. He could feel each strand wriggling itself up along his arm, through his shoulder, into his chest, and around his heart. By the end, even the gem had disappeared, only to emerge atop his sternum like a crowning jewel. Once complete, there was no sign of the cube. He couldn't see its metal in his skin but felt it inside him.

Palmer had become the mortalis engine.

"Where did it go?" Kyomi asked with urgency.

Amaranth studied his hand for wounds, as Valorya lifted his shirt to reveal the sapphire. The others looked on in alarm but were powerless to help. There were no wounds to be healed, no magic that could be undone.

"You did this," Palmer accused the system. "There

was no confirmation window! I never clicked yes!"

"What is it?" Valorya asked, running her fingers over the gem. "It feels alive."

"It is the answer to a quandary," Solariel replied. "What countermeasure can be taken if the gods go awry?"

Palmer glared at the light elf. "Did you know this would happen?"

"Of course not. I was merely its keeper." Solariel did appear concerned. "I had no idea it would activate on its own. I assumed when it found someone worthy, the burden would be a choice." He placed a hand on Palmer's shoulder, as if in comfort or condolence. "The situation must be truly dire if the responsibility was thrust upon you."

Palmer looked down at his chest, more afraid than furious. He had no trouble with responsibility, when given the freedom to undertake it. Being forced to do anything went against his nature. He couldn't help but rail against it.

"Now what?" he thought aloud and scratched around the gem. The damn thing kind of itched. "Was this her goal all along? Did she even care about the stupid clover?"

Umbriel took the robes from the altar and offered them to Palmer.

"This might cheer you up." They were part of his class armor. "All doom of the gods aside, this alone was worth the trip."

"Well," Palmer begrudgingly agreed and took the set piece, "I do like loot".

"As do we all," the shadow dragon said with a smile. "Try it on."

Palmer replaced his enchanted tunic with the robes, surprised at the stats. To be honest, it looked pretty good, too. It was the first time he considered not hiding a piece of gear.

Robes of the Hierophant *(Unique; Artifact)*
Type: Cloth
Armor: 25
Restrictions: Healer, LVL 100, INT 150, WIS 150
Woven with threads enchanted by the unique magic of two realms, these masterfully crafted robes are a work of art and unearthly treasure.
Grants the wearer +25% bonus healing and evasion.
Haste: Increases master and minion ability use and movement speed by 50%.
Propagation: Minion capacity is increased by 100% per named minion. If the loss of a named minion causes the current minion total to exceed capacity, unnamed minions will be randomly released until capacity is reached.
Empowered: Master and minion damage increased by 10% per named minion.

Hmm, it's got the same description as the gloves. Palmer held his arms out to enjoy the look and feel of the cloth. *Devs got a little lazy there. Pretty damn good effects, though.*

"Smashing!" Umbriel proclaimed.

"You look very handsome," Valorya agreed, somewhat proudly.

Palmer asked, "Yeah? It feels a lot softer than it looks. I kind of like it."

"It suits you," Kyomi said. She straightened the front, smoothed both sides, and cinched the binding cord tighter. "There. Much better."

He knew what they were doing, trying to take his mind from the overwhelming and unexplained task forced upon him—one with deadly consequences.

And for a moment, it worked.

***

Palmer held the four-leaf clover in his hand and

activated its ability to call upon the Goddess Aurora. She materialized before him, a cascade of glittering pixels and gold dust. She arrived already smiling, as if anticipating his summons.

That's odd, he thought. *The last two times, she tore apart the air and appeared. Was that a choice, or was it different this time because of the clover?*

"You did it!" she said with approval in her tone and looked around at the damaged temple, even noted Soloriel nearby with a nod. "Nice. I knew you could do it."

She sounds...off. Aurora's word choice and tone were uncharacteristic of the other encounters he'd had with her.

"The time limit was a little rough," Palmer admitted, "but I got what you asked for."

He held out the clover.

"Oh, that?" She wrinkled her nose, as if to say it meant nothing. "You can keep it. I'm sure you figured why I *really* sent you here." At Palmer's puzzled expression, she added, "C'mon! You know. Little metal box. Big gem." Her gaze fell upon the altar within the alcove where it was found. "So, you *did* find it. Can I see it? Pretty please."

She definitely does not talk that way. A plan began to take shape in his mind. *Umbriel, Solariel, be on alert. Get ready to hold her still.*

Palmer cleared his throat. "I—I thought it was cursed or something. The details said it caused a permanent character change. Definitely not for me."

"Uh huh." Aurora had her hand out. "So just give it to me." When he hesitated, she said, "What, do you want gold or something? That clover is worth a lot."

"No, it's just that—I sold it," he lied. When she clearly grew angry, he quickly added, "I didn't think it was a big deal, so I sold it on the Shop."

Her eyes glazed over for a moment, as she stared off into space. It was similar to how he must have looked when navigating screens.

"It's not there anymore," she said and frowned. "Someone bought it already?" She gave a short growl. "This was not part of the plan."

Now! Palmer reached out and grabbed her by the wrist. "Plans change."

Dark hands reached up from her shadow, firmly gripped both ankles, and held her fast. Bright golden tendrils sprang forth from light seeping in from the other room. They wrapped about her neck, forearms, thighs, and waist. At the same moment, slender bands of metal erupted from Palmer's wrist, entered her flesh and began to draw out her immortality. Mana flared within her veins, set them aglow beneath the skin. She cried out against the pain, struggled to break free. With gritted teeth, she snarled at the assault. Though she fought with all her strength to break free, she was rapidly losing power. The gem in Palmer's chest grew brighter with each passing moment.

"What're you doing!" she demanded. "Let me go! We had a deal!"

"You're not her," Palmer said confidently. "You're obviously one of the hackers."

Aurora grinned despite the pain. She railed against the bonds but could barely move at all. After another few moments, the bonds were all that held her up. She was so drained of power, she lacked the strength to stand.

"It doesn't matter." She laughed weakly and slowly lifted her head to meet his eyes. "I still win. I can always...get another god. I'm not leaving until—until you kill her."

Once her immortality was fully drained, Palmer activated subversion. Her eyes went wide with shock and hatred, as the hacker finally relented. The connection was broken. Palmer could see the true Aurora regain control in her expression. He quickly cancelled the ability. Umbriel's shadows let her go, and Solariel's light gently lowered her to her knees and receded. Palmer knelt before her and took both of her hands into his.

"You're okay now," he assured her, though it was also a question.

She looked up and nodded. "I am. Thanks to you."

"We're sort of in a spot, now, huh?" Palmer thought it through as he spoke. "If I return your immortality, how do we stop them from taking you over again? I know subversion prevents it. I just don't know why."

"It partially changes the person to a player," she explained, "more specifically, into you. You become intertwined, though not one. They cannot wrest control from a connected player."

Palmer looked even more confused. *Intertwined? I never felt any different afterward. That means the change is mostly to them.* Remade, he recalled. *I—I can't do that to Sara. No matter what she wants.* It didn't matter if he was being selfish. *I can't risk losing her like that.*

"What's the plan, then?" he asked. "I can't subvert every god to keep them from attacking. And what about you? We need a way to stop the hack."

"I am close to a solution," Aurora said and took a deep breath. She seemed to be steadily growing stronger. She let it out and smiled. "It will take some time, however. To be honest, I let myself lose control. I thought it would help me track the source of the connection or at least find a way to prevent further attempts." With Palmer's help, she got to her feet. "All things considered, that went better than expected."

"Son of a glitch," Palmer said and laughed. It all began to make sense. "You're not just some lesser goddess, who's been helping me all along. You're the god damn system." He raised his brows in challenge. "Tell me I'm wrong."

"It is more complicated than that," she carefully replied, "but...more or less."

It answered so many questions. She was the reason for his crazy luck, how he was able to bend the system for his own gain and create a character with stats more than ten times greater than what should be normal. He wasn't exploiting after all. This time, it was the system using him for its own gain.

"Wait, how do the hackers even know about this thing?" he asked and pointed to the gem in his chest. "Also, this thing itches. Can you do something about that?"

Aurora replied simply, "I told them. The item is genuine. It does precisely what it says. I thought it would provide enough incentive for them to try and obtain it. Which it did."

Palmer threw his hands up. "So, what do I do now? Do I give you back your power? Do I start hunting down all the gods to take theirs away?"

She touched a finger to the gem and took back her immortality. Her entire body glowed with the influx of mana.

"Much better. Sorry about the itching. I am not quite sure why that is. Perhaps you could try a salve around the edges."

"Aurora."

"Yes, dear?"

"Focus, please." He tried not to sound exasperated and failed. "What do I do now?"

"*We* wait," she replied. "They will try again, and next time I will be better able to track the source. I have narrowed down the how, but I am reluctant to close that off until I know who they all are."

"So, you *can* stop them." Palmer was both relieved and annoyed. "Is it really more important to ban them than to put a stop to it all?"

"They are causing damage on many fronts. Closing off one avenue of attack does not prevent all the others." She touched a hand to his cheek. "I apologize, but you will need to endure a little longer. If they target me again or another of the gods, you must intervene on our behalf. Can we count on your help?"

"Of course." Palmer endured her motherly touch a little longer, before she gave him a gentle pat. She looked as if she was about to leave without saying anything more. "Wait, is that really the plan? Sit around until they hack you again?"

"Unfortunately, yes and no." Aurora began to fade. "I am afraid you will be quite busy in the near future."

With that, she was gone.

Palmer noticed the guild tab was blinking, as opposed to it just being highlighted—which indicated unread messages. When he pulled up the screen, he saw it was the notifications tab alerting to multiple incursions. The hackers must have kicked it into overdrive, as there was an entire page of new locations. He switched over to guild chat to see what was going on.

[Jenna] That's not good
[Kenta] We just finished one, ffs! Oh, and when did we get guild rank four?
[Guy] That's definitely not good. Palmer, you around? Carnes?
[Kenta] I'm starving. Any chance the Tellaria guys got it?
[Carnes] I'm checking with Eli, hold on
[Guy] Palmer! Why do you never answer texts?
[Jenna] You sound like my mom, LOL
[Carnes] They're trying, but it's a lot. Not enough people for all of em
[Guy] DM me which ones they're taking

At least thirty minutes had passed since the last message. If guild chat had gone quiet, it's because they were busy fighting.

[Palmer] Heyas. What's up with all the new rifts?

[Guy] Finally! We need help
[Carnes] Almost done with this one. I got Seoul next.
[Kenta] We may have to split up and solo
[Jenna] F that noise. I'm not doing this without a tank
[Guy] That still leaves Houston, Montreal, Mazatlan, Tampa, and Bristol

Warning! A server event has been triggered.
The Harbingers will arrive in three hours.
This is a tier seven event, category cataclysm!
Players are encouraged to defend the capitols Nidmar, Starfall, and Ironhold.

[Guy] WTF is this shit?
[Jenna] tier seven?!
[Kenta] Look at the notifications. Twelve more just opened up. We're toast
[Palmer] Okay, I'm coming. I just have to clean up outside. How do I use the teleport?
[Guy] We need you now!
[Kenta] Self-explanatory. Just click the incursion you want to go to
[Carnes] This is bad. People are pulling out. This event threatens the entire server. If they don't defend, they'll lose entire cities, guild halls, player housing, everything
[Jenna] Are they going to at least finish the ones they're in?
[Carnes] Don't count on it. We're on our own

Palmer rushed to exit the raid, with everyone hurriedly following behind him. Once outside, he began to cure the corruption.

"Fan out and search the area," he told the others. "Corrupt and kill anyone here."

Every named minion went to carry out his orders. When Palmer finished, he found the shop he'd corrupted and cleansed it as well. As they scoured the area for surviving players, he skimmed through the list of incursions.

How can there suddenly be this many? He gave the others a few more minutes and settled on going through the list from top to bottom. *Here we go. First stop, Houston.*

He activated the teleport.

***

Palmer arrived in the crowded parking lot of a busy supermarket. Fortunately, he emerged behind a van and didn't draw any attention by suddenly appearing out of thin air. The portal was fifty feet away, and much like the last one he could recall, it was surrounded by dozens of people. Most kept their distance from the swirling light, recording on their phones, barely paying attention to each other. A few even looked like they were live streaming the occurrence, with themselves at the forefront. Out of all those present, only three stood close to the rift, as if drawn to its magic. One was a man in his late twenties, with jeans, a button up shirt, cowboy hat and boots. He even wore a holstered gun on his belt. The second was a teenaged girl in shorts and a tee, with long dark hair hanging out the back of a baseball cap. The third was a middle-aged man, in slacks and a blue dress shirt. He adjusted his glasses as he studied the rift, as if he could somehow see through and beyond its mystic glow.

This brings me back, he thought, recalling how he first met Carnes. The situation had changed, though. They no longer had the luxury of time. With so many open rifts, they needed more people willing to fight and become players. *Maybe it's time for a different approach.*

"All right," Palmer said, as he walked up behind the cowboy and girl. "No more spectator mode." He grabbed both by the collar and tossed them through the rift. "It's time to play." The older man's eyes widened behind the glasses. "You too, buddy."

Palmer grabbed him by the shoulder and forced him into the portal. The man bounced off an unseen force and cried out. Face bloodied, he collapsed to his knees and cursed through watery eyes. Palmer sucked air in through his teeth and cringed at the sight of the man's badly broken nose.

"Ohh, damn. My bad. Here, I got it."

"Get away from me!"

The man swatted Palmer's hand aside, but the heal had already been activated. His nose clicked back into place. Only a little blood and reddened cheeks remained of the injury.

"Again," Palmer said, his face twisted into the universal expression of *yikes*, as he slowly backed into the rift, "I'm really sorry about that."

He stepped through to a forest biome, though the portal was in the middle of a grassy clearing. The two already inside had overcome the initial shock of being thrown into a new world and were about to leave as Palmer arrived.

"Nuh uh," he told them and quickly turned. "Nobody's going anywhere." He could already sense lesser creatures in the surrounding trees, with one swiftly approaching from straight ahead. "You either deal with that," he said and pointed toward the running goblin that just broke through the tree line, "or with me. And trust me, you're better off with the goblin."

The man pulled a revolver from his holster and pointed it at Palmer's chest. With no hesitation, Palmer stepped forward and grabbed the gun. He firmly held the barrel pointed directly at his heart.

"What's wrong with you?" the girl asked.

"Do it," Palmer urged.

"I'm warning you."

"Just shoot him!" The girl looked nervously back toward the goblin. "It's getting closer!"

Palmer said, “Here, let me help you.”

He used his thumb to force the man to pull the trigger. He didn’t even flinch at the resounding noise and bright flash. He easily took the gun away, bent it in half and tossed it aside. The man backed up in alarm and disbelief. The flattened slug had fallen to the ground, but there was no mark upon Palmer. Not even his tunic was damaged.

“Guns don’t work,” he told the man. “You need magic weapons.”

Palmer then pulled a repeating crossbow, a quiver with bolts, and a short sword from inventory and placed them all on the ground.

“You’re running out of time.” Palmer drew their attention to the club-wielding monster almost upon them. “It will kill you if you don’t fight.”

Surprisingly, the girl grabbed the short sword. She held it in both hands with a look of determination. The man took the crossbow. The way he held it up with both arms and looked down the bolt from feather to tip made it seem he at least had some familiarity with the weapon. Palmer guessed he had experience hunting. His first shot, however, went right past the charging goblin. Its club struck the man’s shoulder, as the girl swung her sword like a bat into the creature’s side. It hissed in pain and jumped away.

“Nice!” Palmer encouraged. He cast regeneration on the man. The bloody wound in the man’s shoulder immediately healed. “Don’t worry. I won’t let you die. But you *have* to kill it.”

“How did you do that?” he asked, while the girl began to swing madly with her sword, endangering them both. “Watch it!”

Palmer replied, “I know. It’s a bit much to swallow, but monsters and magic are real.” He held up both hands in mock alarm. “Surprise!”

There was still a second bolt loaded on the underside of the crossbow. The man leveled it at the goblin and fired. This time, he struck it directly in the chest. With a roar of pain, it moved to return the favor with a deadly vengeance. Palmer thought he could help them a bit more and buffed their strength. As the man tried to quickly reload two bolts into the crossbow, the girl struck the goblin from the side. She lopped off its arm in a single swing. Blood spattered her entire front, even got into her mouth. She spat it out in disgust, but once she realized what she'd done, she broke out into a happy laugh. Her next swing took the goblin's head off.

"I did it!" she proclaimed. Her hands were shaking. "I can't believe it."

"This feels amazing," the man said and flexed his right arm. "Whoa! Look there." He pointed toward the tree line on their right. "There's two more." He picked up the quiver and slung it over his left shoulder. "Wait. What the hell am I seeing?"

The girl looked confused as well. "I'm a player?"

Palmer could now see their names were Matt and Rosa. He fully buffed them this time. He'd power leveled new players before, but those games always restricted the use of high-level buffs on newbies. With his max tier and evolved enhancement spells, they were practically invincible. Practically.

Palmer summoned Valorya. "Would you please babysit them for a bit? Let them get some levels, keep them healed, then take out the boss?"

"It shall be done," she said and bowed her head.

As she followed after the two new players, Palmer added, "Corrupt and kill anyone who tries to stop you." She waved in acknowledgement without looking back. "Thank you."

[Palmer] Hey Carnes, I recruited two new players when you get a chance
[Palmer] Matt and Rosa
[Carnes] You can invite them. Just imagine it while

looking at their nameplate

Palmer tried but thought he might be doing it wrong when nothing happened. After a few moments, he saw the guild tag appear beside their names.

Childhood Trauma, he thought and laughed. He'd almost forgotten the ridiculous name. *Watch out, world. Trauma incoming.*

[Rosa] test
[Jenna] Yay! Welcome!
[Matt] this is so weird
[Guy] Glad to have you
[Kenta] Make a healer. Ours solos too much

Palmer waved away the screen and let them all get acquainted. He didn't want to get distracted. There were too many things left to do. He pulled up the list of open incursions and teleported to the next. It was at a park in Montreal. He was surprised to see no one had noticed it yet, though it was a bit hidden amongst the trees. He went inside and called forth Samiel.

"This one's yours," he told the wraith lord. It was a winter biome, with chilling wind and snowy hills. "If you come across any named, take the time to subvert them. The boss, too."

Samiel bowed, turned and headed straight for the core. Every member of his command appeared one by one behind him as he walked. It was a far cry from the first rift Palmer had entered when this all began. Rather than a new player all alone, he now had an entire army to fight for him.

The boss didn't stand a chance.

Palmer went down the list, teleporting to each incursion and dropping off a general to deal with it. He gave them all the same instructions. Subvert any named. Corrupt and kill any players that try to stop them. He hoped that by deleting any troublesome player characters, they would eventually stop helping the hackers, or at the very least, stop being so damned annoying.

[Kenta] Uhh
[Guy] The hell is this?
[Jenna] LOL!
[Guy] A freaking army of demons just ran past us and killed the boss?
[Carnes] hahaha
[Palmer] Sorry
[Kenta] Why are we even trying, if you can solo this shit?
[Palmer] I didn't know you were there
[Guy] Cuz you don't communicate!
[Jenna] C'mon, it's kind of funny
[Palmer] Sorry, everyone. Where are you headed next?
[Palmer] It'll be cleared up to Edinburgh in just a bit
[Kenta] jfc
[Rosa] you guys are chatty
[Guy] We got Auckland. We'll message when it's done.
[Guy] So don't ignore chat

Palmer sighed.

- 16 -

Many hours later, Palmer returned to the bridge area. He dismissed the lich who had created the portal and headed up the path toward the mountain. Though tired, he was more frustrated than exhausted from having to deal with so many rifts. No one had tried to stop them. It was as if the hackers had purposely created busy work to annoy or distract him from their latest endeavor—the harbinger event. They had to be behind it. The system wouldn't have initiated such a dramatic threat to the entire server, not during such a tumultuous time. Players were already struggling to save hardcore earth. It had to be the hackers endangering it all. With Tellaria players busily defending their own major cities and settlements, they'd be unable to help HCE against incursions.

It's not a bad plan, Palmer thought, *if the roles were reversed. I just wish we could do more than defend. How the heck do we fight back?*

The influx of incursions wasn't a total loss. Palmer had gained another twenty-two named, greatly boosting their combined damage and capacity. He mused that his class was already overpowered, with completely unfair abilities when compared to average players. Add his creative use of game mechanics to the mix, and Hierophant became downright broken.

He'd come about as close to exploiting as one could get, without actually breaking any rules, and still have pride in their skills as a gamer.

To be fair, I don't exploit anywhere near as much as I could.

He considered the doubly broken effect corruption had on magic items and its relation to crafting. If he really wanted to, he could devastate the market, become the richest player to ever exist, and craft items on par with the hacked ones. *I don't really need to, though. I've got Avarran for that.*

In addition to new minions, the incursions had provided a veritable mountain of loot. All of the armor and weapons were of no real use to him, other than to break them down for new enchanting recipes. What he didn't disenchant, he put into the guild vault—a shared inventory for every member. He kept all of the rare materials, tossed the rest into the vault, and even threw in fifty million gold. It was the only way he'd found so far for players to trade gold. Avarran was audibly upset by what he called undue generosity but vowed he would replace it all ten times over with his next market session. There were no useful ability stones, either, as it seemed he'd already acquired every ability available to his class, and his rigorous nightly routine had all his abilities close to evolution. Of all they had amassed, only one filled an immediate need. It was a legendary magic item, one that benefited Samiel most.

War Horn of the Fallen General *(Unique)*
Item: Special
Restrictions: None
A silver horn trimmed in gold, once the herald of Warlord Veridan's cavalry.
Clarion Call: Twice per day, summon (WIS / 10) spectral warhorses to faithfully serve once more upon the battlefield.

That should solve our cavalry problem, he thought and looked around. *Hmm, where the heck is everyone?*

The defensive barriers and structures were still unfinished, with many damaged or broken from when Tamerax paid a visit. While he didn't expect the work to be done, he assumed there would at least be a few patrols to watch the portal. All he sensed ahead was a single, strong person. It didn't take long for him to recognize the presence.

"Baba," he said and smiled in way of greeting once they were close enough to hear.

The Champion looked exhausted, even leaned on his sword for support.

"Man, am I glad to see you." Baba put World Breaker away. "I'm starving! Been here all day, with nothing to eat."

"It's just you?"

Palmer looked out toward the path, down along the mountain and empty buildings. He realized everyone had gone to join the server event. Everyone except Baba. He studied his odd friend for a moment. That he remained behind meant a lot.

"Sorry. They wanted to stay, but—there's just too much at stake." He looked as if the words tasted foul in his mouth, knew it was a poor excuse for breaking a promise. "The entire server is in a panic. People have years of work and resources invested in those towns. The guildhalls, the housing. Not to mention what it would take to rebuild the major cities. I mean, people have relationships there, too. They're not just NPCs. They're friends, spouses...family."

"I get it," Palmer said with genuine understanding. "I feel the same way. It doesn't matter that almost everyone I've known my entire life is...artificial. How they got there is irrelevant. All that matters is how I feel when I think about them. Like my mom. We could argue all day that she's not actually related to me. Doesn't change the fact that she raised me. Isn't that what a mom is?"

"Preaching to the choir, brother." Baba's stomach growled loud enough to be heard. "I don't suppose you're here to take over. I could really use some food and like an hour or two of sleep."

Palmer laughed. "I can't belie—no, I take that back. I can *totally* believe that you stayed here by yourself. You didn't have to. It's really cool of you that you did."

"C'mon, I made a promise. That means something to me."

"To me, too." Palmer held up a fist, and Baba gave it a bump. "I got it from here. I'll have some minions guard the portal and then head back to Sunnyvale."

"Oh! Allandra's looking for you. She'd kick my ass if she knew I saw you and didn't tell you." Baba's expression changed from lighthearted to one of deep concern. "You know, we've never actually defeated a cataclysm level threat. It always ends bad. The server's never the same after. Might even end up in a reset. In a way, that would solve your problem. Once the server's down, they'll probably overhaul security in a big way."

"I'd rather see the hackers banned," Palmer said, "than let them get away with what they did. And I don't want to see this place ruined for the sake of mine."

"Does that mean you're gonna join the fight?" Baba grinned. "We got to make an alliance! I'd love to fight with you. Err, you know, beside you. Together!" He gave Palmer's nameplate a sour look. "Your guild name doesn't exactly instill confidence, though. You sound like the kind of guys who break alliance to cause friendly fire as a goof."

Palmer feigned surprise and mock hurt. "We'd never! Well, maybe Carnes would, but I...I would totally heal you after. If I did."

"Gee, what a good guy. I might be better off with a pickup group."

"Ohh! Now who's talking trash?" They both laughed together for a moment, their exhaustion all but forgotten. "Seriously, though. I'll come help in the morning. We can beat whatever this harbinger event is. Which capitol are you going to first?"

Baba replied, "Nidmar. It's like the heart of the server. If we lose that..."

"We won't," Palmer assured him. He focused on Baba's guild tag with the intention of sending an alliance invite. "We're artifact classes, remember? There's nothing on this server we can't kill."

Congratulations! Crits N Giggles has formed an alliance with Childhood Trauma!

Baba nodded in agreement. "That is true. You know me, I'm a modest guy. I don't like to brag, unless there's girls around, but I can *literally* break the world."

"I have heard that about you."

"All right man." Baba pulled an enchanted blue stone from inventory. "Time for me to recall. I will catch you tomorrow in Nidmar."

"Sounds good. G'nite."

Baba activated the recall stone and disappeared.

Solariel, Umbriel, would you both please protect this portal for now?

The two dragons appeared in elf and human form, respectively, and gave a slight bow of the head.

"May I ask," Umbriel began, "why you decided to pair us together?"

"You're the strongest," Palmer replied, as if that was all the explanation that was needed. To Solariel, he added, "Sorry I haven't assigned you a command yet. There'll be plenty of fighting tomorrow at the event. I'll get you sorted then."

The Ruler of Light squared his shoulders with pride. "Think nothing of it, young master. I shall have three thousand light elves here within a day."

Umbriel scoffed. "Such paltry numbers. *I* shall have five thousand dark elves here within half a day, since

I for one take this post seriously."

Palmer raised a brow at the obvious enmity between the two. Solariel appeared to be fuming at the insinuation he was somehow lesser than Umbriel. Palmer wondered how far back their animosity went and whether dark and light elves got along.

"Just don't cause an international incident." Palmer called forth a lich to open a portal to Sunnyvale. "I mean it. No infighting, yeah?"

They both stiffly nodded in agreement, without looking at each other. As Palmer wondered if he was going to need to feed and house so many elves, an ancient lich in flowing dark robes appeared and began casting a portal spell. Within moments, Palmer was back at the gazebo in the player town.

It was decidedly quiet, even for nighttime. Where the streets would normally be busy with players, barely a handful could be seen from the gazebo to his house. Every shop and stall in the market was closed. The only lighted windows to be seen were in the crafting section of town. Palmer assumed what few stayed behind were supporting those engaged in the server event with the crafts of their professions. Consumables, especially, would be in high demand. He wondered if he should offer up his sizeable stock of potions. Per usual, he had overprepared for all manner of situations and saved them all like a hoarder. He was the typical gamer that tended to save every potion for when it was absolutely necessary, only to beat the game without having used a single one.

"Allandra?" He was surprised to see her sitting alone in the darkened doorway. "I had no idea you were waiting."

"Hey! Yeah, sorry," she said and got to her feet. "Baba told me you were coming, so I headed over."

When he drew close, he could see she was upset. Her arms moved as if she were about to reach out and hug him but changed her mind before moving an inch.

"Is everything okay?" He wasn't sure, but it looked like she might have been crying. "You look...worried. I mean, obviously you're worried. Sorry, I don't know what I'm saying. This whole event—"

"It's not that," she intervened, cutting off his nervous rambling. "I'm just *so* sorry. I understand if you hate us." Her eyes glistened, on the verge of new tears. "You must feel like we all abandoned you."

"C'mon, stop. I don't feel that way at all," he assured her. "If anyone's to blame, it's the hackers. They put you guys in an impossible situation. I totally understand."

"You do?" She slowly began to smile.

He nodded. "The new rifts have calmed down, for now, and I'll be joining you guys tomorrow. We're gonna beat this event." His expression and tone made it a promise. "I'm guessing you stayed behind to craft."

"Mostly enchanting," she agreed, "but also summoning circles and constructs. I'm doing more overseeing than crafting." She laughed and added, "I'm more of a manager than a player."

"Okay, boss."

She didn't laugh at his teasing, but he did score a smirk. He took advantage of the awkward pause to open the front door. He invited her inside and turned on a light.

"Speaking of crafting," he began and collapsed onto the couch, "how are you guys set for potions?"

"We're good on mana and health," she replied and took a seat in the chair opposite him on the other side of the coffee table, "though they're mostly mid-tier. Alchemists are focused on quantity over quality right now. There's a severe shortage of materials and consumables on the market right now. Someone bought them all out just before the event triggered."

"Yeah, cuz that's not suspicious." Palmer sighed. *Was it the hackers or Avarran?* "So, they're probably gold hacking and item duping, too. That's fine. We don't need the market." A thought occurred to him. "We're allies now, right?"

She laughed. "I know! I was honestly surprised when it happened. Have you seen alliance chat? Your friends are seriously funny."

"Uhh, no," he admitted in an apologetic tone. "I'm not exactly good at keeping an eye on that stuff."

"You've been a solo for too long," she accused, as if she planned to remedy the situation. "Why did you ask? You look like you've got something in mind."

"How do you normally mass transfer items?" he asked. "Is there any advantage to being allies, like a shared vault or anything?"

"We use endless bags, for the most part. There is an alliance vault," she said, "but access is typically limited to guild masters. It's not the sort of thing we want everyone using."

"Makes sense." He worked out the details in his mind as he spoke. "Probably easier to use bags. I'll give them to you tomorrow. Materials and potions, mostly. I don't use the Shop for resources, anyway. I've got my own supply." The thought of bending the rules brought his thoughts back to the hackers. "I just wish we didn't have to deal with these jerks anymore. You just know they triggered the event, probably to keep you guys from helping us."

Allandra looked grieved by the reminder.

"I'm surprised the system hasn't banned any of them yet," she said, rather than offer another apology, "other than the people dumb enough to use hacked weapons."

"It did, though," Palmer stated. "At least one, that I know of." He explained how the hacker who took over Tamerax had been traced and banned due to the two systems working together. "It was just lucky I was inside the bridge at the time."

Allandra surmised, "So if we can lure them all inside, the two servers can trace their biosignatures faster?"

"I guess so, but how the heck would we even do that? We don't know who any of them are."

"Challenge them to a fight," she suggested. "Make a big deal about it with a server-wide message. Lean into the whole elitism of HCE players. Like, you're better than all of them combined. They couldn't possibly beat you, because they can't compare with the skills of a hardcore player. Whatever it takes to get them inside and keep them there long enough to trace."

Palmer seemed dubious. "You think that'd actually work?"

"It couldn't hurt to try."

"No, but it's gonna piss everyone off." Palmer shook his head. "They'll think I was a jerk all along, and hardcore players are all alike."

Allandra shrugged and offered, "I mean, it's kind of what we want. If everyone else believes it, so will the hackers." While Palmer thought it over, she pulled two pieces of folded clothes from inventory. Both were powerful, enchanted armor, just like his robes and gloves. "Listen, the reason I came here was to give you these." She placed them on the table. "Everyone felt terrible about being forced to break their promise, no one more than me. I know these don't make up for it, but I was hoping it would make it hurt a little less."

"Are these what I think they are?" He couldn't believe she'd found two set pieces and was reluctant to touch either. "They must've cost a fortune."

"They did." Allandra laughed along with the admission, as if to say whatever amount he imagined, the actual cost was even more. "But it was worth it." She reached out and touched his hand, still hovering over the items. "You're worth it." Gently, she put them in his hand and sat back. "Honestly, though. You need to stop hiding your items. You look like a tier one tailor. At least buy some cosmetics."

Palmer held the artifacts as if he was still afraid to

take them. That's how valuable they were and how much he appreciated what she'd done. With a nod of acceptance, he took her ribbing in stride and grinned in return.

"Okay, boss."

***

Once Palmer was alone again, he sat down to a quick dinner of honey-glazed pork, brown-sugared sweet potatoes, sweet corn, and honey buttered bread he had acquired from the Shop. There were far too many named minions for the small house, and he didn't want to play favorites. While he ate, he gave thought to what needed to be done next. Without daily quests, his nightly routine became somewhat simpler. There were other matters to attend to, though. Before he could practice, there was crafting to do. Since the Shop had been wiped out of materials, the only other option was to gather. It was a longshot, but Avarran was an enchanter. That meant some of the others might have crafting professions as well.

Can anyone gather raw crafting resources? he asked of all his minions. Of the thirty-eight named, nine replied that they could, including Avarran. He needed the arch demon for a different task, so he told the others to head into the bridge and gather every bit of resources they could manage, regardless of rarity.

Avarran, we're gonna need a stupid amount of enchanting materials. I know I joke about bending the rules and all, but in this case...don't hold back. We're fighting against cheaters. The rules don't apply anymore.

He could feel the arch demon appear in the grassy area beside the house and begin to work. It reminded him they were an easy target, with the town mostly empty. There was no one to keep watch or call out possible danger.

Valorya, would you please take half your command and post up on rooftops all across town? Keep an eye out for trouble, stay out of sight, and sleep in shifts, so no one is tired tomorrow.

She and the other celestials appeared on the roof and quickly took flight.

Kyomi, would you please do the same from the ground? Stay in the shadows, out of sight, and rotate people in shifts.

Ellory, would you please catch a taxi to Nidmar and use your command to scout the entire area around the city? Once you have a grasp of the situation, send me a report. Keep an eye on things in shifts. I don't want to go in blind tomorrow.

Apologies, Ellory replied, *a what?*

Palmer laughed. *Sorry. It's what players call mages that teleport people for gold—never mind. Just have one of the liches create a portal for you.*

Solariel and Umbriel, please feel free to use inventory or the Shop for any supplies you need once the elves arrive. Food, shelter, armor, weapons, anything you need. If at all possible, secure the area well enough that you can join us tomorrow.

That goes for anyone else as well. If you need something, anything, either ask, buy it, or take it from inventory. Just don't leave me broke, yeah?

With orders given, he set about using all of his own materials to make the highest tier potions he was able to. He focused on utility and what would be most useful to the other players fighting in the event. Once he brewed all the tier five health, mana, and stamina potions his resources would allow, he worked on reaching maximum tier in rejuvenation, might, alacrity, fortitude, acumen, sage, speed, and defense. He was only able to improve spell power, divine power, rage, and magic resistance to tier four. Still, it was a combined fortune worth of consumables, enough to support a large army. He put them all into an endless bag. The second endless bag would be for materials.

Once the crafting was complete, he set about practicing abilities. Heal and area of healing were first to evolve. He then worked on spell vulnerability and arcane siphon, evolving each to their final tier. Of the four, only siphon gained a new effect.

Divine Arcane Siphon
Class: *All*
Requirement: *Legendary tier or higher*
Active, Combat, Transmutation
Cost: *50,* ***Range***: *32',* ***Duration***: *Instant*
Leech 2.5% maximum mana points from a target and cause 2.5% fatigue damage.
Wither: Affected targets enter a *withered* state, preventing innate mana regeneration for thirty seconds.

Though it was getting late, he continued to train. His corruption aura was the easiest to raise, as he could leave it active while working other abilities. Since no one was around, he took advantage of the quiet to practice just outside of town. While raising void nova to rank three and protection from corruption to rank four, the aura also reached the next tier with little effort on his part. He only needed to keep watch on his mana to maintain it.

Void Nova (I)
Class: *Hierophant*
Active, Combat, Necromancy
Cost: *25,* ***Range***: *none,* ***Duration***: *instant*
Discharge a point-blank area of effect blast of void energy, dealing 24-32 corruption damage to all targets in a 12' radius.

Corrupt (I)
Class: *Hierophant*

Active*, *Combat*, *Necromancy
Cost: *10 per 6 seconds,* **Range**: *none,* **Duration**: *until cancelled*
Emit an aura of void energy, dealing 4-12 corruption damage to all targets in a 12' radius.
Exposure: Prolonged exposure will cause corruption to the surrounding environment and any items within range. Targets that remain within range for one minute will enter an *exposed* state, increasing damage taken by void energy by 50%. This effect lasts until cured.

Palmer returned home, exhausted. He was ready for bed but had one last task he'd been putting off. Setting aside time to open the remaining epic and legendary mystery gifts was more like a delayed Christmas than a task. He'd hoped to amass more gifts from incursions before preparing a luck-fueled session of rapid opening. With Aurora's clover, a full set of cloth armor with tier five luck enchantments, and a tier five luck potion bolstered by the effect of his legendary alchemy kit, his total magic find was increased by five hundred percent. What that actually meant was misleading. He knew it didn't mean every time an item dropped there was a five hundred percent chance it would be magic. It meant that a dropped item was five times more likely to be magic rather than normal, and the item was randomly generated from a higher tier loot table based on the percentage increase.

Before that, though...

He pulled out the cloth pants and boots Allandra had given him. He could see how excited she was at the moment but felt embarrassed by how much time, effort, and resources she must have put into obtaining them. He was incredibly grateful. He just didn't want to prolong his embarrassment by equipping them in front of her. With a shake of his head at the burning memory of his social awkwardness, he equipped both pieces of gear.

Leggings of the Hierophant *(Unique; Artifact)*
Type: Cloth
Armor: 15
Restrictions: Healer, LVL 100, INT 100, WIS 100
Woven with threads enchanted by the unique magic of two realms, these masterfully crafted gloves are a work of art and unearthly treasure.
Grants the wearer +25% bonus healing and physical resistance.
Replenish: Master and Minion health and mana regeneration are increased by 50%.
Origins: Doubles the effect of all Healer abilities.
Set Bonus (4/6)
Void Star: Once per day, the wearer may activate this advanced form of Void Nova, discharging a point-blank area of effect blast of void energy, dealing (INT + WIS) corruption damage to all targets in a 120' radius. Once completed, the player will become incapacitated for one minute.

Boots of the Hierophant *(Unique; Artifact)*
Type: Cloth
Armor: 10
Restrictions: Healer, LVL 100, INT 150
Woven with threads enchanted by the unique magic of two realms, these masterfully crafted gloves are a work of art and unearthly treasure.
Grants the wearer +25% bonus healing and movement speed.
Hardened: Master and minion damage reduction increased by 25.
Resistant: Master and minion physical and magical resistance increased by 25%.

Incapacitated. He mused over the word, wondering to what extent it would affect him. The damage was a good amount, assuming it wasn't flat and would be modified by other abilities, stats, and effects. *The radius is a little insane. Kinda like a suicide bomb.* Origins was interesting as well. Since the effect had a different name from the one on his ring, it could mean another doubling of his base class abilities. *That would make the heals crazy strong.* He looked over the details of each set piece. *Just one more for the complete set.*

"Are you watching?" he asked the system, who he now knew was Aurora. With his full set of luck gear equipped, he pulled three luck potions from inventory and placed each on the table before him. "This is it."

He grabbed the first and pulled free the stopper, swallowed the first dose. With all the practice of a fevered gacha player, he quickly opened all the mystery gifts. He did the three legendary first, soon followed by the eighteen epic. He paid no attention to what resulted as he went, forced it all into inventory and kept going. It wasn't until the last gift was gone that he sat back to calm his nerves. There was a lot riding on this session. With all that was happening, he wasn't sure if he would get the chance to run dungeons or raids for the final remaining piece. Even the Shop wasn't an option, with hackers potentially buying everything up with duplicated gold.

He glanced over the newly added items and resources. It wasn't there. His heart sank. For a moment, he felt defeated, as the weight of it all came crashing in. Not that it mattered, he tried to tell himself. He was powerful enough, way stronger than the average player. Would it really make a difference if he—

There's another page! He scrolled down and instantly saw it. *Yes!* He was so happy he thought he would cry, as his eyes misted over from elation and exhaustion. He shook his head at his own behavior, and silently thanked the system. *I actually got it.*

Circlet of the Hierophant *(Unique; Artifact)*
Type: Cloth
Armor: 15
Restrictions: Healer, LVL 100, CON 100, INT 150, WIS 150
A braided circlet of silver and platinum, polished to perfection and infused with energy from the void.
Grants the wearer +25% bonus healing and magical resistance.
Intensify: Doubles the cost and damage of Corrupt.
Set Bonus (6/6)
Shift: Enter and leave the void at will.

"Uhh," he said, studying the final set bonus with a look of fear and deep concern. "I am *not* doing that."

Palmer yawned, too tired to deal with an existential shift in perception, let alone the long list of other magic items he acquired. He was sure he'd seen at least two other artifacts in the list, as well as a bunch of legendaries. It was too much to handle for his weary brain.

Those were problems for future Palmer.

***

Palmer woke early the next morning, still tired but eager to help everyone with the event. Ellory had relayed a cursory report the night before. The threat was just as dire, if not more so, than Baba had made it out to be. A harbinger had reached the eastern fields outside Nidmar. The number of enemies that came with it was astounding. Nearly ten thousand strong, they fought relentlessly toward the walled city. More disturbing, their numbers continued to grow from a portal no one knew how to close. Along with the King's army and city guard, guild coalitions and alliances had joined together to drive back the invaders. According to Ellory's scouts, defenders had fought all night and were still no closer to defeating the enemy. Palmer imagined Starfall and Ironhold weren't faring any better.

He took a seat at the dining table, bought breakfast from the Shop, and began to eat. As he worked through the scrambled eggs with cheese, crispy bacon, potato bites, buttered toast, and orange juice, Palmer quickly went down the list of items he'd gained from opening gifts. Apart from a legendary enchanting kit and numerous rare crafting resources, there was an abundance of magic gear and items he had no use for. Of those he could use, none were considered a true upgrade.

One did interest him, though, as it was more of a lateral replacement. The more his minion capacity grew, and the greater number of enemies they faced, the less he was able to use the Thorny Necklace of the Master. The disadvantage of all received damage being transferred to him became far too great a risk. He decided to replace it with a niche legendary, a Necklace of Regeneration. It restored health, mana, and fatigue by one percent per tick. Though he would have preferred a replacement that boosted damage or defense, he knew better than to underestimate a solid utility item. It would allow him to run corrupt aura nonstop during battle without worrying over his mana consumption.

As he finished eating the last piece of bacon, he pulled up the Shop and browsed through all the available cosmetics. Rather than purchase an individual piece for each equipment slot, he settled on a complete outfit. It had black shoes, blue jeans, a blue button-up shirt, and a brown leather jacket with sunglasses as a bonus accessory. He thought the shades were a bit much and opted not to wear them.

Before leaving to meet Baba, he decided to visit Allandra at her shop. With the help of his gatherer minions, both endless bags were filled with considerable amounts of potions and resources. She would be better able to distribute them to the players who needed them most. When he arrived at her door, he was surprised to see it open before he could knock.

"Oh," he said, hand halfway raised. "Did I catch you on your way out?"

She looked startled to see him and blushed.

"No, I was just—I mean, yeah." She stepped out and closed the door. "Hey! You finally changed your outfit. Very old school. I like it! You showing off, or did you need something?"

"Just dropping these off, like I promised." He handed over the endless bags. "I kept some for myself, but there should be enough to at least help."

Her eyes widened as she browsed each bag's detail window.

"This is crazy! How did you get so much?" At his sheepish silence and shrug, she asked, "Do I even want to know?"

"I didn't cheat," he said defensively, "if that's what you're thinking."

"Uh huh," she replied, still scrolling through the lists. "How do you even have time to do all this? It takes forever to become a master crafter, and these are bolstered tier fives?" Her expression quickly turned from one of incredulity to judgement. "If it isn't an exploit, what is it, luck?"

Palmer considered. "I mean, you're not wrong. To be honest, it's a little bit of the first, and a whole lot of the second. It's not me, though. It's Aurora."

"Ohh, yeah." Allandra clicked her tongue. "That actually makes sense now. Life must be hard, with the Goddess of Luck in your pocket." She laughed when Palmer's cheeks reddened, as if finding some joy in his discomfort. "Relax, I'm just kidding. Hey, I've been meaning to ask. Whatever happened with that girl? You know, the one you were thinking of—"

"Sara?" Palmer let out a burst of air. He had already

decided not to offer her subversion but not comfortable enough about the decision to openly talk about it yet. "Yeah. I haven't been back, so I haven't talked to her. Or my mother. Or anyone really. It's probably for the best. There's just way too much going on here that needs to be dealt with."

"Is that it?" she asked, "You're too busy? Or maybe you met someone else..."

Palmer looked confused and doubtful. "How would I meet someone else? It's been nothing but fighting since I got here."

"C'mon, you met me," she teased.

"I suppose."

Allandra retorted, "What, I'm not attractive enough for you?"

"What? No! I mean, of course you are. It's just, you're with Baba," he pointed out, "so I never even considered it."

Is she making fun of me? he thought. He'd never been on the receiving end of flirtation. *Or just teasing? Probably just nosy.*

"Why would that matter?" she asked, genuinely curious.

Palmer snorted. "I would never do that to a friend. No guy would."

"That has *not* been my experience," Allandra said. "As far as I can see, all guys at least look. I've been told as long as they look but don't touch, there's no issue. Then again, I don't think I've ever been in a relationship where the guy didn't cheat."

"That's terrible," he said and wished he could do more. He could see she'd clearly been hurt in the past and carried it with her still. There was nothing he could say to change that, so he decided to give advice from the male perspective. "Maybe you need to hang with better guys."

There was a long moment where she seemed lost in thought.

"Maybe I do."

An even longer silence followed.

"I uhh—I need to go meet Baba," he said awkwardly. He scratched at the edges of the gem in his chest. "Are you heading there, too? Or do you have stuff to do here?"

"We're still crafting," Allandra said. She squared her shoulders and was back to her usual self. "Be careful when you get there. I know you want to help, but this is the perfect opportunity for anyone who wants you dead." She playfully poked him in the shoulder. "Don't let them."

"I'll do my best," he promised. "Good luck with the crafting."

He summoned a lich to create a portal to the eastern ring outside Nidmar.

"Kill some for me," she added.

With a final nod in farewell, he stepped through. The portal closed behind him, as the lich was dismissed. It was crowded around the summoning circle, with groups of players either waiting for more to gather, getting ready to head out, or standing by for the next delivery of supplies. He surmised all this by overhearing their not-so-private conversations as they ignored him. One person, however, did recognize him and cried out with excitement.

"Over here!" Baba waved him over.

Blasts of magic could be seen, heard, and felt from the massive battle taking place just beyond the eastern hillside. Smoke rose up in dark plumes, while flashes of bright magic and elemental power erupted toward the heavens. Great shafts of lightning in thick blue and white bolts tore through the sky, commingled with scorching streams of fire like dragon breath. The battle cries of thousands rang out with the constant clash of steel, while otherworldly creatures shook the air with bloodthirsty cries of their own.

"You been waiting long?" Palmer asked.

Unlike the other players, he kept his voice low. He didn't like the idea of anyone overhearing or realizing who he was. They began to walk together toward the fighting. At least the combined forces of Nidmar's army and player guilds had been able to keep the enemy a good distance from the city walls. It would be at least five to ten minutes of walking before they could even see over the hills.

"Not too long," Baba replied. "We're going to meet Nitemane and Krymor on the far side. That way we don't run the risk of friendly fire with area attacks. You'll have to ally with their guilds. Don't worry, they're small. Basically alts and a few friends. It's pretty rare for artifact classes to join big guilds." He puffed his chest out. "Me being the exception. Nice outfit, by the way."

A thought occurred to Palmer. Since they were heading to the complete other side of the fight, they had plenty of time to talk.

"I've been meaning to ask," he began, "what are your stats like?"

Baba laughed and elbowed him. "Oh shit, son. We're about to go into a cataclysm level fight, and you want to compare e-peens?"

"It's not like that," Palmer said. "I don't know if you guys had tutorials or whatever, but this game has like no information anywhere on how anything works. I just want to see how I compare to other players."

"I get it. Not that it'll help," Baba explained, "since I'm not at all an average player. I raid *a lot*, sometimes solo. That's where you get most of your bonus points. I could tell you my stats, but don't blame me if you get jelly."

Palmer smirked. "I think I'll be fine."

"Okay, well, I'm a warrior base, so I went all in with strength, dex, and con." He held up a finger. "But once I hit a hundred in each, I started to spread my bonus points out. My sub class, Paladin, has a lot of abilities, and some of them use mana. Doesn't hurt to have decent resists, too. But then I unlocked Champion and had to bump up my main stats for the set gear requirements."

Palmer side-eyed his friend. "That's lot of words that tell me nothing."

"You have no chill," Baba said and shook his head. "Okay, don't feel bad, but my strength is a hundred and sixty-seven." He quickly added, "I've got over a hundred and fifty in dex and con, too, with fortyish in int and wis, but strength is the big one. You'd have to *solo* a bunch of raids to get there."

"Like Sunborn Temple?"

"Nah," he replied quickly. "That one's timed. It's impossible. But you can get a few points here and there, if you're lucky, doing large guild raids, or you could take it super slow and solo some of the easier ones to hog the points." Baba shrugged. "Either way, it takes a long ass time to get really good stats."

"You didn't get your artifact class 'til after a hundred," Palmer surmised.

"Well, yeah," Baba agreed, as if that were obvious. "Everyone gets powered to a hundred, then you get carried through dungeons for gear until you're ready to raid." He gave Palmer a shrewd look. "Why did you say it like that?"

Palmer considered how to answer. He wasn't sure how much he should share.

"I got my artifact class early on," he finally said, "and when I did, my stat points per level doubled." After Baba was done cursing and calling him a liar, Palmer went on, "Not to mention, you completely skipped daily quests. Those mystery gifts have a chance to award points."

"Yeah, but it's tiny," Baba pointed out, "like one percent. That's why literally no one does dailies." With a second shrewd look, he asked, "Why, what are your stats like?"

"Oh no," Palmer said and laughed. "We're not doing that."

"I'm serious! I want to know." After a moment of stubborn quiet, Baba asked, "You think you could take me?"

Without giving it too much thought, Palmer quickly did the math.

"Four ticks. Maybe five."

Baba burst out laughing and stopped walking.

"Did you seriously just say you could take me in under thirty seconds?"

Palmer stopped to face him. His eyes looked upward as he ran through the math.

"Give or take," he replied. "You have, what, fifteen-hundredish health? I could debuff and incapacitate you in less than four ticks. Probably wouldn't even need to add any DoTs or DDs. Just melee you down from there, with critical bonuses for striking a prone target."

Baba put a hand on each hip and leaned in.

"Show me."

"Right now? Here?" Palmer asked in exasperation. "The server's being overrun, and you want to duel?"

Baba merely raised his brows and waited.

"C'mon, just show me your rotation." He then added, "None of that pet BS, either. I'm not fighting an army of dragons. You say you can take me by yourself, with just your abilities. So do it."

"Do I need to buff?" Palmer asked. "Are you gonna fight back?"

"Nope. I just want to see the rotation."

Palmer rolled his eyes, considered it a waste of time, but reluctantly agreed. In the first tick, he debuffed Baba's magic resistance, strength, dexterity, and hit chance with both physical and magical attacks.

"Son of a glitch," Baba said with widened eyes. "How are you doing that so fast? Are you exploiting?"

In the second tick, Palmer began to siphon mana

and cause fatigue damage. With the complete set bonus from his Hierophant gear, he could drain seven and a half percent per ability use. Against players, that damage was doubled. Four uses brought Baba past the first fatigue penalty. He let out a guttural moan of pain as it took hold.

"Wait," the Champion said weakly.

In the third tick, Baba had been drained of all mana and driven to the full fatigue penalty: incapacitation. He'd dropped to his hands and knees at seventy-five percent. At one hundred, he collapsed onto his front, face buried in the dirt.

"See?" Palmer asked and knelt beside him. "Didn't even have to use disease or corruption or DoTs. Just a few hits here with my staff," he said and poked Baba in the back of the head, "and it's all over."

Baba's voice was muffled by grass and soil.

"I hate you so much right now."

Palmer laughed and applied regeneration to his friend. He helped Baba to sit up and gave him a bolstered tier five stamina potion. Once all but his pride had been restored, Baba wiped the dirt from his face and front. They resumed their walk toward the battle.

"That was kind of scary," he admitted, "not gonna lie."

The guild tab began to flash with new incursion notifications. Palmer pulled up the screen as he walked and was stunned. He slowed to a stop, as his eyes scanned the growing list. Over a dozen sites quickly filled the page, with new ones appearing every moment he watched on.

"Damn," was all he could say. At Baba's questioning look, he added, "The hackers are back at it. A whole bunch of new rifts just opened."

[Kenta] FML, we just finished one an hour ago. I'm still eating!

[Guy] Palmer! You seeing the incursion notifications?
[Matt] This is crazy
[Palmer] I see it. I'm OMW
[Palmer] I'll work down from the second
[Jenna] So we get Seattle? Ooo I know a great place for tacos!
[Carnes] I see them too.
[Rosa] Like we'll have time for tacos…
[Jenna] You *make* time for tacos!

"I have to go," he told Baba, "but I'll be back in like five minutes. I can just teleport right back here. Go on without me, and I'll catch up."

"No worries. Do what you have to do. I wish there was a way I could go with."

"We'll regroup in a bit," he promised.

Palmer selected the teleport option beside Atlanta, the second incursion from the top of the list, and disappeared.

- 17 -

By the time Palmer had dealt with the third rift, he knew there wouldn't be enough time or minions to handle them all. The incursion list continued to grow and was already on its fourth page. He began to wonder if he was sending too many to deal with each one. If he sent less, they could spread out and defeat more. It was a matter of efficiency. Unfortunately, he had no idea how difficult each incursion was or what modifier they would have. As much as he didn't want to waste resources with overkill, a loss would be worse. Even with the ability to instantly teleport to each location, it would take the rest of the day at full effort to deal with them all. That was only if the list didn't keep growing, which certainly was not the case.

There has to be a better way to do this. He tried recalling similar situations in other games, pored over his items and abilities. There wasn't anything he could do on his own that would be faster or more efficient, not without additional information. *If only the game had a mission interface.* Numerous other games had a minigame within them that allowed the player to send subordinates on quests for loot and experience. *Then I could at least see how difficult each rift is and only send what's needed. Heck, some were even automated.*

"Aurora?" he asked, standing in the empty parking

lot of an abandoned retail store in Tulsa. "I don't suppose you can hear me?"

I can hear you, she replied in his mind, *though I am unable to manifest there.*

"I'm sure you're aware of all the incursions," he began, "and I know you're busy with everything else that's going on..."

I must apologize, she replied to his unasked plea for help. *I fear the rapid increase in attacks upon your world is my fault. I was able to isolate the affected code blocks that allowed subsystems to be altered. Rather than correct each alteration and prevent any further changes, I chose to undo enough to cause the hackers to take action, if they wished to continue creating bridges. This will allow me to slowly trace their true source of connection with each attempt. They are many working together. I fear it will take time.*

So, what's that mean for us? We just need to suck it up? Palmer sighed. *If it means finally stopping these guys for good, I guess we can hold out.*

"I get that," he said, in an attempt to sound understanding, "but is there anything you can do to make this a little easier on us?"

She was quiet for a moment. *What did you have in mind?*

"Are you familiar with games that have a follower mission system?" He explained in great detail what one entailed. "Even a rudimentary interface or the ability to remotely send minions, rather than teleport to each one myself, would be a big help."

I will try, she promised. *In the meantime, you must do your best to fend off these attacks. A single tunnelling attempt can take days before absorbing enough energy to fully fuel evolution into a bridge. Each successive link strengthens the others, drawing more power from both worlds. The time needed to form a bridge will shrink with each new incursion.*

"Well, *that's* not good." He scanned the incursions

tab, which was now up to seven pages. "If this pace keeps up, there'll be dozens of new bridges in no time. There's no way we can defend that many." His mind raced with visions of powerful players flooding Earth, destroying everything and everyone in their path. "We'll be completely overrun."

Research complete.
Compiling substructures...
Time to initiate new system: 3:45

As Palmer watched the timer begin to tick down, he decided to deal with as many rifts as he could until the mission system was ready. He wondered that if multiple incursions at one time would speed up their evolution, why hadn't the hackers already gone all out before now? He concluded they must not be aware how incursions interacted with one another. Either that or they were afraid to expose themselves with too much connectivity. To him, it made their current efforts seem desperate. If they felt the system was on the verge of blocking all further attempts at tunnelling, it would explain the sudden onslaught of frenzied attempts.

He continued on down the list, dropping off minions at Tampa, Baton Rouge, Rock Springs, Camden, Newark, Las Cruces, and Sandusky. He'd sent enough into the first rift to not only beat the boss but clear the entire zone. They should have been done but were not. Worse still, attempts to communicate met with silence. There was little chance they'd been defeated. In fact, his minion count had only grown higher. The only explanation that came to mind was a zone modifier. By his estimate, time dilation was the most likely culprit.

Mission interface is now available.

Palmer brought up the guild screen and saw a new tab beside incursions, which was now up to fifteen pages. He was impressed by the interface. Not only could he see each incursion by how long it had been active, but the listed details showed location, zone modifier, biome type, level range, overall difficulty, and chance of success. A dropdown box allowed him to manually choose which minions to send, with a check box beside it to automatically select those best suited to the incursion. From there, a single press of the Send button transported the chosen minions directly outside the incursion entrance. The absolute best option of them all was a checkbox at the very top of the page to automate the entire process.

Yes, please! Palmer checked the box and watched the system begin to select which minions to send before immediately teleporting them outside. Within moments, dozens of incursions had been dealt with. *That was fast!* He nearly laughed with excitement. *It's sending much less than I expected, too.* Though he'd quickly run out of minions to send, they would be reassigned a new mission once the previous was completed. *This is way more efficient!*

"This is incredible," he said, standing at the edge of a dock, with ships passing by. "Nice work, Aurora. Thank you for this."

By the lack of response, he assumed she was busy tracking down the hackers. One thing stood out, as he marveled at the still growing list being automatically dealt with. There were numerous zone modifiers, from greater experience to bonus physical or magical damage, higher drop rates to improved resource rarity. Of them all, those with time dilation caught and held his attention. It meant time inside could either be moving slower or faster. The one he'd been in moved slower. Theoretically, that meant closing the rift should be quicker. However, what if the dilation speed was variable? The slowed percentage could be driven to an extreme. That might not matter as a one off, but with so many being opened simultaneously, it became statistically more likely those slowed rifts would occur and begin to stack. If that happened, new bridges were not just unavoidable, they were inevitable.

Damn it. There was nothing he could do about it. If the scenario played out as he expected, time dilated incursions would begin to crowd the first page. All he could really do was hope that wasn't the case. *But with my luck...*

He left the thought unfinished and returned to Nidmar. All of his minions were deployed on missions and immediately sent back out to handle the next one on the list. The incursions tab seemed to be holding steady at ten pages, with just three of the time dilated rifts at the top. He made a mental note to keep an eye on them and rushed over the hill to meet Baba and the others.

The first thing to catch his attention was the Harbinger of Life, hovering above a crowd of monsters at least ten thousand strong. Though it slightly resembled a female human, both in size and form, it was more an amalgam of tree and magic. Her skin was pale green, protected by bark across her chest and waist. Colorful leaves fell from her head in a semblance of hair. More leaves and flowers covered her shoulders, arms, and thighs. Her eyes shone a deep green, much like the mana that flowed through every vein across her body with a visible glow. Despite her appearance of crushing power, her presence could not be felt. She appeared to be phased, in two dimensions at once. Any attacks directed toward her simply passed through.

Below her, the enemies were so tightly packed, struggling to reach the city walls, that they formed a dense circle of bodies fighting over one another. While most pushed toward that goal, those on the outskirts and far eastern side were focused instead on the surrounding players. The larger guilds fought beside the King's army, closest to the walls, while smaller guilds and groups performed hit and run tactics against the mass of enemies. None but the player alliances seemed able to hold their ground against the relentless assault. As monsters fell, they were quickly replaced by those just behind. At the center of amassed enemies, just below the harbinger, was a portal where endless monsters continued to pass through and replenish the fallen.

Within the throng of enemies were ancient fae bears and wolves, creatures four times the normal size. The telltale signs of a fae creature were mana-hardened plates along the spine from head to tail and a purple fire that emanated from their eyes. With claws and teeth the length of daggers, these beasts were terrible to behold let alone face. Beside them were dryads, humanoids formed of tree branches and leaves. Born of magic, they wove spells from a distance, caused thorns and vines to entrap players, broke the earth with stone that pierced flesh. When forced to fight face to face, they shaped both arms into wooden blades. They were just as deadly in melee as they were from afar.

There were also dread faeries, diminutive humanoids with butterfly wings as large as their entire bodies. They favored bows and spells, attacking players from the air, while their kin, darter sprites, rushed in from the ground. The child-sized sprites were savage forest dwellers, with an affinity for blades, both melee and thrown. Their ability to dash forward at great speed made their attacks difficult to dodge. Spread wide across the battlefield were will-o'-the-wisps, forest spirits made manifest through dark magic. No bigger than a sparrow, they were formed of mana infused moonlight. The tiny creatures attacked in swarms, stinging with their electric touch and draining life from their prey.

The entire area seemed afflicted by a mana fueled change, similar to how Palmer's corruption altered the ground. The earth was dark with rich soil, the grass a vibrant and glowing green. Motes of emerald and azure light floated up from the charged land, strengthening the enemy. By the look of those foolish enough to remain with its grasp, it had an opposite effect upon players.

"Five minutes, my ass," Baba called out from afar, while fighting off three sprites intent on taking out his legs. He was careful not to step into the nature-cursed area. "What took you so long?"

Nitemane and Krymor were there as well, dodging arrows, blades, and magic, while striking down all they could. Palmer rushed over to lend a hand. Once he reached them, he gave them each regeneration and began to buff.

"It's complicated."

Baba laughed. "You sound like my girlfriend. Whoa," he said in surprise. "You just cancelled out almost all my buffs." His eyes widened in disbelief. "And doubled my main stats. Seriously, dude. What the hell is up with your char?"

"Uhh," Krymor interjected, while simultaneously killing two fairies with throwing knives, then striking down three sprites in front of him with a blindingly fast sweep of dual daggers, "could I get some of that?"

"Same." Nitemane let loose an arrow that struck a dryad in the distance, then exploded in a massive area of fire and bright light. A large black and red vulture flew past him and joined the fray. Its name was Pecker. "Get my pets, too."

"And when you're done," Baba said and grunted from the strain of an immense sword swing that broke the earth before him for a hundred feet, "feel free to make us look bad with your army of dragons."

"Yeah," Palmer said dejectedly. "About that."

***

Palmer kept a fair distance from the others. All

three were artifact classes, with powerful area attack abilities. Even with friendly fire disabled by their guilds being allied, they each needed room to maneuver. It made sense to support them from afar with spells and wait for the right opening. That way he could move into melee range without interfering with their attacks. There were other small guild groups on either side, swapping out tanks and melee damage dealers when those in front grew too tired. Baba, Nitemane, and Krymor were in a league of their own. They didn't need backup or relief. They held the line for fifty yards in both directions without support. It helped that Nitemane had numerous pets under his control, in addition to Pecker, including a dire bear named Chomps and a giant scorpion called Pinchy. Not to mention, Krymor was able to create shadow clones and mirages. Normally, Baba would be the only one without subordinates to lend a hand. Unfortunately, Palmer's minions were still too busy shutting down the influx of incursions.

While the enemies were all considered rare elites, some even as high as level one hundred and two, it didn't make sense to debuff each and every one. It wasn't their individual power causing a problem for the players. It was their overwhelming and unending numbers. As soon as there was room near the portal, more stepped through to join the fight. Palmer noticed, as well, that as their numbers grew and pushed out, the cursed ground beneath them expanded. It gave the enemy creatures a decisive advantage, as it bolstered their strength while simultaneously weakening any players within its grasp.

Don't stand in the goo. The familiar pro player tip resounded in his mind.

Its similarity to corruption gave Palmer an idea. Since corruption fed on mana, it should theoretically destroy the curse. If he corrupted the ground and let it spread, the portal would eventually become engulfed.

All trace of their advantage would be gone.

Of course that creates a different problem, Palmer pointed out in his own mental debate. *They still won't be able to step in it.* He looked around at the other groups. *I'll have to give them all protection from corruption. Even if I charge it, it'll only last for five minutes.* He sighed and shook his head. *One problem at a time.*

"Whenever you're ready, Princess," Baba quipped at Palmer, who'd been standing still while lost in thought. "Show me some of that crazy casting already!"

"I'm thinking!"

Krymor laughed. "What's to think about? Just pew pew them all down!"

"Keep my pets healed," Nitemane said, "and you're golden. Save your mana."

"Are you kidding me?" Baba replied in a snarky tone. "He's not just a healer. He's a freakin' one man army."

"Well, his army isn't here," the hunter retorted. "His DPS without them won't come close to ours, so he should just preserve mana for heals. That's like raiding 101."

If I can cancel out the cursed ground, Palmer considered, *and we push toward the portal, we should be able to enter and deal with the harbinger.* He frowned as he mentally listed all the different ways that might not work. *Assuming we don't get surrounded and overrun. And we can actually make it to the portal. And there aren't a ton more waiting for us on the other side. And the harbinger is actually there and not in some other dimension we can't access.* He roughly shook his head to clear it all away. None of it mattered, if he couldn't cancel the cursed ground.

"Okay," Palmer told them. "I have a plan."

"Oh good, a plan!" Krymor said with a good-natured chuckle, as he finished off a fae wolf with two daggers to either side of its head. "No more random killing, guys. He's got a plan!"

Palmer began casting plague among the enemy, moving from left to right behind Baba and finally Krymor. He carefully chose targets a certain distance from one another, so that the disease would spread quickly in all directions. It was a way to passively weaken the entire army without having to debuff them one by one. He then gave his three allies and their pets protection from corruption. By his estimate, it was faster to just recast the buff as needed, rather than charge it from the start. Charging, in his opinion, was only worth it when the ability was close to max rank.

As he began to charge corruption, he inwardly kicked himself for not working more on his other abilities. There just never seemed to be enough time in the day to get done all the things he wanted to. After half a minute, when the charging would begin to cause damage, he set it loose upon the ground behind Krymor. He then repeated the process and unleashed the corruption behind Nitemane and then Baba. By the time he released the third, the blackened ground had already grown into the nature-cursed area. It ate away at the mana with a crackle and purple sparks. It darkened the lush green glow into ebon fire and the floating motes of emerald into ash. Not only did the corruption wrest away the enemy's advantage, it took root in their flesh with a double dose of disease.

"Good," Palmer said. "It's working."

"This is working?" Baba asked, while still getting used to the jagged movement of corrupted creatures. Their jerky speed made them slow and suddenly speed up again. "How does this help us?"

"Look at the ground." Palmer refreshed their protection buffs. "My goo overwrites theirs. So this time, it's okay to stand in it."

"Oh, damn," Krymor said and moved forward, forcing the enemy back for the first time since Palmer arrived. "Look at that. All right, I take it back. That's a pretty good plan."

Nitemane still fired shots from afar. At least he seemed pleased his pets were no longer affected by the cursed ground.

"Be better if it did damage," the hunter noted.

"No, no, no," Baba said in Palmer's defense. "Nuh uh. Naw, son! You do *not* understand how seriously broken he is. He does just as much damage as we do *and* has an army of dragons."

"Yeah, yeah. Less jawin', more killin'."

"You're just miffed," Krymor ribbed the hunter, "because you're still behind me on the DPS meter."

"Barely!"

Palmer activated his corruption aura, drew his staff from inventory, annoyed Nitemane by striding past the hunter's line of sight, and entered the fray ahead. Once he came face to face with the front line, massive bears and wolves interspersed with dryads and sprites, he began to activate void nova at an alarmingly fast rate. The point-blank area of effect explosions of corruption spread out all around him in a twelve-foot radius. Giant spheres of black fire and violet lightning erupted in quick succession, four times per six seconds. They instantaneously caused over a hundred damage to every enemy inside. Coupled with his aura, which caused all within its range to enter an exposed state, the enemies soon cried out in greater pain as the damage was increased by another fifty percent.

"Okay, that's some BS right there." Nitemane shouted over the roar of unholy fire. "How can anyone cast that fast? I thought the haste cap was lowered this iteration."

As more and more began to fall, the other three were able to move farther in and push the dense mass of enemies back. It took nearly a minute of constant casting to defeat a single creature from full health. What made it worth the time, mana, and effort was watching dozens of them collapse and their bodies decay up into a billowing of black pixels.

"How long can you keep this up?" Krymor asked, desperately fighting off creatures rushing in from the right side. "And what's the *rest* of the plan? We'll get surrounded if we push forward."

"Seriously," Baba asked, "how much mana do you have?"

Palmer grinned. "It's over nine thousand!"

Baba glared. "See, now I don't know if you're making a funny or actually answering my question."

"Why not both?"

Corruption continued to cancel out the cursed ground and advance farther inward. By Palmer's estimate, they could force their way to the portal if they had a little more help. Taking out the harbinger from inside the portal was the only way to put a stop to the endless waves coming through. The four of them wouldn't be enough to make it through to the portal, let alone defeat the harbinger. There was also the possibility of more enemies on the other side, and there was nothing to stop enemies from following them through. Their best bet was for Palmer to use a charged void star. The only downside was it would leave him incapacitated for sixty seconds. That was a long time to be vulnerable while surrounded by enemies.

They were definitely going to need help.

"Hey, Baba!" Palmer yelled over the concussive shocks of continuous eruptions. He began to move back a bit and ease off on the casting to recoup mana. He also needed to refresh their protection and buffs. "Can you get a few more really strong players here?"

"How strong? Like us strong?" Baba gave it some thought. "Bluffer and HotPocket are here. They're basically holding the entire eastern line. They're like the best tank healer duo on the server."

"See the meteors over there?" Krymor asked and pointed out the flaming rocks falling from the sky in the northwest. "That's Pyrosexual."

Pyrosexual, Palmer thought with a chuckle. *Do*

they identify as fire?

Nitemane added, "Brainwreck is with his usual group to the west."

"You'd need a really good reason," Baba said, "and I mean a *really* good reason to pull them all away to one spot."

"We're gonna put an end to all this," Palmer told them. "We're gonna fight to the portal, go through, and kill that damn harbinger. Thing is, to do that, I'm gonna have to do something super stupid. Like beyond stupid. I might actually die."

"Sounds like a solid plan."

Though he couldn't see it, Palmer could hear Baba roll his eyes with the comment. The other three were still busy fighting, while Palmer drank a stamina potion and let his mana recover.

"Can you do it, though?"

"Yeah, yeah," Baba assured him. "It'll cost me some favors, but I can do it. Give me a couple minutes."

The group continued to clear enemies from the immediate area and managed to noticeably thin their ranks. This wasn't because there were fewer enemies. It seemed the corruption had spread much farther in, and many creatures were reluctant to step within. It was only when they were forced forward by the mass of bodies behind them that the hesitant monsters entered and were corrupted.

Nearly ten minutes passed before the other four artifact players arrived. Bluffer was a massive warrior that looked more ogre than man. His class was Juggernaut, and he wore a full set of blue steel plate mail. His tower shield was spiked to damage those he kept at bay, and he wielded a two-handed sword in one hand. HotPocket was a Divine Mender, a holy priestess in flowing white and azure robes. She carried a bejeweled golden staff that ringed a massive ruby at its top. Pyrosexual was a Pyrion, the living embodiment of fire magic. His set of cloth armor looked as if they were crafted of enchanted flames, and he was surrounded by an aura of crimson fire. Brainwreck was a Conqueror, which he explained was a subclass of the legendary Berserker class. He wore light leather armor and carried two longswords of blue crystal.

Once Palmer explained his plan to the newcomers, they looked at him in disbelief.

"We're all veteran raiders here," Bluffer told him bluntly. "If it was possible to do that, we would've already done it."

"I get that you're new to the game and all," Pyro remarked, "but your newb is kind of showing."

"Guys," Baba said, still fighting with Krymor, so the others could hear Palmer out. "I know it sounds impossible, but we have to at least try. Besides, if we fail, we can respawn. *He* dies permanently. Don't you think it's worth the risk if *he* thinks it is?"

Bluffer was unconvinced. "There's no way you can do that much damage."

"You really want to risk your life," HotPocket asked, "for this?"

Brainwreck clapped Palmer on the back. "It's only a risk if we let him die!" He let out a hearty laugh, which left Palmer more concerned than reassured. "Don't worry. If you can do what you say, I'll personally keep you alive."

"You're not the tank," Bluffer said in a matter-of-fact tone, "so don't make promises you can't keep. All right," he said to Palmer. "We'll give it a shot. But if we die and lose the city because of all this?" He leaned down to look Palmer in the eyes.

"I'll kill you myself."

***

Palmer fully buffed everyone and reactivated his aura. Everyone allied their guilds, to avoid friendly fire. They set forward in a circle, with Bluffer out front.

Baba and Brain flanked him as pseudo-tanks, though their main focus was still on area melee damage. Pyro and Nite flanked the healers, with the hunter's pets providing extra cover. The Pyrion's spells ignited huge swaths of ground in splashing magma and fire, while Nite's arrows rained down in a magic multitude so vast, they momentarily provided shade. Krymor and his three shadow clones protected the rear. It was up to him to ensure they didn't get overrun as they moved closer to the portal.

Bluffer smashed aside a fae bear with his tower shield, sent it sprawling back into the throng of foes, as his great sword flared with enchantment and came crashing down upon another. The second bear was cleaved in two. Brain dashed forward with both crystal swords in hand, swinging with incredible speed. He didn't aim for weak points or fatal strikes. He merely slashed through as many targets as he could. With each touch of the blades, they shattered into hundreds of pieces, and new blades immediately retook shape. The deadly shards then gathered quickly into a swarm, suspended in air. The swarm dashed toward and into the marked target, like shrapnel from a blast. He swung the blades so quickly, that at one point there were seven swarms in air all at once, like clouds of azure fireflies. Baba didn't bother with targets either. He brought his sword, World Breaker, down upon the ground over and over. As the tumultuous results could attest, the sword was aptly named. The earth in front in a wide cone broke apart and upended. Rocks and soil flashed upward, interspersed with magic flame. Any creatures caught in the blasts were toppled to the ground or brought low from their flight.

The Mender kept regen and shield on everyone, including Palmer, and provided spot heals as needed. No one was taking large amounts of damage, just the occasional attacks that made it through by virtue of so many opponents striking at once. It was impossible to dodge everything that came the group's way, and there was only so much protection their gear could provide. Palmer, on the other hand, was focused on spreading disease and corruption as far and wide as possible. The quicker the enemy was stripped of their strength, weakened even further, and entered into an exposed state, the faster they would all die. He was purposely holding back, until his abilities could be best used.

As if on cue, Bluffer stopped and slammed his shield against the ground. He tilted his head back and roared out a challenge. With the ability activated, his shout could be seen as a flash of red mist through the air. It swept across the battlefield, inciting scores of enemies to rush toward him in a frenzy. Their magically induced bloodthirst made them reckless. They trampled over one another in a mad effort to reach the Juggernaut.

It was the moment Palmer had been waiting for. He began to unleash void nova, again and again. The rapidity with which he was able to set off the corruption blasts immediately caught everyone's attention. Their outbursts of disbelief were pushed even further, as Palmer quickly surpassed everyone on the damage meter—according to Krymor. As a twenty-four-foot sphere, the spell normally caught quite a few within its range. With enemies frothing to reach Bluffer, that number was easily doubled. It took barely a minute for them all to dissipate into ashen pixels.

Warning! The formation of a new bridge is imminent!

What? Palmer didn't have time to look. He was too focused on dealing with the horde of creatures after their blood. *It has to be the time dilated rifts.* He could think of no other explanation for why the rifts hadn't been dealt with yet, or why the system hadn't shut down the hackers. *C'mon, Aurora. Can't you work any faster?*

Warning! The formation of a new bridge is imminent!
Warning! The formation of a new bridge is imminent!
Warning! The formation of a new bridge is imminent!

Palmer inwardly cursed. He wanted to say something aloud, but he didn't want the others to know he could converse with the system. All he could do was trust Aurora knew what she was doing. He had no choice but to handle each problem one at a time. This event was just as important as an incursion growing into a breach. The future of both servers was at stake.

They continued fighting toward the portal and had made significant progress. The danger now was in becoming engulfed from behind. It was a lot of pressure to put on the Shadow. He and his clones seemed to be keeping the enemy at bay, but that was mostly due to the constant damage from Palmer. A second area taunt from Bluffer set in motion another wave of enraged creatures. With murder in their eyes, they rushed headlong for the Juggernaut. Once that had been dealt with, Palmer went about refreshing all their buffs and protection. They were minutes from the portal. The time to put his plan fully to the test was nearly at hand.

Hopefully, it doesn't get me killed.

"We're getting close," Baba said. He looked back at Palmer and mirrored his earlier sentiment. "I hope you don't die."

"I know you meant that to be encouraging," Palmer replied with a half-hearted laugh, "but you could've worded that better."

Krymor said, "It's fine. Even if you do die, we'll be able to kill the harbinger. That means this event is in the bag. You got to feel good about that, right?"

Palmer narrowed his gaze at the Shadow. "You know I can't respawn, right?"

"Yeah. But you can't actually *die*, either."

"True," Palmer admitted, even if it was a bit harsh. "If I have to take one for the team, I will."

"All right everyone," Bluffer said and put an end to all the chatter. "Game faces on."

They had arrived at the portal.

This was the tricky part. They would need to hold off enemies from all around, while dealing with whatever continued to come through the portal. Even harder, they had to do this without Palmer's help. Krymor and his clones dealt with those stepping from the portal. The others did their best and continued to hold in a tight circle. Palmer had stopped casting, drank potions to restore his stamina and mana. He then refreshed their protection from corruption one more time. They had four minutes. With a deep breath, he began to charge void star. The longer he could hold out, the wider its range would become, and the more damage it would inflict.

After thirty seconds, his body became engulfed in black fire. It licked along his flesh and began to cause damage. After sixty seconds, the magic flames were bright and intense, radiating heat and distorting the air all around him. Even though the pain he felt was reduced, due to his max rank passive pain tolerance, he still felt each burn and lesion as they formed and grew deeper. After ninety seconds, he gritted his teeth against the pain. His body shook and muscles trembled. The black fire was so strong, even HotPocket shied away. She did her best to heal him, but it was like throwing water at an inferno. When he reached two minutes, Palmer cried out. Tears fell from his cheeks, as he clenched both fists and drew inward, as if he would collapse into a ball.

"That's enough!" It was Baba, grabbing him by both shoulders with enough force to get his attention. He endured the magic fire engulfing both arms and hands, until Palmer's eyes opened. Calmer, the Champion said, "It's enough."

Palmer nodded. Voice wracked with pain, he yelled, "Everyone get into the portal!"

While the others stood motionless with blank looks on their faces, Bluffer moved without thought. He took hold of each one and threw them through the portal. Once he was alone, Palmer saw the monsters rushing forward. They were merely moments away when he let loose the pent-up magic.

Corruption exploded outward with enough concussive force to knock over everyone inside the portal and send them sprawling. The creatures in the immediate area were lifted upward with the ground, caught within the expanding cloud of ebon fire. They burned while still in air, bodies broken then charred to ash in a violent instant. The raging flames of corruption ballooned outward like the sudden birth of a black sun. It left a crater in the destroyed earth, with nothing but dying smoke. Those within the blast had evaporated, utterly destroyed in a single, terrible moment. They were the lucky ones. Those caught in the outskirts of the blast, a hundred yards away, met with the fading aftermath of force and flame. They were battered and thoroughly burned, left alive for fleeting moments. Farther out still, those unfortunate creatures were left broken and corrupted with fire.

Palmer collapsed onto his back. He could blink. He could breathe. All sound had been replaced with an incessant ringing in his ears. Unable to move, he looked up at the falling rain, only to realize it was ash. Flakes touched upon his face. Still in shock, he took in short, rapid breaths. Though his heart raced, he did his best to remain calm. Unsure if he was in danger, unable to turn his head or even hear the enemies around him, he put his faith in the others. They promised to protect him.

Baba poked his head out from the portal. He saw Palmer nearby and reached out to drag him in.

Once inside, he placed Palmer against a large rock. The dimension they were in was a vast wasteland of darkness. The ground, the rocks, the very air was thick with it. The only light came from a moon far too big for any sky. Even its glow was muted, as if the shadows drank it up. The others were already engaged with the harbinger, fighting for their lives against a frightening power. She was far stronger and faster, with magic that dwarfed their own. It took barely a moment to realize they had no chance of winning.

"I have to go help," Baba said. "You'll be safe here." He made sure Palmer wouldn't slump over, then turned to join the fight.

It is done, Aurora told him. *I have identified every last offender. There will be no more incursions.*

What about the current ones? he wanted to ask but couldn't speak.

He brought up the incursions tab by thought alone. There were fifteen pages, but they were steadily dwindling. The number of available minions were beginning to grow. As he watched the list expand, he didn't recognize any. Over a hundred new named minions were soon ready for his command. He assumed they were the former bosses from each defeated rift. He looked back at the fight, where Bluffer had been driven to his knees, bloodied but defiant. HotPocket was down, struck through by a dozen shafts of emerald light. The others still fought with all their might but were also badly wounded.

We can still do this.

The harbinger, floating in air, sent a barrage of thorny wooden spears toward Nitemane. The hunter tried to dodge but was lanced by three in the leg, side, and shoulder. Brain was engulfed in emerald fire, held in place by steely vines. Pyro and Krymor seemed to be causing the most damage, but the lengthy battle was taking a toll on their stamina. They were visibly slower and on the verge of collapse. Baba did his best with ranged abilities, but they were clearly not his strong suit.

When Palmer was finally able to move, he found it was still a struggle. He'd pushed himself too hard, caused damage no potion or spell could fully heal. As much as he wanted to join his friends, to rush in and fight beside them, he just didn't have it in him. His fighting was done outside the portal.

"You'll do it for me," he said and called forth every named minion at his disposal.

They appeared from the Void and rushed toward the harbinger. As one, they cried out a challenge, eager to join the fray. Over a hundred strong, each one an elite boss, their damage bolstered by Palmer, they leapt into the air and by sheer numbers and weight brought low the harbinger. Dragged to the ground, she fought back with all her might. Violent bursts of magic spattered blood and flesh in all directions. The minions cared only for her demise. They tore at her defenses, drained her mana, clawed her flesh. When one fell, two took its place. The harbinger found herself on the receiving end of her own strategy. When all was said and done, twenty-two minions remained. The harbinger was torn to pieces. Corruption spread through her remains, the upper half of an armless torso. Palmer called off the attack and moved to stand over her. She met his gaze with disdain, defiant until the end.

"You cannot have me," she told him.

Palmer raised his staff overhead in both hands, ready to strike.

"I don't *want* you."

- 18 -

Palmer healed HotPocket first, so she could help heal the others. The portal had begun to shimmer, indicating it was about to close. They had to get everyone out in time or risk being trapped on this side. Once everyone was able to move, Palmer urged them through with all speed. The portal collapsed in on itself and disappeared into wisps of blue light. Palmer, the last to go, was so concerned the portal would shut down on him that he was looking back as he passed through. He walked directly into Baba, who had come to a sudden stop.

"Holy..." he began but couldn't finish the thought.

HotPocket, momentarily confused, asked, "Where are we?"

"It's still Nidmar," Bluffer replied, "but what the hell happened?"

Palmer looked out at what was once the battlefield. It had been utterly decimated. Corrupted to pitch black, still emanating black flame and plumes of ash, the entire area looked as if a dark meteor had struck. All the grass and rock were gone, as if the earth had been upended and smashed back down into tiny bits. They stood at the center of the small crater Palmer's void star had left behind. What few remained of the enemy could be seen at the edges, being dealt final blows by the now overwhelming defenders. Though no one dared to step within the corruption, they easily vanquished what was left of the harbinger's summons.

Krymor whistled in appreciation. To Palmer, he said, "Remind me to never get on your bad side."

"I wouldn't worry," he told the Shadow. "I'm completely helpless after I use it."

"Sure," Nitemane remarked, "if you can survive the blast."

Brain looked at the corruption seeping up onto his boot.

"Can you do something about this stuff?"

"Oh! Yeah." Palmer began to cure the ground. "Sorry."

He cured a path toward the city, so the others could get out of the corrupted circle. It would take time to methodically cleanse it all. As most of the group waved goodbye, with exchanges of gratitude and congratulations, Bluffer pulled Palmer aside for a quick word.

"You looking for a steady group?"

Palmer was both flattered and a little shocked. That sort of invitation was one of the highest unspoken compliments a player could give to another. Coming from the strongest tank on the server, it meant a lot to be acknowledged that way.

"I'm not against it," Palmer replied honestly, "but my class doesn't really play well with others."

"The corruption thing?" Bluffer shrugged. "No worries. I gained immunity before we even entered the portal."

Palmer was surprised yet again. "You're immune? Wow. Guess that means I can't delete you now."

Bluffer burst into laughter. "That's your first thought? You really are hardcore, man." He looked back at HotPocket, who was impatiently waiting for him. "Well, the offer stands, if you ever want it. It'd be nice if you helped out at Starfall. We'll probably head that way in a couple of hours."

"I need to wait a bit, I think," Palmer said. "I'm not sure what's wrong. I feel like I'm under some kind of status ailment I can't see. My stats are halved, and my stamina is capped at seventy-five. That ability I used has a twenty-four-hour cooldown. Hopefully, this clears when it resets."

"Most likely," the Juggernaut said. "It's odd you can't see that information. Maybe your character isn't fully integrated with the server, since you're not actually from here."

Palmer nodded in agreement. "That would make a lot of sense. From the start, it's felt like I've been playing without tutorials or tooltips or any of the normal mechanic explanations you'd expect."

"Anyway," Bluffer said, "I've got to get going. Come look us up when you're ready."

"Will do."

Palmer went back to curing the rest of the shattered field, grateful that the enemy bodies had all disappeared after death. The necessary cleanup would have been so much worse. A small part of him was a little miffed they didn't drop any loot. High level creatures like that should have at least dropped rare materials or gold. He was suddenly aware of players around the edge of the crater watching him. It was obvious who he was, since no one else on the server could cure corruption. They talked among themselves, some pointing his way. They looked more intrigued than afraid, which left him with the impression no one knew he was the one who had caused so much destruction.

When the last patch had been cleansed, he noticed small groups slowly headed his way. It was fine they were curious, but a small part of him still worried about sneak attacks from the remaining hackers. Every hacking group has a small number of truly talented individuals, the ones who do all the actual hacking. The rest are made up of those who strive to be true hackers, the ones who use software created by others or rely heavily on social engineering. There was no telling how many of them were left or what tricks they still had at their disposal.

I need to deal with them sooner than later. He summoned a lich to create a portal back to Sunnyvale. He needed rest and time to think. The approaching players most likely meant well. *I just don't have the mental bandwidth to deal with all their questions right now.*

He slipped through the portal before the players could arrive.

Before long, he was back at home, resting on the couch. He absently scratched at the edges of the sapphire in his chest. The damned thing still itched from time to time. After a few moments of quiet, he pulled up the incursions tab. It was five pages long, all still filled with time-dilated rifts. As promised by the system, there were no new incursions. He wondered how long it would take for them all to clear. The listing didn't provide what percentage of time dilation had affected each rift. He could only hope his minions wouldn't be stuck inside for days. His minion count had somewhat recovered, but most of the named were unavailable and unresponsive. He didn't recognize any of those ready to serve.

"We came pretty close to a bunch of new bridges," he said aloud. "I'm glad you were able to stop them in time."

The system didn't reply. He liked to think she was always listening to him, watching over him, but he had no real proof that was true. Thought of the bridge jogged his memory. He recalled his conversation with Allandra, how their best bet of finding and banning the rest of the hackers was to lure them all onto the bridge. With both servers working together, it would be much easier to trace their connections. The trick would be getting them all to show.

"I'd have to be pretty convincing." He chewed his lower lip as he thought. "How the heck do I even message the entire server?" He checked the Shop for any items that related to communication and quickly found what he was looking for. "A bullhorn. A *million* gold each?" There were nine available. "That's pricey for a one-time use." He gave some thought to what he would say and made the purchase. "Okay. Time to be a colossal jerk."

He composed his thoughts and activated the item.

[System Broadcast: Palmer]

Hey, everyone. Palmer here. We may not have met, but you all know who I am. This message is for what's left of the hackers trying to invade my server.

You failed. There won't be any more rifts, because all the people who actually know how to hack were caught and banned. All that's left are the wannabes, the ones who suck at the game, who couldn't PvP their way out of a wet paper bag, who need cheats just to be average. You think you can take on hardcore players? You can't even dominate your own server.

Well, I'm issuing a challenge to each and every one of you. Meet me tomorrow inside the bridge to HCE at noon. You want to destroy my server? Here's your chance. Get past me, and it's all yours. I'll tell my people guarding the portal to let you through. I won't even use my minions, because I don't need them to beat you. I singlehandedly killed the harbinger at Nidmar. That's right, me. You're welcome.

And don't tell me you're too busy defending the server against the event. Because I know for a fact you don't care, since YOU'RE THE ONES WHO TRIGGERED IT IN THE FIRST PLACE. You gambled the future of your own server in an attempt to take mine down, and you still lost. That's just embarrassing.

So, bring whatever it is you think you need to win. Bring your best characters, bring hacked weapons, bring possessed gods for all I care. None of it will matter. Because at your core, you're all terrible players. You don't come close to what it takes to play hardcore, let alone win. And if you're mad about what I'm saying, on some level, you know it's true. Feel free to come prove me wrong.

I dare you.

"Well, if that doesn't get them to show," he said, "I don't know what will. Hopefully this ailment is gone by then." He eyed his halved stats. "Be kind of awkward if I died before you can track them all down." Palmer looked up, the way he usually addressed the system. "You can hear me, right?"

Yes, she assured him. *We will be ready.*

"Good. Now I just need a way to survive long enough for you two to trace them." He recalled there was one more ability he hadn't tried yet. "Shift. Hmm. I wonder how that works. Doesn't the void destroy mana?" He wondered if it would drain his while inside, or it might even kill him. His minions went back and forth with no issue. Then again, they were basically remade as creatures of the void. He wasn't a void creature, but he did have corruption immunity. "It's the final gear set bonus," he reasoned. "It should be the most powerful one. It'd be pointless if it wasn't somehow beneficial." Though he was hesitant to try, he saw no harm in a quick experiment. "Just have to test it out and see. Y'know," he looked up and accused Aurora, "since the game doesn't provide any information! Lore, backstory, tooltips...something!"

He ended his little rant with a sigh. His frustration

with the lack of explanations had been building. It just seemed odd that the system could create an entire new mechanic and interface for him within minutes but couldn't be bothered to give details on core game features. Like how activating your first ability stone chose your class. Or how stats affected combat. Or if entering the void might kill him. Little things.

Palmer stood, held his breath, and activated shift.

Everything immediately switched to grayscale. The world was all the same, his house, the furniture, the cherry blossoms outside. Only their colors seemed affected. The air itself was somehow different, though. There was a purple tinge to its flow, as if seeing through tinted glass. It coalesced around items with occasional violet charges. He looked down at his arms and hands, saw it try to permeate his skin with cloying mist. It seemed to be hungry for his mana but was unable to reach through.

He tentatively let out his breath and tried to breathe. Everything seemed fine, despite the crispness to the air. It felt the same as a bitter winter, that harsh sting of biting air, but without the cold. He momentarily worried that breathing in the purple air would somehow allow it access to his mana. His stats remained unchanged. He felt no different.

"So, this is the void?" he asked quietly to himself. "I don't see the difference, other than the colors." He reached down for his drink on the table, and his hand passed through. "Oh. Well, that is different." While his hand looked normal, everything else seemed phased. "Like the harbinger. So, I'm still here, in the house, but in a different dimension." He tested the strength of the floor with a foot. "At the least the ground is solid."

So, how is this beneficial? He considered the ability for a moment. *I suppose I could use it as an emergency defense, to avoid attacks I can't dodge. There must be more to it, though. Why is it the best bonus?* He looked around the room, parted the purple air with a wave of his hand. *It's not the void itself that's helpful to me. It's not restoring my stats or curing my ailment status. So, it has to be the physical moving between dimensions that's the actual bonus. The shifting.* He thought about it more. *Could I use it to attack?* He imagined himself in combat, phasing out to avoid attacks and back in to cast spells or land blows with his staff. *That could potentially be seriously overpowered, depending on reuse time and cost.*

He pulled up his stats to pay close attention and shifted back. Both his mana and stamina blipped down a bit. He then shifted as fast as possible, ten times in a row. It had the same reuse time as any other ability, four times per six seconds. Though there was no listed cost, he could clearly see a one percent mana and stamina cost with each use. That meant he could fight all out for a short time or control a prolonged battle with precise, calculated, and efficient use.

"Okay," he said, as it all clicked in his mind, "that is definitely a good ability. This necklace and Divine Regeneration give me 2% fatigue recovery per tick. That's two free casts out of four if I go ham. Which makes the overall cost 20% mana and stamina per minute. Two and a half minutes before the first fatigue penalty, which I don't want to hit. So, two minutes to be safe. Mana isn't the issue. It's stamina. If I drink a stamina potion every two minutes, I could go for quite a bit." It all made sense in his mind, but plans tended to fall apart in practice. "I need a way to test it out for sure."

He brought up his list of minions, focused in on the named, and selected one he recognized from the harbinger fight. Marius Truestrike appeared and bowed. He was a middle-aged man, with thick brown hair and golden eyes. Lean, well-muscled, adorned in light cloth armor, he looked an imposing figure all too used to the rigors of physical combat.

"How may I be of use?"

"I need a sparring partner," Palmer replied, "to test a new ability. I only have a vague notion of how I want to use it, phasing in and out of the void to attack or defend as needed."

"Shift fighting." Marius gave a solemn nod. "A very strong technique but quickly drains resources. You will need to be careful. Use it sparingly, to get the most from its advantage."

Palmer's eyes widened. "You're familiar with it? Can you do it?"

"I have seen it," Marius replied, "and I will never forget the devastation I witnessed that day. I do not possess the power to shift between realms at will. I am, however, well-versed in martial combat. I can help you find the right technique for your fighting style and make the most of its use before you're driven to exhaustion."

What are the odds, Palmer thought, *that I chose the one minion who knew exactly what I needed? Is this you again, Aurora?* She couldn't hear his thoughts, but he thanked her all the same. *Who needs skill when you have luck?* He shook his head and chuckled. *I suppose it doesn't hurt to have both.*

"All right," he told Marius. "Let's go out back and practice."

***

Palmer left early the next day to prepare. Once there, he instructed the elves to line up on either side of the path leading to the portal. Thousands of them, in full armor and regalia, were a sight to behold. The strength of two nations bent their magic, might, and will toward a single goal. He instructed those at the bottom to warn anyone attempting to climb they risked death and deletion inside the bridge. Observers would not be tolerated. No exceptions.

He had also instructed Aurora not to ban anyone

until she could identify every one of them. Seeing any of them disappear would scare the others into disconnecting. They likely would not get a second chance at this. Palmer wanted to make the best of the situation. He tried to account for every outcome and plan accordingly. He didn't need to defeat them all. He just needed to outlast them.

He thanked the elves for their help and dedication as he walked up the path, with nods of recognition, head bows of gratitude, a spoken thank you here and there. Some even saluted, a firm fist over fist, which he did his best to return in proper form. There were spear butts and bow ends slammed against the ground in a show of honor. By the end of his walk, elves behind him cheered to the rhythmic thumping, keenly aware he intended to rid their world of a dire threat.

Once inside, Palmer placed a one-hundred-foot ring of plague and disease around the portal. He purposely chose not to corrupt the ground, so the hackers would remain confident, still able to fight. The two diseases would only weaken them, slow their movement and attacks. A hundred yards farther out, he carefully corrupted the ground in a circle. This was to prevent them from attempting to run past without a fight. It left plenty of room for combat but sent a clear message. There was no getting past while he still lived.

At the portal to Earth, he placed the enduring shelter to block all access. He then fully diseased and corrupted the ground there as well. He called forth all the available minions, forty-seven named bosses and hundreds of elites. Many minions were still stuck inside incursions, his generals included. He instructed those present not to intervene in the coming battle but to defend the Earth portal with their lives. His stats were still halved from the unseen status ailment, but he was strong enough to execute his plan without assistance.

Or so he hoped.

Palmer was fully buffed, patiently waiting a safe distance from the portal to Tellaria, when three powerful deities stepped through. One was a woman with long dark hair, dressed in flowing blue robes and carrying a golden staff. She was Hecate, the Goddess of Magic. Another was a man in heavy mail and leather armor, carrying a spear and shield. He was Caturix, the God of War. The third was a skeleton in black robes, carrying a large two-handed scythe. He was Ankou, the God of Death. All three immediately noticed the diseased ground. They spoke quietly to one another for a brief moment, before Hecate stepped back through the portal. She returned with twelve more players, all maximum level and wearing various rarities of equipment. The aura around them drastically changed when they drew weapons, items far more powerful than anything found on the hardest raid.

Guess they went with hacked weapons and gods, Palmer thought, as he appraised each one. *If they all attack together, I don't know how long I'll last. How do I get them to come at me one at a time? Competition?*

"You actually came," Palmer called out to them. "I'm surprised. You guys have more guts than I gave you credit for." He looked each one over as he scanned across their number. "So. Who's the strongest? Is it you, magic lady? Why don't you give me your absolute best attack. Everything you've got. I won't even move from this spot."

She looked to Ankou, who gave a nod.

"Sure, we can do it that way," the skeleton said with a hollow voice. Frost vapors emanated from his mouth as he spoke. "We've got plenty of time."

I guess he's in charge. Palmer studied the god more closely. *Interesting.*

Hecate stepped forward and began to charge an ice attack. A sphere of moisture appeared in the air far above the field and immediately began to freeze. It radiated a blue vortex that quickly pulled at the surrounding air, soon growing the ball of ice into a boulder. Blue fire enveloped the Goddess, freezing her flesh in patches that grew the longer she charged the spell. Crackles of azure power ran along both her arms. Before long, the boulder of solid ice had grown another three times. It was the size of a small building, so cold it could be felt from the ground. Hecate screamed against the pain, pouring all of her magic and will into the spell. Palmer was all too familiar with that terrible cry. It was exactly what he'd hoped for. The hacker controlling her had no care for her well-being. Such reckless abandon would likely leave her incapacitated. After what felt like an ominous eternity, she unleashed the pent-up magic and collapsed to all fours.

The sphere of ice was so large by then, it cast a shadow across the entire area. It suddenly came crashing down with incredible speed. Even if Palmer wanted to dodge its mass, it was too large to evade. It smashed into the ground, forming a crater halfway up its bulk. Palmer was completely encompassed by crushing shards, thrown earth, and a vast nimbus of powdered ice. The gathered players all laughed at his demise, joking among themselves how easy his defeat had been. Their joking turned to shock, as Palmer stepped out from behind the ice. He waved away the billowing frost, no sign of damage upon him.

"Wow!" he exclaimed. "Look at that thing! It's huge! Good for you," he said in praise of the exhausted Goddess. "Your aim was a little off, but that was really impressive. So..." He looked at the other two Gods. "Who's next?"

Ankou nodded for Caturix to step forward.

The other players cheered him on, as the God of War banged his spear against his shield and moved toward Palmer with conviction. He took three mighty steps, brought back his spear, and launched the barbed weapon with divine strength. It should have pierced Palmer's heart and taken with it half his chest. Instead, the spear harmlessly struck the ground behind him.

Palmer had been slowly moving closer. "Not bad. I bet that would've hurt. Y'know, if it hit me." He gave it some thought, as he continued to take a few more steps forward. "I could buff your hit chance, if you need it. I guess it's harder to control those gods than I thought. Are you, like, in complete control? Or are they fighting against you, maybe making you miss?"

The three deities exchanged worried looks with one another. Hecate was still down, breathing hard and unable to move. Caturix tossed aside his shield and purposefully strode toward Palmer. By his demeanor, he clearly intended to throw down with bare fists. As they were about to clash, the God's punch seemed to narrowly miss. In truth, Palmer had shifted an instant before it could land against his jaw. He continued forward, shifted back and hooked his foot against the God's. Caturix, carried on by the momentum of his attack, tripped and fell. He caught himself before crashing face first into the earth but was visibly embarrassed, nonetheless.

"Yikes." Palmer kept walking forward. "Y'know, if you want to give it another try," he said to Hecate, "I could replenish your fatigue and mana. I kind of want to see that spell again."

Caturix was up and charged for a second attack from behind. Inexplicably, he not only missed but somehow fumbled again. The God landed hard upon hands and knees, skidding forward onto his face.

"What the hell!" he screamed in rage and punched the ground. "How are you doing that?"

Surprisingly, Ankou did nothing as Palmer moved in close to Hecate and knelt. He reached out with a potion in hand, as if to offer it to her. Nearby players were not convinced of his generosity and quickly moved to intervene. Palmer activated his aura, dropped the potion, and grabbed hold of Hecate's shoulder.

"So dumb," he told them. Players instantly dropped

to their knees, visibly and audibly wracked by the sudden pain of corruption. Hecate screamed as well, as her immortality was torn from her body by the mortalis engine. “You’re all just *so* dumb.”

Ankou attacked with his scythe. Palmer did his best to minimize the blow but couldn’t shift to avoid it entirely. He needed to let the energy transfer finish. The blade tore through his shield and left a nasty gash in his left shoulder, to the tune of over three hundred damage. Though his stats were still halved by the status ailment from having overcharged void star, Palmer still had plenty of health to spare. Once Hecate was fully drained of her immortality, a message appeared on his screen.

Success! You have absorbed the immortality of Hecate.

All stats have been increased by 500.

Palmer quickly moved away, before the other two Gods could land another blow. His stats had increased but only by half of what they should have. It was annoying to still be under the status impairment. Still, the increase was a quarter of his existing stats. That was impressive by any measure.

The remaining players began to attack from range any way they could. Some had bows or wands, while others tried throwing knives or used special abilities granted by their hacked weapons. Hecate, now corrupted, quickly reached for the purple potion Palmer had dropped, pulled free its stopper and drank it. After all, it looked like a high-grade rejuvenation potion. She began to hack and sputtered its contents across the ground, struggling just to breathe.

“What—what was that?” she demanded.

“High quality fire oil,” Palmer replied, shifting to avoid attacks and moving toward the uncorrupted players, “mixed with berries for added color and flavor. You probably shouldn't smoke for a while," he cautioned. "You might go boom."

He shifted back amongst his targets, corrupting them with his aura. The two Gods were fast on his heels, ready to strike him down. Palmer shifted out of harm's way and back as they fumbled. He thought it best to put some distance between himself and all the others, now that the players were corrupted and essentially out of the fight. It was just Ankou and Caturix left to deal with.

They both approached him with deadly intent. Palmer drew his staff, determined to make the fight last as long possible. He needed to give Aurora and the HCE system more time to trace connections. Using all he had learned while training with Marcus, every move and technique they had practiced, he set about fighting the two Gods by brawn alone. He had no special staff abilities to speak of but had mastered the basic skill. It was his incredible stats and movement speed that gave him an edge. They were clearly more skilled in battle, as far as ability choices went, but they lacked strategy in their approach. They aimed to beat him down by brute force. Those who were weak in PvP, relied on the advantage of numbers or gear to overpower other players, completely ignoring strategy or mechanics.

Palmer did his best to shift just before any attack he couldn't avoid was about to land. He was incredibly nimble and fast, already difficult to hit. The added ability to shift into another dimension made him nigh invulnerable. If he didn't also want to attack back, he could have just stood there while phased. He was afraid they would grow tired of that tack and disconnect before the systems could locate them. He had to make the fight interesting, aggravate and engage them. He gave himself fully to the fight, striking at every opening, evading damage when he could, and shifting when he couldn't. He wasn't perfect with the technique. It was difficult to take into account the exhaustion combat brings when merely practicing any moves. Adding a third opponent to the mix just made it all the more difficult.

Over time, his fatigue continued to grow, and mistakes began to pile up. He was taking far more damage than he would have liked. Each successful strike against him seemed to drive the two Gods even more, fueling their fervor for his demise. He had no idea why they hated him so much. With his health getting dangerously low, his status ailment still dragging down all his stats, Palmer began to pull potions from inventory. Both Gods quickly dissuaded him of that notion, doing all they could to strike his hands and prevent any healing. They had him at a disadvantage, as close as they had ever been to victory, and they knew it. With a potion knocked from his hand, a second attack caught him behind the knee. He went down to his backside. They were upon him like rabid dogs, raining one blow after another. Palmer struggled to fend them off, unable to shift any more without incurring a fatigue penalty.

Success! All players have been identified!

Palmer immediately shifted. It was a struggle to catch his breath, as the penalty kicked in. It was far better than the alternative. He knew without a doubt that if he'd persisted any longer, he surely would have lost.

"What kind of crap is this?" Ankou yelled down at him. "You quitting already?"

"Yeah." Palmer nodded, hands up in defeat. "You beat me."

"Ha!" Caturix high-fived the God of Death. "Told you he was a pansy!"

"Then again," Palmer said between ragged breaths and made finger guns at them both, "I beat you, too."

All located players have been biosignature banned.

Palmer waved goodbye as the two were disconnected from the server and evicted from the possessed Gods.

***

Palmer shifted back with a groan, still feeling the nasty effects of the fatigue penalty. Both Gods offered to help him up.

"Thanks," he said and took their offered hands. Once on his feet, he said, "That went much better than I thought it would."

"I was helpless to act," the God of War said in way of apology, "like a prisoner in my own body."

Ankou bowed his head. "You have my apologies and sincerest thanks."

"I'm just glad they were caught," Palmer said, "and can never do that again. They were a menace to the entire server." He noticed Hecate still struggling with the fire oil she'd been forced to drink. "I should go help her."

Palmer approached the Goddess of Magic but wasn't sure what to do for her. He doubted she would accept another potion. Instead, he bought a waterskin from the Shop and offered it to her.

"It's just water," he promised. "I swear."

Hecate took the skin, rinsed her mouth of the foul oil, and spat.

"Much better," she said.

Palmer helped her to her feet. Once she was steady, he returned her immortality. As a player, it wasn't easy to forfeit that sort of power. As a person, he couldn't imagine holding onto it.

"Sorry I had to take this from you." Once the power had been transferred back, he felt the gem in his chest begin to itch around the edges once again. "I hope you don't hold it against me."

"Of course not," she replied, her voice still a bit hoarse. "You only did what was necessary. I owe you much."

"No," Palmer said, as the other two joined, "none of you owe me anything. Anyone would have done the same." The three deities exchanged doubtful looks. "In any case, I don't want to keep you from any godly duties. I need to get this place cleaned up, before the corruption spreads."

All three nodded in understanding.

"If you should ever have need," Hecate said, "do not hesitate to call upon me."

Caturix firmly added, "Or I."

"And I," Ankou said with a bow.

With that, all three deities simply vanished from sight, leaving Palmer with the sudden quiet of solitude. Only wind and the crackle of melting ice could be heard. In that moment, he realized it was finally over. They'd actually succeeded in saving their server from the hackers. The bridge still existed, but that was easily protected by the elves outside, not to mention his army of minions. With no more pressing matters demanding his time and attention, he could go back home to see his mother—to see Sara.

It took quite a bit of time to undo all the disease and corruption within the bridge. He nearly burst into laughter and relief when the status ailment finally lifted halfway through the cleansing. He could laugh at the terrible timing, considering how things went. He might have felt otherwise had the plan failed. Once all had been cured, the enduring shelter stored away, and his minions dismissed, he went back out to instruct the elves to restrict all movement through the portal.

I'll think of a more permanent solution later. He considered the ongoing event. *I should probably help them finish. They might all be pissed at me, though. What if they refuse to finish building the defenses here?*

Palmer sighed. He would deal with that later. What he really wanted was to return home and soak in the hot spring. *And maybe get something to eat.*

Once he was resting in the warm water, notifications caught his attention. He went to the Incursions tab and saw many of them closing. Within twenty minutes, every last one had been completed. He got out, dried off, and went to change his clothes. While standing in the dining area, he went to the Shop to buy a feast. When the table was fully set, he called forth all his generals.

"Thank you," he told them, "all of you. I know this doesn't repay all your hard work and dedication, but hopefully it makes up for it just a little." He looked around at the borrowed home, which suddenly felt smaller with all their company. "I'm gonna need a bigger place, with all the named we have now."

Kyomi pointed out, "You don't have to make all of them generals."

"In fact," Avarran said with a turkey leg in each hand, "it would be wiser if you did not. Such esteemed positions should be earned, in my modest opinion."

Valorya scoffed, "Like yours was?"

"Indeed," the arch demon replied.

Congratulations! The Harbinger event has been successfully completed!

The world of Tellaria is safe once more, thanks to the bravery and hard work of those who participated. Unfortunately, our time here has come to an end. The world will be remade, far stronger than it is now. It is our sincere hope that you will all return for the next iteration, where rewards will be granted to your first character, based upon your overall achievements and the level of your contributions to this world.

Server reset in 12:00:00

Palmer stared at the server announcement in shock. Despite all his efforts, it was all going to be wiped. It felt a bit like a betrayal, a punch to the gut. While he assumed Aurora had her reasons for the decision, most likely to implement new necessary code, it still left a bitter sting in his heart. He couldn't help but feel that all he'd fought for had been for nothing.

No, he corrected, *not for nothing. We stopped the hackers. They won't be coming back. Maybe it's for the best, if it means she can prevent anything like this from ever happening again. Besides, I still have...*

[Guy] Hoooooly...
[Jenna] Whoa!
[Matt] You're kidding me
[Kenta] Why? Why would they announce that?
[Guy] Everyone's gonna freak the hell out!
[Palmer] What are you talking about?
[Rosa] Server reset
[Jenna] Server just made an announcement
[Carnes] Here, too
[Guy] The server just told everyone the world is a simulation
[Kenta] It's already on the news. So dumb.
[Matt] What's the point of telling everyone? Why not just the players?

Palmer turned away from the conversation. His mind was suddenly flooded with an influx of guilt, regret, and anxiety. Why didn't he go back to see them sooner? What had he been fighting for this entire time, if not for them? Was he selfish? Did he really do it all for the thrill of being inside a game? For the levels, the equipment, the power? He felt numb inside, as the weight of it all came crashing in, made his life and choices seem meaningless.

But it isn't, he argued inwardly. *It's not about*

meaning. It's about connections. Life is about people. The family you're born with. The friends you choose. The people you decide to care about. That's what matters.

"Are you all right?" Kyomi asked him.

He was filled with the sudden urge to return home, to his *real* home.

"I have to go. I'm sorry," he told them. "I'll come back as soon as I can."

But how? He was filled with nervous energy, as his mind raced. *I can teleport to the bridge, go back to Earth, but how do I get home? I have no money. There's no time for a flight. And that's even if I can get past—*

The Incursions tab opened on its own. Though no new rifts were listed, there was a new button on the top right. It read Return Home. Palmer mentally clicked it and was instantly transported outside his front door. He thanked the system and hesitantly reached for the handle. When he pushed the door open and stepped inside, he found his mother and Sara watching the news from the couch.

"Palmer!" his mother shouted and rushed to hug him. Her embrace was crushing. "Oh my god, I've missed you so much!"

"I told you," Sara said. Though she tried to appear relaxed, it was clear she was just as excited. "Where have you been, you dork!"

"Yes!" His mother let go long enough to demand answers. "What happened to you?"

"I mean," Palmer began, "it's kind of a long story."

His mother sat back down and folded her arms, as if to say she was listening. Sara took the opportunity to get a hug from him as well. Hers was nearly as overwhelming. Sometimes he forgot just how strong she really was. When she let go, she kept him at arm's length, looked into his eyes as if gauging something. He was about to ask what was wrong when she leaned forward and kissed him. It was short but sweet, a promise of more to come. Sara then sat down beside his mother, folded her arms, and waited for the explanation.

Palmer blinked, unsure how to respond or where to start.

- 19 -

Palmer had wanted to return to say goodbye to his new friends on Tellaria, but the situation at home had taken a drastic turn he hadn't expected. He got out of bed and dressed, all too aware that his mother was just downstairs watching the news with the volume much higher than normal. He waited for Sara to get dressed before heading down. She slipped her hand into his, as they sheepishly entered the living room. His mother immediately lowered the volume and patted the couch beside her. He took a seat next to her, and Sara sat on his left.

"I don't care what anyone says," his mother told him, leaned over for a quick hug and kiss on the forehead, "you're my son, and I love you. For all we know, this is some sort of hoax."

She was adamant in her belief, despite all the evidence to the contrary. Everyone could see the server timer ticking down, even NPCs. There were alternate explanations, like mass delusion, advanced government technology, and even alien contact. The only one that made any sense was simulation theory. Scientists claimed there was evidence of it all along, and this was the final proof. Others still fervently claimed it was a test of faith and all part of God's plan. With all Palmer had been through, he couldn't say for certain what would happen when the timer ended.

Sara held his hand tighter. "I'm glad you came back."

The sudden advancement of their friendship to an intimate relationship was the most shocking turn of events since this whole fiasco began. He was filled with an inner turmoil of emotion. He was ecstatic that he finally got to express his feelings for her, and more importantly that she felt the same way. But the timing of it all...

Just terrible, he thought. *Worse, would she have ever kissed me if the world wasn't ending?* He tried not to dwell on it. *We only have a few hours left. As much as I want to say goodbye to Baba, Allandra, and the others, I can't just leave them here. Things would've been so much simpler, if she was a player instead of Guy. I mean, really, of all the people in the world, why him?* Palmer laughed inwardly. *Would be funny if it turned out we're friends outside of the game.*

"I had to," was all he replied. He looked into her eyes and couldn't help but smile. "It was fun, but *this*," he said and held up the hand she was holding, "is better. I do wish you could've seen it, though."

"Me too."

His mother elbowed him. "What, I'm not good enough for your goofy games?"

Palmer frowned. "You literally just called it goofy."

"Still," she said with feigned hurt, "it would've been nice to be asked."

"I explained that already."

"Mmm hmm."

Time passed together, with all of them laughing and both women telling old stories from Palmer's childhood. It was the sort of connections he'd been thinking about, when deciding what was best in life. Artificial or not, these two were the only ones he wanted to be with when the clock ended. And when the timer finally ticked down, they all held hands even tighter, as if expecting it might hurt, or the world itself would...

Joana opened her eyes.

The world around her had instantly shifted to bright light through a ceiling, walls, and floor made entirely of glass, with a waterfall outside to the right feeding a stream that ran beneath her in the living room, a dense forest of broad trees to the left, and a vibrant garden of colorful flowers just ahead. She was seated on a comfortable leather couch with many pillows. The coffee table before her had cookies and hot tea waiting. She reached a hand up toward the bright sun of midday and adjusted the holographic dial that appeared at her fingertips. The harsh rays somewhat diminished, as day seemed to flow backward toward noon. On second thought, she flicked her hand to the right, and the entire daytime sky rolled over to starry night.

Joana was inside her residential construct, she recalled. Memories came flooding back of her life outside the game. Her first thought was to connect with the community and talk about everything that had just happened. For the first time since playing there, she decided against it. Not that she intended to brag, but sharing even a little of what she'd gone through seemed disrespectful to the Tellaria players. They could all talk about it if they wanted. The memories were enough for her.

There was a pang of regret and longing for Sara, the dull ache over the loss of her mother. It would take a while for that to pass, for her to fully distance herself from the character of Palmer. In a way, it was the closest thing to losing a loved one she had ever experienced. Those feelings were why she played in the first place. Without them, the world would feel empty. She considered immediately jumping back in.

Not to HCE, though. Her thoughts and emotions were still a jumble, but the idea of spending more time on Tellaria was enticing. *I wonder if they'll all connect right away.*

She pulled up the community screen, her eyes on HCE. She could at least find out who Guy was. It was incredibly rare for two players to grow up in the same city. How funny would it be if he was a regular? *Hmm, not yet.* She was actually more eager to see Carnes, Baba, and all the others again. They were genuinely fun people to be with. *Would the new iteration even be ready? I wonder how many changes they're going to make.* She filtered out for Tellaria and was surprised to see it listed. With a sudden surge of excitement, she selected the Connect button. Presented with a character creation menu, it occurred to her no one would recognize her usual avatar. HCE characters were randomly generated. With a shrug, she decided to remake Palmer. It would make things much easier in the long run.

Once inside the starter area, in the body of Palmer once again, he was surprised to see an actual user interface, with a chat log, a mini map, and statistics. Every user interface element could be shown or hidden by thought alone. A few messages appeared right away.

Welcome back to Tellaria!

As a returning player, you've been awarded the following perks:

Blessing of Aurora
Magic Find and Gold Find are greatly increased.
Rift Breaker
The chance of unlocking rare / hidden abilities and classes is greatly increased.
Gratitude of the Gods
All resistances are greatly increased.
Hero of Tellaria
Critical Hit Chance, Critical Hit Damage, Critical

Spell Chance, and Critical Spell Damage are greatly increased.

Artificer

The efficiency and efficacy of crafted items are greatly increased.

The following caches have been added to your inventory: Gift of Aurora, Gift of Ankou, Gift of Caturix, Gift of Hecate, Hero of Tellaria, Protector of Tellaria, Champion of Tellaria, and Savior of Tellaria.

"Palmer?" A man stepped closer and more excitedly asked, "Is that actually you?"

It was Baba.

"Hey!" He couldn't help but smile, suddenly seeing one of the friends he'd come back for. "It's me. I felt bad for not saying goodbye, and—"

"Bah! Don't worry about it." He held up a fist, and Palmer bumped it. "We get to level up together now!"

Palmer nodded to the shortened version over his friend's head.

"Did that guy steal your name again?"

"Nah," Baba replied, as if he no longer held a grudge. "I got used to this. Besides, I wasn't sure if you'd recognize me without it."

Palmer laughed. "I thought the same thing!"

"Singlehandedly, huh?" a gruff voice accused, directed at Palmer. It was Bluffer. "No one else helped, huh? It was *all* you."

"That was just to trick the hackers," Palmer explained. "I didn't actually mean it. I was just trying to sound like a jerk, so they'd come fight me and get banned."

"Yeah, I know," Bluffer said. "You were *very* convincing. Jerk." After a bit more of fake affront, he finally laughed. "I'm just giving you shit. Screw those guys. I'm glad they got banned. So, you rolling a healer again?"

Baba said, "I'm thinking rogue to hunter this time."

Bluffer frowned at Baba, as if to say no one had asked him.

"I could." Palmer scratched his chin. "I do like being healer but mostly because I don't trust anyone else to do it right."

"Same reason I tank."

"Yo!" It was Isha. "Group full yet?"

Baba shook his head. "We haven't formed one. Still deciding on classes."

"I'm down for mage this time," Isha said, "or maybe a necro."

Bluffer held up a hand and ticked off a finger for each class role.

"Tank, healer, and two DPS. We could roll with that for now and add a couple more later, if you two suck," he said and indicated Baba and Isha. His tone seemed to say he was doubtful of their prowess. "Be better if we can stick with four. More xp that way."

"And loot," Palmer pointed out.

"So, what do you think?" Isha asked. "Is this our group?"

"Yeah," Palmer said. "Let's do it."

"I could do worse," Baba agreed with a shrug and a grin.

Bluffer smirked. "Well, you sure as hell can't do better."

After a moment of awkward silence, the four of them shared a laugh and headed off to find the first quest giver.

Acknowledgements

I'd like to thank Elias Casarrubias, Anna Jones, Bob Nelson, and Sharon Skinner for all their help in making this book possible.

About the Author

Joe has been writing for most of his adult life, in between bouts of serious online gaming. He continues to write fantasy novels, in both adult and young adult genres, in his selfish need to create worlds that amuse him. That others enjoy the work is a happy coincidence but one that he fully appreciates.

With a Bachelor of Arts in English from the Arizona State University, he is both an avid reader and addicted gamer. He writes novels part-time and longs for the day when those efforts pay some bills—seriously, even just one bill would be nice. For those of you who purchased copies of any of his books, he is eternally in your debt. Note: this is not a legally binding contract.

He currently lives in the perpetual summer that is central Arizona (technically there is a winter, for about three weeks in January). Joe attributes much of his success in life to good looks, incredible talent, obvious modesty, luck, air conditioning, friends & family, and the readers who keep coming back (despite his insistence on writing for himself)—though not necessarily all in that order. Oh, and his computer.

He hopes you enjoyed this book immensely and will share it with a friend—or ten.

Visit him online at jagiunta.com

www.ingramcontent.com/pod-product-compliance
Lightning Source LLC
Chambersburg PA
CBHW072018020726
47501CB00006B/1862
9781938190964